THE
ICARUS
NEEDLE

THE ICARUS NEEDLE

TIMOTHY ZAHN

BAEN

THE ICARUS NEEDLE

This is a work of fiction. All the characters and events portrayed in this book are fictional, and any resemblance to real people or incidents is purely coincidental.

Copyright © 2024 by Timothy Zahn

A Baen Books Original

Baen Publishing Enterprises
P.O. Box 1403
Riverdale, NY 10471
www.baen.com

ISBN: 978-1-9821-9379-9

Cover art by Dave Seeley

First printing, December 2024

Distributed by Simon & Schuster
1230 Avenue of the Americas
New York, NY 10020

Library of Congress Cataloging-in-Publication Data

Names: Zahn, Timothy, author.
Title: The Icarus needle / Timothy Zahn.
Description: Riverdale, NY : Baen Publishing Enterprises, 2024. | Series:
   The Icarus Saga ; 5
Identifiers: LCCN 2024029036 (print) | LCCN 2024029037 (ebook) | ISBN
   9781982193799 (hardcover) | ISBN 9781625799913 (ebook)
Subjects: LCGFT: Science fiction. | Novels.
Classification: LCC PS3576.A33 I288 2024 (print) | LCC PS3576.A33 (ebook)
   | DDC 813/.54--dc23/eng/20240628
LC record available at https://lccn.loc.gov/2024029036
LC ebook record available at https://lccn.loc.gov/2024029037

Printed in the United States of America
10 9 8 7 6 5 4 3 2 1

THE ICARUS NEEDLE

CHAPTER ONE

Selene and I had been working for Admiral Sir Graym-Barker and the Icarus Group for about two years when we suddenly weren't.

We didn't know it right away, of course. It was one of those things that sneaks up on you. All we knew at the beginning was that we'd been brought to the group's super-secret headquarters outside an unnamed city on an unnamed planet to meet with the newest member of their top brass.

"So," the newest member said, gazing across an ornate desk at us. "You're Gregory Roarke."

"Yes, sir," I said, resisting the urge to point out that Graym-Barker had given him our names a grand total of five seconds earlier.

Actually, on second thought, it wasn't that hard an impulse to resist. The man sitting stiff-backed behind the desk wore an Earth-Guard army uniform with shiny general's insignia on the epaulets and more medals on the chest even than Graym-Barker's own full-dress outfit. Topping off the general's ensemble was a five-kilowatt glare that appeared capable of piercing general-purpose armor plate. It certainly had no trouble suppressing any thoughts of flippancy.

"Gregory Roarke," he repeated. "The organization's wild card. The man who finds and loses alien portals on a regular basis."

His glare notched up another couple of kilowatts. "The man who unilaterally made the decision to hand over one of our portals—one of *our* portals—to the Patth. Tell me, Mr. Roarke: Can you give me one good reason why I shouldn't have you arrested and thrown in prison for treason?"

"I believe all the relevant information is in my report," I said, forcing my voice to stay calm. I'd been called on the carpet plenty of times through my various careers, but getting dragged halfway across the Spiral for that dubious privilege was a new one. Most of the time whoever was mad at me settled for expressing his annoyance over a StarrComm screen like everyone else in the Commonwealth. Apparently, the general preferred to do these things in person.

"That's not what I asked," he said. "I asked you to give me a reason not to lock you away in a deep hole somewhere for your crimes."

I looked over at Graym-Barker, standing stiffly at the side of the desk. "Actually, I can give you three reasons," I said. "But I believe the admiral was still in the middle of the introductions."

I'd thought the general's glare was already at full strength. Apparently, he was the type who liked to keep a little in reserve. His eyes narrowed, the muscles in his face hardened, and his lips compressed into a thin pale line. Clearly, that had been the wrong thing to say.

Which was of course why I'd said it. As my father used to say, *If the bear already plans to eat you, a show of bravado won't cost you anything, and might just make him wonder if you're as easy a mouthful as he thought.*

"So he was," the general said. His face still held that angry bear look, but there was now a hint of something that an incurably optimistic observer might interpret as grudging respect. "EarthGuard Field General Josiah Leland Kinneman. The new director of the Alien Portal Agency. You were about to offer me some excuses."

"No excuses necessary," I said. So the Icarus Group had become the Alien Portal Agency?

That wasn't good. I'd never yet met anything that called itself an agency, bureau, or department that wasn't peppered with incompetence, laziness, bad communication, and—worst of all—internal politics. Suddenly all my past head-butting with Admiral Graym-Barker over various issues didn't look so bad. "Reason one: We gained previously unknown information about

Patth society and the relationship between their public leadership and the more shadowy power of their established families."

"Information that is completely useless," Kinneman interjected.

"With all due respect, I would suggest that *all* information eventually proves useful," I said. "Reason two: We've now added a bit more strength to our unofficial relationship with Sub-Director Nask and Expediter Huginn."

"A relationship you've never been authorized to make," Kinneman growled.

"'Boots on the ground,' I believe is the proper phrase," I said. "I thought soldiers were trained to watch for unexpected opportunities."

"You really think the Patth will feel more kindly toward you because of this?" he demanded, apparently deciding that my lack of military experience made my soldier comment way too easy a target.

"You mean the Patth in general?" I asked. "Probably not. But if you mean Sub-Director Nask and Huginn, probably so. If for no other reason than they see me as someone who can help them get what they want."

"Which is exactly what you're *not* supposed to be doing."

"I have no problem helping Nask if we also gain in the process," I said.

"You'll forgive me if I don't think some vague philosophical mewings are worth giving them a portal," Kinneman bit out. "Especially a portal that should have been ours."

"Which conveniently brings me to reason three," I said. "Because of your decision to pull our backup, Selene and I didn't have a snowball's choice in the matter. Nask had Huginn and a swarm of Patth and Iykams. Selene and I had no one."

"And whose fault is *that*?" Kinneman shot back. "You deliberately and irrevocably jumped up onto the public stage. If the agency hadn't pulled back from you, it could have suffered the same fate."

Beside me, Selene stirred. "Gregory had nothing to do with that," she said quietly. "All of it was because—"

"The reasons and history are irrelevant," I cut her off. I knew where she was going, and she was *not* going to throw herself on this particular grenade. Even if it would do us any good, which I was pretty sure it wouldn't. "What *is* relevant is that it was a moral decision, we're in it together, and as you say it's irrevocable."

Kinneman's eyes narrowed a little more—

"On the other hand," I continued, "just because it's on the

Commonwealth's official record doesn't mean anyone will actually remember it for very long. I'd make you a small wager that you could mention our names on the street or even in the lofty heights of academia and ninety-nine out of a hundred wouldn't have a clue as to who we were."

I looked at Graym-Barker again. His face was expressionless, but there was a glint in his eye that told me he'd already been over this ground with Kinneman and hadn't made any more headway against the general's unreasonable annoyance than I was.

Except that I was a lowly minion and wasn't supposed to be able to influence a general's conclusions. Graym-Barker was an admiral, and should at least have a decent shot at doing so. The fact that Kinneman was still riding this particular horse suggested he was the type who didn't take advice from anyone.

As my father used to say, *There are people you respect, people you trust, and people you obey. Good leaders go for all three. Mediocre leaders settle for the third.*

"My point is that there's really no danger of the Icarus Group getting pulled into any of this," I went on. Just because Kinneman wanted to call it the Alien Portal Agency didn't mean I had to. In fact, it was almost the exact opposite. "I could also mention that you still need Selene and me to hunt you up portals that the Patth haven't already found and laid claim to."

"We may need Selene," Kinneman said pointedly. "We don't particularly need *you*."

"I think you'll find we're a package deal."

"That remains to be seen." Kinneman touched a key on his intercom. "Send him in."

Behind us, the door opened. I turned—

And felt my throat tighten. The newcomer was late middle-aged, with a receding hairline and the slightly leathery skin of someone who's spent a lot of time under a myriad of alien suns. But his eyes were bright and alert, and his expression held the calm half smile of someone totally at ease with himself and the universe and wanted all those around him to find that same inner serenity.

And as my father used to say...

"Hello, son."

I sighed. "Hello, Dad," I replied, hearing the resignation in my voice. "Why am I not surprised?"

CHAPTER TWO

"Actually, Gregory, you *should* be surprised," my father said as he stirred extra cream into his coffee. "I haven't been with the agency very long. Not officially, anyway."

"Long enough for a full briefing, though," I pointed out, looking around the cozy meeting room as I took a sip from my cola. Kinneman had followed my father's somewhat melodramatic entrance by kicking the three of us out of his office and sending us here, having apparently gotten whatever reaction from me that he'd been looking for. At least he'd had the decency to stock the room with drinks and a reasonable selection of snackage.

Though as we left he'd warned us to keep our reunion brief, with an underlying hint that he wasn't through with us yet.

And so of course my father had now gone with his favorite gambit of picking up on an unfinished conversational thread from several minutes earlier, a technique designed to disconcert people who weren't familiar with it.

Fortunately, I was.

"Because I note the general didn't lay any restrictions on us about our conversation," I continued. "That tells me you're cleared to know anything Selene and I can tell you." I cocked my head. "Though I presume it doesn't go the other direction?"

"Not at the moment," my father confirmed. "Maybe later."

He smiled at Selene. "My apologies, Selene, at our dereliction of hostly duties. I'm Nicholas Roarke, Gregory's father. I'm pleased to finally meet you."

"And I you," Selene said, her nostrils and eyelashes working the air. *Probably establishing a baseline for my father should she need to read his emotions at some future date.*

I wished her luck with that one. As far as I'd ever been able to establish, my father didn't have *a baseline.*

"Though I must admit to some surprise at your appearance," Selene continued. "From the way Gregory speaks of you, I assumed you'd passed on."

"Did you, now," my father said with an air of private amusement. "Let me guess. He quotes me often enough, probably dredging up some of the aphorisms I like to use, but otherwise never speaks of me?"

Selene's eyes flicked to me. "Yes."

"Oh, don't worry, I'm not offended," he assured her. "And no, it's not you, or even him. It's me. You see, for the first few years of Gregory's life he was mostly ashamed of me. In the years since then..." He paused, his half smile slipping a bit. "Let's just say he still isn't completely sure."

Selene looked at me again, and I could see her trying to sift through the tangle of emotional scents I was undoubtedly broadcasting. "At least now you're somewhat more legit," I said.

He raised his eyebrows, the smile reestablishing itself. "Only somewhat?" he asked in a mock wounded tone.

"You seem to be high on Kinneman's list of minions," I said. "That raises a few question marks. No offense."

"None taken," he assured me. "On the other hand, you know as well as I do that I don't necessarily get to choose who I work with. I also understand you didn't always get along with Admiral Sir Graym-Barker when you were working with him, either."

"Not always," I conceded. "But mostly."

"I'm sure it looked that way from your side of the table," he said. "From the agency's point of view, though, I have to tell you there's a certain range of opinion as to how much you were working *for* the admiral and how much you were working *against* him."

"I think that's a bit harsh," I said, feeling a fresh tightness in my throat. There were a lot of topics I didn't want to discuss with my father, especially not in a conversation I assumed as a matter of course was being monitored. But there was something in his expression and tone that made me want to explain myself, a subtle challenge-and-hook he'd spent decades perfecting.

Plus, if Graym-Barker and Kinneman were listening, this might be a good time to clear up any lingering doubts about me. "I never fought him on anything of importance," I said. "Mostly it was a clash of personalities. As a high-ranking military man, he's used to giving and getting orders, all bundled neatly inside the strict and well-defined military way of doing things. Naturally, he was equally used to expecting everyone around him to do the same."

"And you're the polar opposite?"

"I'm not sure I'd go *that* far," I hedged. "But...look. You saw how my school-age assortment of odd jobs came and went. I *do* know how to follow rules and instructions. For one thing, I've got a very high regard for the laws of physics."

"And the law of averages?"

"That, too," I agreed. "And I'm okay with most of the Commonwealth's laws. It's just that when someone tells me to do something I need to see some reason and logic behind it. If I don't, I usually go with what I see as the spirit of the order."

"Whereas military people are obsessed with the precise and specific words involved?" he suggested.

I felt my lip twitch. "Something like that. You disapprove, I'm sure."

"Not as much as you might think," he assured me. "It's really not a bad rule of thumb in general. What happens if there isn't any discernible spirit?"

"Then I go with whatever benefits Selene and me," I said. "Survival of the family, clan, and neighborhood. It's kind of built into us humans."

"It is indeed," he agreed. "And if all of that is still a wash?"

"Then I do what's best for the universe at large, I guess," I said. "Assuming I can figure out what that is."

"Mm." My father pursed his lips, looking once at Selene and then back at me. "And yet, despite your admittedly casual approach to authority, you feel you should have been taken more deeply into the agency's confidence instead of being kept at arm's length?"

I took a careful breath. This was another of his favorite gambits, one I'd played through a hundred times with him. He would throw out a challenge to something I'd said or implied and force me to defend myself. "Our value to the Icarus Group isn't predicated on how well I follow orders," I said. "It's a matter of how clearly I can see the bigger picture and anticipate the consequences of various possible actions."

"Such as?"

"Such as keeping our hands off the Fidelio Gemini portal," I said. "Earth—hell, the whole Commonwealth—could have ended up on the wrong end of a Patth transport embargo."

"There's also Maijo," Selene offered.

"Exactly—case in point," I said, pouncing on the cue. "A couple of months ago, Maijo blindly obeyed an order that left us hanging on Alainn. The direct result of that was that Kinneman lost any chance of getting his hands on the damaged portal he somehow thinks Selene and I could have gotten for him."

"Yes, I've spoken with Maijo," my father said thoughtfully. "He disagreed with that order, if it helps any."

"But he still followed it," I pointed out. "Which isn't to say I necessarily blame him. If *that* helps any."

"Not really," my father said, giving me a wry smile. "Regardless, General Kinneman is now in charge of the agency. If you want to continue on here, you need to accept that and figure out how to work the change with a minimum of friction. As I always say, *A subordinate needs the boss to be happy if he wants to get the job done.*"

"Funny," I said, giving him an exaggerated frown. "*I* remember that one being, *A subordinate needs the boss to* think *he's happy if he wants to get the job done.*"

My father shrugged. "Po-tay-to, Po-tah-to, as they say," he said. "Either way, the bottom line is to get the job done. What do you know about the DeepSix B33?"

Yet another of his standard tricks: an abrupt switch of topic. I knew that one, too. "It's a high-end atmosphere bioprobe," I said. "Bigger and a *lot* fancier than the ones we usually carry aboard the *Ruth*, with considerably more range and a phased transponder lock for better grav-beam acquisition. It can go deeper into a planetary atmosphere, stay down longer, and bring back a bigger sample. They're also horrendously expensive. Why, are you thinking that buying a couple of them for us will make Kinneman happy?"

"Yes," he said. "*And* no." He stood up, his genial half smile back in place. "Come on. It's time to introduce you to the rest of Project Needle."

CHAPTER THREE

Selene and I had been to the Icarus Group headquarters a couple of times, but we'd never been allowed very far from the centerpiece of the place, the massive portal itself. This trip settled neatly into that same pattern, with my father and our four EarthGuard Marine escorts taking us only a couple of corridors from our small meeting room to the larger conference room I remembered from my first visit here.

The crowd awaiting us this time around had a similar makeup. Along with Kinneman and Admiral Graym-Barker were Jordan McKell, Ixil and the two outriders squatting on his shoulders, and Tera C, whose full name and exact relationship to the group I still didn't know. Two other men and a woman in EarthGuard uniforms were also sitting together at one end of the table, all three of them wearing the unit insignia of the 555th Engineer Brigade.

"Let me introduce the Needle department heads," my father said as he ushered Selene and me to chairs facing the three engineers. "Colonel Kolodny, head of the bioprobe assembly team; Major Ganic, heading the grav-beam operations team; and Lieutenant Shevrade, chief grav-beam operator."

"Nice to meet you," I said, nodding to each of them in turn. "Interesting job descriptions. Especially yours, Colonel."

"How so?" Kolodny asked, his pleasant baritone in sharp contrast to his weathered face and wiry hands.

"I always assumed bioprobes came from the factory fully assembled," I said. "What did you do, take one apart just so you could put it back together again?"

"As a matter of fact," Kinneman put in, "yes, they did."

I frowned. "Excuse me?"

"Which should really have been obvious," Kinneman said, clearly enjoying the moment. "You of all people should know the limited size of a portal's receiver module hatches."

I stared at him a moment longer, then shifted my gaze to McKell. "So you really did it?" I asked.

"We did," he confirmed with a nod. "I assume you're suitably impressed?"

"I think we're a couple of grades above just *suitably*," I murmured as the memories came rushing back. Selene's discovery of what turned out to be one half of a directory to the Icarus portal addresses, my suggested reconstruction of the long-past events that might have led to that finding, and my even more tentative conclusion that the directory's other half might have been dropped from the orbiting Alpha portal to the unexplored planet rotating silently beneath it.

And if Colonel Kolodny and his team had really gone to all the trouble Kinneman and McKell just said they had..."I *did* only say that the other half *might* be down there," I reminded them.

"Understood," McKell said. "But your reconstruction of how LH ended up where it did seemed reasonable. It was discussed at the highest level, and the decision was made to do some follow-through." He gave me a small smile. "Don't worry, no one's going to blame you if the search comes up dry."

"Oh, good," I said. Though I doubted that grace would extend to Kinneman. "So we're calling our half of the directory *LH* now?"

McKell shrugged. "It's easier to say and write than *the left-hand half of the portal directory*."

"Plus it's a more opaque name if the Patth happen to be listening in?" I suggested.

McKell and Ixil, as I'd long ago discovered, had excellent control of their faces. But Pix and Pax, crouching on Ixil's shoulders with their long claws tapping into his nervous system, weren't nearly as inscrutable. The two ferret-sized creatures gave simultaneous twitches, small but obvious if you knew what to look for. Clearly, Patth monitoring of the Spiral's communications in general and the Icarus Group's in particular continued to be a sore spot with the upper brass.

"Plus that," McKell agreed, his voice as unreadable as his face.

Kinneman wasn't nearly as good, or else he just wasn't trying. His eyes narrowed, and I could tell he wanted to say something, probably an accusation that my contacts with Sub-Director Nask had been what had put the Patth onto the group in the first place. But for once, he decided to let that one lie.

Or else knew perfectly well that it wasn't true and didn't want to look stupid in front of the rest of the assembly.

Regardless, it was time to move the conversation off that subject. "So what's the plan?" I asked.

"We spend the rest of the day here," McKell said. "You and Selene need to be briefed on the equipment and the proposed schedule, and be fitted with vac suits. Tomorrow, we head to Alpha and you and Lieutenant Shevrade will see if you can make some history."

"Okay," I said cautiously, eyeing Shevrade. "So the lieutenant will be operating the grav-beam generators. Who's operating the bioprobe itself?"

"I was given to understand it's not so much *operating* as it is *monitoring*," Kinneman put in.

"Correction noted," I said, inclining my head to him. "So who's *monitoring* the bioprobe?"

"You are, of course," Kinneman said. "It's what you've been doing for the past few years, isn't it?"

"Yes, except that Selene and I usually do it from the *Ruth*'s control room," I pointed out. "This will be entirely different."

Kinneman gave a small snort. "I don't see how."

"Plus I've never operated a DeepSix before," I continued. "It may take more than a single afternoon to learn how to properly run one."

"It's a bioprobe," Kinneman said, his limited supply of patience starting to run even lower. "You'll watch the lieutenant send it into the atmo, and then watch her bring it out again."

"Of course." I turned to Colonel Kolodny. "Colonel, I assume your engineers use dirt-moving equipment on occasion?"

"Of course," Kolodny said.

"Ever dealt with a Drovni-Kalib twelve-mark?"

His eyes narrowed a bit. "Drovni-Kalibs are a Drilie machine."

"Yes, they are. So that's a no?"

"Your point is well taken, Gregory," my father jumped smoothly into the conversation. "I think we can consider the schedule Colonel McKell offered just now to be only the first of several options. You and Selene will certainly be given whatever time you need to feel comfortable with the DeepSix."

"Thank you," I said, keeping my own face and voice casual. McKell was a *colonel*? There'd never been even a hint of a military connection in any of interactions I'd had with him. "I presume, Colonel Kolodny, that you have a full manual available?"

"We do," Kolodny confirmed, a hint of relief in his voice. He, at least, knew better than to throw a complicated machine at someone without proper training. "We also have a second B33 available for you to look at—fully assembled, of course—plus a simulator you can use for operational practice."

"Excellent," I said, nodding my thanks. "Thank you."

"In the meantime," my father continued, "since we're already assembled here, I suggest General Kinneman continue his briefing, along with the proposed timeline once you're ready to proceed with the operation." He gestured to Kinneman. "General?"

"Yes," Kinneman said. He still didn't look happy, but at least he wasn't glaring anymore. "The bioprobe and grav-beam generators have been mounted on the outside of Alpha's receiver module." He keyed his info pad, and a schematic of Alpha and the planet appeared on the conference room's displays, complete with a dizzyingly complex series of orbital pathways and insertion vectors in half a dozen colors. "Here's how and where the probe will do its first pass."

The briefing took an hour. After that, Colonel Kolodny took us to a large and well-equipped machine shop where the promised DeepSix B33 was sitting on a workbench. A computer desk beside it held the operations manual and simulator program.

Kolodny stuck around the whole afternoon, answering our questions and generally making himself useful as we got up to speed on this particular bioprobe's set of quirks. McKell dropped in twice to see how we were doing, though he then went off to presumably attend to other duties. At one point I asked Kolodny to call in Ixil so that he could send Pix and Pax through some of the B33's larger conduits, just to confirm that the manual's diagrams accurately described the gadget we were working on.

I found it particularly interesting that neither Ixil nor Kolodny took any issue whatsoever with my borderline tech paranoia, whereas I guessed Kinneman probably would have considered it a waste of time. Clearly, our two advisors had both had the experience of documentation and reality not synching up.

Selene and I had missed lunch, but dinner more than made up for it. Most of the people from our earlier meeting were there, plus a dozen additional EarthGuard junior officers with the same 555th patch, presumably the rest of Kolodny's engineering team. I picked a table that was close enough for us to eavesdrop on the latter group, under the reasonable assumption that the people who were handling the project's nuts and bolts would have the most interesting conversations. As my father used to say, *It's not a coincidence that* ear to the ground *and* boots on the ground *are two of humanity's most enduring idioms.*

Unfortunately, in this case the gambit gained me nothing. The engineers mostly chatted about what they were going to do when they were finally given a few days' leave, and their many and varied suggestions for that liberty strongly suggested that they didn't know where we were any more than Selene and I did.

My father and General Kinneman, I noted, were conspicuous by their absence.

Kinneman had assigned us a nice suite, consisting of two bedrooms, each with a private bathroom, and a good-sized living/ conversation area in the middle. The bedroom where Selene's luggage had been laid out, I noted, had an extra set of filters on all the ventilation grilles. Either someone was worried that the base's odors would be offensive to the incredibly powerful Kadolian sense of smell, or that same someone was concerned that those odors might provide clues as to where the Icarus Group had set up shop. Given Kinneman's overall attitude toward us, I leaned toward the latter.

And with the two of us finally alone, I was able to ask the question I'd known I had to ask. The question I'd been dreading ever since our arrival.

"So," I said with an effort at casualness I knew was pointless. "What do you think of him?"

"Your father?" Selene gave a small shrug. "He seems pleasant

enough. A good negotiator, and also very quick. He saw how
you were setting up to slam Kinneman with your Drovni-Kalib
question to Colonel Kolodny and cut you off before you could
do so." She considered. "Though he *does* know you, so of course
he would have an awareness of your methods. What exactly is
his job, if I may ask?"

"You already said it," I told her. "Negotiator. Though I believe
he usually just calls himself a *Fixer*."

"That sounds like the kind of title that would be used by a
criminal organization."

I felt my stomach tighten. "Yes," I agreed soberly. "It does."

Abruptly her pupils went all stricken. "Oh, Gregory," she
breathed. "I didn't mean—are you saying he's a *criminal*?"

"No, no," I hastened to assure her. "Well, maybe, depending
on how you define the term, and whether or not you were on
the losing side of a negotiation. But yes, he did start out in the
Spiral's criminal underground."

"Is that why you were ashamed of him?"

"I wasn't *ashamed* of him, exactly," I said, trying to call back
my emotions and mental state of those long-past years. "But
my mom was worried about his safety, dealing with all those
crime bosses, and I think I picked up on her stress." I shrugged.
"Though we were probably worried about nothing. Once he'd
moved up the ladder to where he was dealing with only the top
crime people they all recognized his value and none of them was
going to risk losing that."

"Especially since everyone else would be angry if violence
was done to him?"

"Especially then," I agreed. "Imagine a scenario where Gaheen
sent Floyd to deliver a message to someone he was mad at. It
would not be pleasant for the object of that lesson."

"No, it wouldn't," she agreed soberly. Abruptly, her pupils
frowned. "*Did* he work with Gaheen? Or Varsi, when we were
still working for him?"

"I really don't know," I said. "Dad didn't talk with me about
his work, at least not when I was young. Anyway, at some point
he started being noticed by corporations and governments, some
of whom decided they could benefit from his fixer services.
Gradually, he shifted into those more legitimate lines of work,
and I gather he's been there ever since."

"And now he's with the Icarus Group," Selene said, her pupils going thoughtful. "I wonder why."

"Or as Kinneman calls it, the Alien Portal Agency," I said, the new title tasting sour on my tongue. "As my father used to say, *Beware of any man, corporation, or country that keeps changing its name.* I assume they brought him in to ease the transition between Graym-Barker and Kinneman."

"So you think the admiral is going to be moved out?"

"I think he *has* been moved out," I said. "Right now he's doing a Ghost of Christmas Past impression to ease any nervousness the change in management might spark in the lower ranks."

"I can see why people might be nervous," Selene murmured. "The last time we were here, the humans certainly held the dominant position, but I could smell several aliens, as well. Kalixiri, mostly, but also some Crooea and Vyssiluyas. Now, all the nonhumans except Ixil seem to be gone."

"Kinneman and his superiors trying to change the portals from Graym-Barker's multispecies organization to something solely under Commonwealth control," I said. "Maybe they're even trying to turn it into something overtly military under direct EarthGuard auspices."

"I don't think that would sit well with the other species," Selene warned.

"Understatement of the year," I agreed grimly. "Especially the Kalixiri. Especially since Ixil was one of the people who brought the Icarus home to begin with and has risked his life numerous times to keep it here. I don't suppose you smelled any resentment on his part during the meeting, did you?"

"Nothing clear enough to catch my attention," she said, her pupils going a little unfocused as she thought back to our recent interactions with him. "Though if the shakeup happened weeks or months ago he may have simply accepted the situation."

"Somehow, I don't see Ixil accepting something like that," I said. "Let's keep an eye on him and see what we can pick up. McKell, too, of course."

"I will." Selene hesitated. "There's one other possibility that occurs to me, Gregory, about your father's presence here. They need us to analyze whatever the bioprobe brings up, and Kinneman surely knows that. Maybe your father was brought in to persuade you to continue cooperating with them."

"Could be," I admitted. "Though bringing him in for just one person seems like a waste of his talents."

"Or else," Selene added, "he came in to persuade Kinneman to keep you part of the team."

I scowled at one of the room's corners. Unfortunately, that one held a much higher level of possibility. Selene could talk about Kinneman needing us; but as the general himself had already pointed out, he only needed *her.*

Still, I'd pointed out in return that she was only interested in working with me, which Graym-Barker had surely already warned him about. The admiral had also undoubtedly realized that Kinneman and I were pretty well guaranteed to lock horns, especially after the Alainn mess. I could easily see Graym-Barker having spent a few of his last official minutes as head of the Icarus Group to call in my father in hopes of keeping Kinneman and me in our respective corners until the job was done.

"Or did the admiral and general miscalculate?" Selene asked quietly into my musings.

"You mean do my dad and I hate each other?" I shook my head. "No, nothing like that. We mostly get along all right. It's just that our lives really don't have much in common, and we've just sort of drifted apart."

"This may be your chance to remedy that."

"Assuming both of us want to do so," I said. "Not sure we do."

"Family is important, Gregory."

"In principle, I agree," I said. "In this case, not convinced." I yawned and stood up. "But that's a conversation for another day. I don't know about you, but I'm ready to turn in."

"I am, too," Selene said, also standing up. "What's the plan for tomorrow?"

"I figure we'll need at least one more day, maybe two, to check out the DeepSix and run some simulations," I told her as I backed toward the door to my bedroom. "Probably another day of simulations after that, and then we should be ready."

"Kinneman won't be happy if you drag it out," Selene warned.

"I don't think Kinneman's ever happy," I said. "Don't worry, I'm not doing any of this to irritate him. Well, not solely to irritate him, anyway. The minute I think we're ready we'll let him know he can get this show on the road."

"All right," Selene said, finally starting to move toward her own bedroom. Apparently she'd needed to hear some assurances before letting me go. "Sleep well, Gregory."

"You, too, Selene."

But once the show was finished, I told myself darkly as I closed the bedroom door behind me, it might be time to reevaluate our place in the scheme of things.

And if my father had truly been hired to keep us with the Icarus Group, this might be one of the few jobs to end up in his failure column.

CHAPTER FOUR

For once, my expectations turned out to be overly pessimistic. With Kolodny still hanging around ready and willing to answer our questions, the rest of our work on the bioprobe proper was done by lunchtime. After lunch came an hour with the vac-suit fitters, and then we were able to tackle the simulator.

I'd never worked with DeepSix equipment before, and didn't know what to expect. To my mild surprise, their simulator system turned out to be so easy and intuitive that by nine o'clock that evening I was satisfied we were ready to move on to the main event.

I figured Kinneman probably didn't want to talk to me any more than he had to, so instead of phoning him I called my father. He congratulated us on our quickness and efficiency, promised to pass the news on to the rest of the team, and told me our Marine escort would pick us up at eight the next morning for breakfast.

As usual, the meal that Kinneman's people had laid out was excellent. But as Selene and I ate I could see that the group assembled in the dining room had more pressing concerns than steak, eggs, waffles, and bacon. Kolodny and the other engineers, I was pretty sure, were running the tech details through their minds, searching for anything they might have missed. McKell,

Ixil, and Tera were conversing quietly at their table, possibly discussing the huge implications of finding the other half of the portal directory, not just to them and the Icarus Group but also to the future of the Spiral. Kinneman and Graym-Barker, seated at a table off by themselves, were eating silently, and I would have laid good odds they were wondering if this whole incredibly expensive gamble was going to pay off or not, and what they would say to the money people if it didn't.

But if Kinneman was feeling nervous, it didn't show in his post-breakfast briefing.

"We'll reconvene in one hour in the ready room outside the portal chamber," he announced, his voice the slightly sonorous tone of someone who knows he's speaking for posterity. "At that time you'll do a final check on your equipment and suit up for the trip to Alpha. Colonel McKell and Brigadier Ixil will go through first, followed by Colonel Kolodny and his team. Mr. Roarke and Ms. Selene will wait until Colonel Kolodny returns with the all-clear, at which point they'll accompany him back to Alpha. McKell will decide when all is ready, at which point Lieutenant Shevrade and Mr. Roarke will begin the mission. Questions?"

By no doubt sheer coincidence he happened to be looking straight at me right then, his expression not so much an invitation as it was a challenge.

And it occurred to me that if my father had been hired to keep the team and me working and playing well together, I should probably at least make him work for his money.

"I have one," I said, lifting my hand as if we were all in school. "All the Royal Kalixiri commandos who were helping guard Icarus the last time I was here seem to have disappeared. Are they all on leave or something?"

Kinneman gave me a measuring look, then made a small gesture toward my father. "This was under your watch, Sir Nicholas," he said. "Would you care to answer Mr. Roarke's question?"

My father cleared his throat, while I took that same brief moment to field the double gut punch Kinneman had just delivered. My father had been involved in the decision to force all nonhumans out of the Icarus Group?

And he was now *Sir* Nicholas?

"Of course, General," my father said. His genial smile was still in place, but I could see small tension lines at the corners of his eyes. "The agency's undergone some reorganization over the past few months, Gregory. Part of that has been a shuffling of personnel and oversight representation. The Kalixiri guard isn't gone permanently, but simply on hold while things settle down."

"I see," I said, a hard knot settling into my stomach. The words were meaningless froth, of course. I was pretty sure we both knew that. But the overall meaning was clear.

Kinneman and his people had indeed taken Icarus for Earth, the Commonwealth, and humankind.

And this time, I didn't see any twitches from Pix and Pax. Clearly, Ixil wasn't surprised by any of this.

"If there are no further questions," Kinneman said, his tone strongly suggesting that there had better not be, "we're adjourned. I'll see you in the Icarus ready room in one hour." Giving a brisk nod that took in all of us, he turned and strode from the room, Graym-Barker and my father close behind.

I looked at Selene, saw the tension in her pupils. Clearly, she'd gotten the same message from my father's bafflegab as I had. "Gregory?" she murmured.

"Not now," I murmured back. We were definitely going to have a conversation about this, but not with the mission to Alpha rushing up to meet us.

As my father used to say, *Picking the wrong time for something will generally cost you more than just those few lost minutes.*

But then, as my father also used to say, *Alliances based solely on money are inherently unstable. If you choose to join such a group, make sure you get paid in advance.*

I made a mental note to ask him later if he'd been paid in advance.

Selene and I didn't have any equipment to prep, and were therefore ready a good ten minutes before the now familiar Marine guard came to fetch us. The omnipresent escort was just one more reminder, if I'd needed one, that we were the unwanted side dish in this little family dinner.

The rest of the team were already suiting up when we arrived, McKell and Ixil halfway into their vac suits, Kolodny and the other two engineers not far behind. Kinneman and my father were off to the side, silently watching the procedure.

Selene and I weren't nearly as expert at the procedure as the others, but with some help from our Marine shadows we were ready only a few minutes behind the others. I noticed out of the corner of my eye that Kinneman was watching us closely, but if he was annoyed at the delay he didn't say anything.

Finally, everything was ready. One by one we rolled through the open hatchway into the Icarus receiver module, my father and Kinneman tagging along behind the rest of us. We all walked around the interior of the huge sphere to the launch module and rolled our way into that one as well. As per Kinneman's earlier orders, McKell and Ixil went first, fastening on their helmets and then riding the extension arm up to the center and vanishing. As the rest of us watched, Kolodny, Ganic, and Shevrade did likewise.

"Any idea how long before Colonel Kolodny comes back for us?" I asked.

"The others will first want to exit the receiver module to the outside," my father said. "An airlock has been set up over one of the hatchways for that purpose. They'll then walk the entire exterior of the portal, both spheres, making sure everything is as they left it and that there are no surprises."

"You mean like someone having moved in during their absence?" I suggested.

"As in like nothing has broken loose or run afoul of a meteor," Kinneman said tersely.

"There's never been any indication of anyone elsewhere in the system," my father added. "Either on the planet itself or in interplanetary space." He raised his eyebrows. "Which, I'll point out, correlates well with your theory that the last Icari to travel there from Meima found themselves in an isolated, dead-end situation."

"Emphasis on the *dead*," I murmured, eyeing Selene out of the corner of my eye. She tended to be sensitive to conversations about the dead, even if those specific deaths had occurred ten or more millennia ago. But aside from a little queasiness in her pupils as she visualized the last days or hours of the marooned Icari she seemed to be holding up okay. "So, what, five or ten minutes?"

"More like fifteen or twenty," my father said. "As I always say, *You want it good, fast, and cheap? Pick two and get back to me.*"

"In this case it's just the *good* part, I assume," I said. In other words, Selene and I could have hung out in our suite another fifteen minutes and not been any farther behind the curve.

My words and tone were just as civil and polite as they could be. But Kinneman apparently heard something he didn't like. "You've never been in the military, have you, Roarke?" he growled.

"I'm pretty sure you know I haven't, sir," I said. "Unless you want to count the time I've spent working with Admiral Sir Graym-Barker and the Icarus Group."

Kinneman grunted. "As Sir Nicholas said a couple of days ago, there's the question of whether you were working *with* us or *against* us. But that's beside the point. The point is that the maxim *hurry up and wait* isn't just a cynical view of how the military does things. Everyone needs to be in the right place at the right time before an operation can begin. Some of those people will be early, and they have to wait for everyone else. Those who are late..." His eyes bored into mine. "Let's just say that they'd better not *be* late."

"Yeah, I get it," I said. "As my father used to say, *A late soldier often becomes a* late *soldier.*"

"When did I say that?" my father asked, frowning. "I never said that."

"Didn't you?" I asked, putting puzzlement into my voice. "Must have been someone exactly like you."

"Really," my father said. He eyed me curiously, then shrugged. "At any rate, General Kinneman is right. All the pieces have to be prepped and ready before the operation begins or you risk losing by default. *For want of a nail...*"

"*...a shoe was lost,*" I finished the first part of the old quote. "You didn't say that, either."

"Oh, I've said it often enough," my father corrected, his half smile going a bit enigmatic. "I just didn't say it first."

Kinneman tilted his head suddenly toward his right ear, the one with the earbud in it. "Colonel Kolodny's here," he said.

I stepped over to the sphere interface and looked down into the receiver module. Kolodny had appeared, all right, drifting downward from the center of the sphere. His faceplate was turned away from me, but his hands were curled in the double thumbs-up that Kinneman had specified for the all-clear signal.

Or course, they hardly needed a hand signal when there'd already been whatever radio confirmation he'd presumably just given to the general. But I'd noticed that Kinneman liked putting multiple redundancies into even the simplest parts of his plans.

Which, I realized suddenly, might be one reason he was so resentful of Selene and me. Selene's unique Kadolian senses, and her refusal to cooperate with the Icarus Group without me, meant that we were a factor that couldn't be duplicated and didn't have a backup. *For want of a nail...* except that the nail we represented couldn't be replaced by a quick trip to the supply depot. For a detail-obsessed person like Kinneman, that had to be both annoying and concerning.

"Over there," the general ordered into my thoughts. "Roarke?"

"Excuse me?" I asked, looking at him.

"Over there," Kinneman repeated, jabbing a finger toward the base of the extension arm.

I frowned again into the receiver module. Kolodny hadn't even landed yet, and furthermore was coming down about a quarter of the way around the big sphere. It would be at least another minute and a half before he could join us, and Kinneman had already said he would be accompanying Selene and me through to Alpha. "I assumed we were still in the waiting part of the hurry-up-and-wait," I said.

"You are," Kinneman growled. "You're going to wait over *there*."

I looked at my father. But he was just standing silently, sending a neutral look in my direction. "Yes, *sir*," I said briskly. Taking Selene's arm, I walked us around the sphere to the extension arm, mentally counting down the seconds.

Sure enough, as I'd estimated, it was another eighty-nine seconds before Kolodny rolled over the edge of the interface into the launch module. He touched a key on his forearm control array—"Everything looks good," his voice came through my earbud as he brought Selene and me into the conversation. "You two ready?"

"Ready, willing, and able," I confirmed. "Though as my father used to say—"

"Stow it," Kinneman cut me off. "Helmets on, and get moving."

Obediently, I lowered my helmet over my head, listening for the click as it engaged the locking collar and then confirming on the chin-level status display that it was secure. I wrapped my hand around the black-and-silver-striped extension arm, waited as Selene and Kolodny did the same, and as that section of the launch module's artificial gravity reversed direction we all floated up toward the sphere's center. We reached the luminescent gray section, and with the familiar tingle and couple of seconds of blackness we arrived in the center of Alpha's receiver module.

The last time I'd been here the sphere had been completely empty, with only the plate that McKell's people had welded over the sphere interface showing that it hadn't sat untouched for the past ten millennia. Now, the place looked like a combination workshop and supply depot. There were a dozen stacks of crates piled in carefully delineated areas all along the interior of the sphere, some of them clustered around workbenches or welding stations alongside tool racks and equipment dollies. One rack held six emergency vac suits, of the no-frills, no-nonsense, blow-up type a person could get into and zip up in twenty seconds flat. Other racks featured Barracuda underwater maneuvering packs, high-altitude ramjet and low-altitude owl-wing flightpacks, and a couple of suits I'd never seen before but which looked capable of a trip through an active volcano. Off to another side were a pair of large weapons lockers. They were closed, so I couldn't see what Kinneman had given his team for possible self-defense purposes, but since most of the people here were EarthGuard or EarthGuard trained I didn't have to use my imagination very much. Directly across from the launch module interface was the big rectangular block of a portable airlock, its power supply and oxygen tanks connected to it by cables and hoses like they were all heading up the Swiss Alps together.

Tethered beside the airlock, bobbing gently in the breeze and looking for all the world like the driveway marker for a child's birthday party, was a thirty-centimeter-diameter helium balloon.

"Love what you've done with the place," I commented. Normally, arriving passengers headed off in random directions toward the inside of the sphere as the interior gravitational field pulled them away from the center. In this case, I'd taken hold of Selene's wrist as soon as we popped in, and as a result we were heading together toward our projected landing spot near one of the workbenches. Kolodny, in contrast, was headed in a different direction, closer to the airlock. "Especially the pointer," I continued. "Someone worried we wouldn't be able to find our way home?"

"Pointer?" Kolodny asked. "Oh—you mean the balloon. No, that's our intruder-deterrent system. When all the legitimate traffic for the day has come and gone, the sentries release the cable and let it float to the center of the sphere."

"Ah," I said, nodding understanding. Solid matter sitting in the center of the receiver module would automatically keep any unwanted company from popping in. "Simple and elegant."

"We like it," Kolodny said. "I'm told you used something similar once to keep out a group of unfriendlies."

"Yes, though the execution was a lot trickier," I said. "Why just one balloon, though? Seems to me a cluster would be even more secure."

"You'd think so, wouldn't you?" Kolodny agreed. "That was actually our first approach, in fact. But it turns out that having a bunch of balloons rubbing against each other builds up static electricity and shortens their lifespan considerably."

"How considerably?" I asked.

"A single balloon sitting by itself will last six to eight months before failing," Kolodny said. "A clump of balloons—or even just two of them—start to fail within a few hours."

I gave a low whistle. "That fast?"

"That fast," Kolodny agreed. "We figure the gravity field somehow interacts with the static charge to enhance the material degradation, but so far the brain people haven't figured out how."

"What if you don't use rubber?" Selene suggested. "Would a nonelectric material avoid that problem?"

"That balloon isn't rubber now," Kolodny told her. "It's a thermoplastic we had specially mixed up for the job. But no. We tried a full range of materials, and none of them was light enough to maintain position in the center of the sphere, non-permeable enough to contain the helium, and able to hold up to the friction degradation."

"Interesting," I said, eyeing the balloon. Still, given how the receiver module's radial gravitational field was configured, one single helium balloon sitting in the center was absolutely not going anywhere and therefore absolutely not letting anyone in. "Requires a very precise timetable to make sure you reel it out of the way so that your own people can get in, of course."

"You might be surprised at how precise EarthGuard engineers can be," Kolodny said with more than a hint of pride. "McKell? We're here."

"Good," McKell's voice came from my earbud. "We're ready for you."

"There in three," Kolodny promised.

Half a minute later we hit the deck, the last meter marking the usual surge of acceleration as the gravity came up to the module's full strength. I glanced at the workbench we'd landed near as we walked past, but the half-disassembled gadget lying on it wasn't anything I was familiar with. We kept going, and reached the airlock the same time as Kolodny. "What do we need to know about operating this thing?" I asked as the colonel swung over the lever that opened the hatch.

"Don't worry, I'll handle it," he said, gesturing us inside. "Go on, get in. There's room for all of us."

The chamber hadn't looked that big from the center of the sphere, but the three of us were indeed able to squeeze inside, though it was something of a tight fit. I watched as Kolodny ran the cycle: first firing up the pumps to remove the air from the box into one of the nearby tanks, then checking the indicators to confirm when the vacuum inside matched the vacuum outside, and finally squatting down and touching the spot that would activate the module's hatch. The hatch swung open, and I saw the starry blackness of space beyond.

"Ladies first?" I suggested, gesturing to Selene.

"Colonels first," Kolodny corrected. Lying down in a sort of fetal position in the cramped space, he rolled through the hatchway and out of sight. "Okay. Selene?"

Obediently, Selene lay down and followed him out. I took her place, settled myself...

And paused, peering at the line where the airlock met the module's deck. I'd assumed it had been welded to the sphere's inner surface, since that was the best way to guarantee an airtight seal. From my current vantage point, though, I could see that the interface wasn't fused metal, but instead a thick, translucent plastic. "Colonel Kolodny?" I called. "This seal. Is it Corcoran Maxor?"

"You've got a good eye," Kolodny's voice came approvingly. "Yes, it is. Best vacuum adhesive on the market. Three centimeters thick and solid as the commark."

"Good to hear," I muttered, making a face. Corcoran Maxor was good enough, I supposed, but it was hardly the best the Spiral had to offer. Informed opinion was that Crooea technology was the platinum standard for vacuum products of all sorts.

But then, Corcoran Maxor was the best sealant produced in

the Commonwealth. Apparently, Kinneman's new *Humans Only* policy also included ignoring equipment or materials made by anyone who wasn't in that elite club.

As my father used to say, *Allies and assets come in all sizes, shapes, and colors. If you let yourself get prejudiced against any of those options, you might as well tie one arm behind your back.*

I doubted he'd mentioned that one to Kinneman. Not that Kinneman was likely to have listened even if he had.

I was starting to *really* hope he'd been paid in advance.

CHAPTER FIVE

Ixil and Selene were waiting when I emerged on the outer hull. The momentum of my roll started me drifting away as the sphere's internal gravity vanished, and left to its own Newtonian devices that movement would send me slowly but inexorably into the black void.

But McKell's team had that covered. Even as I floated upward I bent my knees, swiveled my hips, and planted the soles of my boots solidly onto the surface beneath me. "Like that?" I asked as Ixil caught my arm and levered me upright.

"Exactly like that," Ixil confirmed. "Though I daresay Selene did it more gracefully."

"I wouldn't say that," Selene demurred.

"No, you probably wouldn't," I agreed, peering down at my feet. The receiver module's outer hull had been wrapped in a thin-strand, close-knit mesh, similar to the one that held the equipment and cables in place in the interior of the launch module, but much finer. According to the prep files I'd been given, magnetic boots didn't work on portal hulls, and Kinneman had apparently decided not to risk the massive and widespread welding that would be required to install a network of anchors. The mesh had been the solution: adhesive enough to grip the soles of our boots and keep us from floating away, but not so sticky that it nailed us to the spot. As long as we kept our steps slow

and deliberate, we should be able to travel more or less normally.
"But just because you wouldn't say it doesn't mean Ixil's wrong,"
I added. "Where did McKell and Kolodny go?"

"We're on the planet side," McKell's voice came in my earbud.
"Come join the party."

"On our way," I said, watching as Ixil started walking across
the mesh. Pix and Pax, I noted, were in their usual places on his
shoulders, encased in little vac suits of their own. It also looked
like their suits had been anchored to the torso section of Ixil's
own suit, probably to keep the outriders from getting lost, but
possibly also to create a seal that would allow their claws access
to Ixil's nervous system.

Though what use that would be out here I couldn't guess. It
wasn't like Ixil could detach them from his shoulders and send
them into some narrow conduit for a quick look. There certainly
wasn't any call for the kind of scouting duties they often per-
formed for him.

"Yes, they can detach from my shoulders," Ixil said.

I twitched, the movement nearly dislodging my feet from
the mesh. What the *hell*? "You've taken up mind-reading now?"
I asked, frowning at the back of his helmet.

"No, just reading human expressions," Ixil said. "You were
wondering if Pix and Pax can be taken off, weren't you? I saw
the way you were studying their suits."

"I was just...oh. Right," I finished lamely. Our helmets were
mostly solid metal with wide faceplates, the bulk of the helmets'
interior layered with various status displays. The outriders' helmets, in contrast, were merely bulbs of clear plastic.

And as I belatedly focused on Pax's helmet I saw that his head
was turned partway around toward me. "So they *are* plugged in?"

"Indeed," Ixil confirmed calmly. "I understand why our
helmets need to be mostly opaque, but I dislike the limitations
that puts on my field of vision. Having Pix and Pax providing
two additional points of view alleviates much of that restriction."

"Sounds handy," I agreed.

Though I strongly suspected that advantage came with a
heavy price. Ixil had never said whether or not it hurt to have
his outriders dig through his skin and into his nerves that way,
and I'd never found a good opportunity to ask him about it. But
I couldn't imagine such a thing being even moderately painless.

"Personally, I prefer having a couple of satellites or drones to watch my back," McKell put in. "But to each his own. You planning to get here sometime today?"

"We're just taking it slow," Ixil assured him. "There—I can see you."

"Likewise," I said as the top of McKell's helmet came into view over the curve of the receiver module. A few more steps, and the whole equipment layout was visible stretched out in front of us.

It was pretty impressive. The bioprobe and grav-beam generators had been set up near the intersection between the two spheres, the generators spaced about twenty meters apart, the bioprobe itself nestled inside a compact railgun launcher sitting midway between them. Set to one side and about fifteen meters back from the bioprobe were a pair of compact fusion reactors. The same distance in the other direction were two wraparound control boards. One of the boards, large and impressively complex, would be the grav-beam controller, while the other far simpler setup would be for the bioprobe. Everything looked to be glued to the hull with the same Corcoran Maxor that sealed the airlock to the interior. Thick power cables and thinner control lines linked everything together, all of it lashed securely to the hull mesh.

Lieutenant Shevrade was strapped into the grav-beam seat, hunched over the board as she presumably ran her final checklist. Kolodny stood behind her, watching her work. The colonel half turned toward us as we came into view, pointed at the two unoccupied seats at the bioprobe board. "You two over there," he ordered.

"Got it," I said, eyeing the control layout as we approached. The arrangement here was somewhat different from what I was used to on the *Ruth*, but we'd run through everything several times during our simulation runs and should be fine with it.

Which raised the question of why Selene and I were out here in the first place. There was only a limited amount of anything I could do with the bioprobe itself, and Selene certainly couldn't do an analysis of whatever it brought up until we were back in atmosphere, either inside Alpha or more likely all the way back in the Icarus base.

Had Kinneman sent us here simply so that we would be out of his sight for a few hours? Or was this my father's way of positioning us as absolutely vital parts of the Icarus team?

In which case, we probably shouldn't undercut his efforts by looking even the slightest bit incompetent. As my father used to say, *Low expectations can be your friend, but don't overuse them.*

Fortunately, in this case, low expectations weren't likely to be a problem. As Kinneman had said, handling the bioprobe during its atmospheric journey was mostly a matter of watching it do its job. Selene and I belted ourselves into our designated seats and started running our own checklist. With the simpler system we had to work with, we were finished well before Shevrade also pronounced herself ready.

"Okay," McKell said. He gave each of our boards one final look and then stepped over to join Kolodny and Ixil. "Go."

Shevrade nodded and keyed the launcher. The railgun's warning lights flashed, and ten seconds later it spat the bioprobe out toward the hazy-edged planet below.

And for the next few minutes, at least, there was nothing at all for Selene and me to do. The planetary surface read out as about two thousand kilometers away, with meaningful atmosphere beginning at about the three-hundred-kilometer mark. I confirmed that the bioprobe was on its designated trajectory, then shifted my eyes to the planet itself.

Alpha's receiver module had a set of viewports that could be opened from the launch module, but I'd never had a chance to look through any of them. For that matter, until that fateful conversation about our newly found directory half all those months ago, I hadn't even known the portal was orbiting a planet instead of simply drifting on its own through interstellar space.

I'd seen a lot of planets from space before, of course. But usually I was busy piloting, or else talking with Planetary Control for a landing field assignment, or was getting the *Ruth*'s two bioprobes ready to fly. This was possibly the first time I'd been able to just sit back and look.

Planets seen at ground level could be impressive, grotesque, or disgusting, depending on where you ended up. They were crowded with humans and aliens, peppered with conversation, noises, and odors, and usually took some getting used to. Some of the people were decent enough company, others did their best to cheat the unwary, and a few seemed to like taking potshots at anyone whose looks they didn't care for.

Planets seen from two thousand kilometers out were the complete opposite: silent, elegant, and majestic. Alpha was currently passing over the terminator line, showing us the blackness of night on one side and the sunlit end of the day on the other. On the lighted side I could see scatterings of white clouds floating over swatches of green and blue, the green areas cut into irregular pieces by the wavy brown lines of mountain ranges or the muted blue of rivers. The larger blue sections, lakes or oceans, sent sparkly reflections of sunlight peeking through the clouds. Stunning, serene, mysterious—

"Gregory," Selene whispered urgently. "Gregory, do you see it?"

I frowned. Was she talking about the general magnificence of the planet? "See what?"

"There." She pointed at a spot on the night side, just barely past the terminator line, where the tops of the highest clouds were still catching the last rays of sunlight. "There, in the middle of that line of clouds."

I followed her extended finger. The clouds were pressed up against a faintly visible dark line, probably a mountain range whose highest peaks were also still catching some of the fading light. In a small gap in the clouds—

"Shevrade!" I snapped, dropping my eyes to our control board and searching desperately for the display and controls I needed even as my fingers reflexively went toward where those spots would be on the *Ruth*'s board. "We need a grav swirl at—damn it—"

"I've got it," Selene said calmly, her fingers punching in numbers on the controls I'd been looking for.

"Selene's getting you the location," I told Shevrade. "You know how to do a grav swirl?"

"Whoa," Kolodny put in before Shevrade could answer. "What are you talking about?"

"A grav swirl," I repeated through clenched teeth. "Shevrade?"

"I don't know what that is," she said, frowning at me through her faceplate.

"I asked you a question, Roarke," Kolodny said, his tone taking on a warning note.

"A grav swirl," I said again. If Shevrade didn't even know what that was... "Never mind," I said, punching my strap release. "Move—I need your seat."

"Stay where you are," Kolodny snapped. "What the hell—?"

"Stand down, Colonel," McKell said, his own voice glacially calm. "You heard the man, Lieutenant. Out of your seat."

"McKell—?" Kolodny began harshly.

"I said *stand down*," McKell cut him off. "Roarke? What is it?"

"Give me a second and I'll show you," I said, easing myself out of my seat and heading for the grav-control board. My brain was screaming for me to hurry, that the longer I delayed the smaller the chance that a grav swirl would do the trick. But I nevertheless forced myself to walk slowly, painfully aware of the fragile grip my boots had on the mesh.

Shevrade was clear by the time I reached her station. "Selene?" I called as I lowered myself into the seat.

"I have it," she confirmed. "Grid position: 35.01.41 north by 111.01.24 west."

"Thanks," I said, punching in the location. Out of the corner of my eye I saw the grav-beam generators shift aim to comply. "Come on over—this will be easier with two of us."

By the time the grav generators had settled onto their new vector and I had adjusted their power level, she was at my side. "Take portside," I told her, moving my hands to the fine-tune control stick for the generator to the right. Kolodny had gone silent, but I could imagine the look he was probably giving the back of my helmet right now. "Ready?"

"Ready."

I nodded and keyed the power. The generators blazed to life, and if I looked closely I could see the slight distortion inside the twin beams as they yanked at the tenuous atmosphere this far out from the planet. "Okay," I said, getting a grip on my control stick and bracing myself. *"Go."*

The distortion as the beams cut through the interplanetary medium had been extremely subtle, visible only if you knew what to look for. The microscopic swiveling of the generators as Selene and I sent them twitching, rotating, and jinking back and forth was even less noticeable. I wasn't expecting any of the others to see anything at all, and I was right.

"Well?" Kolodny growled.

"Keep an eye on the far end of the beams," I told him. "You can pull up a visual overlay on your—"

"I know how to do it," the colonel cut me off. "What am I supposed to be looking at?"

"The clouds at that spot," I said. "They've closed in now, but Selene and I saw something there. Swirling the beams like this sometimes clears them away, just enough."

"At two thousand klicks' distance?" Kolodny scoffed. "What do you think they are, military-grade tractors?"

"Don't worry, they're strong enough," I assured him. "I've done more with less."

Of course, the times I'd made this trick work I'd always been a hell of a lot closer to the cloud layer in question. But Kolodny didn't need to know that. I kept the stick moving, mentally crossing my fingers . . .

And then, like a gift handed down directly from heaven, the clouds parted. Just for maybe a second or two, but long enough.

There, right where Selene and I had seen it—

"I'll be damned," McKell breathed. "Is that a *light*?"

"That's a light," I confirmed.

And felt a hollow feeling settle into my stomach. An uninhabited planet, Kinneman had said. Ours for the searching, ours potentially for the taking.

Only it wasn't.

"Apparently," I distantly heard my voice say, "we aren't here alone."

"No," Kinneman said flatly. "It's not possible. We've been watching that planet for almost eight years. Whatever you saw down there, it wasn't some indigenous people or lost civilization." He glared at me as if this was all *my* fault. "No, we've got company."

"I don't think we can be quite *that* definitive, General," McKell said. "Up until Project Needle, our surveillance mostly consisted of brief and fairly casual eyeball and sensor readings of the planet, usually in conjunction with the various physical measurements we were taking. A low-tech, isolated culture could easily have escaped our notice."

"Particularly in that location," Ixil added. "It's only about ten kilometers west of a high mountain range, with the prevailing westerly winds coming off a warm ocean current less than a hundred kilometers farther away. I've looked at some of the weather archives we've collected over the years, and that region is frequently hidden under a dense orographic cloud cover."

"Maybe that's how surveillance was handled before I arrived," Kinneman said pointedly. "Not anymore. We've been watching the planet closely for over six months, and I can assure you there were no signs of anyone down there during that time."

"What about natural phenomenon?" McKell suggested. "What we saw could have been a tight cluster of flames, maybe from the early stages of a forest or grass fire."

"Did you see any flickering?" Kinneman asked. "Or smoke?"

McKell and Ixil exchanged looks. "No to both," McKell conceded. "But a couple of seconds' worth of observation doesn't really count as a significant sample."

"As to smoke, it would have been difficult to distinguish between smoke and the cloud cover," Ixil added.

"Not after Roarke churned up everything in sight, anyway," Kinneman agreed sourly.

"I think that's a bit unfair, General," I said. Out of the corner of my eye I saw McKell flash me a warning look, but I didn't care. "If we hadn't swirled the clouds out of the way, you still wouldn't know there's someone down there."

"You think it unfair, do you?" Kinneman said. "Well, let's flip the coin over and look at the other side, shall we? Up until twelve hours ago, whoever's down there also had no idea we were flying past them on Alpha. Now, they probably do."

I looked at McKell. The warning look I'd seen a few seconds ago had turned into a sort of resignation. "I don't think that necessarily follows," I said, turning back to Kinneman. "At that distance those grav beams were too weak to affect anything solid or liquid. Unless our visitors were looking up at that exact spot at that exact time, they would have missed the show completely. Plus it was night. Stargazing is a popular pastime. Cloud gazing isn't."

Kinneman said something under his breath. "Sir Nicholas?" he invited, waving a hand toward where my father was sitting by himself in a corner of the room. "You want to explain the facts of life to your naïve offspring?"

My father stirred. "I think the point General Kinneman is making," he said, "is that a civilization advanced enough for star travel is likely to have the kind of instruments that can detect the presence of grav beams overhead, no matter how weak."

"*If* they're tourists," I countered. "As McKell's already pointed out, we still haven't established they aren't locals."

"Or they may be something in between," Kinneman said, his voice going a very unpleasant shade of black. "Tell me, Roarke: What exactly have you said to your Patth friend Nask about the portal directory?"

The room was suddenly very quiet. "I've said nothing," I said into the silence, carefully enunciating my words. "I've hinted nothing. I've offered nothing."

"Really," Kinneman said, his eyes boring into me. "I only ask because you've not only offered him a couple of portals, but delivered on that promise."

"One of those portals, I've already explained, I had no choice about," I reminded him, holding tightly onto my temper. As my father used to say, *Your temper is like a small bird: very hard to catch again once you lose it.* "The other I did for Earth and the Commonwealth."

Kinneman raised his eyebrows. "You did it for *Earth*? *That's* how you're going to pitch that debacle?"

"I suggest you ask Ixil sometime what a Patth transport embargo means to a planet," I said. *Since he's the only Kalix still here,* I wanted to add.

I resisted the temptation. As my father also used to say, *It's even harder to find someone else's temper when you're the one who goaded him into losing it.* "As for Sub-Director Nask being my friend, I think he would laugh his little mahogany-red butt off if he heard you say that. I'm pretty sure his main plan is to squeeze me for everything he and the Patth can get."

"And he seems to be doing a damn good job of it," Kinneman growled.

"Only if you look solely at his side of the balance sheet," I said. "If you look at *our* side, I would submit that we're holding our own pretty well."

Behind me, the conference room door opened, and I turned to see one of the Marine guards at the door usher Selene inside. "This conversation isn't over," Kinneman warned me as he shifted his eyes to Selene. "Well?"

Selene's pupils gave a reflexive wince at the sharpness of his tone. A second later their expression shifted again, this time set-tling into a calm determination. "Nothing," she said.

"*Nothing?*"

"Nothing," she repeated. "No Icari metal, either the portal or directory variants."

"But there *was* a sampling of biomass, I assume?"

A slight frown crossed Selene's pupils. "Yes, of course," she said. "Your people have already taken it away for analysis."

"Good." Kinneman's eyes were still on her, but I had the sense that he was thinking about something else entirely. "Good enough for now, anyway," he amended. "You and Roarke are dismissed back to your suite. The Marines will pick you up in an hour for dinner."

"When will we be going back to Alpha?" I asked as I stood up.

Kinneman frowned. "To Alpha? What for?"

"The next bioprobe survey," I said, frowning back. "Our current data is from a hundred kilometers away from the light show. We'll want to do a flyby of that particular spot as soon as possible."

"Perhaps," Kinneman murmured. "We'll see. Dismissed."

CHAPTER SIX

An hour later, our guards got the word and escorted us to the dining room. Several of the other staff were there, including Kolodny and his engineering team. Kinneman, McKell, Ixil, and my father, I noted, were elsewhere, possibly some exclusive dining area.

Selene and I ate quickly and returned to our suite. With the prospect of a quick bioprobe turnaround hovering in front of us, we made sure to hit the sack early.

I'd half expected to be awakened in the middle of the night with orders to return immediately to the Icarus ready room. We weren't. Next best guess would be for us to be summoned at our usual waking time, or during or after breakfast, or during or after lunch.

None of those happened, either.

In the middle of the afternoon I tried calling McKell and Ixil. No answer. I tried leaving them messages. Neither of them messaged back. I tried getting our door guards to take us somewhere—anywhere—where we might run into someone else who could tell us why we'd suddenly been put on ice. Nothing.

It was an hour before dinner, and I was seriously considering trying to make a break for it, just to see how far the Marines were willing to go to keep us penned up, when our isolation finally lifted.

Though not in the way I'd expected.

"I just wanted to drop by and tell you that all bioprobe surveys have been suspended indefinitely," McKell said, waving us over to a group of four chairs at one side of the conversation area. He watched us seat ourselves in two of the chairs, then set off on a wandering path around the room, looking for all the world like someone in an interesting new environment who's casually checking out the décor.

Having been cooped up here far longer than anyone would ever have wanted to, I could have told him there was nothing at all interesting in the place.

"I also wanted to make sure you two weren't going stir-crazy in here while the general figures out what to do with you next."

"I thought we were the Icarus Group's original one-trick pony," I pointed out, looking sideways at Selene. She'd clearly picked up on McKell's odd behavior, and her pupils were showing the same growing apprehension I was feeling.

For her, her uneasiness would be coming from the subtle changes she could smell in McKell's scent. For me, it was all about the way he was searching for bugs and other monitoring devices without being too obvious about it. "Our trick being that Selene finds the RH directory, wherever it came down, while I cheerlead from the sidelines."

"Sounds like your usual gig," McKell said. "Of course, that assumes RH *did* come down here. Or was ever here to begin with."

"Assuming all that, yes," I conceded. "So is the general having trouble wrapping his mind around Selene's abilities?"

"It's more like he's trying to figure out how to add a second trick to your repertoire," McKell said. "He's had the rest of us sequestered in a very private room since yesterday's meeting, in fact, brainstorming possibilities."

"Of course we'll look forward to hearing whatever you come up with," I said. Best guess as I listened to him and watched his meanderings was that he was trying to stretch out the froth part of the conversation until he concluded it was safe to switch to whatever it was he'd really come here to tell us. If that was the case, I was more than willing to play along. "We've thought about branching out into lie-detector work, but so far that hasn't taken off."

"Yes, I remember you pulling that trick on Tera back when

we first met," McKell said. "Seemed very effective. But I don't think that'll be something we can use here."

"Why not?" I asked. "Kinneman seems pretty paranoid about the Patth and people dropping hints to them. Maybe we could check his staff for him and see if any of them, shall we say, have been talking out of turn into the wrong ears."

"That's a serious accusation," McKell warned. "You have anything to back it up?"

"Oh, no, I'm not accusing anyone of anything," I assured him. "But we know how the Patth have backdoors into StarrComm and a lot of planetary communications networks. It wouldn't be a stretch for them to add human intel assets to that mix."

"Well, if someone here is feeding anything to the Patth, I wouldn't want to be in those shoes when the general finds out," McKell said. He came to a halt in the middle of the rug and gave the room one final, careful look. "But you're right about the Patth passion for intel gathering. I suppose the power-hungry are always like that."

"The power-hungry, and the paranoid," I said. "I think it's a toss-up as to which crowd the Patth land in. You finished?"

McKell pursed his lips, then nodded. "Yes," he said, coming over and sitting down across from us. "The brainstorming I mentioned finished up about an hour ago." His lip twitched. "The bad news is the hill it landed on. General Kinneman has decided on a military incursion."

I felt my mouth drop open. "A *what*?"

"You heard me," McKell said grimly. "A full EarthGuard HOTSPUR assault. The only question is how many platoons he'll be able to commandeer and how fast they can get here."

"With all due respect, he must be out of his mind."

"I don't like it either," McKell said. "But whatever the state of his mind, it's completely made up."

"What's HOTSPUR?" Selene asked.

"High Orbit To Surface Pursuit," McKell told her. "Basically, it's a military team suited up in what amounts to tiny rockets who drop unexpectedly into and through a planetary atmosphere, and hit the ground ready to kill people and break things."

"That seems...dangerous."

"It is," McKell agreed. "HOTSPUR soldiers are among the most elite in EarthGuard, right up there with the LOGI—that's Low

Orbit/Ground Infantry—and SOLA—Space Ocean Land Air—units. They're highly trained, highly motivated, and highly respected."

"And you say they're strapped into their *rockets*?"

"Personal rockets complete with thrusters and retros," McKell said. "Plus a generous coating of ablative material to absorb some of the atmospheric friction."

"It still sounds dangerous," Selene said, the apprehension in her pupils taking on some puzzlement. "Once they're down, how do they get back up?"

"Normally a shuttle is dropped to pick them up after the mission's been completed," McKell said. "If they're needed elsewhere in the same operations theater they'll be moved via ground or air transport."

"Only here none of those options are available," I said grimly. "They're stuck until... well, until they die."

A look of horror flooded across Selene's pupils. "They're being sent on a *suicide mission*?"

"It's not quite that bad," McKell said, an odd reluctance in his tone. "The plan is to bring a shuttle through in pieces and assemble it at Alpha. Once that's done, they'll be able to go down and bring them back."

"Really," I ground out. "Excuse my cynicism, but *saying* you'll do something is a lot easier than actually doing it. Out of curiosity, how long did it take to get the bioprobe and grav generators pushed through the Alpha hatches and assembled?"

McKell's lip twitched. "About five months."

"Five months," I repeated. "I'm hardly in Colonel Kolodny's class, engineering-wise, but even I can see that putting together a shuttle is a couple of magnitudes harder than doing the same thing with a bioprobe. Or am I being too pessimistic?"

"No, that's basically the estimate Kolodny came up with," McKell agreed.

"So," I said. "Two orders of magnitude up from five months gives us... about forty years, give or take."

"Unless someone comes up with a faster technique, yes."

"It's good to have goals," I said sarcastically. "So basically, their choices are to die from native spears, starvation, or old age. Or whatever predators are down there. Did I miss anything?"

"*Now* you're being pessimistic," McKell chided. "You're forgetting that the railgun we used to launch the bioprobe is already in position. We can keep up a steady stream of ablative-shielded supply pods as long as the team needs them."

"Right," I said. "Because people high-tech enough to spot a grav swirl in the clouds will *certainly* miss a procession of half-ton pods parachuting into their forest. The HOTSPUR team might as well put up a beacon announcing their location."

"Or the natives might simply intercept or destroy the pods before the team even gets to them," Selene murmured.

"Actually, we discussed that possibility," McKell said. "Our analysis of the bioprobe contents indicates that the native flora and fauna should have all the necessary amino acids and micro-nutrients to create a reasonable human diet. If the landing team can get a farm set up, or even just manage a sustainable hunter-gatherer system, there's a good chance they could live off the land until the shuttle is ready."

"I feel better already," I said. "Somehow, I'm still not seeing a crowd of eager volunteers clamoring to sign up for a forty-year mission."

McKell shrugged uncomfortably. "The general assures us he'll be able to pull together more resources to throw at this than Admiral Graym-Barker was given for the bioprobe setup. If that helps any."

"Of course he says that," I said. "See my earlier comments about *talking* and *doing*. But fine. Halve that forty years all the way down to twenty. You're still not going to get a lot of volunteers."

"I agree," McKell said heavily. "Which is why I gather the general isn't planning to ask."

I stared at him. "Does he really think he can sell a conscript semi-suicide mission to the Commonwealth and the EarthGuard senior generals?"

"*He* thinks he can," McKell said. "And to be honest, the handful of officers and politicians who've been read into Project Needle are apparently *very* eager to get their hands on RH. If Kinneman can convince them that he can deliver, I get the feel-ing they'll give him carte blanche."

He seemed to brace himself. "And here's where it goes from bad to worse." Almost reluctantly, he looked at Selene.

And suddenly my blood went cold. "No," I breathed. "*Hell* no."

"It's the only way this makes even marginal sense," McKell said. "The HOTSPUR team isn't going down for an extended vacation or to plant the Commonwealth flag. Kinneman wants RH, the Commonwealth wants it, and the only way to get it—"

"Is if I'm down there with them," Selene said quietly, her pupils brimming with fear and horror.

"No," I repeated, emphasizing the word even more. "I'm not letting him sentence Selene to what amounts to a lifetime exile."

"I don't want that either," McKell said. "Neither do Ixil and Tera. But this isn't Admiral Graym-Barker's Icarus Group anymore, and we don't have the influence with Kinneman that we had with him. And as I say, he and everyone else wants a full portal directory."

"Then let me put this in terms they can hopefully grasp," I said softly. Those first blinding flashes of disbelief and fury had faded from my mind and soul, leaving a hollow but deadly resolve in their place. "Selene isn't going. Period. Not under those conditions." I looked at her, then back at McKell. "Before I let that happen, I will personally and permanently take her off the table."

I saw a flicker of black amusement cross McKell's face, the look of someone who's hearing hyperbole and prepared to accept it as such. A second later, the full meaning of my threat seemed to hit him squarely across the face. "Roarke—"

"After which," I cut him off, "I'll kill myself." I gave a small shrug. "Which will be a shame. I'd have enjoyed hearing Kinneman try to explain that one to his precious Commonwealth supporters."

"Roarke, let's think about this before we go off the deep end," McKell said carefully.

"Oh, I'm thinking," I assured him. "And I'm certainly not taking any irrevocable steps until they're absolutely necessary. I just want to impress on you that no matter what Kinneman does, he's not going to end up with the big win he's looking for. I trust you can deliver that message?"

"I can deliver it," McKell said reluctantly. "But I don't think he'll listen."

"I'm sure he won't," I agreed. "So here's Plan B. I want you to pull my father aside and tell *him* how this is going to end. Maybe you and I can't get through to Kinneman, but maybe he can."

"Assuming *he's* willing to listen to me," McKell warned.

"Oh, he'll listen," I assured him. "He's always been good at that. Whether he'll be able to do anything is a different story. But he's always been a survivor, and I can't see him keeping his wagon hitched to Kinneman's donkey if he sees that donkey about to get booted off his lofty peak and go splat on the ground. Who knows? Maybe my father publicly bailing on Project Needle will be enough to make Kinneman reconsider."

"Maybe," McKell said, sounding doubtful. "Interesting turn of phrase, 'booted off his lofty peak.' What was that old line? *I saw Lucifer fall like lightning from heaven.*"

I frowned. "Excuse me?"

"It's from the Bible," McKell explained, standing up. "Lucifer, an angel of light, on his way to becoming Satan, the devil. It's sounding more and more like Kinneman's future career path."

"Maybe," I said, frowning as a sudden thought struck me. *Booted off his lofty peak...* "Any idea how long before Kinneman can get this future fiasco up and running?"

"It'll be at least a few days before he can announce it," McKell said. "His people are still working out the logistics to present to the Commonwealth, and Colonel Kolodny needs to put together a full mark-sheet of how his engineers would get a shuttle out to Alpha. And of course, he can't just call Earth on StarrComm to discuss it with EarthGuard and the Commonwealth. Not with the Patth eavesdropping everywhere."

"Okay," I said, thinking hard. A few days should be enough to at least figure out if my idea was even theoretically possible. "Do me a favor, will you? Come back and see us again tomorrow. Any time will do. Under the circumstances I doubt Kinneman will be letting us wander outside checking out the local sights."

"If there are even any local sights to see," McKell said. Even here, even under these circumstances, his automatic response was to not say anything that might give us a hint as to where we were. "I'll aim for this same time."

"That'll do," I said. "And bring Ixil and Tera if you can."

"I will," McKell said, giving me a speculative look. He'd seen some of my harebrained ideas before, and he knew how far off the charts those ideas could be.

But he'd also seen that more of them panned out than the laws of probability would reasonably predict.

"In the meantime, try to get some rest," he added, heading toward the door. "And if anyone asks, I just dropped by to say you wouldn't be needed on bioprobe duty for the near future."

"Which Selene and I were both relieved and disappointed to hear," I said, nodding. "See you later."

He nodded back and crossed to the door. As he opened it, walked through, and closed it behind him I caught a glimpse of the Marines standing their silent vigil.

"Yes," Selene murmured.

I looked at her, wincing at the sadness and determination in her pupils. "Yes, what?"

"If it comes down to only those two choices," she said quietly, "yes. Please kill me."

"It won't," I promised her. Standing up, I went over to the table where we'd left our info pads. "Come on. We've got work to do."

It was two hours before dinner the next day when McKell, Ixil, and Tera knocked on our door. We greeted each other with the friendly humor and camaraderie all five of us knew would help lull the guards away from any suspicion they might have about our meeting. Tera, in particular, had thought to put additional icing on the cake, bringing a couple of bags of grainory chips and a bottle of Dewar's scotch for me, plus a bottle of Selene's favorite sauvignon for her. Just a group of comrades-in-arms touching base with each other on a lazy afternoon.

Distantly, I wondered how many of them would still consider themselves my friend after this.

I'd already drawn a fifth chair into the original ring of four, waiting until the others had seated themselves before doing likewise. "Let's begin with the bad news," I said as I lowered myself into the remaining chair. "At least I assume it's bad news. McKell?"

"I talked with your father," he said. "He's fully aware of the seriousness of the situation, and agrees that sending you and Selene is not the right thing to do."

"But he won't talk to Kinneman?"

"He won't talk to Kinneman," McKell confirmed, "because he believes that if the general knew of your scorched-ground threat he would immediately separate the two of you. He might even put you both in restraints."

I grimaced. He was probably right, too. "Nice of him to at least allow us the illusion that we have freedom of movement."

"As opposed to the reality of having none at all?" Tera pointed out.

"I suppose," I conceded. "I should have thought that through a bit more. Lucifer to Satan—right, McKell?"

"If you're hoping to mend fences with the general," McKell said with a touch of dry humor, "I'd keep such comparisons to yourself."

"Don't worry, he won't hear it from me," I assured him. "Anyway, I think I can give him a far better reason to hate me. Actually, it was your comment that pointed me in the right direction."

"I can hardly wait," McKell said. "So what's your plan?"

"We take away Kinneman's motivation to send Selene and his HOTSPUR crew to the planet," I said. "And if we're lucky, he still gets to win everything."

I braced myself. "Like Lucifer in your quote, we're going to kick Alpha out of heaven and bring it crashing to the ground."

CHAPTER SEVEN

I'd half expected barks of derision, cries of outrage, or gasps of disbelief. But these were the people who'd successfully snuck the original *Icarus* out from under the collective nose of the Patth, and who had played a quiet and mostly successful game against them ever since. They were people of thought, consideration, and speculation. Reflexive sounds of anything weren't how they were built.

Ixil was the first to speak. "I assume," he said, "there's more to it than that."

"Oh, there is," I assured him. "Selene?"

"We ran some numbers," she said, pulling up the file on her info pad and handing it to Ixil. "This is Alpha's orbit now compared to what it was eight years ago when you first found it."

"Yes, I've seen these," Ixil said, glancing at the numbers and diagrams and then handing the info pad to McKell. "Nearly perfectly circular, strongly implying it was deliberately placed in orbit rather than being the result of gravitational capture."

"Indeed," I agreed. "But look again. The distance to the planet hasn't changed so much as a millimeter in the past eight years."

"That sounds right," McKell said, handing the info pad in turn to Tera.

"But it *should* have changed," I pointed out. "The atmosphere two thousand kilometers up is thin, but it's still there. Not to mention solar wind and possible micrometeor impacts. Even in just eight years the orbit should have shown a noticeable decay. If you're right about the Icari having disappeared ten millennia ago, Alpha should have fallen out of the sky by now." I raised my eyebrows. "So why hasn't it?"

"It's possible it started out much higher," Ixil suggested.

"And was able to maintain a nearly circular orbit the whole time?" Tera pointed out. "Seems unlikely."

"It also doesn't work," I said. "At least not if our backtrack program is correct. If we take the theoretical air resistance into account and run the timeline backward, we get Alpha to a distance where it would be too far away to have been gravitationally bound to the planet at all."

"I presume you have an alternate explanation?" McKell asked, handing the info pad back to Selene.

"We have *an* explanation," I said. "Whether it's the correct one we're not yet sure." I gestured to Selene. "Selene?"

"We know the portals have their own internal gravitational fields," she said, pulling up a different page and again handing the info pad to Ixil. "Fields with two distinct focal points, one at the center of each module. I don't know how to do the physics properly, but the simulation I was able to create suggests that the portal would interact oddly with a planetary gravitational field."

"You mean like it disconnects from it?" Tera asked, frowning.

"Not *disconnects,* exactly," Selene said. "The planet's gravity still holds it in a stable orbit. It's just that small perturbations like air resistance seem to be compensated for."

"You may be right," Ixil said, peering at the info pad. Pix and Pax, I noted, were crouched with unusual stillness on his shoulders. "Yes, I see where you're going with this. If the portal resists changes in its orbit, then nudging it inward might result in a measured path to the surface instead of an uncontrolled death-spiral crash."

"That would be handy," Tera agreed. "It would also be suspiciously convenient."

"Maybe not all *that* suspicious," I said. "I mean, there have always been hints in that direction. All the other portals we've found have been undamaged, with no indication that any of them blasted to the ground at an uncontrolled eleven kilometers a second. We've also never found one in the center of the kind of crater an impact like that would normally throw up."

"Though ten thousand years adds up to a *lot* of erosion," McKell said, taking the info pad from Ixil. "Alternatively, the portals could just be really, really indestructible."

"Which would get us to the same end," I pointed out. "It would put Alpha on the ground where Kinneman's HOTSPUR team or whoever could come and go at will."

"At least once they climb out of the two-hundred-meter crater they just made," McKell said dryly.

"Actually, Jordan, I think Gregory's right," Tera said thoughtfully. "Even if the blast rim eroded away, there should be tectonic cracks or subtle ray systems or *something* still measurable if an object that big hit the ground that hard. In fact, now that I think about it, I remember reading a report a few years ago where that absence was noted and that exact question was raised."

"Maybe," McKell said doubtfully as he handed the info pad to Tera. "I'm still not ready to buy into this."

"McKell—" I began.

"So let me get this straight," he interrupted, locking eyes with me. "You want us to smuggle a bunch of explosives to Alpha, figure out where to put them so we can knock it out of orbit, set them off, and hope like hell it doesn't end up a pile of twisted alien metal that we'll never see or use again. That about sum it up?"

"Mostly," I said cautiously. Put that way, it *did* sound pretty insane. "Except that you won't need any explosives. Everything we need to change Alpha's orbit is already in place."

"Wait a minute," Tera said, frowning up from the pad. "You're not talking about the grav generators, are you?"

"I am," I said, nodding.

"I thought the beams were too weak to do anything at that distance."

"They were strong enough to haul the bioprobe up from the stratosphere," I reminded her. "No, Selene and I just cranked down the power when we swirled the clouds."

"He's right," Ixil said. "All we need to do is point them at something solid like a mountaintop, fire them up—"

"At the *right* mountaintop," McKell muttered.

"Yes, the *right* mountaintop," Ixil agreed, "then just let Alpha and the planet pull themselves together. If you do the calculations and positioning properly, you should be able to land the portal wherever you want."

"Which I assume is how the Icari settled them onto their designated planets in the first place," I said.

For a long minute the room was silent. I watched Selene, but whatever she was getting from their scents all I could read in her pupils was nervousness.

"I assume you understand the full range of possible consequences of what you're asking us to do," Tera said at last. "If you're wrong, Kinneman ends up with a tangle of useless scrap metal on a distant planet that we'll never see again, and we end up executed for treason. Even if you're right, we'll probably still be brought up on charges."

"And if you're *half* right," McKell added, "Alpha survives the landing but something breaks loose and it no longer functions properly. Depending on the specific damage, we may never be able to use it again or—worse—we can go through but can't get back."

"Again stranding the landing party," Tera said. "Only there'd never be a way to get them a shuttle."

"Or anywhere for them to go if we did," Ixil pointed out.

"Exactly," Tera said soberly. "Nor could we send them supplies unless someone hand-delivered each package."

"Why not?" I asked. "Can't you just strap something to the extension arm and let it go?"

McKell shook his head. "You can't send inanimate objects through all by themselves. You need a living hand to trigger the launch sequence."

He paused, and I saw that all three of them were staring at me. "I agree it's a horrible risk," I said into the silence. "Graym-Barker gave lip service at least to the idea of his underlings taking the initiative. I'm guessing Kinneman doesn't even go that far. That's why all we're asking you to do is run some numbers, or just get us access to a program that'll let us figure this out on our own. After that, we'll ask you to go off somewhere and establish alibis. Selene and I will do the rest."

"What about the Marines outside?" McKell asked, nodding toward the door.

I shrugged. "We get past them, we get to Icarus, we get to Alpha, and we get it done."

"And we all hope together that it works," McKell said.

"Yes," I said. "And whether it does or not, Selene and I take the consequences. At least we'll have the consolation that Kinneman didn't send a bunch of elite soldiers on a one-way mission when we go to the gallows."

Again, the three of them looked at each other, and I could sense the wordless communication. "All right, we're in," McKell said as they turned back to us. "You still have those knockout pills you used to carry around?"

"That I *still* carry around," I corrected. "How many do you need?"

He pursed his lips, apparently doing some private calculation. "Five should do it."

I frowned, throwing a sideways look at Selene. Whatever he was up to, she apparently wasn't getting any details.

Still, if this was a ploy to confiscate every weapon at my disposal before he handed me over to Kinneman, he really ought to have asked for all six. Pushing up my sleeve, I worked the release at the wrist of my artificial left arm and popped open the hidden compartment. "You sure you don't want all of them?" I asked as I pulled out five of the pills.

"No, five should do it," he said. "How fast do they work?"

"Pretty fast," I said as I handed them to him. "Always within a minute, usually within a few seconds. Be sure you bear that in mind when you work out your lead time."

"Got it," he said, carefully tucking the pills away in an inside pocket. "How long does the target sleep?"

"About six hours," I said. "A bit more or less if his body mass is smaller or bigger than average."

"Or you can put one in a bottle of wine and make everyone extra groggy," Tera offered.

"Thank you, I *do* remember that one," McKell said dryly as he stood up. "Okay, Roarke, you're on. We'll be in touch. Probably not for four or five days, though, so be patient."

"All right," I said, eyeing him closely. There was something in his voice and expression I didn't like, but I couldn't pin it down. "Remember: the numbers or the program. We'll handle everything else."

"Got it," McKell said. "We'll be in touch."

I watched as they filed out of the room, their speech and manner suddenly back to the casual banter they'd been faking on their way in. If they were planning to turn us in, at least they weren't going to sic our Marine guard on us here and now.

I waited until the door was closed. "What do you think?" I asked Selene.

"They mostly agree with our plan," she said, her pupils running through several expressions as she sifted through the changes in scent she'd experienced over the past few minutes. "Though I don't think any of them particularly like it."

"Well, that makes five of us," I said. "The big question is whether this agreement of theirs is going to translate into action."

"I think it will," Selene said, her pupils settling into a frown. "But there's something more. Something I can't get a handle on."

"Well, work it out as best you can," I said. "But do it fast."

I looked at the door. "If McKell's pulling one of his famous off-kilter surprises here, I'd prefer to know about it before we get to the *hey presto!* part."

The next two days dragged by. We spent most of that time in our suite, only being let out for meals. My requests to our guards to allow me to see or at least message my father were politely received, then completely ignored.

Still, it wasn't a total loss. Selene found a computer file she was able to access that showed part of the base's floor plan. It only included the areas we'd already been allowed into—the rest was marked as classified—but still it gave us more of an overall perspective and feel for the layout than we'd had before.

I also found a way to use one of our water glasses to enhance the muffled sounds coming in through the door. I usually couldn't get full conversations, though I could pick up individual words here and there if the Marine in question was talking loudly. But the varying tones were clear enough, and I made copious mental notes as I gauged from the casualness or precision of the voices which of them took their boring guard duty perhaps more seriously than the others.

The enhancement was also good enough for me to note the additional foot movements and multiple voices that signified a shift change. I made careful mental notes on that, as well. By the time McKell was ready with the data, I would hopefully know which ones I had the best chance of sneaking past.

In the popular mind, the middle of the night was an ideal

time for jailbreaks and other forms of mischief. What the popular mind failed to realize was that prison guards and other security types also knew that, and therefore made it a point to be extra alert during the hours of darkness when most people were asleep. I naturally knew better than to try anything that blatantly obvious.

McKell, apparently, didn't.

My only warning was a sudden whisper of air wafting across my face warning me that my bedroom door had just been opened. I got my hands under the blankets, preparing to loft them up into my visitor's face while I simultaneously rolled off onto the floor and hopefully out of immediate reach. I heard stealthy footsteps approaching—

"Don't just lie there, Roarke," McKell's stage whisper came in the darkness. "Up and at 'em."

"You're joking," I protested, still lofting the blankets but now only far enough for me to get out from under them. "At—?"

"Two-thirty in the morning," he supplied, flicking on a flashlight whose beam had been adjusted to be just bright enough to remind me where I'd left my clothes. "Come on. Alpha awaits us."

"*Alpha?*" I echoed, grabbing my trousers and glaring into the darkness behind the pale glow where I estimated his face would be. "I told you to get us the numbers and then get out of the way."

"I don't recall ever being told to take orders from you," he said. "Come on, snap it up. It'd be very embarrassing if Selene's ready before you are."

"You woke her up *first*?" I demanded, pulling on my shirt.

"Didn't wake her up at all," he corrected. "I'm pretty sure she got the message without any help."

I muttered a curse under my breath. Of course Selene already knew McKell was here. The suite's air flow system was quite efficient.

She wouldn't just have gotten the simple fact of his presence, either. The urgency I could hear in his voice would have also altered his scent in a way that she would have picked up on and correctly interpreted.

I didn't mind losing a dressing race to my partner. Actually, the idea of such a contest struck me as pretty stupid. What I objected to was McKell dragging her into whatever the hell he was up to without clearing it with me first. She might well be indispensable to Project Needle, but there was no guarantee Kinneman would remember that when he found out what we'd done. As my father used to say, *Enlightened self-interest often goes out the window when that cheery light turns into the blaze of white-hot fury.*

McKell waited until I was ready. Then, gesturing me for silence, he led the way into the conversation room. Sure enough, Selene was waiting by the door, fully dressed. "Jordan?" she asked softly.

"We're heading to Alpha," he murmured back. "Just play along."

I couldn't see Selene's pupils in the dim light, but I knew she'd already have sampled my scent, run her analysis of my thoughts and mood, and concluded that McKell and I had already discussed this and that I was on board.

Which was unfortunately only partially true. But with him already halfway to the door, any reticence or confusion on our part would only risk sabotaging whatever he was planning.

Losing was bad enough. Losing by default was always worse. All we could do now was hang on tight and hope he could pull this off.

He reached the door and pulled it open. "Sergeant," he said briskly as he stepped out into the small cluster of Marines waiting in the corridor. "We're heading out. Should be back within the hour."

"Yes, sir," one of them said, his eyes flicking to me and then Selene as we followed McKell through the doorway. Other than the four of them, the corridor appeared to be deserted. "You sure you don't want us to accompany you? I'm told this character can be a handful."

"He can, and if it were up to me you'd all be invited," McKell said, a hint of annoyance in his voice. "But the admiral insisted we keep this quiet, and the last thing we need is for someone to wander past and notice their guard is missing. Don't worry, I can handle him."

The sergeant gave me a cool once-over. In return, I gave him my best mix of no-nonsense determination and driven-snow innocence. "Whatever you say, Colonel," he said, still clearly not happy with the arrangement. "Whistle if you need us."

"I will." McKell gestured to us. "Come on, you two."

I waited until we were well out of earshot of the Marines. "You didn't really rope Graym-Barker into this, did you?" I muttered.

"Of course not," McKell murmured back. "He just cut the orders I needed to get you out of your cell."

"The *admiral* did that?"

"Maybe not him personally," McKell conceded. "But his computer did. Close enough. Selene?"

"No one else nearby," she said, her eyelashes fluttering. "Six more Marine guards down the corridor around the next corner. Two are at the next intersection past the corner, the other four are about fifty meters farther. What do you mean, 'his computer did'?"

"Don't ask questions," I advised, visualizing the partial floor plan we'd been able to pull up. The intersection Selene had mentioned would be the cross corridor heading off to an area I'd tentatively tagged as either the base's administration complex or officers' quarters. Typically, I'd noted, there were one to two pairs of Marines watching that point. The four guards farther away were almost certainly standing at the entrance to the Icarus ready room and the portal beyond. "It's called plausible deniability. You have a plan, McKell?"

He nodded. "Same one you just saw."

"The admiral's computer talking to them, too?"

"Something like that. Ready for Act Two?"

"Do we have a choice?"

"Do you want Kinneman to maroon Selene on Alpha's planet?"

I glared at the back of his head. But he was right. Especially since this whole thing had been our idea in the first place before McKell and the others started tweaking it. "Point taken. Lead on."

I'd expected this next pair of Marines to be more disinclined to let us pass than the group outside our suite, if only because we were heading into genuinely sensitive parts of the base. But they merely exchanged nods with McKell as we approached and let us continue on without challenge. Apparently, McKell had prepped the ground on his way to our suite. The ready room door and its four guards, who'd come into view the second we rounded the corner, eyed us as we approached, and I found myself wondering if McKell had an exit strategy if this group didn't buy his Admiral Graym-Barker story.

But whatever message had come down the pike from the admiral, it had apparently been something no one was willing to argue with. Once again, the Marines made no move to impede our activity. They exchanged silent nods with McKell, watched as he keyed in the door's passcode—it would be changed daily, of course, possibly even hourly—and as the lock snicked open they stood aside and watched us file in.

"Where is everybody?" I asked, looking around as McKell led the way toward the rack of vac suits. The last time Selene and I had been here the place had been buzzing with techs and Marines prepping for their upcoming trip to Alpha. Now, it was like a small, self-contained ghost town.

"I assume they're all tucked away in their beds," McKell said. "Dreaming of sugarplums or however that poem goes. Kinneman put all bioprobe operations on hold, remember?"

"And no one thought it strange that you and two questionables suddenly were being ordered to go in?"

"Never underestimate the power of bureaucratic mud," McKell said. He pulled my suit off the rack and handed it to me. "Triple that if it's a military bureaucracy. Generally speaking, orders only go to the people who need to know or who those orders supposedly affect."

"And such orders can always be overridden?" I suggested as I started to climb into my suit.

"Not always, but usually," McKell agreed as he handed Selene her suit and then got his own. "It helps if your name has a senior rank in front of it, of course."

"Or if you can borrow someone else's," I said with a grimace. "Poking Kinneman with a sharp stick wasn't enough for you? You had to poke Graym-Barker, too?"

"No way around it." He gave me a tight smile as he started putting on his suit. "I'm waiting for the appropriate aphorism from your father's collection. Something like, *It's easier to ask forgiveness than permission,* maybe?"

I shook my head. "Too easy," I said. "Probably more like, *If you push people hard enough and long enough, sooner or later you'll find yourself in so much trouble that there's really nothing more they can throw at you. At that point, you might as well just relax and keep going.*"

"Ah," McKell said. "Nice."

"But inaccurate," Selene said quietly. "There's always something worse someone can do."

"Such as?" McKell asked.

"There are still Marines inside Alpha." She pointed at a rack of armored vac suits with five missing. "One of them might shoot us."

"You want to respond, McKell?" I asked.

"Don't worry," he said, a hint of humor in his voice. "They've been dealt with. Very cleverly, too, if I do say so myself."

But to my ears he didn't sound entirely certain. I looked at Selene, saw my same doubt in her pupils. "What if they haven't?"

"They have," McKell said, more confidently this time. "And if they haven't... like your dad said, we just keep going."

"Fine," I growled. I sometimes forgot how irritating McKell's confidence in himself could be. "Just remember that when the shooting starts, you're the one Selene and I will be hiding behind."

"I wouldn't have it any other way," he said, all hints of lightness abruptly gone. "You two are indispensable to finding RH. I'm not. If it comes to a life-for-life trade, that's exactly how it plays out."

I looked at Selene, saw her pupils flinch. "I suppose we'll just have to make sure it doesn't come to that kind of trade," I said.

"Certainly wasn't something I had my heart set on," McKell agreed. "Ready? Good. Let me double-check your seals and we'll go."

CHAPTER EIGHT

Three minutes later, we were inside the Icarus launch module. McKell knelt down at the control board and punched in Alpha's address, and we headed up the extension arm toward the glowing gray section.

I found myself staring at my gloved hand as we floated toward the sphere's center, McKell's comment a few days ago coming suddenly to mind. "You said something living had to be touching the extension arm in order to trigger the launch," I reminded him. "How come we can do it with vac-suit gloves?"

"I said you needed a living *hand* to trigger it," he corrected. "I didn't say the hand had to be touching it directly. And no, I don't know how the portal knows the difference between a vac suit around a living hand and a vac suit around nothing. But it apparently does."

"Convenient," I said, frowning. Back on Alainn, Selene had spoken of the portal there being dead. I still didn't know if that comment had been literal or figurative. But if the mechanism could detect life through a vac suit, that might be a strong vote toward the literal side of that question.

Or it might simply be sensing heat, a pulse, a subtle electromagnetic field, or any of a dozen other factors that life had and nonlife didn't. Chasing down all of that was presumably on the Icarus Group's to-do list.

Luckily, it wasn't on mine. I knew how we got from here to there and back again, and that was all I cared about.

We reached the gray section, I felt the tingle as the universe went black, and we found ourselves floating in the center of Alpha's receiver module.

With vac-armored Marines lying on their backs at five different spots around the curved deck, heavy military-class lasers at the ready.

My whole body went stiff, a flash of panic flooding over my brain, the old phrase *shooting fish in a barrel* flashing to mind. Five EarthGuard Marines against the three of us. Them armed and in fixed positions, us unarmed and floating helplessly in the middle of a forty-meter sphere.

"Ixil?" McKell's voice came in my earbud. "How's our timing?"

"Still within our window," Ixil's voice came back. "But I need Selene out here as soon as possible."

"She's on her way," McKell said as we began drifting toward the surface.

Still no response from the Marines. I frowned down at them, wondering what they were waiting for.

Only then did my eyes and brain pick up on what I should have spotted right away. The men lying on their backs down there were indeed heavily armed, but none of their weapons were pointed at us. In fact, now that my reflexive panic was lifting, I could see their lasers were only loosely gripped in their gloved hands and were merely lying across their chests.

And McKell *had* only wanted five of my knockout pills. "I can't wait to hear how you got all five of them to drink with you," I said. "What was it, a toast to the new Alien Portal Agency?"

"Hardly," McKell said. "While we're inside Alpha these suits draw from the local air supply, keeping the tanks in reserve for contaminants or emergency decompression. Did you know that if you grind those knockout pills into an exceedingly fine powder, your target can inhale them without even noticing? And that they work even faster than if you dissolved one in their drink?"

"Didn't know that, no," I said, peering down at the Marines and wishing I could see the slow rise and fall of their chests to confirm they were still breathing. But of course that kind of subtle movement was impossible to see through vacuum armor. "I hope you tested a sample first to make sure it was safe."

"We did," McKell assured me. "Which means Nhu over there will probably wake up a few minutes before everyone else."

"Okay," I said, still a bit doubtful. I'd never tried using the knockout pills that way.

"The alternative was for you to sneak up behind each one, crouch down, and let one of us push him over you," Ixil offered.

"Point taken," I said, tucking my concerns into a back corner of my mind. McKell and Ixil had been working this game a long time. They presumably knew what they were doing. "What's next?"

"Ixil is outside with the grav generators and all the relevant numbers and vectors," McKell said. "Selene will go out and help him set everything up while you and I lug the Marines across to Icarus."

"And then?"

"Then we all high-tail it back home," McKell said, "and cross our fingers really, really hard."

"Probably while in custody," Ixil added calmly. "That part will be for General Kinneman to decide."

"Probably," I said, rather pleased at how calmly that word had come from my lips. Calm, determined, and confident.

And a complete lie.

But McKell and Ixil wouldn't know it until it was too late. And for once, with all of us encased in airtight vac suits, I didn't have to worry about Selene and her hypersensitive nose catching on.

We landed on the inside deck and Selene immediately headed for the boxy airlock, moving as quickly as the vac suit allowed. "You sure you don't want me out there instead of her?" I asked as I headed for the nearest snoozing Marine. "I'm usually the one handling the grav beams on the *Ruth* while Selene pilots."

"Is she as good as you are at shoving a hundred fifty kilos of vac-armored Marine up into a launch module gravity field?" McKell countered.

"Probably not," I conceded. Selene had many superhuman abilities, but massive upper-body strength wasn't one of them.

Which was a shame, because that would have made things easier. "Okay, let's do it."

By the time Selene was settled into position at the grav controls on the portal's surface, I had lugged my first sleeping Marine across the sphere, dumped him there, and was lugging my second in the same direction. By the time Ixil announced that they'd activated the beams, McKell was in the launch module and we had the first of the five Marines floating gently in the interface.

"You sure the beams are working?" I asked, frowning as I took stock of my body's responses. Inner ear, balance, weight—nothing felt the least bit different. "I don't feel anything."

"You wouldn't," McKell said. "Not in here."

"Trust me, they're working," Ixil said. "The instruments out here aren't affected by the internal gravity fields, and they show us decelerating precisely on the correct vector."

"Sounds good," I said cautiously. "What *is* that vector, by the way? You never told us."

"We wanted to land Alpha somewhere near the light we saw during the bioprobe run," Ixil said. "It's the best way to get a look at who our natives or visitors are."

"And hopefully not squash their town in the process?"

"That was something else we decided early on," McKell said. "Fortunately, there was an obvious answer."

"Our single clear look showed those mountains east of the lights to be fairly rugged," Ixil said. "We decided that was the area most likely to be uninhabited."

"Wait a minute," I said, frowning. "You're bringing Alpha down in the *mountains*?"

"On their western slope, yes," Ixil said. "That will unfortunately put us ten to fifteen kilometers from the area of interest. But with our height advantage and the proper ranging instruments, we should get a reasonably clear view."

"And if we decide to visit, it'll all be downhill," McKell added. "You ready?"

"More or less," I said, getting a grip on the bobbing Marine's oxygen pack.

"On three," McKell said. "One, two, *three*."

I shoved down on the pack with my full weight. McKell, on the other side of the gravity flip, pulled upward.

We got nowhere. My side of the portal wanted to push him through to McKell's side, while McKell's side wanted equally hard to shove him back to mine.

"Try bending him over at the waist," I grunted, trying to hop up on the underside of the sleeping man's oxygen pack to add as much of my weight as I could. "Or maybe I should come in there and we both pull?"

"Hard to bend him with the vac armor on," McKell said with a grunt.

"Can we get him out of it?" I asked. "I don't know why we need vac suits in here anyway. Is Kinneman worried about the airlock seal or something?"

"Let's just say he's cautious," McKell said, peering at me through the gap between the Marine and the edge of the interface. "Bonding between known and unknown materials can sometimes be a little tricky. Hang on—let me try something else."

He moved away out of sight. "McKell?" I asked, shifting around and trying to look past the Marine.

A waste of effort. With his military vac armor far thicker and bulkier than our civilian models, he was blocking most of the view. "McKell? Where'd you go?"

"I'm lying on my side with him facing me," McKell said. "I'm going to get a grip on his arms, roll away from him, and try to pull him through."

"Sounds good," I said, getting a fresh grip on the oxygen pack. "Say when."

"I'm set," he said. "On three. One, two, *three*."

Once again I shoved with all my weight. This time, instead of the Marine floating back toward me, he slid neatly through the interface and disappeared into the launch module.

"Did it work?" Ixil asked.

"Like a large and very lumpy charm," McKell confirmed. "Okay, Roarke. Roll the next one into position while I drag this one out of the way."

It took us another fifteen minutes to get the other four Marines into the launch module. "We're ready to start sending them back," McKell reported. "How are things going out there?"

"Looking good," Ixil confirmed. "Fourth braking sequence is done, and the instruments say we're right on course. Two more to go, and we'll be ready to head in."

"Good," McKell said. "Roarke? Time to send our sleeping friends back down the rabbit hole."

I'd been wondering exactly how we were going to pull this off without one or both of us having to babysit the travelers back to Icarus and then return to Alpha for the next load. With the unavoidable delay generated by a passenger's leisurely decent from the receiver module's center to the floor, a couple of round trips would cost minutes that I wasn't at all sure we could spare.

Fortunately, McKell had a plan. First step was to punch Icarus's address into the control board, double-checking as usual that he'd done it correctly. Then, working together, we got the first Marine to the extension arm and more or less upright in McKell's grip. With one hand, McKell wrapped the man's gloved hand around the black-and-silver arm, then wrapped his own free hand around the arm above the Marine's, and as the gravity reversed they both floated toward the center of the sphere. McKell waited until they were just to the arm's gray trigger section, then let go with both of his hands, leaving the Marine's hand pressed loosely against the arm as the only contact. An instant later, the launch sequence triggered and the Marine vanished.

"Okay, that worked," McKell said with relieved satisfaction as gravity once again reversed and he floated back down to join me. Apparently, he hadn't been a hundred percent sure of his plan, either. "Go ahead and tee up the next one."

He was headed up the extension arm with the final package when Ixil reported that he and Selene were coming in.

"Everything look okay?" McKell asked.

"According to all the readings, Alpha is precisely on target," Ixil confirmed. "Whether the calculations Tera gave us are accurate is, of course, an entirely separate question."

"She seemed pretty sure," McKell said. "I guess we'll know soon enough. Any reason I shouldn't just go through with our last Marine?"

"None that I can think of," Ixil said. "You can go too, Roarke, if you want."

"Thanks, but I'll wait for Selene," I said.

"No problem," McKell said. "Ixil, make sure they get back all right. I'll see you back at base."

"We'll be there shortly."

I watched as McKell and the Marine reached the gray section and vanished. Then, making my way to the interface, I rolled into the receiver module and headed to the airlock.

Or rather, to the blockade balloon tethered beside the airlock. It was floating three meters above the deck, bobbing gently in the breeze created by my movements. The end of the cord was fastened securely to the deck, and I took special note of the quick-release knot holding the balloon in its current lowered position.

Yes. This should work.

I was facing the airlock hatch, watching the monitors run through their cycle sequence, when it swung open and Selene stepped out. "You all right?" I asked, taking her arm and peering through her faceplate. The tinting obscured her pupils somewhat, but I could see a calmness there. Whatever doubts she might be feeling about her part in this dangerous path we'd set ourselves on, she seemed to have come to terms with it.

"I'm fine," she assured me. "It looks like we'll have about ten minutes before Alpha starts hitting noticeable atmosphere."

"Time for us to go, then," I said as Ixil exited the airlock and closed the hatch behind him. "I don't suppose we've got time to bring in the grav generators or bioprobe?"

"Hardly," he said, the outriders on his shoulders looking around as if searching for McKell. Probably just wondering when this would be over and Ixil would get them out of their vac suits. "One of many things about tonight's work that General Kinneman won't be happy about."

"He can run us a tab," I said, turning toward the launch module. I wasn't sure how well Ixil could read my face, but I knew Selene was dangerously good at it and I didn't want either of them getting even a hint that I was up to anything. "Better get moving. You know how McKell worries."

One by one, we rolled in turn into the launch module and then gathered around the extension arm. "Fingers crossed," I said as we all took hold of the extension arm and started up. "I wonder if they've got McKell in custody yet."

"Hard to tell," Ixil said. "The orders we sent from the admiral's computer should have kept everyone out of Icarus for another hour, but there's always the chance he or Kinneman or someone else might have gotten a heads-up and decided to investigate."

"Spurious orders can do that," I agreed, watching our ascent carefully. The timing here had to be perfect. "All it would take would be a flag query to Graym-Barker for the balloon to go up. Figuratively speaking, of course."

"Hopefully *only* figuratively speaking," Selene said. "Ixil, you checked that the balloon was securely tethered, didn't you?"

I tensed. Unintentionally, Selene had just handed me the

perfect opening. "Maybe I should go double-check," I suggested before Ixil could answer. "It would be the final ironic line on our tombstones if it broke free and blocked entry to Alpha for the next five years."

"It wouldn't come to that," Ixil assured me. "As Colonel Kolodny mentioned when you first arrived here, the balloon will fail within six to eight months. It was deliberately designed that way so that such a long-term blockage couldn't happen. But don't worry," he added as I let go of the extension arm. "I checked it before I went outside, and it's fully secure. Grab on again—we need to be going."

"Right." Briefly, I wondered if I should try grabbing lower down on the extension arm, which might give me a bit of additional time.

But I really didn't know if shifting my grip would make a difference. More importantly, since I was still floating upward at the same rate of speed as the others, the only way I could take hold anywhere except where my hand had originally been would be both obvious and suspicious. I couldn't afford either of those, especially with several seconds yet to go. Making a face inside my helmet, I took hold of the arm again.

Nearly there. I found myself watching Pix and Pax as I counted down the seconds, the odd thought striking me that I wished I could be there to see the outriders' reaction when this was over. My mental countdown reached zero—

And with maybe a quarter second to go, I opened my hand, letting go of the extension arm. Before either Ixil or Selene had time to react, they hit the gray section and disappeared back to Icarus.

I tensed. No, *not* Ixil and Selene.

Just Ixil. Facing me from the other side of the arm was Selene, her own hand wide open where she'd also let go.

"What the *hell*?" I demanded as gravity reversed and we started floating back downward. "Selene? What are you doing here?"

"I could ask you the same question," she said coolly.

"You need to go," I told her stiffly. "Grab the arm—come on, *grab* it."

"You know that won't work," she said. "It has to complete its cycle before it can send anyone else."

I clenched my teeth hard enough to hurt. "Selene, you have

to get out of here," I said, anger, frustration, and fear tumbling together in my voice and brain. "It's not safe. If we're wrong about Alpha, you could die."

"So could you," she countered.

"I have to," I said. "I don't—look—"

"And while we argue," she interrupted calmly, "Ixil will be screaming at the top of his lungs for McKell. If we don't get the balloon back in the center of the receiver module, none of your reasons will matter."

Because we would both be unceremoniously hauled back to Icarus the minute Ixil or McKell could get here. "Yeah," I ground out. "Okay. Balloon first, talk later."

We hit the deck and hurried toward the interface. I got there first, rolled into the receiver module, and took off toward the balloon at a dead run. A tug on the tether's quick-release knot sent it soaring rapidly toward the center of the module. I watched it go, pulse pounding in my throat, wondering if McKell or Ixil would pop in at the last second.

But they didn't. The balloon reached the center of the sphere and stopped, the radial gravitational field holding it firmly in place.

And with that, Selene and I were free to stay.

To stay, and perhaps to die.

"All right, we're here." Selene lowered her eyes from the balloon and focused on my face. "Tell me why."

"It's—okay, it's probably silly," I confessed, suddenly feeling intimidated. I'd run all the possibilities through my mind a hundred times, but I'd never thought I would have to say any of this out loud. "I'm worried that the collision will break Alpha in such a way that people will still be able to get here from Icarus but won't be able to get back. I thought . . . well, I decided I was the logical test case. I mean, if I can't get back it's not a huge loss. If McKell or Ixil can't, it is."

"It would be a big loss to *me*," Selene said quietly.

I winced. When I first decided on this crazy scheme I'd tried to tell myself that if this didn't work she'd be fine without me.

But down deep, I'd known all along that wasn't true. The Kadolian remnant moved around the Spiral a lot, and in the years since Selene and I teamed up she'd gradually lost track of them. I was really and truly all she had left.

Which meant, if I was being completely and brutally honest

with myself, I'd been willing to risk a friend's life in order to save a stranger's.

As my father used to say, *In the end, friends are the most precious treasure you will ever find, and the one thing you will absolutely regret losing.*

"I know," I told her, feeling as bad as I'd ever felt in my life. "I'm sorry, Selene. I wasn't thinking about...look, there's still time to go back to Icarus if you want. For both of us to go back."

She looked up at the balloon. "No," she said, her voice low. "If this doesn't work, I'll probably lose you anyway. Won't I?"

I hesitated. But even with my scent blocked by my vac suit she would probably know if I tried to lie. "Probably," I said. "We'll both go to prison, or I'll go by myself while Kinneman keeps you working for the agency. Either way, you'll be mostly on your own. But at least with Kinneman you'd be safe and living in a civilized society."

For a moment, she was silent. Then, reaching up, she unfastened her helmet. "You, too," she said. "Take off your helmet. Please."

"Sure," I said, though I didn't know what gauging my emotional state was going to prove. As my father used to say, *Facts usually don't care about your opinion about them.* She let her helmet dangle from one hand, I tucked mine under my arm, and we stood gazing at each other while her nostrils flared and her eyelashes fluttered.

"Civilization means nothing to me except that it's the structure within which you and I live," she said at last. "If you truly believe the Icari built their portals strong enough to survive crash landings—and you *do* believe that—I'm willing to accept the risk."

"I'd feel better facing this unknown if I knew you were safe," I said, trying one last time.

"As would I," she said. "But since neither of us can have that assurance, I would prefer we face it together."

I sighed. "All right," I said, conceding defeat.

And if I was again being completely honest with myself, I had to admit I was glad to have her here. If for no other reason than that if this was to be our last hour together, we'd at least have a chance to say good-bye. "Any suggestions on where we should settle in for the ride?"

She looked around the receiver module, and I saw her eyelashes again fluttering. "I think we should be in the launch module."

I looked around the hull at all the workstations and storage cabinets, my stomach tightening. I'd gotten so used to the way portal gravity fields casually hung stuff over my head that I'd mostly forgotten what would happen if those fields ever failed. "I see what you're thinking," I said. "If the things in here aren't secured, and the gravity fails during or after the descent, they'll all tumble to the bottom of the sphere."

"Where you and I will also be if that happens."

"Right." Though if the gravity cut out on our way down we were likely to have deeper worries than just a bunch of expensive equipment raining down on us. The problem inherent in an eleven-kilometer-per-second impact with the ground, for one. "Launch module it is."

"Yes," she said.

I looked closely at her. The word had been confident enough, but her pupils looked oddly disturbed. "Something?" I prompted.

"I don't know," she said, that strange look still there. "It's just that...that's not the main reason I wanted to be in the launch module. It sounds crazy, but I think Alpha is...frightened."

"Frightened," I repeated, listening to the word bounce around my brain. I was accustomed to her reading emotions and intentions, mine as well as everyone else's.

But up to now those insights had been with *people*. Humans, mostly, since that was who we usually hung out with, but also a whole range of nonhumans.

Now, she was pulling this feeling from a *machine*? A machine, moreover, that was similar to one she'd once declared dead?

"I know it doesn't make sense," she said, her pupils going all defensive as she picked up on my confusion and doubts. But there was also an intensity there that warned me not to simply brush it aside. "But I think—I *feel*—"

"It's okay," I said, taking her arm and heading for the launch module. "Truth to tell, I'm not feeling all that brave myself right now. If Alpha wants some company, I'm more than willing to hunker down in there."

"Thank you," she said quietly. "I wish I could explain it."

"As I said, no need," I assured her. "Any idea when we're going to hit the heavier atmosphere Ixil mentioned?"

"We already have."

I frowned. Everything felt exactly the way portals always did. "You sure?" I asked. "I'm not feeling anything different."

"Neither am I," she said. "But that was Ixil's timetable." She hesitated. "There's also... the air smells a little different. Like the portal is... I don't know. Straining?"

As in straining against the wind buffeting against the outer hull? Maybe fighting against the increased heat or gravity? Maybe all of the above? "Hopefully, that's a good sign," I said. "Or at least not a bad one."

We reached the interface and I gestured to it. "Ladies first," I invited. "Let's go in and see what the end of the world looks like."

She shivered as she lay down by the interface. "Yes," she said quietly. "Let's."

CHAPTER NINE

The minutes trudged along. I settled down flat on my back beside Selene—it seemed as good a posture as any to be in if anything in here twitched or failed—and gazed up at the various displays curving around the inside of the sphere. Most of them meant nothing to me, their blinking or pulsating lights equally meaningless. I knew where to program in the address of the portal you wanted to go to, I knew where the display was that showed the address of the portal you'd just left, and I knew the extension-arm procedure. Aside from that, I was about as ignorant as I'd been when Tera and her buddies first popped into our lives and tossed us unceremoniously into this thorn patch.

More than once I wondered how many secrets Admiral Graym-Barker and the Icarus Group had coaxed out in the eight years since McKell, Ixil, and Tera delivered it to them. Not too many, I guessed. Alien tech was like that.

I wondered, too, if it was the slowness of that progress that had persuaded the Commonwealth money behind the project to dump Graym-Barker and bring in Kinneman instead.

Kinneman, and my father.

What would my father think when Selene and I didn't come home from this final gamble with the universe?

Maybe he would mourn me for at least a few days before life

and business once again crowded out everything else. I would like to think he would. Maybe he wouldn't. Either way, I could at least hope I would show up as the object lesson in some future aphorism.

I doubted Kinneman would either mourn me or invoke my name in some cleverly crafted wordplay. My best hope for acknowledgment from him would be if he turned my name into a new curse word that drill sergeants could use to intimidate recruits.

I was mentally running through a list of people who'd be sorry I was dead, most of them bounty targets I'd tossed into prison who no doubt wanted to kill me themselves, when Selene stirred. "Gregory?" she said tentatively. "I think we're here."

I frowned, checking the vac suit's chronometer. Forty-five minutes had passed since Selene and I settled down. "So soon?"

"Ixil told me the landing would take thirty-six minutes once the portal hit the heavy part of the atmosphere," she said. "Unless his calculations were off, we should be on the ground."

I took a deep breath. Up in the mountains above our City of Light, if Ixil had gotten that part of the calculations right, too. "That's great," I said cautiously. "It *is* great, isn't it?"

"I don't know," she said. "The smell in here has changed again."

"Good or bad?"

"Just different."

"Okay," I said, trying to think. If we'd landed sometime in the last ten minutes, shouldn't we have felt something? I'd handwaved a good theory to McKell and the others about how Alpha's artificial gravity should work and play well with the planet's more traditional gravity field, and we'd had the data to back it up. But I'd never believed the portal could slam into the ground without a jolt or bump or *some* kind of announcement to that effect.

Yet here we were, sitting in the middle of Alpha's usual radial grav field, without so much as a flicker in the lights to herald our arrival.

Did that mean we *hadn't* arrived? If Tera's calculations had been off in one direction we would presumably have slammed straight into the surface without coming in along a curve that we'd hoped would cushion our impact a bit. In that case, shouldn't we be dead? Alternatively, if the numbers had been off in the other direction, Alpha might still be in orbit, either running an elongated ellipse or tracing out a descending spiral.

Which left us with a crucial decision. If we were in a more

or less stable ellipse, we needed to go back outside and use the grav beams to give us an additional nudge. But if we were spiraling toward the surface, we might step outside just in time to get squashed as Alpha tore a monster rut in the planet's crust. "I don't suppose you know how to open the receiver module viewports, do you?" I asked.

She shook her head. "Sorry."

"Yeah, me too," I said. "Unfortunately, as long as things in here don't change, I don't think there's any way to tell if we're down, still on the way, or in an altered orbit."

"The outer hull must surely heat up during an atmospheric descent," she pointed out. "There's a lot of spare equipment out there. Maybe we can find a temperature sensor and attach it to one of the hatches."

"That assumes Alpha descends fast enough for that kind of frictional heating," I said. "The whole point of this gamble was the assumption that it would come in slowly enough that it would survive the trip and the impact. Besides, even if the outer hull gets hot, that temperature change might not make it inside. The Icari had some weird engineering tricks up their sleeves."

"You're right about that," she conceded. "So?"

I looked around the launch module, straining all my senses to find something—*anything*—that looked or felt or sounded different. But I couldn't. "How's the scent now?"

"It's changed again," she said, sniffing the air. "Not much. Actually smells a little better than it did a few minutes ago."

"All right," I said, once again consulting my suit's chronometer. "Let's give it...let's say thirty more minutes. You keep track of Alpha's scent, and if nothing has changed by then we'll revisit our options."

The minutes ticked slowly by. I tried closing my eyes, hoping lack of sight would enhance my senses of hearing or touch, quickly decided that not seeing what was happening—even though what was happening was exactly nothing—only enhanced my twitchiness. I tried staring at the displays, but the slow shifting of lights meant nothing to me, and try as I might I couldn't see any pattern to the changes. I tried watching Selene, but the rhythmic movements of her nostrils and eyelashes were just as useless to me, plus they underlined the frustrating fact that she was doing something constructive and I wasn't.

Plus the minor annoyance of seeing that she didn't seem to have any problem keeping *her* eyes shut.

We'd used up twenty-four minutes of my suggested thirty when Selene suddenly stiffened. "Something?" I asked.

"I think so," she said. "It's like Alpha's suddenly gone weak."

"Weak, like it's breaking down?" I asked, feeling my heartrate picking up.

"No, more like...maybe *quieting down* is a better way to put it. It's almost like a long-distance runner who's finished a race and is feeling the strain—"

Right in the middle of her sentence, the diffuse light that seemed to come from nowhere and everywhere disappeared.

And an instant later I found myself sliding helplessly along the module's curved inner surface in total darkness as gravity suddenly shifted to my right. I heard Selene gasp, felt mesh-covered cables and display board corners grabbing briefly at various parts of my vac suit. Through the interface I heard a cacophony of crashes and crunches as the equipment and workstations that had been resting peacefully on the deck all tumbled to the portal's new definition of *down*. Apparently, a lot of stuff in there *hadn't* been glued down. I reached the new bottom of the launch module, grunted as Selene slid into me—

And then all was silence.

With an effort, I found my voice. "You all right?"

"I think so," Selene's voice came in the darkness. I felt a hand touch my side, move up my chest to my chin. "You?"

"I'm fine," I assured her, digging into my suit's small hip pouch. There should be a flashlight in there somewhere. "That was fun."

"I can't find my helmet," she said, her searching hand brushing my hair as it probed the deck beside my head.

"Do we need them?" I asked, a sudden tightness in my throat. She would know instantly if something had gone wrong with the air in here. *Had* something gone wrong? "Is the air going bad?"

"No, it's still fine," she said. "I just don't know where it went."

So if the air was still good, why this sudden need to find her helmet? "Just relax," I soothed. "You stay put here. I'll find it." My fingers found the flashlight. I pulled it out of the pouch, flicked it on, and played it around the sphere.

From the sounds of crashing Marine property in the receiver module I'd expected the landscape here in the smaller sphere to be pretty messy. To my mild surprise, it wasn't. Aside from a couple of cables bulging a few centimeters through the mesh above us, plus all the displays and lights being off, everything looked pretty much as usual. I swept the beam around some more and finally spotted our helmets sitting together at the base of the extension arm. "There," I said, pointing. "They're over—"

I broke off. The helmets weren't caught on something, as I'd assumed, either the mesh or some of the equipment beneath it. They were just *sitting* there.

Which meant that while the main part of the portal's internal gravity had failed, the generator around the extension arm, the one that expedited travel to the center of the launch module and thereby the full teleportation procedure, was inexplicably still operating. "Selene?" I asked, wiggling the flashlight beam over the helmets for emphasis.

"Yes, I see them," she said. Her pupils, faintly visible in the backwash from my light, looked thoughtful. "I thought that's where they would be."

"You *thought* they'd be by the extension arm?"

"Yes," she said, her pupils shifting to an odd sort of puzzle-ment. "*Why* did I think that? It has to have been the scent."

"Okay," I said, trying to keep my voice casual. "So the scents in here are multicolored enough that you can get that level of precision out of them? Why haven't you been able to do that before?"

"Because the scent inside the portals we've visited has never changed before," she said. "Not until Alainn."

I pursed my lips. Not until Alainn, and the portal she'd declared dead.

On the other hand, this was a phenomenon I was already familiar with: the *Ruth's* status displays assuring me that everything was working properly even as a subtly altered scent emanating from one of the systems warned Selene that it was about to go gunnybags on us. The monitors always caught up, but without Selene's advance warning there'd been one or two occasions when we could have been in serious trouble. Was she using a similar technique to root out Alpha's status?

Maybe. But for the moment the *how* of it wasn't the ques-tion uppermost in my mind. The more urgent issue question was—"So what does that mean?" I asked. "Is Alpha sick? More to the point, is it sick and getting better? Or is it—?" I stopped, suddenly reluctant to say the word out loud.

"Dying?" she asked quietly. "I wish I knew, Gregory. But right now I don't. Alpha's been through a horrible experience. I think we just have to give it time to rest and recover."

"Okay," I said, gazing at the dull metal and muted displays at the far end of my flashlight beam. "Any idea how long before we know?"

"No," she said. "We'll just have to wait and see. I'm sorry."

"No need to apologize," I said, reaching over and briefly squeezing her gloved hand. "We wouldn't know even this much without your abilities and insight. As my father used to say, *Everything has its own time and its own rhythm. Try pushing either of them faster, and you'll just annoy everyone involved.*"

I yawned, fatigue suddenly pulling at my eyelids. "I don't know about you," I added, "but my brain still thinks it's four o'clock in the morning. As long as we're doing nothing right now anyway, I vote we do that same nothing with our eyes closed."

I stood up, eyeing our wayward helmets. They were hanging a quarter of the way around the sphere above us, but with a climbable mesh stretching across everything it should be easy enough to retrieve them. "And we should probably put our helmets back on if we're going to sleep," I added, hooking my flashlight into one of my suit's connectors so that it would continue to light my way. "In case something goes wrong and we lose our atmosphere."

"I can't," Selene protested. "I can't keep track of Alpha's progress unless I can smell it."

"Not a problem," I assured her. "Remember how the Marine vac suits can use outside air until and unless the tanks are needed? Ours can do the same thing. We'll program them to leave the vents open unless the pressure or oxygen content drops below a specified level."

I snagged the helmets without trouble, though reaching through the edge of the field into full gravity did momentarily throw me off balance. I climbed back down to Selene and after a couple of minutes' trial and error was able to activate the failsafe programming I'd described.

And with that finished, there was nothing more we could do.

"Try to get some sleep," I advised as I shifted myself into as comfortable a position as the mesh and underlying equipment allowed. "We'll get some rest, let Alpha do likewise, and by the time we wake up everything will be back to normal."

"Yes," Selene murmured. "I'm sure it will."

I closed my eyes. As my father used to say, *It's surprising how often a lie turns out to be nothing but a thin layer of deceit wrapped around a secret and all-but-abandoned hope.*

I hoped Alpha would pull through. Not just because I wanted us to live, but also because I didn't want my last words to Selene to be a lie.

Four hours later, I was awakened by a sudden glare of light in my face.

I snapped my eyes open, my right hand reflexively going to my hip where my plasmic would normally be holstered. The whole launch sphere was ablaze with light. "Selene!" I barked.

"I'm here," her voice came back calmly.

I turned my head. She was sitting cross-legged beside me, her helmet sitting on the deck beside her. Her face was turned upward and her eyelashes were fluttering. "What's happened?" I managed, working myself up into a sitting position.

She looked at me, her pupils puzzled. "What do you mean?" she asked. "Alpha's waking up."

"Oh," I said. "Right." And now that my eyes were adjusting, I could see that what I'd taken to be unnatural brightness was simply the portal's usual steady light. "So it's working now?"

"Partly," Selene said cautiously, her pupils going a little worried. "The lights and gravity are back, but the launch controls are still dormant."

I looked over at the display that usually showed the destination address. Where there were normally four rows of twenty red squares that could be changed to yellow or black when programming in your destination, all the squares were now a sort of pasty white. The previous-portal display on the deck just below it was the same. "So I'm guessing we shouldn't plan to be back at Icarus for lunch."

"No, I don't think so," Selene said. "The scent hasn't changed for the past few minutes, either. I think it's . . . I don't know. Resting? Regrouping?"

"Let's go with *resting*," I said. "Sounds more optimistic. We can work on the diagnostic terminology later if we need to. What about the hatch controls? Are they working?"

"I don't know," Selene said, looking at me with wariness in her pupils. "Why?"

"I was thinking I should step outside and see what the planet looks like from ground level," I said. "Or rather, ground level plus a thousand meters if we landed in the mountains Ixil was aiming for."

"What about disease organisms? We can't stay in these suits forever."

"There *is* that," I conceded. The vac suits would protect us just fine while we were outside in the alien air. But as soon as we opened one of the portal's hatches we'd be inviting all manner of buggy things inside. If there was something dangerous in that mix, if and when we were able to go back to Icarus some of those ickies could teleport back with us.

Bad enough that my memorial plaque might read DISAPPEARED AND LOST IN ETERNITY. I really didn't want ALSO UNLEASHED DEVASTATING PANDEMIC UPON HUMANITY added to the fine print.

"On the other hand, as you pointed out earlier, there's a lot of very expensive equipment out in the receiver module," I said as I got to my feet. "Good chance that one of those items is a backup biothreat sampler."

"Let's go see," Selene agreed as she stood up beside me. "We should also make sure the balloon's out of the way for when Alpha's able to receive travelers again."

I looked at the dead, pasty-white display. Selene had said *when.* Distantly, I wondered if the more appropriate word would have been *if.*

But there was no point in being overly gloomy about it. As my father used to say, *Pessimism can be useful when formulating backup plans, but it makes for a depressing life philosophy.*

"Good idea," I said. "You go do that, and I'll go find that sampler."

We'd heard the equipment in the receiver module go crashing to the deck when Alpha's gravity shut down, and as we walked to the interface I wondered how long it would take to dig through a literal mountain of large and heavy tools and crates of supplies to find what we were looking for.

Fortunately, it wasn't as bad as I'd expected. The supply cabinets were indeed piled together at what had temporarily been the bottom point of the big sphere, their packages of food, water, and spare equipment modules scattered around like oversized confetti. But the heavy equipment—machining tools, workstations, and the like—were still spaced around the hull right where we'd left them. Either Colonel Kolodny hadn't trusted Alpha's internal gravity to remain steady or else his engineer's natural distrust of vibration and other unwanted motion had persuaded him to anchor down his heavier pieces of equipment.

So while finding what we needed was still going to be an Easter Egg hunt, at least I could be fairly sure it hadn't already been squashed by a quarter ton of falling table lathe.

It took nearly an hour of wading through the scattered debris and prying open jammed cabinet doors. But it was an hour well spent. In the end I found not just a spare biothreat sampler, but also a standalone analyzer, which would relieve us of the burden of trying to locate the necessary programming in the main computer.

"Okay, here's the plan," I told Selene as I double-checked the connections on the fresh oxygen tank I'd loaded into my vac suit. The old one was still showing half full, but with the uncertainties of an outside trek looming ahead of me, basic caution dictated that I start with a full tank. "I'll go into the airlock, open the hatch, and wait there while this thing takes its samples. If I'm reading it correctly, the analyzer should transmit the data and results directly to the computer."

"Are you sure you don't want to wait a little longer?" Selene asked, her pupils showing concern. "The biothreat data from the probe's last trip is surely already in the computer. We could try to find that first."

"We could," I agreed. "And you're more than welcome to keep hunting while I'm in the airlock. But that data was taken from the stratosphere or upper troposphere, and the situation may be different here at ground level."

"I know," she said reluctantly. "I just..."

"You're worried about predators and native spears," I said. "To be honest, I'm not exactly thrilled about this myself. But we can't just sit here until Alpha brings its teleport system online. Besides, I've got this." I tapped the holstered Sigurd plasmic I'd borrowed from the weapons locker. "If I need to scare someone or something away, I won't have any problems."

Her pupils told me exactly what she thought about that line of reasoning. But she didn't comment. I finished my checks, locked my helmet back on, and tucked the sampler and analyzer under my arm. "Am I coming through okay?" I called.

"Yes," Selene's confirmation came through my earbud. "You'll describe everything you're doing, won't you?"

"Of course," I assured her as she held the airlock hatch open for me. "Don't worry, you'll get the full running commentary. By the time I'm back inside you'll probably be sick of my voice."

Again, she didn't say anything. I stepped inside the airlock and waited while she closed the hatch behind me. I confirmed that the seal was solid, then knelt down and set the sampler on the deck.

Portal hatches could be set to open either inward or outward, and given the uncertainty of the landscape outside we'd opted for the first. Bracing myself, trying to ignore unpleasant mental images of tigers and native spears, I touched the control spot. The hatch started to swing inward—

And to my utter surprise, a surge of water burst through into the airlock.

"What the *hell*?" I snapped, jerking back upright as I stared in disbelief at the water pooling around my ankles.

"What is it?" Selene's anxious voice came back.

"Water," I said. I couldn't feel the temperature through my vac suit, but the stuff looked cold. "We've got water coming in."

"*What?*"

"You heard me," I said, staring down at the water, my mind trying to get a grip on this unexpected development. "Alpha didn't come down in the mountains. It came down in *water*."

"You mean like in a lake or river?"

"Or like in the ocean," I said grimly. "Remember the ocean a hundred kilometers west of the mountains?"

"Oh, no," Selene breathed. "Oh, Gregory. If we're that deep . . ."

"Okay, let's not panic," I said, trying mightily to take my own advice.

Because Selene was right. If we were even a hundred meters below the surface, we might well be doomed. I didn't know what the decompression tables were for this kind of situation, but I *did* know that an ascent with pressurized oxygen had to be done very carefully if the diver was to avoid getting the bends.

Not to mention the more immediate problem that vac suits designed to hold in pressure against vacuum might fail spectacularly against heavy water pressure coming at them from the other side.

"Can you get out of there?" Selene asked. "Come back in here, I mean?"

"I think so," I said, frowning at the gently bobbing pool around my ankles. "But I don't think I need to. The water's stopped rising. Looks like about twenty centimeters deep, maybe twenty-five."

"That's all?" Selene asked. "It must be a *very* shallow ocean."

"I think it's more a case of the water pressure hitting equilibrium with Alpha's gravity," I said, eyeing the sloshing water.

"Can you see any light out there?" she asked. "If you can, that might tell us how deep we are."

"Yeah, hang on."

I eased myself down into the water and maneuvered into a position where I could stick my head through the hatchway. I did so, looked around, then pulled myself back in again. "Nothing," I reported as I got back to my feet. "But from the feel of the gravity, I think I'm under Alpha's curve. It could be blazing sunlight out there and I wouldn't be at the right angle to see it."

"So one of us is going to have to go outside."

"Eventually, yes," I said, gazing thoughtfully at the pool sloshing around my feet. "But before we do that, maybe we can use the water's equilibrium depth to calculate how deep we are."

"Do you know how to do that?"

"Not a clue," I said. "But that's an EarthGuard engineering computer you're sitting at. It ought to have the relevant equations in there *somewhere*."

"I'll see what I can find," she said. "What about you?"

I looked down at the biothreat sampler, its top just visible above the water. "As long as the sampler and I are in here anyway, I might as well run some of this water," I said, reaching down and lifting the device out of the pool. "Let's see which of us comes up with some good news first."

I ended up winning the informal race, mostly because my data search was fully automated while Selene had to hunt manually through the computer for the equations she needed. But both our results were gratifying enough that neither of us cared who'd won.

"So nothing dangerous in the water," she said, running her eyes over the data dump from the sampler. "And you say that's not just the water?"

"Nope," I confirmed, leaning over her shoulder and pointing at one of the lines. "We got water and atmosphere both. Turns out there's a lot of dissolved air in the water, and the sampler got good readings on both. And it gets better." I reached past her to the computer's controls and scrolled down another couple of pages. "There was enough biomass in the mix to get readings on those, too."

"And there's nothing dangerous?"

"Nothing the sampler could find," I said, feeling way more satisfied with myself than I should be, given that my only contribution to this information treasure trove was scooping water into the sampler and keying a few switches. "Like McKell told us, life here is built on the same amino acid spectrum that we are. But none of the resulting microbes seems to have been put together in a configuration that'll be a problem for us."

"And if there *is* something like that the sampler didn't catch, we just have to trust our wide-spectrum immunities to keep us covered?"

"That's the theory," I confirmed. "Actually, given how many biospheres we've run across during our travels, and how seldom either of us has gotten sick from one of them, I'd say the theory is pretty solid." I gestured to the computer. "I'm done. Your turn."

"My findings may not be as solid as yours," she warned as she keyed for a different file. "But if the formula I found was the correct one, and if I did the calculation right, the airlock is between twenty-five and thirty meters below the surface."

I frowned over at the airlock, rising up from the deck in the middle of the small puddle that had spilled out when I came back into the sphere. It was a little less than a quarter of the way around the sphere from the pile of supplies that presumably still defined planetary *down*, putting it about midway up the receiver module's diameter.

But that diameter was forty meters. If the distance to the surface of the water was twenty-five to thirty... "Are you saying we're only five to ten meters underwater?"

"From the top of the portal, yes," she confirmed. "But again, my calculation could be off."

"I'm sure it's close enough," I said, my earlier nightmare scenario of a hundred-meter upward swim vanishing into dawn's comforting light. "Ten meters will be trivial to deal with. Five meters will be even easier."

"I'm more worried that your vac suit won't be able to handle full immersion in water," Selene warned. "Just because it can keep air in doesn't mean water won't get somewhere it shouldn't."

"There's that," I agreed reluctantly, looking down at the control bars on my suit's forearms. Civilian vac suits were designed to be simple, fail-safe bags of air for untrained people, and the variety Kinneman had supplied us with were even more idiot-proof than the more upscale ones we had on the *Ruth*. "On the other hand, all the exterior controls are this molded flexible plastic with no openings where water can get in," I pointed out. "They should be all right."

"What about the joints and connections?" Selene persisted. "Will water do anything to them?"

"I don't know," I admitted. "It shouldn't, but that doesn't mean it won't. But the option is for me to float up naked and hope I can hold my breath long enough to get back down to Alpha again."

She gave a soft sigh. "So you're going alone?"

"I have to," I said, wincing at the quiet pain in her pupils. The whole reason we'd both ridden Alpha down from orbit was so we could face these horrible threats together. Now, I was heading off to face one of them on my own. "There are too many variables in play for both of us to take that risk. Don't worry—a quick look, and I'll be right back."

"All right," she said, clearly still not convinced. "We need to figure out the best way to get you outside and back in again."

I grimaced. "Yes. Let's definitely make sure I can get back in again."

CHAPTER TEN

It took us about half an hour to find some heavy-duty line in one of the supply closets and dig out four empty water bottles from the trash bin. While I rigged up a traveling harness to anchor me to the line, Selene wove the bottles into the upper end for buoyancy.

Somewhere along the way I remembered the Barracuda maneuvering units lying in a pile halfway around the deck. But they were military-grade gadgets, I'd never used one before, and this didn't seem like the right time for a practice run.

"All right," I said as I fastened the other end of the line to the leg of one of the workstations. "That gives me fifteen meters out from the hatch. Enough to cover your estimate, plus a margin for error. A quick look around—a *quick* look," I emphasized, noting the nervousness still in her pupils, "and then come back in. Okay?"

"Okay," she said. She still didn't like this, I knew, but knew it had to be done. "Give me two tugs on the line when you're up, just so I know you're safe. And if something goes wrong with your suit and the earbuds don't work, give four sharp tugs on the line and I'll pull you back."

"Got it," I said, noting the irony of the situation. All of modern technology at our fingertips; but if the earbuds didn't function through ten meters of water, our backup plan was the ancient nonverbal techniques of Earth's pre-spaceflight mariner past. "See you soon." I sealed my helmet, knelt down, and opened the hatch.

Once again I was greeted by a surge of water. It churned for a moment, then settled down into a rippling puddle as the water pressure came into balance with Alpha's gravity field. The puddle here was smaller and more shallow than the one that had invaded the airlock, I noted, a direct result of this hatch being higher up and the water therefore having less pressure to work with. I shoved the float end of the tether through the hatch, watched it disappear into the murky water, from my perspective looking as if it was going straight down.

"Any light?" Selene asked.

"Nothing I can see," I told her. "But the water's kind of cloudy, so that might not mean anything. Okay. Here goes." Smiling encouragingly at Selene through my faceplate, I rolled through the opening.

I'd already noticed that the water seemed murky. It was only as I completed my exit and followed the buoys toward the surface that I realized part of the cloudiness was due to the fact that the water was both flowing and churning. Definitely a river, then. I tried to remember the images of Ixil's target area, but aside from the mountains I couldn't remember any topographic details.

All of which assumed we were even in that area, of course. If Tera's calculations had been wrong, or if Ixil and Selene hadn't fired the grav beams correctly, we could be literally anywhere on the planet.

Above me, the water was getting lighter as I neared the surface. But not *all* of the water. There was an odd shadow hanging over part of it, to my left as I faced downstream. A dock? A ship?

A large and hungry predator?

No way to know until I was there. Unfortunately, there was also no way to know if the plasmic belted at my waist would work after being immersed in water. I slowed my ascent, trying to figure out if the shadow was moving...

And then, with a muffled splash, I broke the surface.

It was a river, all right, flowing past me at a good clip. The shadow turned out to be coming from a five-meter-tall, shark-tooth-shaped rock poking out of the water to my left, its presence in the flow probably part of the reason for the turbulence I'd felt on my way up. The right-hand bank was about a hundred meters away, its edge thick with some kind of reedy plants. Beyond it in the distance I could see a line of grayish-brown mountains. The ones Ixil had been aiming for?

"Selene?" I called. "I'm on the surface. A river, not too wide, with a big rock in the middle that we seem to be pressed up against." I paused. "Selene?"

Silence. Apparently, our fears about the earbuds not working through this much water had been justified.

No problem. Shark Tooth Rock was blocking my direct view of the left-hand bank, but it shouldn't take long for me to maneuver around it and get a look at the other side. If I was lucky, I'd see the village or campfire or whatever had been showing the light that had sparked this operation in the first place. If not, Selene and I would have to start the tedious task of figuring out where exactly Alpha had landed. Either way, in a few minutes I'd be able to head back down and report to her in person.

I gave the line the two-tug all-clear signal, then unfastened my harness and hooked the buoy mesh around a convenient crag on the rock where the current wouldn't carry it away. Holding onto the rock, keeping a careful distance from the jagged sur-face, I maneuvered around the upstream side to where I could see the bank.

And there it was. A village—a small city, actually—starting at the riverbank and extending inland a few kilometers along a low ridge that led in turn toward a set of forested foothills. Beyond the hills, I could see that the sun was close to the horizon, its reddish light peeking through the layers of clouds already form-ing above me. Morning or evening, though it wasn't immediately obvious which it was.

Still, if those were the right mountains, and this was the right city, then that direction was west and it was evening. And if it *wasn't* the right city, at least it had a similar weather pattern and geographical positioning.

So why had we seen only a single light? A city this size should have lit up the sky.

I looked back at the buildings closest to the river... and as I focused on them I felt a shiver run through me. All of them seemed to be in various stages of decay, from heavily dilapidated to barely identifiable piles of rubble. The structures at the other side of the city were too far away for me to see much, but from their asymmetric silhouettes against the distant hills I guessed most if not all of them were in similar shape. Whatever this city had once been, its glory or power had long since faded.

So if the place was deserted, why had there been any lights at all?

I looked up. I'd already noted that my rock had a rough, pitted surface where it stuck up above the water level, and that jaggedness gave it an abundance of hand- and footholds. If I was careful, I should be able to climb to the top without damaging my suit. Sliding back around to the rock's far side where my progress wouldn't be visible from the city, I picked out a pair of handholds and started up.

As anticipated, the climb was pretty straightforward. I reached the top, planted my feet securely on a narrow ridge, and eased my helmet over the top.

As my father used to say, *Time is the best tool for altering someone's perspective. If time isn't available, try altitude.* In this case, he was absolutely right. From my new vantage point I could see that, while the rest of the city was in much the same shape as the riverside section, there was an area of maybe fifty or sixty two- to four-story buildings in the center of town that not only weren't heaps of ruins but also looked well-maintained and quite livable. They were grouped in a ring around a wide grassy area dotted with tall bushes and stands of flowers that looked like it had once been the city's main park. In the center of the grass, where one might expect to find a statue or maybe a children's adventure structure, was an ornate, brightly colored building shaped like a truncated cone towering over all its neighbors. Outside the park and functional-looking buildings, as if it had been set up to be the border between the good part of town and the ruins, was a ring of low hills.

So that was that. Mystery explained. A remnant of the city's original denizens was still here, shining a light in forlorn defiance of the darkness.

It was depressing in the extreme. It also strongly suggested that this wasn't where we should expect to find the RH directory Kinneman was hoping for.

Which he was only hoping for because *I'd* suggested it.

I sighed. No matter what happened from this point on, I might as well get used to living under a rain cloud.

Living under one, or possibly dying under one. Depending on how angry Kinneman was at what we'd done, there were probably two or three capital crimes he could legitimately charge me with if he felt like filling out the paperwork.

Assuming Alpha finally came back to life, of course. If it didn't, Kinneman and his anger would be the least of my problems.

I focused on the ring of hills, trying to force my mind away from depressing thoughts of execution and exile. It was a bit difficult to tell from my low viewing angle, but they seemed to be too uniform in size and too precisely spaced to be natural formations. Burial mounds, maybe? The last resting places for whatever passed for kings here?

No. I'd met enough people of power to know none of them would settle for something so drab and commonplace. The big fancy central building was more likely where the high-priced crypts were located. Maybe the mounds were for the kingly spouses, servants, or pets.

Or maybe they were the tombs of enemies or former friends who'd fallen out of the king's favor. It would make a certain amount of macabre sense for those graves to ring the town center as a warning to everyone else.

I was staring at the mounds, wondering if Kinneman had his own private morgue or if he would have to outsource my body to someone else, when I spotted movement along the riverbank.

Instantly, I ducked down, pressing my torso against the rock, leaving only my eyes and the top of my helmet still exposed to view. Half a dozen aliens had come into sight in the area beyond the ramshackle buildings, striding purposefully along a path through the reeds toward the river.

Whether or not those city mounds were tombs, the locals must have *some* place to dump dead enemies... and a lot of cultures included trespassers and spies in that category. The last thing I wanted was to find out the details firsthand.

Fortunately, for the moment the aliens didn't seem to have noticed me. They were walking through the reeds, apparently aiming for a short stone dock I hadn't noticed before that stuck a couple of meters out into the river.

I peered through my faceplate, wishing I'd tried to talk Kinneman into giving us Marine vac suits instead of these pitiful civilian things. Not only were the military versions fully armored, but they had a whole range of optical enhancements, from telescopic to infrared to starscopes. Here and now, all I had was my own eyeballs.

Still, the aliens were close enough for me to see that they were a species I'd never seen or heard of before: tall and lanky, their faces wide with long snouts, their entire bodies covered with armadillo-type scale armor. Their hands were wide, each with four fingers and an opposable thumb, like many of the Spiral's bipedal species. Unlike those, though, these aliens' hands had two long fingers and two much shorter, thicker ones.

Conventional wisdom among anthropologists and conmen was that reading a person's clothing was the first step in evaluating and understanding that person and their culture. In this case, both of those groups would have had to be content with light browsing. Four of the six aliens wore long tunics with wide kilts below them that extended from waist to mid-calf. The other two were dressed similarly, but had added hats to the ensemble. The hats, at least, were moderately interesting: wide-brimmed, with tricorn-style points on four corners plus a pair of brightly colored feathers that rose from the front brim and crossed each other in a way that reminded me of a military rank badge. Those two aliens also carried flat boxes with top-mounted lids and handles.

Worst-case scenario was that this was a police or military patrol, sent to scout the city's perimeter with an eye toward spotting intruders. Fortunately, that didn't seem to be the case here. None of them carried obvious weapons, though it was possible they had small firearms tucked away out of sight. There was certainly nothing military I could see in their gait. Best guess was that they were fishermen heading for a dusk appointment with the local river trout.

They were approaching the last line of reeds when half a dozen ferret-sized creatures popped into view, scuttling enthusiastically around their feet.

My first reflexive thought was that they were some variant of Kalixiri outriders. But as one of the creatures turned around to look behind him I saw that, like the aliens themselves, these creatures had scales instead of fur. Pets then, joining their masters for the evening's labors? The alien in the lead, one of the ones with a hat, reached the end of the reed patch and turned toward one of the others.

Abruptly, his head snapped back around, twisting back and forth as he gazed up and down the river.

I ducked out of sight, cursing myself for my carelessness. The sun was halfway down the horizon, but there was still enough light left to glint off my faceplate. Time to disappear into Alpha before he decided his eyes hadn't been playing tricks on him and headed out into the water to investigate.

I climbed back down the rock as quickly as I could, grabbed the line and unhooked the buoy mesh from the rock. I attached my harness—

And stiffened. I'd looked straight at the city's ring of mounds and even made some idle speculation on their purpose . . . only there was one, utterly logical, almost inevitable purpose that I'd somehow never even considered.

It was time to get back to Alpha, all right. It might even be too late.

Three hours later, I was once again rising through the dark water. This time, Selene was at my side.

I took the ascent slowly, painfully aware that if the alarm had been sounded there were likely to be patrols all along the bank. Even worse, if *I* was running security for the city, I'd have tagged Shark Tooth Rock as an ideal place to set up surveillance or a mid-river command post. The last thing I wanted was to bump into an anchored boat on my way up, or to grab for a handhold that was already serving as someone else's foothold. I reached the surface and cautiously raised my eyes above the water.

Nothing leaped out at me, or dropped down on me, or screeched a warning at me. If the glint I assumed they'd seen earlier had indeed been spotted, apparently whoever was in charge had decided it was just a trick of the fading light.

Still, a minute of quiet recon was definitely called for. I worked my way around the rock, watching for boats or other signs of life. The clouds that had been gathering earlier had mostly dissipated, and while there was no visible moon the stars gave enough of a glow for me to see by.

There was also no light showing from the direction of the city. Whatever it was we'd spotted from orbit had either been a onetime event or something that was routinely shut down shortly after nightfall. Returning to my starting point on the eastern side of Shark Tooth Rock, I gave the double tug on the line that signaled Selene to join me.

A moment later, her helmet popped into view. I took her hand and guided it to a grip on the rock. "You okay?" I asked.

"Yes," her voice came in my earbud. "Give me a minute to recover from the change in pressure."

"No problem," I said. "Nothing out there is going anywhere."

"So you say," she said, and I could imagine some crossness in her pupils. "You *could* have told me why you wanted me here, you know. Or you could tell me now."

"I know, and I'm sorry to be so mysterious," I said. "I just didn't want to prejudice you by trotting out my own theories or preconceptions."

"Preconceptions don't affect me," she said. "They're not an issue with Kadolians. And it isn't like this would be the first theory you've come up with."

I winced. She didn't actually add the words *half-baked*, but she might as well have. "I know," I said again. "I just wanted to be especially careful on this one."

"I understand," she said, and I pictured her crossness fading a little. As my father used to say, *Humans are a tightly wrapped bundle of contradictions and neuroses, and the sooner everyone else in the Spiral figures that out, the less annoyed they'll be.* Certainly Selene had had plenty of personal experience with that. "All right, I'm ready. Should I take off my helmet, or will opening the vents be enough?"

"Probably should do it full open-air," I said. "Hang onto the rock and I'll get it off you. And be sure to keep your shoulders well above the ripples. We don't want water coming in your neck."

Half a minute later, I had her helmet tucked under my arm. "Okay," I said, watching her pure-white hair moving restlessly in the eddy breezes coming around the rock from the direction of the city. It looked even more ethereal than usual in the starlight. "Tell me what you smell."

I held my breath as her nostrils and eyelashes began sampling the air. If I was right...

Abruptly, she stiffened. "Oh, Gregory," she breathed. "Oh. No."

I felt the knot in my throat tighten a little more. I'd hoped I'd been wrong. But I hadn't. "They're portals, aren't they?" I said quietly. "All of those mounds. They're portals."

"I don't know if it's the mounds," she said. "But there are definitely portals in or near the city. But it's worse."

I frowned. "Worse?"

She gave a long, lingering sigh. "I'm also smelling a human." She seemed to brace herself. "And at least three Iykams."

"Terrific," I muttered, a hopeless, impotent rage settling into my gut. All the trouble we'd been through—crashing Alpha here, risking our lives, all of us including McKell and his friends hanging by our thumbs over a figurative lava pit. And all of it for nothing.

The Patth—the damned Patth—had gotten here first.

I don't know how long we hung to the rock in silence, staring at nothing, wrapped in the starlit night and our own individual thoughts. A minute at least, maybe two. The only way the Patth could have gotten here was via a portal of their own, presumably popping into one of the ones Selene was smelling.

Which meant either they'd already taken possession of the portal ring or else had the necessary personnel and resources on the way. Even if Alpha came back to full function tonight— and Selene's latest evaluation on that wasn't very promising—I doubted Kinneman could throw together a team fast enough and big enough to do us any good.

"Okay," I said at last, trying to filter the frustration out of my voice. "I guess we're on to Plan B, then. Whatever the hell Plan B turns out to be."

"Maybe not," Selene said, her nostrils and eyelashes still working. "The human and Iykams *were* here. But I don't think they are anymore."

I frowned at her. "You're joking. They found a whole ring of Icari portals and just *left*?"

"I agree, that seems strange," she said. "All I can tell you is that the scents are weak, probably several days old. For whatever it's worth, I don't smell the kind of cooking or stored food odors I would expect if they'd settled in, either."

"Okay," I said again. "Well, I suppose that's something. Anyone we know, by the way?"

"I can't tell," Selene said. "The scents are too weak to sort out from the native aromas layered in on top of them."

"Understood," I said. It was a frustrating scenario—more frustrating even for her than for me—but one we'd run into on more occasions than either of us liked. The only way around the impasse was to either get closer to the scent or to let her get familiar enough with the local unknowns that her brain could edit them out.

I leaned back a little to look around the rock at the dark and silent city. A sudden, unpleasant thought had just occurred to me. "Odd and slightly disturbing question," I said. "What if the intruders are dead?"

"That depends on how they died," she said, taking the question in stride. "The scent of blood is very distinctive and tends to linger. If they were stabbed or shot, I would probably know it. If they were choked or smothered, the signs wouldn't be as obvious."

"So, inconclusive."

"From out here, yes," she said. "When we get closer, I'll be able to tell more."

"You mean when we get closer to people who might have already taken out a human and some Iykams?"

"That's one way to put it," she said. "But I don't smell firearm residue or the scorching and charring from plasmics or corona weapons."

I frowned at the city. "Which is pretty odd all by itself. It's hard to imagine Iykams being chased out of anywhere without firing their weapons at least once."

"Unless they were ordered not to."

"There's that," I conceded, frowning as something belatedly struck me. "You said there's human and Iykam scent. Did you forget to mention Patth scent? Or isn't there any?"

She sniffed for a few seconds. "No, no Patth," she confirmed, sounding puzzled. "There's another group of aliens, probably the ones you saw earlier. But no Patth. You're right, that doesn't make sense. Why would there be Iykams and not Patth?"

"Because this wasn't an invasion," I said as the mix of details finally began to coalesce into something solid. "It must have been a quiet probe or scouting expedition. Nask sent in a human, probably an Expediter, along with an Iykam escort to take a look around. They did so—in fact, maybe they were the light we saw—then hightailed it back to report."

"Yes, that would make sense," Selene said. "If that's true, what's our response?"

I chewed thoughtfully at my lip. "I don't see a lot of options," I said. "We could wait for Alpha to reactivate and send for McKell and a bunch of EarthGuard Marines. Unfortunately, we have no idea when that might happen. We also don't know what Nask's schedule is. If we delay too long, we might roll up to the city to find the Patth already have it buttoned up."

"You're saying you and I are it?"

"For the moment, yes, I am," I said heavily. "And given our lack of numbers and resources, I only see two possible courses of action. One, we walk into the city tomorrow in broad daylight and try to open a conversation. Two, we sneak in tomorrow night and... actually, I have no idea what we'd do in that one."

"Well, we certainly aren't going to sneak out with one of the portals," Selene said, with a touch of dark humor. "I don't think either option is going to get us very far, though."

"I suppose that depends on whether or not the natives are friendly," I said. "I guess we're mostly talking recon mission."

"Recon *and* first contact," Selene said. "I'd say we go with your first option. At least walking in during the day doesn't make us look guilty of something before we even meet them."

"Not looking guilty is always a good way to start negotiations," I agreed. "I suppose the other option is for *me* to walk in while you stay behind in Alpha. That way—"

"No," she interrupted.

"That way," I continued stubbornly, "you'd be able to give McKell a preliminary report when he finally shows up."

"We can leave him a note," she said. "We go in together, or we don't go at all. Staying together was the fundamental reason we didn't leave with Jordan and Ixil in the first place."

I sighed. "Fine. My chivalrous side would object, but it's too tired to argue. Let's get some food, some sleep, some more food, and in the morning we take a swim. Hold still and let me help you get your helmet back on."

She was silent while I reattached her helmet and checked the seals. "Looks good," I said. "Let's go."

"Yes," she murmured, her hand still gripping the rock. "Gregory...you said they had scales like armadillos?"

"That's what they looked like from here, yes," I said, wondering why she was bringing this up now. "Why?"

"Just getting it clear in my mind," she said. Letting go of the rock, she took hold of the line and started pulling herself down toward Alpha.

It was only as I began to follow that it occurred to me that right now, in the darkness of night and with our helmets in place, would be the only time she could ask a question and know that I couldn't read anything in her pupils.

And the question she'd chosen to ask was about the aliens in the portal ring.

She didn't talk much about her past, or the past of her people. But there'd been a few times she'd mentioned Kadolian stories and legends. None of them had struck me as being either good or pleasant memories.

I wondered if any of those legends talked about scale-armored creatures.

CHAPTER ELEVEN

The river that Alpha was submerged in flowed largely south to north, coming out of the mountains and presumably winding its way to the ocean a hundred kilometers to the west. My original plan had been to strap ourselves into a couple of the Barracuda maneuvering packs, swim upstream underwater for a kilometer or so, then head to shore. We'd find a place to bury the packs and suits and approach the city from the south. Part of the logic was that if we had to leave in a hurry it would be easier and less detectable to let the current carry us back downriver to Alpha than having to travel upstream from the other direction.

But in the light of day, as we floated beside Shark Tooth Rock, I realized that wasn't going to work. Both sides of the riverbank, in both directions, were crowded with the reeds I'd seen the previous evening, and while they shouldn't be much trouble to get through, our point of exit from the river would be obvious to anyone with half a brain and decent eyesight. There might be better crossing points upriver, but I hated to count on that. Even if there were, a quick exit from the city would then require us to travel a hefty distance on foot before we could get back to our gear and into the water. Plus there was still the fact that neither of us had ever used a Barracuda before. Civilian gear like our vac suits was generally intuitive and simple to operate. Military versions generally weren't.

Which left a single and obvious option.

"We could go straight across to the dock," Selene suggested as I paddled around the rock. "That would get us past most of the reeds, and it looks like there's enough room to store our suits underneath it."

"I know," I said, peering across the river at the eastern bank, the one on the far side from the city. Not only was the bank lined with reeds, but just a little ways inland was the edge of a fairly substantial forest. If we swam over there, punched through the reeds however we had to, hiked upriver, then swam back across to the city side...

"If we stay between the reeds and the forest, we'll be in view of the city the whole way," Selene pointed out, correctly interpreting my musings. "If we go into the forest, we'll be hidden but will have to deal with whatever dangers might be in there."

"Plus we'd have the same problem of coming ashore once we crossed back to the western bank," I conceded, turning back toward the city. "So. The dock, you say?"

"I don't see any better entry points."

"Neither do I," I said. "Problem is that the natives probably use that dock on a regular basis." I frowned as another thought belatedly struck me. "Selene, why are those reeds even still there? Why weren't they knocked flat by the mini tsunami when Alpha hit the water?"

"Because it didn't hit the water here," Selene said, her pupils showing puzzlement that I had to ask. "It hit the mountains way to the south, rolled down into the river, then traveled underwater until it hit this rock and stopped."

"You're kidding," I said, squinting upstream. There was nothing in view that indicated something like that had happened. "How do you know?"

"I can smell the crushed and scorched vegetation in that direction," she said. "And as I think back, I can interpret some of Alpha's shifting scents as corresponding to the changes from orbit, atmosphere, landing, then underwater travel."

"So Tera's calculations were bang on target."

"Except landing us a few kilometers too far south."

"Coming from two thousand kilometers up with a whole planet to aim at, that counts as bang on target," I said. "Well, there's no guarantee that going downstream wouldn't give us the same shoreline reed issues, plus I don't fancy a long exit jog if things go sideways. Let's head for the dock and hope for the best."

"All right." She ducked her head under the water.

"Just keep an eye out for those ferret things," I warned as I submerged alongside her. "I don't know if they're pets, symbionts, or parasites, but I'm not willing to assume friendliness on their part."

"We shouldn't assume friendliness on *anyone's* part," Selene said.

I frowned as I pushed off the rock and headed for the dock. There it was again. Just like when she'd asked her armadillo question last night, there'd been something in her voice that went past just normal caution or even random speculation. "You know something about these people that I don't?"

She didn't answer. I let her have her moment, focusing my full attention on my swimming. I'd noted yesterday that the vac suits had a tendency to float, and had added some ballast to both our outfits before leaving Alpha today. But even with neutral buoyancy this was harder than I'd expected.

For one thing, the last time I'd done anything like this I'd had swim fins that let my legs do most of the work of propelling me through the water. The vac suit's boots were pretty much useless in that department.

Worse, my helmet and faceplate were designed to give me a clear view of the world when I was standing or sitting upright. Here, stretched out prone with my face pointed downward, I had a terrific view of the water beneath me but only a hint of what was directly ahead. Given that my hands were busy stroking their way through the water, I could only hope that my restricted vision would warn me of obstructions before I slammed helmet-first into them.

"I might," Selene said reluctantly. "Do you remember me telling you there are stories of Kadolians being recruited as assassins?"

Like I would somehow have forgotten a bombshell like that. "Yes, of course," I said. "Were these armadillos involved in that?"

"The stories are...unclear," Selene said. "Some say that armored creatures were the ones who sent the assassins on their missions. Others say those creatures were the assassins' targets."

"Or it could be both," I offered. "After all, the whole reason we're here is our theory that there was a big dustup on Meima, and that one side of it sent half of the directory here. Depending on how deep and how nasty the fight was, it's possible people on one side sent assassins to attack people on the other."

"Those assassins being us," Selene said quietly.

I winced at my mental image of what her pupils must look like right now. Selene was bad enough with just ordinary death. Death that her people might have been deliberately involved with would be far worse. "Or the stories might just be rumors started to implicate you and maybe alienate you from one side or the other," I pointed out. "The only reason I brought it up was to ask if you thought the people here might themselves be Icari."

"I thought the Icari disappeared ten thousand years ago."

"All we know is that they stopped making buildings in the Spiral around that time," I pointed out. "We don't know if they all disappeared after that or are still hanging around in the shadows. Or if the main group is gone but a remnant got left behind."

I made it another couple of meters before she spoke again. "I don't know," she said. "If these people are Icari, how did they work the portal controls?"

I scowled. That was one of the questions I'd wrestled with ever since the first time I'd taken a ride in one of the things.

I could understand why all the portal launch module displays were flush with the inner hull, essentially set into the module's floor. Human designers probably would have mounted them on stands or consoles, but that was mostly because we liked looking at things that were waist-high or higher. But the Icari could easily have had different preferences, and standing over a display was an equally reasonable setup.

For me, the sticking point was that all the controls were down there, too, including the four-by-twenty array of squares where you punched in the portal's destination address.

Did the Icari just crouch down to reach them? Did they lie flat on the deck to punch the keys? Both postures were workable, but they seemed starkly at odds with the sense of dignity inherent in towering over the displays.

A better guess was that there was something about Icari physiology that made such an arrangement both logical and practical. "I asked McKell about it once," I said. "He told me the Icarus Group thought the Icari either had very long arms—like, you know, gorilla-long—or else had tentacles or elephantine trunks they could use to reach the controls."

"The skeletons on Shiroyama Island and Meima didn't have any such appendages."

"I know," I said. "Though I suppose any tentacles could have been non-bony and decayed along with the rest of the soft tissue. Anyway, that was McKell's theory."

Selene was silent another few strokes. "You're thinking the local aliens here might fit the skeletons?"

"Not a clue," I admitted. "They have all that armadillo armor and those extra-long fingers, but I suppose ten thousand years of decay and scavengers could account for those discrepancies with the skeleton record."

"Especially since we don't know what those body parts are made of," she said. "Cartilage scales might disintegrate more quickly than bone, and what you thought were fingers might be short tentacles."

I pursed my lips, thinking back to the brief look I'd had. Those appendages hadn't appeared to be anything except fingers, but given my distance and the short observation window, what Selene was suggesting was certainly possible. "They'd have to telescope pretty far in order to reach the controls," I said. "That much extension would leave them really thin at the end. But I suppose it doesn't take *that* much effort to punch in a code."

"It's also not possible to know a being's strength merely by looking at him," Selene said. "Is that the dock?"

I paused in my swimming and arched my back to angle my faceplate as far forward as I could. Through the murky water I could just make out a set of pilings rising from the riverbed below to a shadowy overhang above. "Looks like it," I said. "Stay back while I check it out."

There were three sets of supports in all, holding up a dock that was about five meters long and three meters wide. The entire structure was made of stone: square stone blocks piled on top of each other for the pilings, a couple of wide flagstones sitting on top of them forming the dock itself. There was about a meter of air between the dock and the rippling water, plenty of room for our vac suits once we were out of them.

Which was going to be the tricky part. Here at the bank the water was only half a meter deep, which meant we could easily undress under the dock's shelter and fasten the suits to the underside with the bungee cords we'd brought. But that would leave us wet from at least the knees down, rather defeating the whole purpose of heading into the city without the inhabitants knowing where we'd come from. In the end we had to set the bungees in place, climb up onto the dock and strip off the vac suits, then lean awkwardly over the edge to maneuver the bundles into place in their supports.

The procedure had the advantage of keeping us dry. It had the disadvantage of putting us right out there in the open, in front of God and everyone. If any of the locals happened to be looking in the right direction at the right time, we might as well not have bothered with the subterfuge. Still, if we kept low enough, the reeds should give us at least partial cover.

"Why is there still a path to those buildings?" Selene asked.

I frowned, following her eyes. Right along the riverbank, a single narrow line of reeds in from the shoreline, there was indeed a path. It led off upstream, toward our left, from the track that the fishermen I'd seen last night had been using. It was a little hard to see through the various stands of reeds, but it looked like it ran past all the decrepit buildings on that side of the water.

And Selene was right. With those structures long since abandoned, why hadn't the reeds reclaimed that section of the bank?

Unless the houses *weren't* abandoned?

"Good question," I said. "Now that I think about it, what I assumed was the lead fisherman turning to talk to one of his companions might instead have been him starting to turn onto this path."

"Which would suggest they weren't fishermen."

"Which would suggest it highly," I agreed. "Any one in particular you'd like a look at?"

"That one," she said, pointing to the debris pile third over from the dock area. It was the largest of the group and also in the best shape, with two walls and part of the roof still mostly intact.

"Okay," I said, giving the area a quick survey. Reeds, bushes, decrepit buildings, no people. "Let's go."

We headed off along the path. "Anything interesting?" I asked.

"There are several strong scents," she said. "Some locals were here in the past day or two. I don't know whether they were inside or outside."

"Not that there's a lot of difference between those two," I said, eyeing the generous gaps in walls and roof. "Any idea whether they stayed or were just passing through?"

"They were here awhile," she said, sniffing a little harder. "A couple of hours, possibly more. I'll be able to tell more once we're inside."

"Okay," I said, an unpleasant tingle running up my back. Maybe the group I'd seen last night hadn't been as quick to dismiss the glint from my faceplate as I'd hoped. If they'd decided to run surveillance along the riverbank, this building would have been a reasonable place to do it from. "Anything else?"

"There's metal," she said. "Not one I've smelled before."

"Another Icari variant?"

"Possibly," she said. "But it smells . . . cheaper, somehow."

We arrived at the building, and I ducked through the drooping opening that had presumably once held a door.

"Do you think we should?" Selene asked, hesitating at the doorway.

"Not exactly breaking and entering when all the breaking's already been done," I pointed out. "Don't worry, we'll be quick."

The building layout was about as simple as such things could get: a single square room with a dirt floor. Over in the corner between the two mostly intact walls someone had torn away the baseboards and dug into the floor beneath the rotting wood, exposing a foundation consisting of a line of stone blocks with some sort of black wire mesh facing on them. Beside the pile of dirt from the excavation were a pair of metal trowels, a wide-blade shovel, and three soft-bristle brushes.

"There's your cheap Icari metal," I said, pointing at the trowels. "Tools."

"Yes," Selene murmured, taking a couple of steps toward the site.

I frowned at her. There'd been something in her voice just then. "What is it?"

She didn't answer, but just continued walking. She reached the excavation spot and knelt down. For a moment she paused, sniffing. Then, picking up one of the brushes, she started clearing away the dirt from the stones at the edge of the hole.

I walked over and stood beside her, feeling a stir of unpleasant anticipation. The last time she'd smelled something through a layer of dirt it had ended up being an alien skeleton. She hadn't taken that particularly well, and she probably wouldn't do any better if she found another one here. The dirt fell away under her brush, rolling down to the bottom of the hole. With her head bowed over her work I couldn't see her pupils, but I could imagine a mix of intensity and dread. She gave the stone surface one final sweep—

I stiffened. Behind the dirt, woven into the black mesh, were two other threads. Not black, these two, but a shimmering, glistening silver. Even in the diffuse light coming through the sagging roof they seemed to glow like strands of living light.

I took a careful breath. "Is that what I think it is?" I asked, trying to keep my voice steady.

She nodded and looked up. There was intensity and dread in her pupils, all right. But flowing across both of them was a sort of disbelieving awe. "It is," she confirmed.

"It's silver-silk."

From the moment Selene smelled the presence of Iykams in the city I'd known this moment was coming. But despite that head knowledge I'd still clung desperately to the hope that I was wrong, that Sub-Director Nask and the Patth had found some other way to get to this world and its cluster of Icari portals.

That hope was now shattered. The presence of silver-silk meant Alainn, and Alainn meant that Nask had been able to reactivate the portal he'd taken from that world. The Iykams had been a strong hint, but now the connection was confirmed.

And if Kinneman was still uncertain whether or not to charge me with treason, Selene and I had just made his case for him.

"Well," I said, hearing the slight trembling in my voice. No use trying to sound casual. Not anymore. "I guess they got the portal working."

"I guess they did," Selene said, turning her face and her pupils away from me. She could follow the logic train, too, and knew as well as I did what this discovery meant for my future. Or more likely, my lack of one.

I took a deep breath. Fine, so I was doomed. But just because I was a walking dead man didn't mean we should just go back to Alpha and sit around singing sad songs until EarthGuard Marines showed up and clapped me in irons. If nothing else, we owed it to McKell and Ixil to gather whatever information we could before they arrived.

"At least we know now why the Icari went to all the trouble

to keep the portal to Alainn open," I said. "Apparently, this stuff has other uses besides just decorating the rich."

"So it would seem," Selene said. "Strange that no one's realized that after all these years."

"Not really," I said. "Not for humans. We have a long history of letting decorative stuff just lie around without bothering to figure out what else we could do with it. Gold, for instance. For centuries we just thought of it as something you could make thrones and scepters out of. It wasn't until we started getting serious about technology that we figured out it was a good conductor, was soft enough to be hammered into thin coatings, was impressively noncorrosive, could reflect EM radiation, et cetera."

"Though to be fair, as you said, there wouldn't have been any reason to look at gold's other properties until you began utilizing electricity and electronics."

"True," I said. "And that's a good point. We know Icari technology is light-years beyond anything in the Spiral, so there really may be nothing else we can use silver-silk for right now."

"Any thought as to what it's being used for here?" Selene asked, gesturing at the glistening threads.

"Not a clue," I admitted. "The way it intertwines with the black wires reminds me of an electrostatic defense grid. But without knowing anything about the other stuff I wouldn't want to put any weight on that."

"And we don't know anything about whatever missing equipment it was attached to."

"That, too," I agreed, looking around the ruined building with new eyes. Strip off the rotting wood, extend the stone foundation up above ground level... "You know, if I were going to make a wild guess, I'd peg this place as some kind of guardhouse. A river in front of me, a city and a bunch of Icari portals at my back, a defense grid"—I pointed to the floor in the center of the building—"maybe a mobile missile cluster or a swivel-mounted laser cannon here in the middle."

"Yes, that could make sense," Selene said, her pupils thoughtful. "You noticed the dock used to be longer, didn't you?"

I frowned at her. "It did? How do you know?"

"There are the footings for other pylons in the mud," she said. "I saw them as we were swimming across. At least, I *thought* they were footings. You didn't see them?"

"No, but I also wasn't looking," I said. "Interesting. So are we talking a longer dock or a full-fledged bridge?"

"I hadn't thought about a bridge," she said, the thoughtfulness deepening. "Where would it go? I didn't see anything on that side of the river except reeds and forest."

"Maybe there used to be another city over there," I said. "If it collapsed faster than the one on this side and the forest reclaimed the land, there could be nothing to see. Or maybe there wasn't a city, but they did a lot of mining and logging in the mountains."

"Or—" She broke off. "Gregory, they're coming," she said, her voice dropping to a whisper. "Three of them. Maybe four."

Reflexively, I dropped my hand to my holstered plasmic. "How close?"

She shook her head. "A hundred meters. Maybe less."

I looked around the ruined building. Not a single scrap of cover in here, though the two mostly solid walls might let us do a duck-and-seek with our new playmates.

But keeping the walls between us and them would be tricky enough to pull off with one or two seekers. It would be nearly impossible with three or four of them, especially if they knew what they were doing. They were also already too close for us to make it back to the dock without being seen or to look for other cover.

Which left only one option.

"Okay," I said, taking my hand off my weapon. "We came here to make contact with the locals. I guess the time has come."

"So it would seem," Selene said. There was tension in her pupils, but she could see the same lack of other options that I could. "Just remember they won't speak English."

"Hopefully, they speak empty hands and smiles," I said, trying to keep my voice light. The history of the Spiral was replete with alien first-contact stories, some of them warm and encouraging, others not so much. "Let's go." I led the way back through the squashed doorway and picked my way through the debris to the city side of the building.

There were four of them, just as Selene had said, fifty meters away now and striding briskly and purposefully in our direction. They were dressed like the fishermen I'd seen the previous evening, except that there was only one in this group wearing a hat. The other three made up for that fashion deficiency with long black rods slung over their shoulders. I didn't spot any obvious reaction to our sudden appearance, but I noted that their angle of approach shifted a few degrees toward us. Possibly someone in the city had spotted our arrival, but had lost track of us between the dock and the building.

And like the fishermen, they had a small entourage of ferret-sized creatures scampering along at their sides.

I eyed the group, wondering if it would look more friendly and less threatening for us to walk toward them and meet in the middle or for us to stand our ground right here. My mental coin flip came up heads; touching Selene's arm, I started walking.

Again, there were no obvious reactions to our approach. Still, I kept my eyes on those staves. If they were just bo sticks designed to club one's opponent into submission, great. If the rods were the sheaths for very narrow swords, I could deal with that, too.

If they were plasmics or firearms, that would be an entirely different matter.

I was still running the possibilities through my mind when I heard a muttered word from the alien in the hat. In perfect unison the other three swiveled their rods around to point at us as they all continued walking.

"Gregory?" Selene murmured.

"Keep going," I said, forcing my hand to stay away from my plasmic. It was perfectly natural for people in an isolated community to be wary of strangers. "Try to look friendly."

We'd made it another two steps when Hat Man muttered again and the four of them stopped. A third command, and the alien on the right-hand end of their line shifted his rod to point at the ground beside him. The ferrets, clearly picking up on the cue, scampered out of the way. One of the alien's long fingers did something to the rod—

And a lightning bolt flashed from the end and blasted into the ground.

I don't know if Selene jumped. I know I did. "Gregory?" she repeated, more urgently this time.

"Keep walking," I said again, lifting my hands to shoulder level. Not quite a gesture of surrender, but definitely emphasizing the fact that I wasn't going for my own weapon. "They're giving us a choice: Keep walking and make contact, or turn and run like rabbits."

"With them holding electrical discharge weapons at our backs?"

"There's that," I conceded. "On the other hand, they could have shot us already if they were in a shooting mood. Let's accept their warning, play it cool, and see where it leads."

The aliens watched as we approached, all three lightning guns now back to being pointed at us. We'd closed the distance to five meters away when Hat Man took a step forward and held up a hand. I took the cue and brought us to a halt. "Hello," I called cheerfully to him. "My name is Gregory Roarke. This is Selene."

For a moment Hat Man stared at me. Then, very deliberately, he turned his face to Selene and said a few words in a melodic, singsong language.

Beside me, Selene stiffened. "What?" I muttered.

"He spoke," Selene breathed. "Gregory, he *spoke.*"

I frowned at the oddness of her comment. Of course he spoke. We'd both heard him saying incomprehensible words.

Unless what she meant—"Are you saying you *understand* him?"

"I—no, not completely," she fumbled, confusion in her pupils. "But some of the words were ours. Or maybe just sounded like ours. Maybe I just thought he was..." She broke off.

"Assume for a moment his words were your words," I said, eyeing Hat Man closely. "What do you think he said?"

"It sounded like..." She hesitated. "Like *you return now from the sky?*"

CHAPTER TWELVE

"Okay," I said, trying to suppress the reflexive urge to look up at the sky and the clouds drifting overhead.

Trying equally hard to stay calm.

The Icarus Group's best estimate was that this system was at least forty thousand light-years from the loose collection of inhabited worlds we called the Spiral. There was a good chance it was even farther than that.

Granted that the locals were sitting on a bunch of portals, at least one of which we knew led to a minor Commonwealth world. But even so, how in the world had they bumped into the nomadic Kadolians? How especially had they bumped into them long enough to have picked up some of their language?

Unless they'd done all that *before* the Kadolians became nomadic. Say, maybe ten to fifteen thousand years ago.

Selene and I had speculated that her people and the Patth had both been clients for the same patron species. Were the aliens here those patrons?

Had we finally found the Icari?

I ran my eyes over them, feeling my sudden emotional surge fade away. Up close, I could see that their fingers were just fingers, not coiled tentacles or extendable trunk-like appendages. Their arms weren't extra long, and there were no other obvious places where tentacles could be lurking. If they were connected to the Icari, they were likely just another client species.

"We should say something back to him," Selene murmured.

"Yes. Right." I pursed my lips, trying to think. "Okay. He talked to you in his language, which had enough Kadolian in it for you to understand. Try saying something in Kadolian and see if he can sort out what he needs from his end."

"All right." Selene began speaking, talking slowly and enunciating each word. I focused on Hat Man, peripherally keeping tabs on the lads with the lightning guns. One of the ferrets detached itself from where it had been crouching at Hat Man's feet and scurried over to me. It sniffed at my shoes, then stretched itself upward, resting its front paws on my shins, and sniffed some more at my trouser legs. I ignored it, keeping my eyes fixed on the aliens. I'd seen Ixil use Pix and Pax as similar diversions, and I was determined not to let my guard down.

Selene finished speaking, and for a moment, Hat Man was silent. Then, he gestured. The other three aliens raised their weapons to point at the sky and moved around to our sides. Hat Man said something, then turned and strode back toward the city. "Selene?" I muttered.

"I think he wants us to follow," she said, setting off after him. "I didn't understand most of that last part, but I think one of the words was *companions*."

"Was he talking about us?" I asked. "Or about me, as your companion?"

"I don't know," Selene said. "All I got was *companions*."

I nodded, eyeing the three aliens flanking us. "We need to get a fast handle on this," I warned. "We won't get anywhere with these people if all we can get is one understandable word per sentence."

"I know," Selene said. "I'm sure he does, too. But there's something else. When you first started speaking—when you said hello and gave our names—their scents changed."

I frowned. "Changed how? Hopeful? Confused? Angry?"

"I don't know," Selene said. "I don't have a baseline for them. All I know is that they had one scent when they first saw us, it changed when you spoke, and then it changed again to something else while he and I were talking."

I thought back to those particular moments. The aliens had

been a good fifty meters away when we first came out of concealment, which was pretty far for even someone of Selene's abilities.

On the other hand, the breeze *had* been coming toward us from behind them. That typically gave her more range. "We'll tuck that away for future reference," I said. "What about the lightning guns? Do they smell distinctive enough that you could find one if we needed to?"

She turned to me, her pupils wary. "You're not thinking...?"

"No, no, of course not," I assured her. "We're perfectly peaceful. Remember?"

She didn't answer. But then, she didn't have to.

We were perfectly peaceful, all right. Right up to the point when we suddenly needed to be something else.

Hat Man and his friends hadn't been visible when we first left the dock after dumping our vac suits, and I'd wondered how they'd managed to sneak up on us so fast. Fifty meters into our hike, I got my answer.

The reeds that lined the riverbank had given way to tall grasses and scrub brush a few meters past the row of ramshackle buildings. Now, as Hat Man led the way through the low foliage, I spotted a ramp angling downward into a tunnel in the ground, our view of which had been previously blocked by a group of waist-high red-leafed bushes.

Hat Man stepped onto the ramp and headed into the tunnel. With guards on either side of us, and with a half dozen ferrets scampering around, Selene and I had no option but to follow.

There were no lights in this section of the tunnel's walls or ceiling, and as we moved away from the entrance the tunnel became progressively darker. Fortunately, the floor was smooth, with no bumps or debris that could pose a hazard to navigation. Forty meters ahead, I saw the first glimmerings of light, right at the point where the ramp flattened out into a metal walkway. "Is all of this Icari metal?" I asked quietly.

"Yes," Selene confirmed. "It's similar to the shovel and trowels."

"Mm." It made sense that an Icari base would be constructed of Icari metal.

The problem was that that was going to make it a lot harder for Selene to zero in on the specific variety the Icari had used in their portal directories. When I'd first proposed this plan to McKell and Ixil, I'd expected that RH's distinctive aroma would stand out from the native flora like a flare on a moonless night. If it was instead in the city somewhere, surrounded by tons of similar stuff, that particular bet would need to be heavily hedged.

The walkway at the bottom of the ramp turned out to be a platform serving a pair of monorail tracks, one on each side. A train consisting of four eight-seat, open-topped cars was waiting on the track to our right. Hat Man climbed into the driver's seat in the front car, Selene and I took the two seats behind him, and the three guards and ferrets settled in behind us. One of the ferrets hopped briefly into my lap, nosed at my holstered plasmic, then apparently decided I was too lumpy or didn't smell right and abandoned me for the empty front seat beside Hat Man. Hat Man waited until everyone was settled, then touched a couple of controls, and we were off.

I'd estimated the city was a few kilometers across, with the portal ring and its central building sitting at roughly the center of the urban expanse. Subways were fairly common in the Spiral's larger cities, and I'd occasionally had the need to ride one.

But those trains had usually had well-spaced-out stops, putting them at least half a kilometer apart. Here, the platforms were much closer together, with only one or two hundred meters between them.

That didn't slow us down any, of course, since most of the stops opened into the abandoned parts of town and we bypassed those without slowing. Still, the arrangement seemed a little odd.

Selene noticed it, too. "I wonder if there used to be a lot of invalids living here," she mused.

"You mean the close platform spacing?" I asked. "Could be. Or maybe they just get a lot of really bad weather. Or everyone was just lazy."

She was silent a moment. "Those mountains to the east. Do you think any of them could be volcanic?"

"No idea. But the winds mostly come from the other direction, don't they?"

"Mostly," she said. "But volcanic ash can spread out in all directions."

"Certainly with a big enough eruption," I agreed. I looked at the next platform as we passed, catching a glimpse of the ramp leading to the surface beyond. This entrance and the one we'd used had both been completely open to the air.

Could they be sealed off in an emergency? If not, a flood of volcanic ash, or even just the rain from a moderately ambitious thunderstorm, could have disastrous consequences for the subway and anyone who happened to be in it.

"There's another possibility," I said, lowering my voice. "They may not have been worried so much about natural disasters as, shall we say, unnatural ones."

I felt her shiver. "Like an attack?"

"That's what we humans tend to worry about, anyway," I said. "If this place can be sealed off, it would make a pretty good bomb shelter. Do the patrons in your legends have any enemies?"

She sighed. "Everyone has enemies, Gregory."

"I suppose."

We finished the trip in silence. Three minutes later, the car came to a halt at the end of the track.

Our marching order as we headed up the ramp was a little different this time. Two of the guards now took the lead, with Hat Man behind them, Selene and I behind him, and the third guard bringing up the rear. I wondered if this was a more ceremonial formation or whether Hat Man just figured that we were far enough in that there was no longer anywhere we could run.

Based on my assumption that the big central building was the government center, I'd expected that the ramp at the end of the subway line would bring us right up to the front door. To my mild surprise, we instead emerged between two of the nicer buildings at the edge of the well-maintained lawn of dark green grass, which put us another hundred meters from the central building. Either government workers had living quarters in there, or else they were expected to get some exercise on their way home.

I looked over my shoulder at the buildings we were passing between. Close up, they looked to be in even better shape than I'd guessed from that first distant sighting. Their walls and doors showed no sign of serious aging, their foundations were mostly free of windswept leaves or other debris, and their windows were clean and plentiful, allowing for brightly lit interiors.

Hat Man babbled a few more words, then turned forward and set off toward the central building. We took the cue and followed. "You get anything from that last speech?" I murmured.

"There was the word *companions* again," she said. "Nothing except that."

"At least they've figured out that you and I are together," I said. "I just hope someone in there is good at charades. Otherwise we've got a really boring afternoon ahead of us."

From Shark Tooth Rock the central building had looked generally conical. Here, closer and in full daylight, I could see it was a lot more complicated than that. The building was divided into five tiers, each one slightly smaller than the one beneath it, each one shaped like a polygon with rounded corners. The windows were of various sizes, their layout suggesting that each tier was comprised of two floors. There were also a handful of taller windows that I guessed were floor-to-ceiling versions gracing some two-story-high rooms.

The strange thing was that each of the polygon shapes was different. Assuming they were regular figures, the number of corners I could see indicated that the lowest tier had eight sides, the next one up seven, the next six, the next five, and the last one four. Sticking out of the top of the final tier was a short windowless cylinder that looked too narrow to have any rooms. The swashes and swirls of color along the sides weren't confined to a single tier, but generally swept over all of them. The aerial view of the place must be interesting, as would be the tower's floor plan.

There were three ornate doors leading into the lowest tier on this side of the building, one built into each of the visible corners. Each was set about two meters up from the base, with a short landing at the top and a ramp leading to the ground. Each door had a pair of aliens on guard duty with lightning guns slung over their shoulders.

But none of these entrances was apparently up to Hat Man's standards. Instead of leading us to one of them he instead veered us off into a path angling around to the left, upriver side of the building. As we came around that side, I saw another corner and another door, this one flanked by four armed aliens instead of the two we'd seen elsewhere. "Selene?" I murmured.

"I'm not getting any change in their scents," she murmured back. "Did you notice that none of the door guards have ferrets?"

I looked back at the door we'd passed, then at the one we were heading for. She was right. "No pets while on duty?" I suggested.

"I don't think so," she said. "There's something strange about the animals' scents. They're similar to the aliens' scents, but not *too* similar."

"Like Ixil and his outriders, maybe?"

"No, Pix and Pax have scents all their own. Here...I don't know. There's some connection, but I can't pin it down."

"You'll get it," I assured her. "I have the feeling we're going to have plenty of time here."

We reached the ramp leading to Hat Man's door of choice and headed up. The guards on the landing watched our approach, but left their weapons on their shoulders. We reached the door and paused while Hat Man and the guards held a brief conversation. One of the latter made a gesture and pulled open the door. Hat Man gestured back, and we headed inside, leaving the four door guards at their posts.

After the building's dramatic exterior, I was mildly disappointed by the room we walked into. The ceiling was low, not much higher than it would be in a standard human-sized building, the floor was made of simple stone, and the walls were a plain and unadorned off-white. Hat Man didn't pause, but continued straight through to another door at the far end. We passed through into a short hallway with a pair of spiral ramps leading off to right and left. Hat Man led us to the left one and we headed down.

An unpleasant thought tingled its way across my brain. In nearly every business or governmental building across the Spiral, the people who ran things were at the top, where they got the panoramic views and the clean air and could flaunt the less-than-subtle reminder that they were above everyone else. The lower levels, in contrast, were occupied by the men and women who toiled for those elite in silence and anonymity.

And the very lowest levels...

I caught my breath. Hat Man had said *companions*...

I moved closer to Selene as we continued down the ramp. "You said earlier that the human and Iykam scents were a few days old, right?" I asked quietly.

"Yes," she said, puzzlement in her pupils.

"And your conclusion was that they'd either left or were dead?"

"*You* were the one who said they might be dead."

"Whatever," I said. "What if they were neither? What if they were locked away?"

"Are you saying *they're* the companions he's talking about?"

Ahead, the ramp was coming to an end. "You tell me," I said. "What are you getting from the walls?"

She sniffed the air. "Nothing. But the entire area's been cleaned recently. Very thoroughly."

"Handy," I muttered. "I wonder if we were expected. Maybe they spotted me last night after all."

"Maybe," she said, still sniffing. "I'm still not getting any human or Iykam scents. If they're here, their cells are very well sealed."

The ramp let us out into another hallway, this one with five doors on either side and a single larger one at the far end. The latter door had yet another pair of guards flanking it.

"I think this area is food storage," Selene said as Hat Man led the way past the first set of doors. "There are several varieties of plants, but there seems to be only one type in each room."

So the locals separated their various crops to make inventory and cooking easier. A fairly standard procedure. "You getting anything that might be cold storage?"

"Nothing that smells like normal refrigerants," she said. "Maybe they don't use cold for long-term food preservation."

I nodded, eyeing the door at the end of the hallway. It had a more elaborate lock and handle mechanism than the others we were passing and the door was edged by a rubbery-looking material. "Those look like hermetical seals to you?"

"Yes," Selene said. "Modified atmosphere preservation?"

"That's my guess," I said. "I just hope they remembered to switch out the carbon dioxide or nitrogen they're using before they tossed their prisoners inside."

We passed the last pair of side doors. Hat Man gave a gesture, and the two guards at the far door stepped aside. Hat Man stopped in front of the door and turned to give Selene a long look. He said something, then turned back and got a grip on the handle. He hesitated a moment, then pulled the handle down. There was a *click* from the lock, a sort of muffled *puff* from the seals, and he swung the panel open.

There, seated on rough crates in an otherwise plain metal-walled room, were the prisoners I'd expected to see. Three Iykams and—

"Hello, Roarke," Expediter Huginn said, his unshaven face twitching in an ironic smile. "Why am I not surprised?"

"Hello, Huginn," I said. "Nice to see you, too. You come here often?"

His smile turned into a sort of half-hearted smirk. "Not at these prices," he said. "Welcome to purgatory. Pull up a crate and sit down."

I looked at Hat Man. He was just standing there, his eyes on Selene, making no move to order or encourage us inside. "You misunderstand," I said. "We're not here to join you. We're here to get you out."

I gestured to Selene. "Or rather, *Selene's* here to get you out."

CHAPTER THIRTEEN

———— ❖ ————

The setup was perfect for a combination prison break and star-thriller hostage exchange. As such, I subconsciously expected it to be dramatic and complicated.

It turned out to be neither. Hat Man waved a hand at Huginn and his friends, waved the same pattern at Selene, then took a step back away from the door. I waited a couple of seconds, then tentatively beckoned to Huginn. "I guess that's it," I said. "He's been talking about companions since we arrived. I'm assuming you're them."

"Not sure why you'd think that," Huginn said, watching the aliens warily as he walked through the doorway, the Iykams close behind. "Or why *they'd* think that."

"I'm just arguing from results," I said. Two of the Iykams, I noted, were also watching the aliens as they followed Huginn. The third was watching me. "You've been locked up here, what, five days? Six? I can't see them releasing you to anyone except a good friend."

"A good *friend*?" Huginn echoed, looking Selene up and down as he stopped in front of us. "I didn't know the Ammei *had* any friends."

I frowned at him. "You *know* these aliens?"

"I know *of* them, anyway." Huginn nodded toward the corridor behind me. "Can we table this discussion until we're free and clear?"

"Good idea." I turned and started back down the hallway, Selene at my side.

I got three steps before our window of opportunity slammed shut. I caught a glimpse of movement on the spiral ramp, and suddenly six more armed guards came tromping into view. They lined up, three by three, and came to a halt at the end of the hallway.

Their lightning guns, I noted, were still slung over their shoulders. Under the circumstances, that wasn't much comfort.

I looked at Hat Man. He and his three guards were just standing there, but Hat Man himself was talking rapid-fire in a low voice. "So much for that," I muttered. "You see a comm or phone? Or is he talking to himself?"

"The comm's in his hat, I think," Huginn said. "Any idea what he's saying, Selene?"

"Not really," she said. "I heard the word *companions* again, and I think he also said *honor* and *arrived*. But I don't know how they fit together."

"I can think of a couple of ways," Huginn said grimly. "None of them good. Shall we keep walking and see if they try to stop us?"

"Selene?" I prompted.

"I don't see why not," she said. "All they can do is block our path."

"Or shoot us," Huginn said. "Let's give it a go."

We made it another three steps before Hat Man, putting on a burst of speed, skittered past us and came to an abrupt halt right in our path. He spun to face us and bit out a few words.

"I think he wants us to stop," I offered.

"Yes, I get that feeling," Huginn agreed. He looked pointedly at my holstered plasmic. "Nice weapon. EarthGuard Marine issue, if I'm not mistaken. They actually let you keep it?"

"I'm a friend of Selene's, remember?" I said. As far as I could tell, the newcomers at the far end hadn't reacted at all to our movement or Hat Man's. "I also haven't been waving it around, like I'm guessing your friends did."

"Touché," Huginn said, looking back at the three Iykams. "Though to be fair it wasn't so much waving as it was cautiously keeping hold of."

"Sure," I said. "'Cautious' is the word I always associate with Iykams. What do you know about these Ammei?"

"Not much," he said. "They live in four tight-knit enclaves, isolated or at the edges of small cities. They supposedly survive by scratch-farming their land and selling exotic fruits and vegetables to their neighbors."

"Given this group is living in the middle of a ring of portals, I'm guessing they can come up with plenty of exotics. All that access to different soils and climates, you know."

Huginn's lips compressed briefly. Maybe he'd been hoping I hadn't figured out that the mounds out there were portals. "Anyway, they're listed in the Patth alien registry, which is why I know the name," he said. "Other than what I just told you, I don't think anyone knows much about them."

"And has probably cared even less." I nodded toward Hat Man. "Until now."

Huginn hissed softly. "Until now," he conceded. "So when and where did the Icarus Group find this new Janus portal of theirs?"

"You're behind the times," I told him, throwing a bit of smugness into my voice to try to cover up my reaction to his question. Just as I'd assumed Huginn had come through the restored Alainn portal, so he was also assuming Selene and I had come through another Gemini dyad to one of the other portals in the ring.

Which meant he didn't know this was Alpha's planet. More important, he didn't know we'd brought the big full-range portal down from its orbit.

And that fact presented us with a huge advantage. If we needed to run, our exit was outside any restraint cordon the Ammei would ever think to set up. They could stack the portal ring three guards deep, and all Selene and I had to do was get out of town and to the river and we were as good as gone.

Unfortunately, that same fact also carried a terrible risk. If Huginn figured out the truth then not only was Alpha in danger but so was Firefall, which had been the Patth's own full-range portal before the Icarus Group swooped in and snatched it away from them.

Worse, if the Patth could commandeer Firefall and also figure out Icarus's address, everything we and the Icarus Group had worked for would fall apart in front of our faces. Probably accompanied by a whole lot of spilled blood on all sides.

"We're not the Icarus Group anymore," I continued even as that horrifying scenario played across my mind. "We're the Alien Portal Agency now."

"Interesting," Huginn said, frowning. "So Kinneman's officially taken over?"

I felt my stomach tighten. How the hell did the Patth know that? "Who?" I asked innocently.

Huginn gave a little snort. "Yes, I forgot how little they tell you. Kinneman, General Josiah Leland, has been positioning himself for the past year or so to take over the Icarus Group. Among his other selling points is the name change you just mentioned."

"Well, if that's all he's got planned, we should be all right," I said, wondering if I dared ask if Patth intel included anything about my father's place in the new command structure.

I resisted the temptation. If the Patth didn't already know he was aboard, best to leave it that way.

"Unfortunately, it's not," Huginn said. "I think you're going to be as unhappy as we are to see Admiral Sir Graym-Barker go."

"You liked him that much?"

"*Liked* him?" Huginn shrugged. "Not particularly. But we knew him, and that's important in a game like this." He smiled knowingly. "Also my theory as to why you always seem to make sure Sub-Director Nask comes out of your interactions with a little something to make him look good to the Director General."

"You're reading way too much into it," I said, picking my words carefully. He was absolutely right about known opponents, and the last thing I wanted was for Huginn or the Patth Director General to wonder if Nask was losing his focus. "My sole concern is the Icarus Group and the Commonwealth. Sub-Director Nask's sole concern is the Patth. It just so happens that it's not a zero-sum game."

"Always nice when that happens. Ah—here we go."

I nodded. At the end of the hallway a newcomer had appeared, walking slowly down the ramp toward us. He was shorter and thinner than the other Ammei we'd seen, and his armadillo armor seemed darker and dimmer. He was wearing the most elaborate hat yet, and I had the odd sense that its weight was bothering him. A pair of ferrets accompanied him, walking slowly to either side as if making sure they didn't outrun him. He passed between the lines of guards and hobbled his way to a spot midway between them and us.

I sighed, bracing myself for more alien speak. I just hoped Selene would be able to get more from this one than just a word or two—

"I greet you, travelers," the alien called, his heavily accented but fully understandable English echoing off the tunnel walls. "I am the Fourth of Three. In the name of the First of Three, I welcome you to Nexus Six and *Imistio* Tower."

In that first rush of disbelief that this creature was actually speaking English, I completely missed the glaring mathematical oddity in his greeting. It took another second for it to rear up and slap me in the face.

Fourth of *Three*?

I looked at Selene, wondering if she'd spotted the strange math, too.

I felt my breath catch in my throat. Her pupils, which had shown a familiar wary calm, had suddenly changed to a mix of surprise and disbelief, tinged with something I could only interpret as horror. I looked back at the alien, then back at Selene, trying to figure out what had startled her that badly.

"Fourth of *Three*?" Huginn murmured. "Someone's math is off."

"It's the schools these days," I said, my focus still on Selene. The horror had faded somewhat, along with whatever shock had precipitated that reaction. But the disbelief remained.

"No doubt," Huginn said, oblivious to the silent drama taking place in Selene's emotions. "I'm thinking the other one—First of Three—sounds like a title. Maybe *Fourth of Three* is likewise, except it's an honorary post?"

"Could be," I said. Selene's pupils were rapidly returning to their original wariness, and I needed to get back to work on the immediate situation. "He also looks like he's waiting for an answer."

"Agreed," Huginn said. "You or me?" He nodded toward Selene. "Or Selene?"

"Or Selene," I agreed. "You game?"

She took a careful breath. Still a little shaken up, I could tell, but there was fresh determination in her pupils. "Yes," she said.

She faced Fourth of Three and drew herself up to her full height. "I greet you in turn, Fourth of Three," she called. "I am Selene of the Kadolians. These are Roarke and Huginn of the humans, and their escorts of the Iykams. We thank you for your greeting."

"You are most welcome, Selene of the Kadolians," Fourth of Three said. "Come. Second of Three awaits you."

He turned and started walking back toward the ramp. I took Selene's arm and started to follow—

And twitched to a sudden halt as one of Big Hat's three guards slashed his lightning gun warningly in front of me. "What the *hell*?" I bit out.

"Second of Three does not welcome Roarke and Huginn of the humans," Fourth of Three said. He'd turned back and was staring at us from beneath the brim of his hat. "Third of Three will welcome them."

"I don't think so," I growled. I pushed away the lightning gun still hovering in front of my chest and started forward. Out of the corner of my eye I spotted the two ferrets at Fourth of Three's feet suddenly come to life, arching their backs warningly—

And I again jerked to a stop, this time by Huginn's grip on my arm. "Steady, Roarke," he warned quietly. "Unless you're ready to take on nine armed Ammei, your best move is to back off."

Every cell in my body was screaming for me to yank out my plasmic and start shooting. But Huginn was right. If the Ammei wanted to kill us there were lots of easier ways for them to do it.

Besides, Selene was in their line of fire.

"He's right, Gregory," Selene said, holding out a cautioning hand of her own. "Don't worry, I'll be fine."

I took a deep breath. "Sure," I said. "But if you need me, just...I don't know. If you need me just scream or something."

"I'll be fine," she repeated. Her pupils took on a hint of amusement. "And I really don't scream very well."

"Try high opera, then," Huginn offered. "It's close enough. Just relax, listen to what they say, and see what you can learn."

"I will." The amusement in her pupils faded and was replaced by concern. "*You* be careful."

"We'll be fine." I threw a look over my shoulder at the silent Iykams. "Assuming Huginn can sit on his minions."

"I'm sure he will," Selene said. "I'll see you later."

"Right," I said. "Fruit and bird?"

"Fruit and bird," she confirmed. Turning, she resumed walking toward the waiting Ammei. "Fourth of Three?" I called. "What about us?"

"Third of Three will welcome you," the alien called back.

"Great," I said. "When?"

"Soon." He waited until Selene reached him, then turned and led her back up the ramp. The six armed aliens fell into step beside them, and then they were gone.

As my father used to say, *Sometimes there are no words for a given situation. Make sure you save a few good expletives for times like that.* I unloaded a quiet but heartfelt curse, then added another one just to round out the session. "Well, we're back to six-to-five odds," I pointed out to Huginn. "That sound any better?"

"Better, but still stupid," he said. "Like she said, she'll be fine. Didn't you see how they marched out?"

"Yeah," I growled. "Surrounding her like a prisoner."

"Surrounding her like an honor guard," Huginn said with exaggerated patience. "Remember what she said about hearing the word *honor*?"

I thought back to the guard configuration. Huginn could be right about that, I had to admit. "It's also the way soldiers march with high-ranking prisoners."

"She'll be fine," Huginn said. "You're a real worrier, aren't you? What was that *fruit and bird* bit?"

"Private joke," I told him. It wasn't, of course—preset security codes were never a joke. But I had no intention of reading him into our system. "Did you see the ferrets' reaction when I started toward Fourth of Three?"

"They acted like guard dogs," he said, nodding. "Very small guard dogs, but they may have some serious teeth tucked away in there. You probably don't want to find out for sure."

"Probably not," I said. "Still, a single good kick ought to be all it takes."

"Bearing in mind we're talking a single good kick apiece," he warned. "You get a mob of them together and you'd be hard-pressed to stay on top of it. What exactly was she reacting so hard against?"

I looked sideways at him. "You can read Kadolian expressions?"

"No, but I can read yours," he said. "So?"

I shook my head. "I don't know. Something back there just poked at a nerve. No idea what it was."

"Interesting," he said. "You'll have to ask her about it later."

I snorted. "I can ask," I told him. "Doesn't mean she'll necessarily answer. There are things she doesn't like to talk about."

"Be persuasive," he said. "By the way, you never told me where you found the Janus portal you used to get here."

He would keep bugging me until I gave him something, I knew. Fortunately, I'd had time to come up with an answer. "We didn't," I told him, mentally crossing my fingers. "We just flew here."

The brief widening of his eyes was all the proof I needed that my bluff had worked. However long he and his team had been poking around before the Ammei caught them, it hadn't been long enough for them to do the star scans that would give them some idea of Nexus Six's location. "You *flew* here?"

"Yes," I said. Technically, of course, that wasn't even a lie, Selene and I *had* flown here. Just not very far, and mostly straight down. "And no, I'm not going to tell you where we are."

"No, of course not," Huginn said, looking troubled.

As well he should. The very nature of portal travel limited the size of any army or weaponry someone might try to bring through. We'd seen that firsthand with the technical and logistic hoops Kinneman had had to go through just to get a simple bioprobe and a couple of grav-beam generators from the inside of Icarus to the outside of Alpha.

But if Nexus Six was close enough to civilization for us to have come here by starship, Kinneman could whistle up a few EarthGuard warships and kick the Patth back to their secret homeworlds before they could even bring a decent defense force to bear. Huginn clearly knew that, and even now he would be sifting through the ramifications.

Of course, if the Patth called my bluff and stuck around long enough for some decent sky analysis they'd quickly realize we weren't anywhere near the Spiral, let alone within an easy flight of civilization.

At which point Huginn would probably be *very* annoyed with me. But I'd cross that bridge when I got there. Right now, worrying about Selene was a full-time job.

We'd been standing there for ten minutes, Huginn likely wrapped in thoughts of imminent Patth disaster, me wondering how fast I could draw and shoot if that became necessary, when the wait finally came to an end.

It came in the form of two Ammei coming down the ramp and walking toward us. The first had the same dulled scales and walking tentativeness as Fourth of Three, characteristics I'd tentatively marked as signs of age, and was wearing an even fancier hat. The other Amme was walking beside and a little behind him, but I could tell he was deliberately matching the other's pace. He also had shinier scales and no hat at all. Pacing them were four more ferrets, again maintaining the same slow gait as the Ammei.

The older Amme took a few steps down the hallway and spoke in a quiet voice. The younger one twitched his fingers and drew himself up. "I greet you, travelers," he said in much better English than Fourth of Three. "I am Rozhuhu. I speak the words of the Third of Three. In the name of the First of Three, I welcome you to Nexus Six and *Imistio* Tower."

"Thank you," I said. "We would like to join Selene of the Kadolians now."

Third of Three spoke again. "Selene of the Kadolians is currently examining the locales of power and authority," Rozhuhu translated. "You shall examine the rest, so as to prepare her for proper comfort."

I frowned at Huginn. "Her proper *comfort*?"

"They hold her in high esteem," he reminded me quietly. "Important people always come with an entourage. That seems to be us."

"I guess so." I turned back to the two Ammei. "We would be pleased to prepare her comfort. Please show us what we may do to serve Selene of the Kadolians."

Third of Three spoke. "Excellent," Rozhuhu said. "The Third of Three approves."

"A question before we begin," Huginn said, pointing to the ferrets. "Your animals. Roarke of the humans is concerned that they might be dangerous."

"They seemed prepared to attack us earlier," I added. I wasn't all that concerned, but Huginn was clearly probing for information and I was willing to look nervous if it helped back him up.

"You need have no fear," Rozhuhu said. "Tenshes are fully tamed."

"Are you sure?" I pressed. "There've been plenty of human pets which, while appearing to be just as tame, have suddenly gone wild."

"You need have no fear," Rozhuhu repeated. "We will begin here, where the food for the Tower and its personnel is stored."

I scowled. So much for finding out what role the animals played in Ammei society. And meanwhile Selene was still way the hell off somewhere.

Still, I *had* wondered what kind of floor plan this place had. This was our chance to start filling in that map.

CHAPTER FOURTEEN

In all, the tour took about three hours, moving from the lower storage levels to the food prep area to more storage areas. We continued upward through the building, again traveling along curved ramps. We were shown meditation rooms, game rooms, music and dance rooms, and conference rooms. Along the way we bypassed a number of closed doors, which Rozhuhu told us were sleeping rooms.

The place was big, well laid out, and elaborately decorated. But given the size of the common rooms and the number of bedrooms, it was clear that the place had been designed to hold and cater to a large population, a hundred or possibly more. The fact that the hallways and rooms were all but deserted laid a pall of sadness over the tour. Echoes of a glory long past, whether the current inhabitants realized it or not.

We were two and a half hours into the excursion, and I was trying to think up another way to ask where Selene was, when we were finally escorted into the room that made all the slogging through kitchens and conference rooms worthwhile. The room I'd been hoping for ever since I first saw the building from the middle of the river.

The library.

"This room is *Imistio* Tower's Center of Knowledge," Rozhuhu intoned as he and Third led the way into the high-ceilinged room. "The truth of the Ammei of Nexus Six is contained within these volumes."

"Very impressive," I said, looking around. The outside wall was a full expanse of south-facing, floor-to-ceiling windows, which on a sunny day would flood the room with light. Even today, with a low cloud cover, there was more than enough illumination to read by. In the center of the room were several chairs and couches, some facing low tables that had room for multiple books to be laid out for study or comparison. Near the windows were a group of six wide-topped desks for more focused study. There were also two consoles, one at either end of the room, that I tentatively tagged as index files.

Which would not just be useful, but utterly necessary... because the shelves on the curved wall opposite the windows were crammed with books. Each book looked to be twenty centimeters high by two thick, all of them bound with black metal. Hints of alien script traced curves along their spines, subtle enough that I could barely make it out.

Which was exactly what LH, the left-hand part of the portal directory that Selene had found on Meima, looked like. And if Rozhuhu was right—if this room really contained all the knowledge of the Ammei—then the RH counterpart we'd come here to find was sitting right here in front of me.

Not having to search the entire planet for our needle was a huge operational coup. Unfortunately, it was still way too early for a victory lap. My quick estimate put the number of volumes here somewhere between five and ten thousand. Even if I could identify the correct one from the writing on the spine—and I couldn't—it could take hours just to sift through all of them. If I had to open each one in order to spot the distinctive colored squares of a portal directory, that task would stretch to days or weeks.

Third said something. "You are impressed by the depth of our truth?" Rozhuhu translated.

"I am indeed," I said. "Selene of the Kadolians, too, treasures stores of knowledge. I would urge you to share this with her."

"She shall see it soon," Rozhuhu said. "Let us proceed. The Pools of Meditation and Grove of Reflection still await."

❖   ❖   ❖

The Pools of Meditation was a room full of glorified bathtubs on the north side of level four, some of them sized for individuals, others built like hotel and spa communal tubs that were large enough for small groups. The Grove of Reflection was on the south side of the same floor, a high-ceilinged room just above the Center of Knowledge with the same floor-to-ceiling windows. It contained clumps of bushes, flowers, and small saplings, with brick pathways winding through the foliage.

With the tour finally complete, Rozhuhu and Third took us to one of the level-two dining rooms we'd passed through earlier, where a light lunch had been laid out. I was hesitant about eating food I'd never had a chance to sample, but Huginn assured me that it was perfectly adequate in the nourishment department and at least made an attempt to be tasty. I tried a small sample of each dish, decided he was right on at least the last count, and dug in.

We'd been at it for a few minutes when Selene and Fourth of Three entered from a different door, accompanied by an Amme in an even fancier hat whom I assumed was our hitherto unseen Second of Three. Selene spotted us across the room, bowed to her two escorts and said something I couldn't catch, then walked over to us.

"Are you all right?" I asked.

"Just peachy," she said. "You?"

"Ducky," I said. Out of the corner of my eye I saw Huginn's small smile as he caught onto the earlier *fruit and bird* mystery. "Enjoy your tour?"

"I did." She nodded toward the buffet. "Could you come show me which ones I'm most likely to like?"

"Sure," I said, standing up. Clearly, she wanted a moment alone. "She has quirky taste buds," I added to Huginn in explanation.

"I know what you mean," he said. He looked pointedly at the three Iykams as they dug enthusiastically into what I'd personally found to be the least appetizing dish on the sideboard. "As long as you're up, how about grabbing me another of those egg-roll things?"

"How about you send one of your Iykams or go get it yourself?" I countered. "I'm Selene's minion, not yours."

"I was just asking," he said mildly.

I took Selene's arm and we crossed toward the buffet. "That sounded a little harsh," she said quietly.

"He didn't want an egg roll," I assured her. "He was just probing to see how badly we wanted privacy. Telling him to get it himself was a signal that we weren't going to discuss anything we didn't want him to overhear."

"Unless he realized you were onto his plan."

"Oh, I'm sure he did," I said. "That's the kind of game where you can go back and forth forever without really knowing where you stand. But as my father used to say, *Even a pointless game is better than sitting in the stands being bored.*"

I glanced back as we reached the buffet table. Neither Huginn nor any of the Iykams had moved. "I presume you got a look at the library?" I asked as we each picked up a plate. "Rozhuhu said Second was going to show it to you."

"Yes, we arrived shortly after you left," she confirmed. "You saw that all those books were bound the same way as LH?"

"Except for the writing on the spine," I said. "The ones I was close enough to see clearly all had different script patterns. Titles or descriptions or something. Did LH have anything like that? I don't remember seeing anything there."

"There was a bit of something on the spine," she said. "But it was faint and completely illegible. Until I saw the books here I assumed it was just discoloration."

"Not unreasonable, given the thing had been packed in dirt for ten thousand years," I said. "Too bad. Might have been useful for sifting out RH if we'd been able to read it."

"Maybe," she said. "But unless the script on LH and RH are very similar to each other, knowing one wouldn't help us find the other."

"Point," I conceded. *Left* and *right* were, after all, two entirely different English words, both in appearance and pronunciation. We could hardly expect the Icari language to have been designed for our personal convenience. "But at least we now have somewhere to start."

"Yes." She paused as she scooped a spoonful of something that looked like blue and green mashed potatoes onto her plate. "I gather from what Fourth said that I was getting the high-level tour while Third gave you the more menial servant version."

"The positions of power and authority for you, Rozhuhu said, the rest for us so that we could prepare you for proper comfort," I confirmed. "Why?"

"Because there were three places where our tours overlapped," she said. "The Grove of Reflection, the ramp leading to the Tower's Upper Rooms, and the Center of Knowledge."

"Interesting," I said, thinking back. The grove and library *could* be considered both royal and peon level, I supposed. But a ramp we didn't climb to rooms we didn't go into? "What are the Upper Rooms like?"

"I don't know," she said. "Second of Three didn't show me into any of them. He just said they were at the top of the ramp."

"I don't think Third said even that much about it," I said. "In fact, I don't think he said anything at all as he walked us past the ramp."

"Maybe he thought you would ask where it went."

"Maybe. Was there anything else?"

"Yes," Selene said, an odd reluctance in her voice. "He said the Upper Rooms had been the living chambers of the Gold One when he was here, but that they hadn't been used for many years."

"Did he say who the Gold One was? Another of their Leaders With Fancy Hats?"

"He didn't say anything specific." She seemed to brace herself. "But from some of the things he *did* say," she continued, lowering her voice even further, "I think the Gold Ones are the Icari."

My first reaction was disappointment that the Ammei themselves weren't the shadowy figures who'd created these incredible portals. Despite their lack of the long appendages that would make sense of the deck-inset portal controls, I'd still privately clung to the hope that we'd finally found the people who'd made our lives so interesting—and complicated and dangerous—for the past two years.

My second reaction was a cautious excitement.

There had actually once been Icari *here*?

"Did he say how *many* years since they were here?" I asked. "Five? Ten? A hundred?"

"He just said it was many years," she said. "The odd thing... I still don't have a baseline for these people. But when Second of Three was talking about the Gold Ones, his scent changed. And he was looking straight at me."

An unpleasant tingle ran up my back. "Meaning?"

"I don't know," Selene said. She paused, her pupils going uncomfortable. "We're not the Icari, Gregory. Really. We're not."

"Are you sure?" I asked, keeping my voice casual and hoping my scent was doing more or less likewise. "They supposedly left the scene ten thousand years ago, remember? Would the Kadolians have anything other than legends about themselves that far back? We humans certainly don't."

"I don't know how far back we have a verifiable history," Selene said. "But you're forgetting what he said: that one of the Gold Ones was *here*. If he was a Kadolian, why didn't they recognize me as being the same species?"

"Maybe they didn't get a good look at him," I said. "He could have worn a robe and hood or something equally obscuring. Maybe they didn't get any pictures and there's no one left who actually saw him."

Selene shook her head. "Second of Three calls them the Gold Ones," she reminded me. "There's nothing golden about us."

My eyes flicked to her pure white hair. "Not unless you count a pleasant personality," I conceded. "You could certainly be called the Silver Ones, though."

"We should get back to the table," she said. "We don't want Huginn wondering if we got lost."

In other words, this particular conversation was shelved until later. "Yes, you know how he worries," I agreed. "Final question. Back when Fourth of Three introduced himself, your pupils went quietly berserk. What was that all about?"

Her pupils went uncomfortable again. "It was probably nothing."

"Glad to hear it. What flavor of nothing was it?"

She closed her eyes briefly. "It wasn't about Fourth of Three or the others," she said. "It was the name he gave this place."

"*Imistio* Tower? What about it?"

"It probably doesn't mean anything," she warned again. "But *imistio* is very close to the Kadolian word *imistiu*. I thought... you realize it's probably just a coincidence."

"Like the Kadolian and Patth names for private currencies—your *cesmer* and their *cesmi*—are coincidences?" I asked pointedly. "So what does *imistiu* mean?"

"Several things," she said. "Point, arrowhead, spear." She seemed to brace herself. "And needle."

I felt something cold walk up my back. "Like Project Needle?"

"There's no way the Ammei could know the Icarus Group's name for our visit here," she said quickly. "It has to be a coincidence."

"Maybe," I said grimly.

But in my mind's eye I saw the rows of books in the Tower library. Did the Ammei know about the portal directory halves, too? Were they looking for the same needle in a haystack that Kinneman was?

Only now the search wasn't a whole planet, but just a single big room. A room the Ammei had had plenty of time to search over the centuries.

So why hadn't they already found it?

"Not a word about this to Huginn, of course," I warned.

"I know."

We took another moment to finish filling our plates and returned to the table. Huginn was talking to the Iykams in what sounded like the Patth language. He broke off and looked up as we approached. "You two have a nice chat?" he asked, switching back to English.

"Yes, we were discussing the weather," I said as we sat down. "You?"

"The same," he said. "Very nice for this time of year. Any idea about the afternoon's agenda?"

"Second of Three said I would be meeting with the Dominants, who I gather are some kind of community leaders," Selene told him. "It sounded like that would take place in one of the buildings in the ring that surrounds the Tower."

My stomach tightened. Bad enough to have us split up for hours inside the same building. Now the Ammei wanted to put a hundred meters of open space between us, too? "Any chance you can persuade them to let your bodyguard tag along?"

"I've already asked," she said. "He seemed very insistent that I stay with him and the rest of you stay with Third of Three."

"Or at least that's what Fourth *said* he said," Huginn reminded her. "I've seen translators make mistakes before."

"Or deliberately lie," I added.

"I don't think he lied," Selene said. But her pupils didn't look entirely convinced. "I'll be all right."

"Heads up," Huginn warned quietly, nodding microscopically over my shoulder.

I turned to look. Second was walking toward us, Fourth toddling along beside him. Behind them were Third and our translator Rozhuhu, trailing the other two at a respectful distance. The six armed Ammei who'd accompanied Selene on her tour had also appeared, but seemed content to wait by the door. "Definitely look like people on a mission," I said. "Okay, I'm going to try something. Let's see what I can shake loose."

"Should we be ready to hit the deck?" Huginn asked ominously.

"I don't think so," I said. "Just look casual."

Second of Three reached our table and stopped, Fourth of Three stopping beside him. The fancy-hatted Amme spoke—"Selene of the Kadolians, it is the hour," Fourth intoned. "The Dominants are assembled for the honor of your presence."

"Thank you," Selene said, standing up. "May I again request that my bodyguard accompany me?"

Fourth spoke, Second answered, and Fourth turned back to us. "That is impossible," he said. "Roarke of the humans cannot accompany Second of Three. He can only accompany Third of Three."

"Then let Third of Three and the rest of us accompany Second of Three and Selene of the Kadolians," Huginn suggested. "Then the Dominants can meet all of us."

"That is impossible," Fourth repeated. "Your duties for the day are at an end, Huginn of the humans. You and Roarke of the humans will be shown to a place of rest until the evening meal."

"If we can't accompany you, perhaps we can watch over Selene of the Kadolians from here," I said. "There must be rooms from which we may gaze down upon her and observe her travels."

Rozhuhu murmured to Second. I flicked a glance at Selene out of the corner of my eye—"Perhaps a place such as the Upper Rooms," I added.

I didn't spot so much as a twitch in any of the Ammei facing us. But the answer came way too quickly. "The Upper Rooms are forbidden to you," Rozhuhu said. "Third of Three will take you to a different resting place."

"As you wish," Selene said before I could answer. "I am ready to meet the Dominants. Roarke and Huginn of the humans and the Iykams await their resting place."

Second spoke. "Come, then, Selene of the Kadolians," Fourth said. "Second of Three is honored to guide you."

On cue, Second turned and headed back toward the waiting guards. Selene gave me a quick look, offering me a view of the confirmation in her pupils, and followed. We all watched in silence as the three of them picked up their escort and the whole crowd disappeared through the door.

Third of Three and Rozhuhu turned back to us. "Come, servants of Selene of the Kadolians," Rozhuhu said. "Your resting place awaits you."

The resting place turned out to be a sort of combination lounge and entertainment center on the northeastern side of level six, the topmost of the two floors that comprised the Tower's hexagonal tier. The windows were decently sized, though not as impressive as the floor-to-ceiling ones a couple of floors below us in the library and Grove of Reflection on the other side of the building. Standing by the window, I could see the ring of buildings we'd walked through earlier after our exit from the subway, as well as the ramp we'd taken to the surface. In the near distance I could see hints of some of the subway's other exits between the outer building rings, and in the far distance I could see the ruined structures near the dock and, partially hidden by the riverside reeds, a bit of the dock itself.

At the very edge of my field of view, to the northwest, I got a glimpse of Selene and her Ammei escort as they went inside one of the larger structures on the inner ring of buildings.

"Pretty fast on the uptake, wasn't he?" Huginn commented from behind me.

I watched the building another moment, as if by sheer willpower I'd be able to see what was going on inside, or if Selene was in trouble.

But she didn't suddenly reappear, running for her life. As for seeing through solid walls, as my father used to say, *Willpower and enthusiasm are no match for the laws of physics.* "Way too fast," I agreed, forcing myself to turn away from the window. Staring after Selene like a moon-sick teenager wouldn't do anyone any good. Better to focus on a plan I could pitch to her when she emerged safe and sound. "I assume you also noted he didn't have to run the double translation."

"I did," Huginn confirmed, eyeing me thoughtfully. "Which means he already knew you were going to ask about that. Why was he expecting it, and what are these Upper Rooms? If it's not a secret."

"Not at all," I assured him. It *might* have been a secret, but there was no point playing coy now that he was already halfway to the answer. "Selene said there were three places that our two tours overlapped: the library, the Grove of Reflection, and the bottom of the ramp that led from the ninth floor to what Second called the Upper Rooms."

"Really," Huginn said, frowning. "How did she know where you and I had been?"

"She smelled us, of course," I said, frowning back. Surely Huginn hadn't forgotten about the Kadolian sense of smell.

"Obviously," Huginn said. "I'm just noting that Selene and her escort left a good ten minutes before we did. How did we get ahead of her on the tour?"

I turned and looked back out at the building the others had disappeared into. That was a damn good question. "I assume you have an answer?"

"Obviously, the Ammei *wanted* her to know where we'd crossed paths," Huginn said. "And, by extension, wanted *us* to know it, too."

"They want to know why we're here," I murmured as the obvious answer popped into my head. "They think we're looking for something and want to know what it is."

"Or it's an entrapment scheme," Huginn suggested. "They want to lure us into going somewhere we shouldn't."

"Why bother?" I asked, frowning. "They don't need to manufacture an excuse. This is their city and their planet. That makes them judge, jury, and possible executioner."

"Does it?" Huginn countered. "Are you sure they don't answer to a higher power?"

"Like who?" I asked. "The Icari?"

"The *who*?"

"The Icari," I repeated. "The species who created the portals."

"Who calls them *that*?"

"We do," I said stiffly. The name had been Selene's suggestion, and I was damned if I was going to let him be snide about it. "So does the Icarus Group. You have a problem with it?"

"You mean the Alien Portal Agency," he corrected absently. "Interesting that we haven't heard that term."

"Nice to know we still have *some* secrets," I said. "Why, what do the Patth call them? The Builders?"

"Actually, yes, we do."

"Our name is classier."

He flashed a sudden grin. "I agree," he said. "The Patth are excellent engineers, but I'll give humans the edge in wordplay any day." The grin faded. "So what do they expect us to find in these Upper Rooms?"

"No idea," I said. "All I know is that he told Selene one of 'the Gold Ones' had been in the Upper Rooms an unspecified number of years back."

"And you think the Gold Ones are Icari?"

"Selene thinks they might be."

"*Thinks?*"

"Yes, and right now that's as solid an assessment as we're going to get," I conceded. "That being said, I'll point out that a lot of Selene's hunches turn out to be right."

I readied myself for an argument, or at least some scornful eye-rolling. But Huginn just nodded. "Like human gut instinct," he said thoughtfully. "A melding of marginal data and subconscious observation that leads to the right conclusion even if you don't know how you got there."

"Basically," I said, nodding back. "I think probably every species has something of that ability."

"Actually, I don't think the Patth do," Huginn said, still looking thoughtful. "Certainly not to the same extent as humans."

"I never heard that before," I said, frowning.

He shrugged. "It's not really a secret. You should probably still keep it to yourself, though."

"Of course," I said. Especially since he could just be setting me up with an intriguing but false tidbit to see how inclined I was to blab about such things to others. "Is that why they recruit so many humans as Expediters?"

"Could be," Huginn said. "Let's assume Selene's right."

"About which part?"

"About all of it," he said. "That the Gold Ones are Icari, that one of them recently dropped in on Nexus Six, and that he might still be lurking around somewhere. What's our plan?"

"*Our* plan?"

He gave a theatrical sigh. "Okay; cards on the table," he said. "First of all, I know you didn't fly here from anyplace in the Spiral."

"You're welcome to believe that if you want," I said as casually as I could. I'd expected him to see through my improvised story eventually, but not quite this soon. "But you of all people should know how many oddball places the *Ruth* goes in the course of our duties."

"Absolutely," he said. "And I know that Selene has a knack of sniffing out portal metal from the barest hint of a bioprobe sample. Unfortunately, I also know that as of three weeks ago your ship was still parked at the Passline Spaceport in Tupnotte on Xathru. I forget which landing slot."

"Your information is out of date," I told him.

"No, I don't think so," he said, his voice and expression showing not the least sliver of doubt. Clearly, the Patth had been keeping very good tabs on Selene and me. "And if you didn't come in your own ship, you'd have come in an EarthGuard ship, and Kinneman would hardly have sent you in alone."

"Who says we're alone?" I countered, trying one more time.

"The point is that you came here via portal," Huginn said, ignoring my question. "I don't know which of the twelve out there you used—of the eleven, rather, since one of them is obviously ours—and right now I don't care. What I *do* care about is that both of us are likely to be seeing backup sometime in the near future, and both our bosses aren't going to be happy if all we did was get a tour of the places the Ammei wanted us to see and then sat around doing nothing." He ran out of air and stopped.

"I'll agree with that last part, anyway," I said. "In fact, I'd take it a step further. If Sub-Director Nask sends in a crowd of Iykams"—I glanced at Huginn's three gunmen, glowering together behind him just within hearing distance—"and Kinneman sends in a squad of EarthGuard Marines, there could be literal hell to pay. And I don't mean just from each other."

Huginn hissed out a curse. "Agreed," he said reluctantly. "The last thing we want is open warfare with the Ammei before we even know what's going on here. I assume you have some thoughts?"

"It's probably too late to stop anyone from either of our teams from coming through," I said. "Especially yours, given that you've been incommunicado for—how long since the Ammei grabbed you?"

Huginn pursed his lips. "They caught us four days ago," he said. "But we'd been poking around for two days before that. That's local days," he added. "They're around eighteen and a half hours long."

I nodded. I'd noticed the day was chugging right along and been wondering how long it would turn out to be. "So you've been gone something like four and a half standard-issue days. Any idea how much longer before Nask sends in the cavalry?"

"Not really," Huginn said. "Our mission was open-ended. But it could probably be any time. You?"

"The same," I said. Though of course that didn't depend so much on Kinneman's patience but on if and when Alpha came back to life. Not that I was going to tell Huginn that. "So it seems to me that what we need right now is to scoop together enough information to keep both sides quiet long enough for everyone to assess the situation before going off half-cocked."

"And then?"

"And then what?"

"And then who gets first dibs on the portals out there?"

I shrugged. "I'd like to think we could just divvy them up," I said. "Half to you, half to us."

"That would be nice," Huginn said. "Very neat, very civilized. Can I have a show of hands from anyone who believes either side will go for that?"

"Okay, so it's unlikely," I conceded. "But we still don't want anyone charging out, plasmics blazing. Agreed?"

"Agreed," Huginn said reluctantly. "Your turn."

I frowned. "My turn for what?"

"Putting your cards on the table," he said. "What got Selene all hot and bothered when Fourth of Three introduced himself?"

"Oh. That." Luckily, I'd already figured out how I was going to answer that question when it came. "It was just the name Fourth gave to this place, *Imistio* Tower. The word's similar to the Kadolian for point, arrowhead, or spear."

"Interesting coincidence," he said, eyeing me closely. "If it *is* coincidence."

"It isn't," I said. "At least, we don't think it is. She'd already caught some Kadolian echoes in earlier Ammei speech. Anyway, the point here was that it was the hint of military in the word that startled her."

"She thinks this place might have been a fortress?"

"Or might still be," I said. "We already know Third didn't show us *everything* that's in here."

"We'll probably want to rectify that somewhere down the

line," he said. "But we might as well start by checking out the places they went out of their way to underline in red for us. You want to take the library, grove, or Upper Rooms?"

"Right now? None of them," I said. "As my father used to say, *There are dumber things you can do than charge across a darkened room, but few of them give you the chance to face-plant quite so spectacularly.*"

"Meaning?"

"Meaning I'd like a better feel for the lay of the land first," I said, pulling out my notebook. "You took the same tour I did. Let's see how you are at spatial memory and sense of scale."

CHAPTER FIFTEEN

—— ❖ ——

By the time Third and Rozhuhu once again intruded on our privacy, Huginn and I had sketched out a reasonably good floor plan of the Tower, or at least the parts we'd visited. Rozhuhu announced that dinner had been prepared, and told us Selene was already there.

We reached the dining room where we'd had lunch earlier to find that all the tables and chairs had been removed except a single four-person table and three chairs set equidistantly around it. Selene was seated in the chair that faced our approach, with Second, Fourth, and the six guards grouped in a loose semicircle behind her also facing us.

And as we came closer, I could see there was tension in Selene's pupils. "Something's wrong," I murmured to Huginn. "Be ready."

"Understood," he murmured back.

"I greet you, servants of Selene of the Kadolians," Fourth said as we came up to the table. "The First of Three sends a message and an order. The escorts of the Iykams must be returned to confinement for the night."

I'd flipped through a dozen different scenarios during those last few steps. That one hadn't even occurred to me.

It apparently hadn't occurred to Huginn, either. He glanced over his shoulder at the three Iykams, who'd come to a stiff halt

145

behind him, then turned back to the Ammei. "Excuse me?" he asked, his voice gone quiet and deadly.

"The escorts of the Iykams must be returned to confinement for the night," Fourth repeated. "They will rejoin you in the morning."

I focused on the landscape visible through the windows behind Selene. The dining room faced northeast, overlooking part of the river, so I couldn't see where the sun was positioned in the western sky. Still, there was only a slight darkening of the cloud layers to indicate that nightfall was on its way. "It's not really night yet," I pointed out. "Can't the escorts of the Iykams at least eat with us before they leave?"

"They will receive food in confinement," Fourth said. "They will leave now."

Again, a declaration without any consultation between them. The verdict had been handed down from on high, and there was no point in arguing it further.

Huginn must have caught the same signals. But he wasn't ready to let it go, at least not without an argument. "If that's your decision, I accept it," he said, his voice carefully neutral. "I would like to see them to their confinement."

"Why?" Fourth asked.

"I'm their superior," Huginn said. "I have a responsibility to assure myself that they're being properly treated."

"Selene of the Kadolians is their superior," Fourth countered.

"He speaks correctly," Selene confirmed calmly. "They are my responsibility." She stood up. "*I* will accompany them to confinement."

The offer seemed to catch everyone by surprise. "That's very kind of you, Selene of the Kadolians," I jumped in before anyone else could say anything. I'd spotted the shift in her pupils from wariness to determination as Huginn and Fourth were talking, and had been pretty sure she was planning something. But I hadn't expected this particular gambit. "In fact, why don't we all go?" I added. "That way there will be no question."

There was brief consultation between Second and Third, with Fourth and Rozhuhu watching closely but remaining silent. Selene also stayed silent, looking first at me, then at Huginn, then at the Iykams behind us. Probably checking our scents and wondering if any of us were going to try something stupid.

She needn't have worried, at least not about me. The Ammei were arranged in a simple fan formation, with the important people in the middle of the semicircle and the armed guards on either end. Even given a plasmic's limited recoil, and the consequently quicker cycling it took for a gunner to shift aim, my chances of taking out all six guards before one of them got his lightning gun into position were extremely low.

If this had been an actual emergency, if Selene had been in imminent danger, I would have risked it, especially since she was in position to create a diversion. Throwing herself at Second or Third would draw the guards' attention and buy me a couple of extra seconds.

Though at that point we still would be faced with the uphill task of getting to the dock and our vac suits before the Ammei could organize pursuit.

Fortunately, such extreme measures didn't seem necessary right now. Selene clearly still held VIP status, and until and unless that changed we would do best to play along and let the Ammei do whatever they wanted with the Iykams.

But then, she and I didn't have the same sense of responsibility to the trigger-happy aliens that Huginn did.

I looked sideways at him. He was still standing motionless, his expression one of grudging acceptance as he waited for the Ammei to finish their conversation. But I could see an ominous tightness in his cheek muscles.

Second and Third finished their conversation, and Second gestured to Rozhuhu. "The Second of Three has decided that such will not be necessary," he said. "You will remain here and eat before you are taken to your places of sleep."

It was my own cheek muscles' turn to tighten. *Places* of sleep, plural? Did that mean they were going to split us up again?

Probably. As I'd just reminded myself, Selene was the important one who deserved special consideration. The rest of us were just extras moving around in the background.

Unless what I'd assumed was privileged treatment was simply the standard care given to a valuable hostage.

I focused on Selene's pupils. If she was a hostage or otherwise believed we were in danger, I couldn't see any evidence of it.

And as if to underline her assessment that no action on my part was necessary, she quietly sat back down.

I sent Huginn another sideways look. If Selene and I were out, he had no choice but to be as well. Without Selene to create a distraction and chaos in the opposition's ranks, and with his own most trustworthy allies standing out of position behind him, he didn't have a hope of coming in anything but second.

As my father used to say, *Shouting* damn the torpedoes *only inspires the troops if they're also not your last words.*

Second waited another moment, as if expecting Huginn to object further. But the Expediter remained silent. Apparently satisfied, Second gestured, and the six guards broke formation and circled around the table, walking past Huginn and reforming around the Iykams. Huginn didn't turn around as the group headed back toward the door, but instead kept an unblinking gaze on Second and Third. I half turned—someone ought to at least figuratively wave good-bye—and watched until the Ammei and Iykams disappeared through the doorway.

"You may sit," Rozhuhu said. "Your food will be brought."

There didn't seem to be anything left to say. Huginn and I sat down, me taking the seat to Selene's right, Huginn dropping into the one on her left. A door in the wall behind where the lunch buffet had been set up opened and three more Ammei appeared, each carrying a large tray with a glass and two covered dishes. They brought them to the table and set out our meals.

I eyed the tray as my waiter removed the dome-shaped covers. One of the dishes was a bowl containing some sort of soup with crouton-like objects floating in it. The other was a large plate holding a selection of the five items from the lunch buffet that I'd found enough to my liking to take seconds of. Selene's and Huginn's plates held different assortments, and from the approving look in Selene's pupils I gathered that selection was also of her favorites.

Clearly, the Ammei had kept close tabs on what we ate, and had planned their dinner menus accordingly. Did that mean Huginn and I were also at Selene's VIP level?

So what had the Iykams done to get themselves kicked out of the club?

The waiters finished laying out the food, then retreated back to the door where they'd entered. They waited there, apparently so that they would be available if any of us wanted seconds.

"Are you all right?" Selene asked.

I opened my mouth to answer. Closed it again. Her attention, and her question, were for Huginn.

"Of course," he said.

"Sure you are," I said. Even without Selene's sense of smell I could tell he was still upset. "Any idea what brought that on?"

He sent me a quick glare, then lowered his eyes to his tray as he worked to suppress the flash of emotion. "No." He looked back up at me. "Unless it was one of you?" he added with sudden challenge.

"Not guilty," I assured him. "Selene?"

"It was nothing I said or did, either," she said.

"You sure?" Huginn demanded, the glare going a little more intimidating. "You don't exactly have warm feelings for them. Or for any of the rest of us."

"One: we're the ones who got you sprung in the first place," I said. "If we'd wanted you left in that walk-in freezer, we'd have told the Ammei right then and there. Two: if we'd reconsidered and wanted you tossed back in, we'd have sent you packing with them. Three: Iykams may not be my favorite species in the whole Spiral, but at the moment, you, us, and them are all we've got against a whole bunch of Ammei who have a private agenda that somehow includes us. As my father used to say, *You can choose your friends, but you can't choose your family. You usually don't get to choose your allies, either.*"

"What Gregory is saying, Huginn," Selene said gently, "is that you're family."

Selene was normally calm and unassuming. Some people in our past had accused her of being borderline boring. She seldom made jokes, pointed out incongruities, or engaged in irony. But on those rare occasions when she did, the results were dead-center bull's-eyes.

Huginn tried his hardest. He was, after all, an Expediter: elite troubleshooter for the Patth Director General, the epitome of all the spies and special agents who filled the ranks of popular star-thrillers. More than that, he was neck-deep in an unknown situation. He didn't want to react to Selene's comment. He certainly didn't want to smile.

But even he couldn't help himself. For about half a second he continued to glower at me. Then, the scowl softened, the tension in his face faded, and he actually gave an amused chuckle.

"That's what they used to call hitting below the belt," he said, leaning back in his chair and giving Selene a mock-annoyed look. "Family, you say?"

"Provided you don't ask to borrow the car," I said. "So?"

"Fine," he said, the brief smile fading again into seriousness. "You're off the hook. But if you didn't engineer this, why did it happen?"

"I have a theory," I said. "But before I talk about it, I need a little more information. What happened before you were first caught and tossed into confinement?"

"We should also start eating," Selene reminded us, her eyes flicking toward the silent waiters across the room.

"Yes, dinner conversation always looks less suspicious when the participants are actually eating that dinner," I agreed, scooping up a spoonful of the soup and carefully touching it to the tip of my tongue. Not too hot, and the taste seemed decent. "Go on, Huginn."

He hissed out a breath as he cut off a section of one of the two egg-roll things on his plate. "As I said before, we arrived six local days ago."

"Via the Alainn portal," I put in.

The corner of his lip twitched. "Yes," he said. No doubt he'd put two and two together and concluded we already knew which of the Gemini portals out there he and his team had used to get here.

Still, as my father used to say, *When you add two and two, always assume your math has been deliberately manipulated to get four.* In this case, Selene and I hadn't had any opportunity to check the portals for human and Iykam scent before we were also picked up by the Ammei. But Huginn didn't know that.

"It was night, and everything seemed quiet," he continued. "We looked around a bit, I assessed the situation and terrain, and we set up a command post in one of the larger buildings on the western edge of the city where we hoped we could evade notice. We spent the day hidden on upper floors, watching the activity in the core area—that's this tower, the rings of houses, and the portals—and checking to see if and when the inhabitants came into the outer parts."

"Did they?"

"No one came close to us," Huginn said. "We saw a little

movement in the areas along the river, but they were too far away for us to get any specifics."

"Yes," I murmured, thinking about the silver-silk retrieval project we'd stumbled onto. "May have been fishermen. We spotted a troop of them heading to the pier around dusk. Them and their little pets."

"Those tensh things," he said, nodding. "Any idea what they are?"

"Far as I can tell, they're just pets," I said. "Maybe they help the fishermen retrieve their catch or something."

"I don't know," Huginn said doubtfully as he scooped up another mouthful. "They're definitely not just pets. There were a bunch of them with the handful of Ammei who were poking around the city's outer areas, too, so they're not just for fishing." He finished chewing and took a sip from the water glass, wrinkling his nose as he set the glass down. "A little heavy on the minerals for my taste. So after nightfall we waited for the beacon to shut off—"

"Beacon?" I cut in, frowning.

"The evening beacon," he said, frowning as he looked back and forth between us. "How long did you say you'd been here?"

"We weren't in observation range during the night."

"Yeah," he said, still eyeing us. "You must have been really out of it. That thing's probably visible for tens of kilometers, especially the way it lights up the lower cloud layers."

"So they just fire it into the clouds?" I asked. Was that the light we'd seen from orbit? "Why not wait until the clouds clear away?"

"I don't know," he said. "Given how old this place seems to be, it could just be that that's how they've always done it."

"You said the beacon shut off," Selene said. "How long did it run? Did you time it?"

"Of course," Huginn said as if that should have been obvious. "Two hours, seven minutes, three seconds. Exactly the same both days."

"Hold it," I said, trying to do the math in my head. "You said the day here was eighteen and a half hours long?"

"Eighteen point six three three hours," he said. "Works out to eighteen hours, thirty-seven minutes, fifty-nine seconds. Boiled down, that means the beacon runs eleven point three-six percent of the day."

"Odd number," I commented. "You sure it's not an even ten percent? Or maybe even twelve point five?"

"Very sure," he said. "Bear in mind that's a sidereal day, and the measurement might be off a bit due to the unfamiliar star patterns. But it's close enough that, no, it's not an even tenth or eighth. Or an even anything else."

"Interesting," I murmured, trying to think. Some fraction of pi, maybe? No—ridiculous. The Ammei wouldn't scale time in the same way anyone in the Spiral did, nor would any of their measurement system match up with ours.

Something that had a special significance to the Ammei, then. But we weren't going to figure that out without more data. "We can work on that later. So the beacon shut off and...?"

"We poked around the abandoned parts of the city a bit while it was dark," he said. "Some of the more elaborate-looking buildings—or rather, the larger ones that looked like they might once have been elaborate—were missing their baseboards and had had the flooring torn up alongside the walls."

"Really," I said, trying to sound intrigued. It sounded just like what Selene and I had seen in the riverfront building.

Except that that one had silver-silk tucked away inside the excavation area. Huginn's buildings didn't.

Or did they? Had there been silver-silk and he was simply withholding that information? That's certainly what I would have done.

Come to think of it, that was exactly what I was currently doing. "But just the fancy ones?" I asked.

"We didn't make a detailed survey of the area," he growled. "But of the nine buildings we looked into it was only the two fancy ones that had been torn up that way."

"Maybe rich Ammei liked to bury their valuables inside their walls," I said. "Or else went in for some very pricey paneling."

"Or it was something else entirely," Huginn said, giving me a hard look. "I thought you were the one who wanted us to work together."

"Let's finish your story before we start ours," I said. "So you looked at some of the buildings. You find anything else interesting?"

"Not really," Huginn said, still eyeing me suspiciously. "I was working on a plan for checking out the core area when about a dozen Ammei suddenly popped up around our building."

"I'm guessing the Iykams wanted to charge to the attack?"

"Iykams are loyal and ready to die for the Patth and their servants," Huginn said, his tone going darker. "They also obey orders. I told them to lower their weapons and surrender, and they complied."

"Under the circumstances, a wise move," I said, studying the tension in his face. He'd surrendered, and now the Iykams under his authority had been summarily hauled away for another night in confinement.

Or worse. We had only Rozhuhu's word, after all, that that was what the Ammei were going to do with them.

Typically, Selene got to the end of that thought before I did. "They'll be all right," she assured him. "They still hold me in high esteem. They won't risk angering me. Not yet."

"Yeah," Huginn said, giving her speculative look. "Maybe."

"Regardless, if they'd wanted you dead, they could have done that before you even knew they were there," I said. "We saw a quick demo of those lightning guns of theirs. Straight shot into the dirt, but even so."

"Maybe," Huginn said, clearly still not willing to concede that his actions hadn't set up his Iykams to be slaughtered. "Anyway, we stayed in lockup until you showed up. Your turn."

"We got here almost two days ago," I said, sorting through what I should and shouldn't tell him. Working together was fine in theory, but his backup was likely to arrive way before ours—if ours ever did—and there were a few bargaining chips I needed to hold onto. "It was already close to sunset, so we stuck around just long enough to look at the Tower and get a feel for the city before we left."

"How close is your portal to ours?" Huginn asked. "Is it nearby, or somewhere all the way across the ring?"

"Come now," I chided. "We can't have your backup getting here first and floating a balloon into the middle of ours to lock it down. Or do you have a different way of keeping out unwanted company?"

"Careful," Huginn warned with a hint of facetiousness. "Giving away state secrets is probably a capital offense under Kinneman."

"It's hardly a state secret," I assured him. "Besides, Sub-Director Nask saw what I did on Fidelio. It's not like he can't extrapolate that to something simpler and more elegant."

"No, he could certainly do something like that." Huginn gave me a sly smile. "Though given the level of leakage from your Alien Portal Agency, it's not like we wouldn't have heard about your methods eventually anyway."

"No, of course not," I said, keeping my voice casual. We'd long since known about the taps the Patth had into StarrComm and other supposedly secure communications networks. But having actual human intelligence assets inside the Icarus Group would raise that game to a whole new level. "I don't suppose you'd like to share any names with the rest of the class."

He shrugged. "As far as I know, there aren't any specific names," he said. "It's all just bits and pieces we've picked up from incautious comments and gossip."

"Ah." Of course, that was also what he would say if the Patth had a whole legion of spies reporting regularly from inside Kinneman's organization. "Anyway, we came back a day later and were poking around the outer edge of the city when we were caught. Though in our case it was more a greeting with an armed escort."

"Because of Selene," he said, again giving her a probing look. "And you get Second of Three while we get Third of Three. What makes you so special?"

"Maybe the better question is what makes humans and Iykams *not* special," I said. The hazy beginnings of a theory were floating around my brain, but I needed way more thought and data before it would coalesce enough to even share with Selene, let alone Huginn. "On another note, I assume you noticed how much better Rozhuhu's English is compared to Fourth's."

"At about the third word out of his mouth," he confirmed. "I assume you have a theory?"

"Remember back on Alainn I told you that someone had been using that portal to get to the Loporr village for the past fifty to a hundred years?" I asked.

"Yes," Huginn murmured, his voice going all thoughtful. "You think Fourth was one of the last people who dealt with the Loporri before the Ammei closed down the operation?"

"Exactly," I said. "Bilswift was barely an outpost at the time, so Fourth's exposure to English would have been minimal."

"Rozhuhu, on the other hand, looks way too young to have been to Alainn before the Janus was shut down," Huginn said. "He must have picked up his English since then."

"Which means he's had at least semi-regular contact with humans," I said. "Which also means the Ammei haven't just been sitting on all those portals out there. They've been using some of them."

"To get to the exotic foodstuffs they pipe into the Ammei enclaves to sell," he said, nodding. "Already figured out that part."

"Good," I said. "Then there's just one other crucial bit of information we need to keep in mind. The Gemini portal you came in through was shut off at the Alainn end, not this one. To me that says the Ammei wanted access to either the Loporri or their silver-silk."

"Agreed," Huginn said. "If they didn't pull the plug, any thoughts as to who did?"

"Not at the moment," I said. "But I can imagine the Ammei being royally pissed off at their private trade route drying up."

"Though apparently not pissed off enough to try to get to Alainn some other way."

"And how exactly would they have done that?" I countered. "They probably never knew the planet's name. Certainly not the name the Spiral calls it by. Add to that the fact that the upstanding citizens who've been exploiting the silver-silk trade all these years kept it a very dark secret, and the Ammei could search for centuries before they figured out where it was."

"Only now they've got a fresh shot at it," Huginn pointed out grimly. "With you and Selene blowing open the question of Loporri sapience, the silver-silk connection is bound to come out."

"Eventually," I said. "But that's not our problem. Our problem is to figure out what's going on here."

"Agreed," he said. "Question: If the Ammei here are making regular trips back and forth to the Spiral, why don't more of them know English? It's one of maybe three main *lingua francas* these days."

"I see two possibilities," I said. "One, it's the Ammei from the other enclaves who do all the trade and language studies while this bunch mostly sit around pining for the glories of the old days."

"The old days?"

"A city doesn't collapse this far without having had some glorious old days," I pointed out. "Or at least days the current populace fondly remembers that way. Second possibility—" I shot a surreptitious look at the three servants, still standing patiently along the wall. "Second possibility," I continued, lowering my voice, "is that they all speak perfect English and this whole happy-natives thing is a huge scam they've manufactured for our benefit."

"Through which they hope to find out why we're here and what we're looking for?" Huginn asked. "Sounds a bit paranoid."

I shrugged. "Just because you're paranoid doesn't necessarily mean you're wrong."

"True," he conceded. "Actually, come to think of it, the whole town doesn't have to be in on it. I don't think we've interacted with more than twenty Ammei total."

"Most of whom haven't said a word," I agreed. "Still, as my father used to say, *The first half of getting through a con is recognizing that it is a con.*"

"And the second half?"

"He said he would leave that up to me," I said. "He liked to encourage resourcefulness. Regardless, I think our best plan is to keep going on as we have, remembering we might still be in option one. It's embarrassing to call B.S. on someone who is completely innocent and has no idea what you're babbling about."

"Especially when it could get you shot," Huginn said. "I still want a closer look at that library and those Upper Rooms."

"Agreed," I said. "But we should wait until Selene's had a chance to fill in her part of the map."

"Map?" Selene asked.

"It's more of a floor plan," I said, again looking at the waiters. I didn't know if they were close enough to hear us, or whether they were among the group of locals who understood English. But they sure as hell were close enough to spot me passing something the size of a folded piece of paper to Selene. "We need to know everything we can about the Tower's layout before we can decide on our next move."

"In the meantime, it's getting close to sunset and our watchdogs are looking antsy," Huginn said. "Ready to put a ribbon on the evening?"

"Almost." I scooped up the last bite from my plate and popped it into my mouth. "I need you to block their view long enough for me to get the map from my right front pocket."

"Sure. Say when."

"When." I lifted my left hand toward Selene and pointed, as if gesturing to something behind her, making sure to keep the hand from getting suspiciously close to her head or body. She picked up instantly on the cue and half turned to look. Out of the corner of my eye I saw Huginn fumble his napkin onto the floor and climb partway out of his seat as he bent down and retrieved it.

And for about a second and a half, I had my window.

I dipped the first two fingers into my pocket, pickpocket style, and pulled out our map. By the time Huginn was back in his seat I had the folded paper palmed invisibly in my right hand. "And now we go?" Selene asked as she turned back to me.

"Now we go," I confirmed. "Kindly be a lady and let your bodyguard help you up."

I pushed back my chair, stood up, and walked around behind Selene. The waiters reacted to my action, two of them stiffening to a sort of attention while the third seemed to be speaking rapidly to no one in particular. An earbud, presumably, or something similar, and I made a mental note to ask for a radio scanner whenever our backup showed up. Even if we couldn't understand their language, knowing what frequency and pattern they were using to communicate could be very useful. I settled myself behind Selene and got a grip on the two sides of her chair, and as she stood up in response to my murmured prompt I pulled the chair back.

And as her hip rose to the level of my right hand, I slipped the map behind her belt and into the hip waistband of her trousers.

I stepped back as Huginn likewise got to his feet. "You!" I called toward the waiters, gesturing the same way I had over Selene's shoulder a minute ago. "Inform the Second of Three that Selene of the Kadolians is ready to be escorted to her place of sleep."

I'd barely finished speaking when the door we'd come in through opened and our entourage marched in. Second led the way, as usual, with Fourth a step to his side and a bit behind him. Third was next, with Rozhuhu holding the same position to him as Fourth was to Second. The six guards who'd escorted the Iykams out of the dining room earlier were also back, fanning out to both sides of the door. Second said something—

"The Second of Three expresses his hope that the meal was

to the satisfaction of Selene of the Kadolians," Fourth of Three translated.

"It was," Selene said with the proper level of calm dignity. "I am prepared to be escorted to my place of sleep. I ask again that my bodyguard be allowed to accompany me."

"That is impossible," Fourth said. Again, there was apparently no need for consultation.

"Perhaps it is impossible for the Third of Three," Selene said. "Is it also impossible for the First of Three?"

For a second, Fourth seemed to freeze. Then he moved a few centimeters closer to Second and began talking rapidly. Second said something back, and the conversation was on.

I glanced at Huginn, saw my own freshly heightened interest reflected in his expression. I still had only a vague understanding of the rules of this hierarchy, but it was clear that Selene's appeal to the top dog wasn't something any of the others had anticipated.

Second and Fourth finished their hurried dialog and both turned back to Selene. "The First of Three cannot be disturbed at this hour," Fourth said. "The Second of Three will discuss the matter with him in the morning."

"How surprising," Huginn muttered. "We going to settle for that?"

I looked sideways at Selene, noting the minor satisfaction in her pupils. Whatever her goal had been in appealing Second's decision, she'd apparently achieved it. "For the moment," I muttered back. I turned my attention to Third. "We are prepared to be escorted to our place of rest, Third of Three," I said.

"We are likewise," Rozhuhu said. Even with the heavy cloak of alienness obscuring his voice and expression, I could swear there was relief there. "The Third of Three will lead you. Selene of the Kadolians, the Second of Three and your escort await."

"Thank you," I said. "Selene, I'll see you in the morning. Sleep well."

"You, too," she said.

"I will."

Which was a promise I had no intention of keeping. If Huginn was right, the beacon would soon be blazing its way into the sky and clouds. Two hours after that, darkness would presumably settle across the city.

I intended to use that darkness to the fullest.

CHAPTER SIXTEEN

I'd thought Huginn and I might be taken to the same level-six room where we'd been sent to rest earlier that day. Instead, we were escorted up to level seven, the lower of the two floors in the Tower's pentagon-shaped tier. Rozhuhu unlocked one of the bedrooms we'd passed by on our tour and we all stepped inside. "I will return at the seventh hour of the morning," he said. "You will eat a meal, then the Third of Three will show you the city."

"Can't wait," I assured him. "What if we need anything before that?"

"What if my Iykams need anything?" Huginn added.

"Everything you need has been provided," Rozhuhu said, stepping to the door. "As have your servants' needs. Sleep well and happily." He left, closing the door behind him.

"You were expecting there would be a summons cord?" Huginn said sourly as we turned to inspect our new quarters.

"Wanted to see if he was leaving a guard outside," I said, walking over and trying the knob. It opened easily, revealing an empty corridor beyond. "He wasn't," I said, closing the door again.

"Or the guard's in one of the other rooms waiting for us to try something," Huginn said.

"I don't think so," I said, looking around. We were in some sort of common room, with a door on either side. "You *do* remember that they want us to look around, right?"

"Doesn't mean they can't be subtle about it."

"I don't think they know *how* to be subtle."

He grunted and fell silent. I thought about reminding him that they still needed our goodwill, which meant the Iykams would be okay at least through the night. But it didn't seem worth the effort. Instead, I kept my mouth shut and looked around our new home.

The suite consisted of two small sleeping compartments, a bathroom that included a long tub, multiple horizontal shower jets, and a slightly alien version of a sink/toilet combination. Beside the tub was what looked like a combination miniature house and a hamster exercise and climbing structure.

It was remarkably similar to the suite Kinneman had put Selene and me in back at the Icarus Group base, or like the sleeping arrangements Sub-Director Nask had put us in aboard his ship. But then, there were only so many ways you could arrange this kind of place, especially if you wanted your guests to be comfortable.

"Interesting add-on in here," I commented over my shoulder from the bathroom. "I'm guessing it's for the outriders."

There was no answer. "Huginn?" I called, walking back into to the common room.

To find that he'd disappeared. Evidently, he'd decided to skip the tour of our new quarters and go hunting.

"So much for worrying about subtlety," I said under my breath.

Still, I wasn't sorry he was gone. I had my own hunt ahead of me, and I'd just as soon not have to make up a story about it.

The common room and both sleeping compartments had spacious windows that looked out across the city. One of the compartments would have more privacy, I decided, and stepped into the one on the left. Pulling aside the curtains, I looked out.

The city was bathed in a faint but uniform glow, probably reflected light from the nightly beacon. I couldn't see anyone in the grassy region between the Tower and the inner ring of houses, but there were some interior lights showing in one of the houses. Possibly Selene's quarters for the night, and I made careful note of the house's location, shape, and color. Despite our cautious optimism about her current status, I'd learned the hard way that such things can change in the blink of an eye.

If the city's inner core was deserted, the area around the Gemini portals more than made up for it. With the dual benefit of height and the beacon's illumination I could see that each of the portals had no fewer than two Ammei standing guard around it, more likely three or four. They'd apparently concluded that their two sets of visitors had arrived on Nexus Six via one of them, and had no intention of letting anyone else pop in without them knowing about it.

I frowned. No; not *all* the portals were being guarded. At the very edge of my viewing angle I could see one that seemed to be unguarded.

Had someone missed a work order? Or had the First of Three run out of soldiers?

I nodded as the obvious answer hit me. Huginn and I had already decided that the Ammei enclaves were using one or more of these portals to travel back and forth. With their own people controlling the far ends of those particular Geminis, there was no reason for the leaders here to waste troops watching them.

Which also meant that such portals were guaranteed doors to at least *some* place in the Spiral, should the need for a quick exit arise.

Of course, arriving in the middle of a group of annoyed aliens was hardly an ideal situation. But it beat the hell out of taking pot luck with everywhere else in the universe.

I shifted my gaze downward. My window was a good twenty-five meters above the ground, but the way the Tower's tiers were laid out I should be able to take the levels one at a time without ever having to face more than a four-meter drop. Still not pleasant, but also no longer a guaranteed set of broken legs or ankles.

Getting back inside the Tower and up to our suite would be an entirely different challenge, of course. But I'd cross that bridge when I came to it. As my father used to say, *Don't go overboard when you're making plans. Most of them will get thrown out the window anyway. Luckily, most of the other guy's will, too.*

The window's fasteners weren't like anything I'd seen before. But once I'd figured them out they were easy to operate. I made sure I could get the window open far enough to get through, then closed it again and lay down on the bed.

Huginn had said the beacon ran two hours and seven minutes. In two hours ten, I would be on my way.

Despite my internal pep talk, I'd had some qualms about this part of the plan. To my relief, it came off without a hitch. Each tier downward had enough width for me to land without the risk of an off-balance moment sending me head-first over the edge, and the roofing material itself was softer than most I'd jumped onto, fallen off of, or been thrown against. Four minutes after I let go of that first windowsill I was on the ground, with only minor aches in my legs and knees to show for it.

I'd anticipated the next part of the night's activities to be trickier. There'd been guards on all the Tower's doors when Selene and I were first brought in, and I needed to find a route that would get me across the lawn, utilizing the bushes and flower clusters wherever possible, without any of them spotting me.

Once again, the execution turned out to be way simpler than I'd expected. Mainly because the door guards had disappeared.

I puzzled at that as I slipped through the darkness across the lawn. The door on this side of the building seemed to be closed and was presumably locked. Did the Ammei consider that adequate security for what seemed to be their most important building? Or had the need to keep a watch on all the portals out there siphoned away the guards who would otherwise have been on duty?

Either way, I wasn't going to complain.

I reached the ramp into the subway tunnel Selene and I had taken from the dock and headed down. The train we'd ridden was no longer where we'd left it, presumably having been put back into service by someone who needed to go elsewhere in town.

Which boded well for my evening's hunt. If the group I'd spotted a couple of nights ago were in fact harvesting silver-silk from that riverside ruin, and if I could catch them at it and then follow them to wherever they were taking the stuff, I might be able to get a better clue as to what they wanted it for.

Still, without the car it was going to be a long walk, and even though much of the trip would be underground it wasn't like I would be completely invisible. There were all those other ramps leading up from the tunnel that someone might happen to look down as I passed. Worse, if anyone happened to wander down here with me, there was zero cover anywhere.

But there was nothing for it but to keep an eye out and try to anticipate any such dangers. I headed out, trying to strike a balance between speed and silence.

The trip quickly settled into a slightly tense routine. I paused at each of the side ramps, looking and listening for voices or other signs of activity, but I saw and heard nothing. I was especially careful near the ramps that led up to the portal ring area, the one place in the whole city that I knew for a fact was crawling with Ammei. But there, too, all was silent.

Which was not only reasonable but pretty much inevitable. If the guards wanted to nab any newly arrived visitors they needed to lure them far enough onto Nexus Six soil that they couldn't beat a hasty retreat back down the rabbit hole. I slowed my pace, focusing on maintaining absolute silence, and kept going.

I kept up my mime act until I was two subway stops past the portals. Then, surrounded now by the ruined and abandoned section of the city, I finally felt safe enough to pick up my pace.

I was approaching the last pair of exits before the final ramp leading up to the riverside when my luck ran out. Ahead, a group of shadowy figures appeared, framed against the faintly lit landscape of the final subway opening.

And they were moving in my direction.

I hissed a curse under my breath, a quick glance confirming that there was still no cover nearby. My only hope was to get to one of the side exit ramps and duck out of sight before the group piled into the car and the driver switched on whatever headlight he had available. With my gaze locked onto the faint movements in the distance, I broke into a full sprint toward the closest right-hand ramp.

Fortunately, the newcomers didn't seem in any hurry to get home. I had reached the ramp and made it a couple of meters up the slope when the tunnel behind me lit up with a soft glow and I heard the sound of the car's engine. I dropped flat onto the ramp, pressing myself against the wall and trying to make myself as invisible as possible. People gazing ahead into a lighted tunnel would normally be pretty much blind to everything alongside them in the shadows, but I didn't put it past this crowd to have people with starscopes watching the darkness around them on both sides.

But the car rumbled past without slowing and without any shouts of sudden discovery. I let them get a couple of seconds past me, then crossed to the other side of the ramp and pressed myself against that wall, just in case someone decided to look back. I waited another few seconds, until the car had made it past the next ramp, then crawled back down to the subway opening. I stroked the thumbnail of my artificial left arm, turning it into its mirror mode, and eased it cautiously into the tunnel.

The car was still trundling its merry way along, with no indication that anyone had seen me or had had their suspicions aroused in any other way. I kept watching, wondering if it would stop at one of the intermediate stations or continue all the way to the Tower. If it stopped anywhere in the ruined part of town, that might suggest they were using the silver-silk for something clandestine, perhaps without the First of Three's authorization. More importantly, given how few of the buildings out here still offered any shelter and privacy, such a move would also severely limit the number of places I would have to search once they were clear.

But no. The car went all the way to the end of the line. It stopped, the headlight went out, and its passengers presumably disembarked.

They were too distant, and the tunnel too dark, for me to see that last part. Outside in the starlight I might have a better chance, but with all the ruined buildings out there sticking up between them and me I would have to be extraordinarily lucky to have even a partial line of sight.

But if I couldn't find out where they were taking their haul, I could at least confirm that they had indeed been to the silver-silk house. I gave them a few minutes to make their way out of the tunnel and to wherever they were settling down for the rest of the night, then stood up and walked the rest of the way to the end of the subway.

I'd gotten used to being at least mostly out of view in the tunnel, and coming out into the night breeze gave me a fresh sense of vulnerability. But I could hardly crawl from here to the river. Hoping that anyone who spotted me would assume I was just another Amme out for a stroll, I headed off through the scrub and bushes toward the sound of rippling water.

The ground cover was as dark as everything else around me, but once I got through them I found that the river reeds themselves displayed a strange shimmer in the starlight. That glow, plus their gentle swaying, made them stand out of the darkness and much easier to see than I'd expected. A nice side effect was that with the reeds visible, so was the gap in the rows that marked the path toward the river that I needed to follow. I reached it and headed in.

It was impossible to walk silently through plants that were swishing against my legs, but I did my best to keep down the noise. It was only an assumption, after all, that the Ammei who had passed me in the subway car were the only ones working this site. If there was another shift hunkered down in the building, or if the Ammei in the subway had been out here for some other reason entirely, I could walk right in on them before I even knew they were there.

I was nearly to the river when I heard a quiet rustling in the reeds.

I stopped short and dropped into a crouch, my eyes darting around as I tried to figure out where the sound had come from. No one the size of an Amme was visible, which suggested it was an animal. Possibly a nocturnal herbivore, possibly a nighttime predator.

Possibly a tensh.

I winced. If it was one of the latter, and if they worked the same way as Kalixiri outriders, the minute this one got back to his boss this quiet little side trip would blow up in my face.

I crouched a little lower, my hand reflexively gripping my plasmic, knowing full well that I couldn't use it. Here in the darkness, with Ammei standing portal guard a couple of kilometers away, a plasma blast might as well be a fully lit adboard proclaiming my presence.

The rustling came again, closer this time. But now I had its location: ahead of me, just off the path. I shifted my gaze to the tops of the reeds, watching for the telltale twitching that would indicate something pushing its way through them at ground level. The plants right beside the path gave a final twitch—

I looked down again, tensing. Something the size of a large rat or small ferret had appeared on the path. It froze in place a moment as it gazed at me, maybe trying to decide if I was too big to eat. Then it stirred and started toward me.

I drew my plasmic, shifting my grip to the barrel. As clubbing weapons went, it would be fairly useless. But if push came to bite it would be better than nothing. The creature moved closer...

And then, barely a meter away from me, it stopped and gave a tentative little squeak. A very familiar little squeak.

I huffed out a sigh of relief. "Hello, Pax," I murmured as I returned my plasmic to its holster. "You come here often?"

Pax gave another squeak, this one sounding more confident, and scampered up to me. "Hello, Ixil," I said, feeling my usual sense of the absurd whenever I used one of the outriders to send what was essentially an organic voice message. "Welcome to Nexus Six. I have lots of news for you, and I'm sure you have a note or two from Kinneman for me. A couple of buildings south of the dock, right along the riverbank, is a building that still has two walls and a partial roof. I'll meet you there."

I nodded, as if Pax would understand the gesture meant I

was done, then gave the little animal a nudge against its cheek. "Go back to Ixil, Pax," I said. "Go on."

He gave one final squeak, then turned and scampered back along the path. I stood back up, looked around, and followed. Distantly, I wondered what Ixil's reaction would be to my news.

I didn't have to wonder at all about the notes Kinneman had undoubtedly sent.

I'd been waiting in the ruined building for nearly forty minutes, listening to the breeze and the rippling of the river and getting colder by the minute, when Ixil finally appeared.

To my complete lack of surprise, McKell was with him.

"Welcome to Nexus Six," I greeted them as they picked their way through the debris toward me. "You and Kinneman hug and make up? Or is this just a short vacation away from the thumbscrews?"

"*General* Kinneman," McKell said, leaning on the rank, "is only slightly less furious with us than he is with you." His eyes flicked around. "Where's Selene?"

"Currently a guest of the locals," I told him. "An honored guest, as near as we can figure. But that could change."

"What about you?"

"Not quite as honored," I conceded. "But there's still a kid-glove feel to this that makes me suspicious. Though come to think about it, Huginn and his Iykams might disagree about the kid-glove thing."

"Wait a second," McKell said, frowning. "*Expediter* Huginn, Sub-Director Nask's right-hand man? *He's* here?"

"He is indeed," I confirmed. "He and his Iykams actually got here a few days ahead of Selene and me. You might want to gloss over that part a bit when you make your report."

It took a couple of seconds for them to track through the dots. Then, Pix and Pax gave a simultaneous twitch. "The Alainn portal," Ixil said. "The Patth got it working."

"So it seems," I said. "And then it gets complicated."

"Does it, now," McKell said, his eyes narrowing. "How so?"

I gestured to the slabs of masonry around the one I was perched on. "Pull up a chunk of rotted building material," I said, "and I'll tell you all about it."

CHAPTER SEVENTEEN

———— ❖ ————

"I'll concede that some of that is speculation," I said as I concluded. "But I think the logic holds together."

"Speculation can be useful," Ixil said thoughtfully, "provided you don't put too much weight on it."

"Especially the tacticals," McKell said. "Like this wholly unwarranted assumption that the Iykams were tossed back in the holding tank because the Ammei don't have enough soldiers to guard their visitors and the portal ring at the same time. Personally, I think First of Three simply wanted to cut down the number of variables and limit your and Huginn's degrees of freedom for the night."

"I agree," Ixil said. "Even if we arbitrarily limit the number of Ammei residences to the houses in the inner ring, they could still have an uncomfortably large force available."

"Not arguing the point," I conceded. "As my father used to say, *Speculation usually includes a high percentage of wishful thinking.* Incidentally, as long as we're talking tactics, do bear in mind that we have no idea what those lightning guns' range is."

"Noted," McKell said. "I'm also not convinced that the Ammei genuinely want you to go looking for something in the library, grove, and Upper Rooms."

"Then why make sure Selene got those same three places on

her tour?" I asked. "*And* why make sure she got there after us so she'd know we'd also been there?"

"Maybe they're just toying with you," McKell suggested. "Trying to lure you into forbidden territory so that they'd have an excuse to drop some consequences on you."

"But who would that excuse be for?" Ixil objected. "The Ammei have full control here."

"Maybe it just looks that way," McKell said. "Maybe these Gold Ones are really the ones in charge, and the Ammei need to make sure and cover their legal butts."

"In which case the Gold Ones are hiding really well," I pointed out. Huginn and I had already been over this ground, but it wouldn't hurt to let McKell and Ixil take their own crack at it. "I haven't seen any evidence they're still around, and Selene hasn't mentioned picking up any spurious scents."

"They could be up in the mountains," McKell said. "If they're far enough away and downwind, even Selene would have trouble picking them up."

"Speaking of Selene, it's possible she's the one they need to impress," Ixil said thoughtfully. "I note that you and she weren't immediately put into confinement like Huginn and the Iykams."

"We noted that, too," I said. "Plus the fact that the Ammei immediately turned Huginn over to us, as if they just assumed Selene was in charge of the whole group. Did Tera pass on my thoughts about the Kadolians and Patth being possibly linked together?"

"You mean because their local currencies have similar names?" McKell asked.

"*And* because the existence of the Patth Talariac Drive meshes nicely with the transportation requirements of the portal system," I said. "Like I said, there's an internal logic here that I think makes sense."

"Let's back up a moment," Ixil said. "Assume that you're right about everything. If the Ammei want you to find something, why not just ask them what it is?"

I shook my head. "Asking a question the other guy doesn't want to answer just buys you a bald-faced lie. It also tips him off that you're on to him and puts him on his guard. I usually find you do better to be oblivious and stupid in the hope of getting your opponent to underestimate you."

"So the Ammei fawn all over you, load you up with bread-crumbs, and watch where you scatter them?" McKell asked.

"Basically," I said. "And like Ixil said, the unexpected arrival of a Kadolian may have ratcheted up their interest and urgency a few notches."

"And we're *sure* the Ammei aren't the Icari?" Ixil asked.

"They don't have the appendages we all assume the Icari have in order to work the portal controls without flopping down on the deck," I reminded him. "Anyway, Selene's money is on the Gold Ones."

"Did she offer any reason in particular for that conclusion?" McKell asked.

"Not really," I said. "She mentioned that Second of Three had made some comments that led her to that conclusion, but she didn't elaborate."

"We need to get that nailed down," McKell said. "If we're on the brink of locating or identifying the Icari, we need to know it."

"Agreed," I said. "Next time we're alone I'll ask her to elaborate."

"We also need to nail down their interest in silver-silk," Ixil said, looking over at the torn-up section of wall I'd pointed out to them. "You're sure they're not using it for decoration? Perhaps woven into their hats?"

"Not a chance," I said. "I haven't seen any evidence of it in the hats, or in any other clothing or decorative items we've seen."

"It could be buried somewhere inside," McKell suggested.

"You don't bury silver-silk inside something," I said. "Its sole purpose in life is to sit out in the light where it can impress your friends."

"From the evidence," Ixil said, "that's apparently *not* its sole purpose."

"Absolutely," I agreed soberly. "I should have said that was its sole purpose for the Spiral's elite. I keep thinking about how gold and silver were just decorative metals before humans discovered electricity. I tried to find technical stats on silver-silk, but there's nothing in our info pads' general files."

"We can look it up when we get back to Icarus," McKell said. "Meanwhile, it sounds like our first job here is to get into the library and see if RH is there."

"*Our* first job, maybe," I said. "Selene's and mine. Not yours."

McKell snorted. "Did I mention Kinneman's feelings about you two going all lone-wolf on him?"

"At least three times," I said. "And I've already told you why we did it. The point is that you two can't suddenly appear out of nowhere, especially when the Ammei have all the portals under surveillance. It'll start them looking and thinking elsewhere, and we can't afford that. Alpha's our one and only ace in the hole, and I have no intention of compromising it."

"*You* have no intention?"

"He's right, Jordan," Ixil said. "You and I can't make any overt moves until we're ready to come back in force."

"Which will be when?" I asked.

"No idea," McKell growled. "Kinneman's furious enough to yank us off the project as soon as we deliver our report." He gave me a tight smile. "Personally, I suspect the only reason he let us come over was that we weren't sure Alpha was working properly, and Ixil and I were the most expendable ones on the payroll."

"Which makes a good case for you two staying put here for a while," I pointed out. "Keep some of Kinneman's uncertainty going. The last thing we want is for a squad of EarthGuard Marines to come charging in with plasmics and lasers blazing. We do that, and we might never figure out what's going on here."

"I don't think that's how the general sees things," Ixil said. "His philosophy is that every problem will eventually yield to sufficient application of weapons and brains."

"You might want to remind him how long the Icarus Group has studied Icarus, Alpha, and Firefall and how little information they've collected," I said. "If that doesn't work, remind him that Huginn's backup could be arriving at any time. He gets his Marines in a firefight with the Patth and we're straight back to serious political and economic fallout."

"He might consider gaining access to a ring of Gemini portals to be worth the risk," McKell said.

"And he would be dead wrong," I said flatly. "Make sure he understands that, too. Or ask my father to explain it to him."

I levered myself off the sloping piece of more or less flat stone I'd adopted as an impromptu seat. "Right now, time rushes on, the night grows short, and I've got a long walk ahead of me before I get back to the Tower."

"Understood," McKell said, getting up from his own slab. "What can we do to help?"

"Right now, just keep Kinneman's wolves on their leashes," I said. "Selene and I may be able to figure out a way to get you two back in, but a full armed presence is the last thing we want."

"How about we split the difference?" McKell suggested. "I go back and report while Ixil and the outriders stay here and keep an eye on you."

"Not sure that's a good idea," I warned. "Going to be hard to keep Pix and Pax out of sight with all those tenshes prowling around."

"They're better at that sort of thing than you think," Ixil assured me. "I agree, Jordan."

"Good," McKell said, as if I didn't have any further say in the matter. Which, realistically, I probably didn't. "Roarke, get going. Ixil, you'll need to find someplace within close-support range to hide out."

"Not a problem," Ixil assured him, snapping his fingers twice. The outriders, who'd been poking around the reeds along the river, scampered back and climbed nimbly up his clothing to their usual positions on his shoulders. "If and when you need to bail, Gregory, just shout *artichoke,* and I'll be there as quickly as I can."

"Got it," I said. I had no intention of bailing, not unless Selene and I were in imminent danger. But I didn't have time to argue the point. "Incidentally, the Tower's architecture is another mark against the Ammei being the Icari. As far as I can tell it doesn't look a thing like any of the Icari ruins we've found in the Spiral."

"Good point," McKell said. "On the other hand, Earth architecture has changed significantly over the ten thousand years or so of recorded history. The Tower here could be very early Icari, or very late Icari."

"Or just something a maverick architect put together," Ixil added. "Not really conclusive either way."

"Good," I said. "Glad we got that settled. I'll hopefully not see you around, Ixil."

"Indeed," Ixil said. "Good luck."

"And watch yourselves," McKell warned. "If you're right about the Ammei trying to play you, odds are the game is running some seriously high stakes."

"I know," I said. "Say hello to my father for me. Oh, and if you get a chance, bring me back a radio scanner."

The subway, fortunately, was deserted. I hurried along the tunnel, glancing up the ramps as I passed, but not bothering to slow to a more silent tread until I was close to the portal ring. Again, I heard nothing from the topside guards, nor did any of them seem to hear anything from me. Two stops later I again picked up my pace, mindful of the passing minutes and the danger of getting caught in the light of dawn.

There was still the problem of getting into the Tower, of course. I'd found a few strong but slender metal shards while waiting for Ixil and McKell, and my tentative plan was to try to wedge them into the cracks around one of the doors to create a ladder, then climb up to the first roof and use one of them to jimmy open a second-tier window.

It was hardly the most solid plan in the world. It wasn't even in the top ten plans I'd come up with on my own. But the only alternative was to sneak into the house where Selene had been taken and try to persuade the Ammei that I'd left my own sleeping room purely out of my sense of duty to her.

Odds on that one were that I would get tossed into the cooler with the Iykams.

I reached the end of the subway and headed up the ramp. The lawn surrounding the Tower was as I'd left it. The Tower itself was also as I'd left it.

What *wasn't* as I'd left it was the slender rope that was now draped along the side that led from the ground to the window I'd left roughly three hours ago.

I stopped beside it, frowning up at the window as I fingered the slender line. Close up, I saw now that it wasn't a rope, but a vine or collection of vines that had been tied or spliced together. Presumably from the Grove of Reflection, almost certainly Huginn's handiwork. The question was whether he'd specifically set it out for me, or whether he was currently off prowling the city on an errand of his own and had left this little back door for his own benefit.

But for the moment the reasons and history didn't matter. The line was here, I was here, and dawn was coming. Sliding my metal shards carefully into the back of my belt, I got a grip on the vine and started up.

I'd noticed the plant's slightly rough feel when I first touched it. What I hadn't realized until I was actually climbing was that the texture was wonderfully suited to the task, with enough bumpiness to keep from being slippery but not enough to scrape into my skin. Wherever Huginn had found this stuff, it was like it had been designed for the purpose.

I hit the first splice midway up level three, a type of knot I didn't recognize but that seemed to be doing its job. I was carefully working my way around it, making sure I didn't loosen it, when an odd fact caught my attention.

The south side of this level, on the opposite side of the building, contained the library, which filled a sixth or more of the tier's floor space and featured a wall of floor-to-ceiling windows. The section I was currently climbing up had those same tall windows.

But on this side, all the windows had been covered over with close-fitting sheets of metal.

I studied the shutters as best I could in the time it took me to get past the splice. It was hard to tell in the starlight, but I had the sense that the coverings were newer than the Tower itself, as if the Ammei had only recently decided to hide whatever was behind them from prying eyes.

Or maybe I had that backward. Maybe the shutters were instead to hide the outside world from whoever was *inside*.

My first night here I'd briefly speculated that the ring of mounds surrounding the Tower were the city's prisons. Maybe I was now climbing past the real thing.

But that would be for later consideration. Right now, I had maybe an hour before the stars faded from the sky over the mountains, and there was nothing to be gained hanging along the side of an alien building. Giving the shutters one final look, I continued up.

I'd sometimes regretted not getting a major strength upgrade when I had to replace my left arm after the Fidelio incident. But even without that, the arm's artificial muscles had the huge advantage of not getting fatigued like the organic ones in my right arm. I could feel my right hand starting to shake when I finally reached the window and pulled myself inside. Working my right hand to ward off any cramps, I peered outside. If Huginn was out there racing for the vine, he was going to cut things dangerously close—

"I was starting to think you'd be out all night," his voice came from behind me.

"Sorry," I said, looking over my shoulder. He was standing in the doorway of my sleeping compartment, an inquisitive look on his face. "I know how you and Mom worry," I added, turning back to the window and starting to pull up the vine. "Thanks for this, by the way."

"No problem," he said. "You can pay me back by telling me everything."

I winced. But really, he'd earned it.

Besides, with Alpha now up and running, and with Kinneman poised to breathe fire and fury all over us, Huginn and I needed to be on the same page if we were going to keep Nexus Six from becoming an all-out battlefield.

"Let me get this in first," I said, continuing to reel in the vine. "How was your evening, by the way?"

"Mildly productive," he said. "I think I've figured out why the Grove of Reflection was on Third of Three's special notice list."

"Because these are in there?" I asked, waving a loop of vine.

"That, and the fact that it's directly over the library," he said. "Apparently, they think that instead of just walking in through the library door we might try to be clever and rappel in."

"We're a Patth Expediter and a former bounty hunter," I reminded him. "We do sometimes tend toward the overdramatic."

"Personally, I prefer the straightforward approach," he said. "But in general you may be right. Which again shows that someone here knows more about the Spiral than they're letting on."

"Or are passing messages and information back and forth to one of the Ammei enclaves."

"Or both," he said, his voice suddenly going all casual. "I also got a look into the Upper Rooms."

"Really," I said, resisting the urge to spin around and stare at him. The big fancy area where the elite Gold Ones hung their hats, and he'd just walked in? "How was it? Nicer than ours?"

"Not necessarily nicer, but definitely different," he said. If he was disappointed that I hadn't reacted with open-mouthed surprise it didn't show in his voice. "It's technically only a single room, though there are chest-high partitions that divide the floorspace into four squares. There are two beds, one each in the north and south sections, a bathroom to the east, and a meal-prep area to the west, though I didn't see any groceries or food-prep implements. Windows all around—great view of the city." He paused. "Plus each of the sleeping compartments includes a small library."

"Interesting," I said, pulling the last length of vine through the window. "Any current bestsellers? Or are they all classics?"

"They were a bit hard to read," he said. "But they look like the books in the main library. So which of the books *are* you looking for?"

"We're looking for everything we can get on the Icari," I said. "Same as you." I paused, pretending to be preoccupied with coiling the vine rope into a tight spiral. Just because I'd convinced myself that I needed to coordinate actions with Huginn didn't mean I had to tell him everything I knew. Especially not the parts that would get me dropped into the deep hole Kinneman had threatened me with at our first meeting, and which was certainly already being excavated. "Though I'm guessing our mandate may be a bit more specific than yours."

"How so?"

I paused, prepping my casual tone as I slid the coiled vine under my bed. "To cut to the chase, the Icarus Group found what appears to be an Icari document."

"On Meima, I presume?"

"What makes you think that?" I asked, making sure my neutral expression was in place as I turned to face him.

Apparently, it wasn't neutral enough. "Thank you for the confirmation," he said calmly. He gave me a lopsided smile. "Oh, don't look like that—you didn't give anything away. We knew from the beginning that you'd made some discovery there."

"Or at least you guessed."

"No, we knew," he said. "You see, you let us have that Janus portal a little too easily."

"I'd already promised it to Sub-Director Nask," I reminded him.

"So you had," he agreed. "Let me restate: Jordan McKell let us have the Janus portal a little too easily. You had to have told him something that persuaded him to back off and let us take the portal and get off the planet, hopefully before we could wonder what that something might be. What kind of document?"

"It was a book," I said. "Couple of centimeters thick, bound in black Icari metal with pages a thinner version of the same stuff, all held together with a magnetic hasp. Sound familiar?"

A minute ago he'd read my poker face with ease. Now, it was my turn. Despite the studied blankness of his expression there was a twitch of tightening in a couple of his cheek muscles that confirmed I'd hit the mark. "Very familiar," he agreed. "Also like the ones in the main library?"

"The edges looked the same, anyway," I said. "No way to be really sure unless I can get a close-up look at one."

"I'll see if I can arrange that," he said. "Have you been able to translate any of it?"

"Not as far as I know," I said. "But then, I'm hardly at the top of the current administration's party-invitation list. They could be reading whole chapters to each other at bedtime and I wouldn't know it."

Huginn grunted. "Stupidly short-sighted policy, if you ask me. You and Selene are as valuable as any other fifty people on their payroll. So what exactly are you looking for?"

"Mostly, I'm hoping to find a dictionary," I said. "Selene told me that Second said one of the Gold Ones had been here some-time in the past few years or decades. If they've been hanging around the Spiral, they must have a working knowledge of English or Patth or something else. Even if the Gold Ones themselves aren't the Icari, they presumably know their language. Maybe they worked up a Rosetta Stone type of thing."

"Interesting thought," Huginn murmured, staring off into infinity in concentration. "Also a real game changer. If we could read those books down there..." His eyes came back to focus. "Though you realize that there's no reason why that particular Gold One had to have been anywhere near the Spiral," he pointed out. "If he popped in via one of the portals, he could have come from anywhere in the galaxy."

"Or from anywhere in any other galaxy," I said, wincing. There was *so* much we still didn't know about the portals. "I don't suppose you took pictures of any of the books' pages."

"They took my phone and all my equipment when they locked us up, remember?" he said sourly, his eyes flicking to the phone case on my belt. "Anyway, we should probably get some sleep before Third and Rozhuhu come looking for us. Any idea what's on today's agenda?"

"You've heard everything I have," I reminded him. "Why? Something in particular you want to see?"

"I was hoping to get a closer look at the portal ring," he said. "We didn't get a chance to check them out before we were grabbed, and I'd like to rectify that." He lifted a finger in sudden thought. "It also occurs to me that we've only got Second's word that it was years since the Gold One he mentioned was here. If it was more recent than that, Selene might be able to pull the scent off whichever portal he came in through."

"Good idea," I said. "Problem: she doesn't know what the Gold Ones smell like."

"Though any unfamiliar scent would be an indicator," Huginn pointed out. He scowled in thought a moment, then suddenly brightened. "Try this. I touched several of the items in the Upper Rooms while I was looking around, including a couple of the books. Maybe she can pull the scent off my hands."

"It would have to have been a *lot* more recent than Second claimed," I warned. "A couple of weeks is about her limit."

"Yes, but that's when she's tracking someone out in the open, right?" he asked. "With weather and a hundred other scents messing with the trail. Here, it's protected and about as pristine as anything she'll ever find. I don't think even the top Ammei ever go up there."

"I don't know," I said doubtfully. "But it's worth a try. I'll talk to Selene at breakfast, assuming they serve breakfast here, and see if she can talk Second and Third into a joint tour."

"Sounds good." He yawned. "Meanwhile, it's been a long day. Sleep well." With a final nod, he disappeared back toward the common room and the other sleeping compartment, shutting the door behind him.

"And sleep quick," I called after him. Kicking off my shoes, I pulled back the heavy blanket and lay down on the bed. Huginn was right about it having been a long day. Unfortunately, it was about to get a little longer.

Huginn had gotten to the Upper Rooms ahead of me. It seemed only fair that I beat him to the library.

CHAPTER EIGHTEEN

———— ❖ ————

I gave him ten minutes to fall asleep. Then, retrieving the vine rope from beneath my bed, I slipped through the door and out into the hallway.

The library was on the south side of level three, four levels below me and on the other side of the Tower. But while I hadn't seen a lot of security inside the building, it was never a good idea to push your luck farther than you had to. The Grove of Reflection was only three floors down, and was conveniently placed above the library.

Even better, I'd noted during our tour that the grove and library both had lower window sections that looked to swivel horizontally open. With Huginn's vine in hand, it should be easy to lower myself from the one to the other.

I didn't see or hear anyone on my way down the ramps and across to the Tower's south side. The doors leading into the grove were unlocked, and I slipped inside.

The room's lights were off, but there was enough starlight twinkling in for me to navigate by. I went to one of the windows in the center of the room and looked out.

There was no movement in the city that I could see. Equally important, the sky to the east still showed starry black. I took a moment to figure out the window's opening mechanism, then swung it in a few centimeters and looked down the side of the building.

Three of the library's windows were also ajar, presumably for ventilation. The nearest one was a couple of windows to the right of my current position; closing my window, I moved over and opened that one.

Perfect. Almost as if the Ammei had deliberately set up an engraved invitation.

As my father used to say, *The plus side of walking into a trap is that they probably won't shoot at you right away.*

One of the nearby vegetation clumps featured a strong-looking sapling. I tied one end of Huginn's vine to its base, then carried the rest of the coil to my window. I got a grip on the vine, worked my way backward through the opening until my legs were dangling outside, and started down. I paused at the ajar library window, worked it the rest of the way open, and maneuvered my way inside.

Here, somewhere, was the RH directory all of us had worked so hard to retrieve.

I looked at the dark rows of dark books, my stomach tightening. Yes. Here.

Somewhere.

I walked across the room, my footsteps sounding unnaturally loud in my hypersensitive ears. Still no sign of anyone lurking about, but I couldn't imagine that convenient solitude lasting overly long. I reached the edge of the shelves and stopped, looking upward at the vast collection.

And as I contemplated the impossibility of the task I'd set for myself, I heard a muffled sound from the direction of the library door.

I dropped into a crouch, half spinning to face the door. The nearest cover was five or six steps away, and the window and any hope of escape even farther. If some Amme strolled in, I had better have one hell of a story to pitch him.

The sound was getting louder. Like distant thunder, I decided, or maybe a cart rolling toward me on one of the Tower's ramps. I could also hear Ammei voices accompanying it. The rolling sound stopped . . .

The seconds ticked by, and the library door remained closed. I could still hear the voices, now accompanied by some soft thuds and the clicking of metal against metal. Taking a deep breath, fully aware that this was dangerously stupid even by my standards, I stole across the room to the door and pressed my ear against it.

There were Ammei out there, all right. At least three of them, from the varying vocal pitches.

I chewed at the inside of my cheek. Across the hall, right where the Ammei were gathered, was the room I'd climbed past earlier with shutters welded over the windows. If the Ammei weren't coming into the library, that must be their destination.

As my father used to say, *Hiding things in plain sight is an art. Most people just settle for putting big obvious locks around the things they don't want you to see.*

There was something in that room First of Three didn't want us to see, and there was clearly no way I could sneak or talk my way inside. But if I was lucky, maybe I could still get a look.

Dropping onto my stomach alongside the wall, I stroked my left thumbnail into mirror mode and eased it under the library door.

The door was thin—doors made of Icari metal didn't have to be thick in order to do their job—and I was able to get a partial look outside. The three Ammei I'd heard were standing beside a low cart and were in the process of carrying a large curved plate toward the door across the hall. Two guards armed with belted hand weapons stood on either side, and as the three approached with their burden one of the guards gave the door a sharp double rap.

The door swung open, revealing a single large room, probably the same size as the library. In the center was a large, vaguely hemispherical object probably eight to ten meters across. Most of what I could see was composed of a loose metal grid, but there were a couple of sections that were solid metal plates perforated with cables, hoses, and equipment boxes.

Rising from the bottom of the mesh, partially obscured by the grid and the Ammei maneuvering their load through the door, was a single slender cylinder.

The door shut, cutting off my view. Silently, I got back to my feet and padded my way back to the book shelves. Whatever the Ammei were building, it clearly wasn't finished and could therefore wait. For now, it was time to refocus my full attention on finding RH.

Unless the Ammei had already done so.

I scowled that depressing thought away. No. Third and Rozhuhu had gone to a lot of effort to quietly pinpoint the library for Selene and me. That whole exercise would be pointless unless they wanted us to find something for them.

But where to start?

Like looking for a needle in a haystack, the old saying echoed through my mind. But as my father used to say, *Better to hide your needle in a tub of other needles.*

The Ammei had had a lot of time to sort through these books before Selene and I arrived, possibly as much as ten millennia. So why hadn't they found what they were looking for?

Had it been disguised somehow so that they couldn't recognize it? Did they not know what it looked like, and kept missing it in their searches?

Or had they not found it because it had never been here in the first place?

I pursed my lips. Because as my father also used to say, *Even better, point everyone at the tub of needles, and while they're looking that direction sneak yours under the nearest rock.*

I couldn't search the whole library. Not with what was left of tonight, not with a month's worth of similar tonights.

But there *was* one place where I could at least take a preliminary look. A place where something could be well and truly hidden and where the Ammei might not think to look.

If you're not sure where you lost something, look where the light is good. If it's there, you'll find it; if it's in the dark you'll probably never find it anyway. As far as I knew, my father had never said that. But he might have.

Retreating to the window, I took hold of the vine and started climbing.

I hadn't paid much attention to the grove on our first visit, barely glancing over the clumps of vegetation and the brick pathways that curved around between them, most of my thoughts and speculations on the library. Now, I took a much closer look.

The plant clusters weren't nearly as uniform as I'd remembered. Each of them seemed to be a unique mixture of various types of bushes, with narrow shrubs, tall plants, and slender but robust saplings like the one I'd used to tie my vine to. The design was reminiscent of a Zen garden or gladed rockery, though somewhat heavier on the plant life and lighter on the delicacy, sand, and stone benches of those formats. Large, ancient-looking flagstones were set into the ground on either side of the main doors, forming spiral patterns that welcomed the visitor and then guided him onto the pathways and into the grove proper. A nice, if slightly shocking touch—not really visible in the faint starlight but something I remembered from our earlier tour—was that while the soil of the grove was black or dark brown the fine dust the flagstones were embedded in was a bright yellow.

I stepped to a spot between the flagstone spirals, gazed across the room at the groups of plants, and tried to think.

If I had something the size of an Icari book to get rid of, where would I hide it?

It wasn't like there weren't possibilities. In fact, with the flagstones, the bricks, and tons of dirt it was another whole haystack up here.

I shook that conclusion away. That was amateur thinking, or the kind of thinking that someone with lots of spare time could afford to indulge in. I wasn't an amateur, and I didn't have the luxury of extra time.

But I also knew I was dealing with a professional, someone who'd done such a good job that the book had gone undiscovered for at least a few centuries. Back in my bounty hunter days, I'd been pretty good at finding people who didn't want to be found, and I had no intention of being beaten by a mere book.

I let my eyes drift across the grove, trying to put myself into the Icari mindset that had given us the clue to the location of the first, LH, half of the directory. Not under the bricks in any of the walkways, I decided. He would have had to take out too many of them, and that much tampering would likely have been noticed. Not in the dirt itself, either, because freshly turned earth was very noticeable, plus he would have had a book's worth of extra dirt to dispose of. Hiding it beneath one of the entryway flagstones would be even worse, given he would have to get rid of that much yellow dirt in a room full of black and dark-gray soil.

I felt a tight smile twitch at the corners of my mouth as something suddenly struck me. *Yellow* dirt. Or maybe *gold* dirt? As in, *the Gold Ones*?

I had no idea whether or not the Icari had a sense of humor.

Or, for that matter, whether they were aware of the Ammei name for them. But if they were, the color scheme here might indicate at least a sense of irony.

My smile faded. *Even worse,* I'd just called the flagstone option. *Flat-out impossible,* someone else might have labeled it.

But as my father used to say, *Most people never think about the impossible. If you want to be invisible, be impossible.*

I focused again on the flagstones. There were two of them, the ones in the centers of the spirals, that were big enough to hide RH beneath. I still couldn't figure out how the yellow dirt displaced by the book had been hidden, but whoever had pulled this off had found a way. Flipping a mental coin, I knelt down beside the right-hand flagstone, pulled out my multitool, and got to work.

For once, Lady Luck was feeling friendly. Four centimeters beneath the flagstone, my multitool blade hit something hard. Carefully, I scraped away the dirt and found myself looking at the distinctive cover of an Icari book. I worked my fingers beneath the edges, visualizing Kinneman's expression when I waved my prize in front of him...

I frowned. The book might have the same cover as LH, but I could tell by the feel that it was much thinner than the book Selene had dug out of the ground on Meima. Some other list, maybe, that someone had been equally eager to bury away from the universe at large? Scowling, I pulled it free of the dirt, popped the magnetic clasp, and opened the book to the middle.

One glance at the metallic pages was all the confirmation I needed that I'd indeed come up dry. There were no diagrams of portal address displays here, no side-margin descriptions of planets or worlds where the address might take an adventuresome traveler. All that was here were lines of flowing script alternating with indented sections that could be chemical formulae, technical stats, mathematical proofs, or even just random quotes or snatches of poetry that the writer had liked.

So what was here that someone had decided it desperately needed to be hidden? And which side of this intellectual tug-of-war should I be on?

As my father used to say, *Picking sides is an art. Learn the technique, but be aware that even the best usually don't do better than sixty or seventy percent.*

I didn't want to pick sides in this. I was here to find RH, and to get out safely with it and Selene. A mystery or feud going back ten thousand years wasn't one I particularly wanted to get involved with.

I frowned at the book. Or *had* it been ten thousand years?

The Gemini portal that had provided the Ammei route to Alainn and its silver-silk had been cut off only a few decades ago. If the stories Selene had heard were to be believed, one of the Gold Ones had been here within that same relatively short time span.

And suggesting that one Icari had deprived the Ammei of an important resource while another completely independent Icari had then come by and hidden an important book struck me as straining the bounds of coincidence.

Worse, simply the fact that I was holding that book in my hands edged me precariously close to that whole choosing-sides thing.

My first instinct was to put the book right back where I'd found it, erase all traces of my presence here tonight, and try to pretend this had never happened. My second instinct was to find a new hiding place, one that would create a third side—me—until I had a chance to gather more information.

But the night was waning fast, and besides I had no idea where to find a better hiding place than the one my predecessor had already created.

But maybe I could have it both ways.

The metallic pages were far tougher than regular book paper. But they weren't indestructible, and my multitool's knife was up to the task. I cut out two of the middle pages, folded them together into a tight wad, and wedged it into the secret compartment just below the elbow of my artificial left arm, the one where Selene and I used to hide bio sample vials. I reburied the book, put the flagstone back in place, and brushed all the yellow dirt that had been displaced back into the cracks between the stones. Then, retrieving the vine rope, I coiled it up and headed back to our room.

The door to Huginn's sleeping compartment was still closed. There was no way to know whether or not he was still in there, or whether he'd noted my departure and kept an invisible eye on me. But at this point I was too tired to care. I stumbled into my own compartment, slid the vine rope back into concealment under the bed, then flopped face-downward onto the mattress.

Huginn was right about getting some sleep while we could. He was also right that between the Upper Rooms, grove, and library the Ammei had the whole Tower sprinkled with mysteries. He was also right about our need to ferret out the puzzles, and do whatever we could to solve them.

But he was wrong if he thought I was going to take his descriptions, analysis, and suggestions at face value. I knew Huginn, I knew Expediters, and above all I knew Sub-Director Nask.

Huginn had some card hidden up his sleeve. I just hoped I could figure out what it was before he played it.

CHAPTER NINETEEN

———— ❖ ————

"I don't know," Selene said hesitantly, scooping up a spoonful of a fruit-flavored gelatin from her plate. "Second of Three is already suspicious. Wouldn't a request like that tip him off that we're looking for something?"

"But he won't know *what* we're looking for," Huginn pointed out. "Besides, we already know they're trying to find out why we're here. If we make it sound like searching the portal ring is a vital part of our mission, they should be more than willing to let us follow up on it, if only so they can watch."

"*My* concern is that they'll think we're trying to run out on them," I said. "We get anywhere near those portals and they'll be watching us like paranoid hawks."

"Which is fine," Huginn said. "All we need is for Selene to get close enough to identify the portal our Gold One came in through."

"*If* he came through recently enough for me to smell him," Selene warned. "That wasn't the impression I got from Second of Three."

Huginn grunted. "Like we can trust them to tell the truth. Drop your napkin, Selene, will you?"

Selene looked at me, her pupils questioning. "Go ahead," I confirmed.

"They also seem very regimented," Selene said. She lifted her napkin from her lap, fumbled it out of her grip onto the floor. Huginn bent down and retrieved it, and as he handed it back I saw him surreptitiously rub his fingertips against one edge. "They may not want their schedule changed. Thank you."

"You're welcome," Huginn said. "You got it?"

Selene lifted the napkin to her face, as if dabbing at her mouth, and I saw her nostrils and eyelashes working the cloth. "All I smell is Icari metal and the various scents of the Tower," she said.

"Try it again," Huginn said. "Maybe it's in there somewhere. Okay. Twelve portals in a ring, equally spaced apart from each other, with a mostly north-south alignment. Right?"

I thought back to the views I'd had from the various Tower windows. The positioning wasn't exactly north-south, but it was close enough. "Right. So?"

"So for our personal convenience let's number them one to twelve starting from the north and going clockwise," he said. "I'm thinking we ask to start at Number Three and work our way counterclockwise around the circle."

"And if they say no?" I asked.

"Then we'll just have to get persuasive." Huginn pushed back his chair. "While you two think of how to do that, I'm getting more of that bacon stuff."

"Be sure to leave a little for the rest of us," I said.

"Forget it," he said. "With breakfast meat, it's every man for himself."

He headed toward the buffet table the Ammei had set up for our breakfast. They'd been able to read yesterday's dinner preferences from our earlier lunch selections, but breakfast had turned out to be an entirely different menu, and they'd thus opted to run another buffet. Tomorrow's breakfast, I suspected, would likely be a repeat of our favorites from today.

"Quick summary," I muttered, holding up my own napkin to hide my lips from the Ammei waiters standing poised by the serving door. "Ixil and McKell came through last night, McKell's gone back, Ixil's still here. I got out of my room by jumping, got back in via a rope Huginn made out of vines from the grove. Question: Did he also climb down and up, or did he just dangle the rope for me and stay in the Tower all night?" I reached over and made a show of brushing an imaginary speck off her cheek, bringing my hand close to her nose and eyelashes.

"I think he used the vine," she said as I withdrew my hand. "Too much of his scent mixed there for just tying pieces together. It also smells a little sweaty, so exertion was involved."

"That could just be me."

"It's also him."

"Figured." So Huginn had snuck out of *Imistio* Tower, prowled around the city's grounds, and snuck back in again, all of which he'd carefully not mentioned to me. As expected, he had some private game going on under the table.

A game that required the three of us to get to one of the portals?

"He's also wrong about the Ammei staying out of the Upper Rooms," she continued. "There are several scents there, all very recent."

"I'm not surprised," I said. "The Upper Rooms are the perfect place to keep an eye on the portals during the day. It's only after dark that they need to put boots on the ground to watch for visitors."

"That seems reasonable," she said. "Any idea why Huginn wants to look at the portals?"

"Not a clue," I said. "Ditto as to whether Three O'clock has particular significance or whether he picked it at random. But whatever it ends up being, it'll make sense."

"To him."

"And for his purposes. Not necessarily for us and ours. Were you able to fill in the Tower map any?"

"I got most of it," she said. "I didn't get into the big room on the north side of level three, though, so I don't know what's in there."

I felt a sudden tightness in my throat. "You talking about the room opposite the library?"

"Yes," she confirmed. "Though I don't know if it's a single room. It could be subdivided inside. What's wrong?"

"I got a quick look inside last night," I said. "Oh, and as a side note it's also got floor-to-ceiling windows that have been covered over with metal plates."

"Interesting. What did you see?"

"Not much," I told her. "There's a curved object in the middle— the place *is* one room, by the way—about ten meters across and mostly made of metal gridwork. Lots of cables and equipment boxes all around, plus a thin cylinder at the bottom pointed upward."

"Interesting," she said, her pupils showing sudden thoughtful-ness. "There's definitely silver-silk inside—I could smell it under the door. There's also a lot of Icari metal."

"Like for books?"

"No, this is one of the heavier-duty versions," she said. "Like they use for portals and lightning guns."

I felt a hard knot form inside my breakfast. "You hadn't mentioned the lightning guns were made of portal metal."

"They're partly portal metal," she said, her pupils gone wary. "Partly other materials. What's wrong?"

I thought back to the brief glance I'd had under the library door. Could the cylinder I saw have been a super lightning gun? Some battlefield-level weapon?

But why build it in the middle of *Imistio* Tower? Especially since they would have to haul it down the ramps and outside if they wanted to give it a full field of fire. They'd do better to build it in one of the houses out there. No, it had to be something else. "Passing thought," I told Selene. "Never mind. Back to last night. I tried to follow the silver-silk hunter-gatherers last night, but they got in and out ahead of me. I'm pretty sure they went all the way to the end of the subway line, though, so they could have brought the night's haul to the Tower. You have the map with you?"

"Yes," she said. "Ready?"

I looked at the waiters. They were focused on Huginn, who was saying something and pointing to one of the dishes on the buffet. "Ready."

Selene set her hand briefly on the table beside me, and when she moved it away I saw she'd put the map there.

But it was no longer the folded piece of white paper I'd given her earlier. Instead, it was a muted shade of reddish brown. "Nice camouflage," I said, moving my hand casually on top of it. "Is that dirt?"

She nodded. "From a flower pot in my sleeping room." Her eyelashes fluttered briefly. "It's from the soil in front of the house. Imported there from one of the other Ammei enclaves, I think. The smell is very intriguing."

"I'll take your word for it," I said, scooping up my last bite of a sort of chocolate-laced pastry and standing up. I'd tried time and again to detect some of the rich olfactory tapestries she routinely sampled, and I'd only rarely been able to do so. On this one, I could get a hint of almost-lavender, but that was about all. "I'm going to get more of that bacon stuff. Want anything?"

I'd fully expected Second of Three to refuse Selene's request, or at least to go into private consultation with Third of Three before making a decision. To my mild surprise, he agreed instantly.

"But you will not be together," Fourth of Three reminded her. "The Second of Three and I will guide you in one direction. The Third of Three and Rozhuhu will guide Roarke and Huginn of the humans."

"What about my servants, the Iykams?" Huginn asked.

"They spent a peaceful night, and have received their morning meal," Rozhuhu said.

"I'd like them to join us," Huginn said.

"I would like that, as well," Selene added.

"That is impossible," Rozhuhu said. "Later, when we have returned to the Tower, they will rejoin you for the midday meal. But they will not join you while you are outside."

"I protest that decision," Huginn said. "They are my servants, just as Roarke and I are servants of Selene of the Kadolians."

"That is impossible," Rozhuhu repeated.

"Is it impossible for the First of Three?" Huginn asked.

Selene had tried that gambit the previous evening, the question precipitating a brief discussion before she was turned down. This time, Second and Third were ready for it. "The First of Three cannot be disturbed," Rozhuhu said.

"Why not?" Huginn asked. "It can't be too late or too early. It's full daylight outside."

"The First of Three cannot be disturbed," Rozhuhu repeated.

Huginn shot me a frustrated look. "Fine," he ground out. "But I want to see them sometime today. With or without the First of Three's permission."

"We will speak of this later," Rozhuhu said. "If you wish to see the ring, we must go now."

Huginn didn't answer, but merely stepped to my side, glowering. "We're ready," I told Rozhuhu.

Second turned and headed toward the dining room door, Fourth behind him, Selene and her usual six-Ammei guard following. Rozhuhu waited until they'd all gone a few steps, then gestured to us. "Come," he said.

Third turned and followed the first group, Rozhuhu falling into his usual position behind him, Huginn and I bringing up the rear.

And as we walked, I kept a close eye on Huginn.

It had been a good performance, I had to admit. His demand to bring the Iykams along and his growing frustration at being denied had been spot on. But to my hyper-suspicious ears, the whole thing had rung just a little bit false. Huginn knew he'd be expected to make such a request, especially after his genuine frustration the night before. But he'd surely expected Second to turn him down.

Which meant that, whatever his game plan was, he didn't need the Iykams to pull it off.

And as my father used to say, *A plan where you aren't needed can keep you out of the line of fire. It can also put you directly into a different one.*

Last night's gentle breeze had turned into a brisk wind blowing from the west toward the river. Second led us across the waving grass and bushes and down into the subway, where the usual four-car train was waiting. Second, Fourth, and Selene settled into the first car, while Third directed our lower-status group to the rearmost. The six Ammei guards took seats in the two middle cars. Fourth got the train moving down the tracks, and a couple of minutes later pulled to a stop by the pair of ramps that led to the north end of the portal ring. We got out of our cars and walked up the ramp back to the surface and the wind.

I hadn't yet been this close to the portal ring, and while the guards formed up around Second and Selene I took a moment to assess the situation.

As we'd already concluded, there were twelve portals, each presenting a dome that was the top part of a half-buried sphere. I'd tentatively concluded these portals were the smaller, dyad-style Gemini type, rather than full-range portals like Icarus and Alpha, and the twenty-meter sphere diameter indicated that it was the receiver modules that I was seeing.

Which was the only way it made sense, of course. The launch modules were crammed with equipment and as far as I knew had no exit hatches, while the receiver modules had a whole grid of them that could be opened wherever was most convenient. Flipping the portals over to put the launch modules on top would have required some kind of underground tunnel network to the receiver modules in order to get inside.

The area of nice houses began about twenty meters inward from the portal ring, forming concentric rings until they reached the lawn that surrounded the Tower. Twenty meters in the opposite direction, outside the portal ring, was the beginning of the zone of abandoned and decrepit buildings that filled the rest of the city.

There were places in the Spiral where the dividing line between affluence and poverty was equally sharp. But they were never anything less than depressing. The contrast here just underlined the bleakness of this place, and made me again wonder what had brought this city crashing down so completely.

"We have arrived," Fourth said formally when Selene and her entourage were settled. "What is here that you wish to see?"

"I wish to examine the portals," Selene told him. She pointed southeast, toward the one at Huginn's specified three o'clock position. "I will begin with that one."

"*We* will begin with that one," Huginn put in before Fourth could reply. "All of us, together."

"That is impossible," Fourth said.

"We need to be with Selene of the Kadolians," Huginn insisted. "It's for her own protection."

"Protection from what?" Fourth asked.

"From the enemies of the Kadolians," Huginn said.

Fourth turned to Second, and once again they held a brief conversation. "Selene of the Kadolians is protected," Fourth told Huginn. "You and Roarke of the humans will begin there." He pointed southwest across the ring toward the nine o'clock dome.

I looked at Huginn, saw a fresh wave of pseudo frustration flow across his face. He scowled at Fourth, then at Third, then at me. Silently, he spun on his heel and stalked across the grass toward the distant dome, Third and Rozhuhu hurrying to catch up with him. I gave Selene a lingering look, noting the mix of tension and dark amusement at Huginn's performance in her pupils, and followed.

As my father used to say, *Sometimes the best way to get someone to do something is to insist that he do the opposite.*

Huginn had gotten about ten steps before the two Ammei caught up with him. I closed to within three meters of them, then slowed just enough to start falling behind. "Slow down, will you?" I called plaintively.

"Speed up, will you?" Huginn growled back over his shoulder. "You want to be out here all day?"

"Is there difficulty?" Rozhuhu asked.

"I have a bad leg," I said, throwing just a hint of a limp into my left leg's stride.

Third said something. "Why did you did not speak of this before?" Rozhuhu translated.

"No one said we were going to be doing wind sprints before," I bit out. "I'm okay—I just need a minute."

"Oh, for—" Huginn swallowed a curse and headed back toward me. "Come on, lean on me," he said, stepping to my side and putting an arm around my waist. "No, you keep back," he added as Third and Rozhuhu started to reverse course as well. "I've got this."

"Thanks," I said, leaning my head against Huginn's shoulder as I measured distances with my eyes. The two Ammei had stopped, and while they were watching us closely they were still far enough away for what we needed. "Do you ever get tired of it being that easy?" I murmured, just loud enough for Huginn to hear.

"Do you?" he murmured back.

"Not really," I said. "What do we want at the nine o'clock?"

"Nothing," he said. "How's your sprinting technique?"

"Adequate. Where are we sprinting?"

"I'll let you know."

"What do you speak?" Rozhuhu called.

"He's telling me it hurts," Huginn called back. "I'm telling him to man up and get his act together."

"I'll be okay," I said, grunting for effect as I disentangled myself from his hands. I didn't much like the idea of charging into someone else's plan without knowing all the details, but we'd already pushed this conversation as far as I dared. Hopefully, Huginn and I would find or make another opportunity down the line to fill in the blanks.

A few minutes later we reached our target portal. "What is here that you wish to see?" Rozhuhu asked.

"Everything," Huginn said. "Every dome in the ring, starting with this one."

"After that, we may want to examine some of those buildings, too," I added, pointing toward the inner ring of houses. "Though that part will depend on what we see around the domes."

Third said something. "That is impossible," Rozhuhu translated.

"What if Selene of the Kadolians wishes it?" I asked.

"That is impossible," Rozhuhu repeated.

"Yeah, we'll see," Huginn said. "Come on, Roarke. Try to keep up."

He began to circle the portal, staying a couple of meters back from the dome's edge. I followed more slowly, mostly also keeping my distance from the portal but occasionally moving in for a closer look at the metal. Once I stopped completely, squatting down and fingering the grass and dirt that was pressed up against the dome.

None of the places I studied looked any different from any of the others, either on the portal or on the ground. But I figured I might as well put on a good show. On top of that, I was curious to see if I could do something that Third or Rozhuhu would declare off-limits or otherwise impossible, which might give me a better handle on what we were and weren't allowed to see or know.

But the chief goal of the exercise was for my slower pace to force the two Ammei to split their attention. As Huginn's faster walk took him away from me toward the edge of the dome, Third and Rozhuhu held a hurried discussion that ended with Third staying with me and Rozhuhu hurrying to catch up with Huginn. A moment later, the two of them disappeared around the side, leaving Third and me alone.

I still didn't know what kind of diversion Huginn had planned. But whatever it was, it would almost certainly be easier to pull off with only one set of eyes watching him.

The magic trick hadn't happened by the time Third and I finished our circle and arrived at our original starting position. Huginn and Rozhuhu were waiting there, the former watching me closely as I came in view. "Well?" he called. "Anything?"

"Not here," I said as Third and I rejoined them. "Maybe the next one."

"Maybe the next one," Huginn repeated. He looked at Third and pointed to the eight o'clock portal. "We'll do that one next."

He got two steps before Third snapped something that sent Rozhuhu scurrying to block his path. "What do you seek?" the Amme asked. "The Third of Three offers his assistance."

"There's nothing he can do," Huginn said.

"It's difficult to explain," I added, trying for a bit more diplomacy. "But assure the Third of Three that we'll know it when we see it."

Third said something else. Rozhuhu answered, and for a moment they talked back and forth. Then, Third gestured toward the portal Huginn had identified. "We will go now," Rozhuhu said, stepping out of Huginn's path.

"Fine," Huginn said shortly and resumed his stride. I followed, remembering to maintain a vestige of my earlier limp.

We reached the portal and repeated our divide-and-conquer routine. This one didn't seem to suit Huginn's diversionary purposes, either. We rendezvoused at the beginning of our separate circumnavigations, I again told them my investigation had turned up negative, and we moved on to the seven o'clock portal.

"Third time's the charm," Huginn announced as we approached the dome. "I have a feeling we're about to get lucky."

"I hope you're right," I said, feeling my heartrate pick up a little. Apparently, this was it. "Just don't get your hopes too high."

"*You* just keep a sharp eye," he countered. "If this is it—" He broke off, giving Third and Rozhuhu a sideways look. "Just keep a sharp eye."

"Right." Whatever Huginn had planned, he was playing his chosen role to the hilt.

We reached the dome and he shifted into his now familiar circular walk. I settled into mine, pausing more often and peering more closely at the dome and the land around it than I had before. Three, in response, seemed to also be paying closer attention to my imaginary studies. We all finished circling the dome.

Only this time I found Huginn and Rozhuhu waiting on the east side of the portal instead of on the northwest side where we'd started. "Over here, Roarke," Huginn called, beckoning as Third and I walked up. "What do you think about this?" He pointed to the base of the dome.

I had just focused on the spot when, without warning, a muffled *crack* came from the western side of the portal, the area directly opposite us. I frowned—

As the whole area exploded into a massive white cloud. For a second the smoke billowed outward and upward, dwarfing the ten-meter height of the portal dome as it clawed its way toward the sky. Then the westerly wind caught it, and the cloud rolled over into a roiling river of white. It flowed over and past the portal toward the four of us, washed over us—

I felt a hand grab my right wrist. "Come on," Huginn's soft voice came, tugging me in the direction of the flow. "Side edge; back hinge."

There wasn't time for questions. I obeyed, taking off into the fog alongside him as he urged us into the sprint he'd hinted at earlier. The gas had some of the same carbonized sugar smell as the smoke shell McKell and Ixil had dropped on us way back on Pinnkus, which meant it was designed to provide visual camouflage and not to kill or disable.

Though right now I was more concerned about the possibility of being killed or disabled by running full-tilt into something solid. Hopefully, Huginn had paid better attention to the landscape and obstacles on our way from the subway than I had and would keep us from a sudden and highly embarrassing death.

Because it was for sure that we weren't going to outrun the smoke. I could still feel the wind against the back of my neck as we sprinted along, which meant the air and smoke were moving faster than we were. As long as we were going this direction we weren't getting into clear air until the stream finally dissipated.

In the distance I could hear alien shouts and rapid-fire sentences, angry or frightened, I couldn't tell which. I hoped part of the frantic activity was focused on getting Selene away from the smoke before her hypersensitive sense of smell was overwhelmed and all but incapacitated her. I'd started off trying to number my steps, but I'd quickly lost track and I now had no idea where we were. I had the vague feeling that we should be close to one of the portals on the far side of the ring, probably either the four or five o'clock, possibly the three or six.

And then, abruptly, a second hand grabbed my left wrist.

My pace faltered with surprise, nearly sending me pitching forward onto my face. Had Rozhuhu found us? Third? One of the Ammei guards?

I was still trying to sort it out when the hand on my left wrist yanked me forward, forcing me back into a run. Two steps later, Huginn's grip vanished from my right wrist.

Again, I had to fight to keep from stumbling as my brain spun with uncertainties. Had Huginn been captured? Three and Rozhuhu should still be well behind us, but with all the houses blocking our view I hadn't been able to see where all of Selene's guards were when Huginn set off his smoke bomb. Had one of them managed to intercept us?

But the mystery hand on my left wrist was still hurrying me along, without any indication that the owner wanted to stop me. Had Huginn passed me off to someone else?

The problem was that the only allies he should have available were his three Iykams. Had they managed to break out of confinement without anyone noticing or raising an alarm?

I started to call to Huginn, realized in time that if we were trying to avoid detection the last thing I wanted was to loudly announce my current position. Clenching my teeth against my increasingly strained breathing, I regained my balance and got back into the rhythm of the run.

Whoever my new guide was, he clearly had a plan. A few steps after Huginn's departure, he gave my wrist a gentle but persistent push, not letting up until he'd shifted our vector a few degrees to the right. I had the sense of other bodies now moving around us—there was a soft but teeth-jarring squeak from somewhere in front of me—

Abruptly, my guide yanked back on my wrist. I took the cue and braked to a halt. He gave me another gentle nudge forward, and two cautious steps later I felt my feet suddenly leave dirt and grass and hit something with the less yielding but slightly bouncy feel of wood. There was another creak, this time from behind me, and the wind that had been pushing steadily at my back was suddenly cut off. My guide swung around in front of me, and with his other hand deftly drew my plasmic from its sheath. The remnant of the white fog dissipated, and I found myself in the middle of a large room in one of the city's dilapidated houses.

And I wasn't alone.

My new guide, the one Huginn had handed me off to, the one still gripping my wrist, turned out to be a woman. She was slender and surprisingly attractive, her black hair tied back out of the way in a short ponytail. But her grip was strong, her bare arms showed a lot of wiry muscle, and her expression was the same coolly calculating global awareness I'd seen time and again on Huginn and other Patth Expediters. Behind her were two Iykams, both with corona guns ready for action. Behind them were a pair of Patth, one of them apparently trying to brush bits of smoke off his elaborately tooled duster tunic, the other more modestly dressed one staring at me.

And the look on his face...

I felt a shiver run up my back. I was hardly an expert on the nuances of Patth expressions, but I'd seen enough pure hatred to know what it looked like.

I cleared my throat. "Hello, everyone," I said as calmly as I could. "My name's Roarke. Welcome to Nexus Six."

"We know," the woman said, still holding my wrist. "Be a good boy and keep quiet, okay? Get over here—"

"Kill him," the Patth glaring daggers at me interrupted.

The woman turned a frown on him. "Excuse me?"

"I said kill him," the Patth repeated. "He is Gregory Roarke. He is a threat to the Patthaaunutth." He slapped the backs of his fingertips insistently against the shoulder of the nearest Iykam. "You will kill him.

"You will kill him *now*."

CHAPTER TWENTY

"Later," the woman said briskly. She twisted my wrist slightly, the move turning me toward a four-meter-wide section of ceiling that had come down and was resting at an angle against the floor. "Over there—that section. Open it up."

"Open it up how?" I asked, my mind flipping between the sudden appearance of this new group, the woman's strange order, and my apparently imminent death.

"He didn't tell you?" she asked.

"You mean Huginn? Of course not—no, hang on," I interrupted myself. Huginn's last incomprehensible words...

I looked at the angled section of ceiling with fresh eyes. *Side edge; back hinge.*

This time I saw it. A part of the ceiling right at the edge that had cracked off from the main part was drooping to the side, conveniently closing the triangle-shaped gap between ceiling and floor. "There," I said, pointing with my free hand. "That's our way in."

"Show me," the woman ordered, releasing my arm.

I stepped over to the collapsed ceiling, studying the suspicious flap. *Back hinge...*

There it was. The hinge was at the upper rear, right where the flap rested against the wall. The hinge itself looked as old as the rest of the house, but I could tell from the area around the screws that it had recently been moved to that position. Huginn and his Iykams had evidently been busy little bees before the Ammei caught them. I looked at the side of the flap opposite the hinge, searching for a hidden catch.

I found it, fumbled at it a moment until I figured out how it worked, then pressed at the proper spot. With a soft click it came free. I got my fingertips under the edge and pulled, and the whole flap swung neatly open. "There," I said, peering into the gap behind the ceiling section.

From the outside, it hadn't looked like there was anywhere near enough room for even a single person to hide in, let alone six of us. But in this case, appearances were deceptive. Looking into the space from this angle, assuming we were all willing to get cozy, there should be more than enough room.

I gestured. "Ladies first?"

"Prisoners first," she corrected. "Go."

I nodded and eased gingerly through the opening, walking sideways all the way to the solid wall at the far end. The woman was right behind me, with the angry Patth, the well-dressed Patth, and the two Iykams following. A few seconds of jockeying for position as we arranged ourselves more or less comfortably in the limited space, and then the last Iykam in line pulled the hidden door closed behind him.

Not a moment too soon. The catch had barely reengaged when I heard the familiar squeak of the door opening and felt the vibration of hurried footsteps through the floor. There was a staccato exchange of Ammei voices, then more hurried footsteps as they rushed off to search other parts of the building.

Beside me, the woman took my hand and squeezed a warning. I squeezed back reassuringly. Whatever Huginn was up to, I didn't want the Ammei catching us in here, either.

The search was brief. Barely a minute after the footsteps charged in they charged out again, the Ammei not bothering to close the door behind them. Their hurry was eminently understandable, given that the smoke from Huginn's bomb would have washed over a lot of real estate before it dissipated. That offered an intimidatingly large number of ruins I could have disappeared into, and they needed to search all of them.

The other possibility being that I'd popped into one of the two or three portals that had been similarly concealed and vanished from Nexus Six completely. That was probably the conclusion Huginn had been trying to guide them to. It would certainly be the logical deduction after all the likely buildings had been cleared. At that point...

I frowned in the darkness. Actually, at that point I had no idea what was supposed to happen. I just hoped that Huginn's plan didn't include one of the Iykams shooting me.

I gave the stillness another two minutes. Then, I leaned closer to the woman and put my lips to her ear. "I hope you were joking," I whispered, "about discussing my death with your friend later."

"I'm *not* joking about strangling you here and now if you don't shut up," she whispered back. "They could still be nearby."

"Sure," I whispered. "Just bear in mind that you still need me. Alive."

She huffed out a quiet grunt and fell silent. I took the cue and did likewise. It was, I decided reluctantly, going to be a long afternoon.

I would have given it an hour before venturing back out into the open air. The woman gave it three. Finally, with a gesture and a whispered word, she indicated the all-clear.

Even then we didn't just stroll casually out. The two Iykams slipped through the secret door, closing it behind them while they presumably checked the house and the perimeter. "No noise once we're out," the woman murmured a warning.

"Wouldn't dream of it," I assured her.

"And once we're settled in," she added, "you can give me your reasons why I shouldn't let Conciliator Uvif kill you."

I winced as the memories abruptly came roaring back. I'd *thought* the angry Patth looked familiar, but I hadn't been able to place him. Not surprising, really, given that I hadn't known Uvif very long and his face hadn't stuck with me.

But the incident in question certainly had. Landon Station; the *Ruth* putting down in hopes of using the crop researchers' private StarrComm center to find out why our passenger Nikki was seemingly being targeted by every bounty hunter in the Spiral; the discovery that the Patth were searching for a portal on the other side of the planet and were effectively in control of the station; Uvif trying to detain us; us outmaneuvering him and escaping.

I hadn't thought much about the incident since then, though to be fair we'd had plenty of more urgent things to focus on. Apparently, Uvif had taken it much more to heart.

Of course, for me it had been little more than a minor speed bump in a highly bumpy few weeks. For Uvif, it had been a humiliation, possibly a loss of prestige or rank, and a generally traumatic event. I would guess that he remembered every millisecond of it.

Small wonder that he wanted me dead.

As my father used to say, *Sooner or later your past will catch up with you. Sometimes it will catch up with you at high speed and try to run you over.*

The door to our hideaway opened. One of the Iykams looked in and muttered a couple of Patth words, and Uvif and the other Patth started easing their way out. The woman tapped my hand and followed. Fleetingly, I wondered if I would be better off if I just stayed where I was, realized it would just make it easier for Uvif to shoot me, and moved out behind her.

The Iykam led us to the back part of the house and a relatively spacious inner room that I guessed had once either been a walk-in closet or an exercise area. There were no windows, the walls seemed to be reinforced, and there was just the one door.

And from the look of the lower walls where the baseboards had been, I guessed the room had also once been the proud owner of a silver-silk mesh.

"Over there," the woman ordered, pointing to the wall farthest from the door. "Make yourself comfortable. We've got some time before act two of this little drama. Tell me why you think we need to keep you alive."

When Huginn first set off his smoke bomb I hadn't had a clue what any of this was about. But three hours standing silently in an oversized crypt had given me a lot of time to think, and I'd finally figured it out.

Or at least, I hoped so. One way or the other, we were about to find out.

"Because Expediter Huginn's plan needs a bad guy," I told her. "Can we have some introductions, by the way? I really don't want to keep thinking of you as Bright Eyes."

Uvif stirred and muttered something under his breath. But the woman merely twitched a small smile. "Huginn's reports don't do you justice," she said. "I'm Circe. You can call me...well, call me Circe. This is Conciliator Fearth, representing Sub-Director Nask. Conciliator Uvif you already know."

"Yes, we had an unfortunate meeting a year or so ago," I murmured. So both Fearth and Uvif were the same rank in the Patth hierarchy.

So why was Fearth dressed so much better than Uvif?

Actually, come to think of it, a bit of tweaking of my theory would explain the wardrobe discrepancy quite well.

"But as I was saying, Huginn needs a bad guy," I continued. "Someone he can point to and loudly declare to be off doing all manner of evil things. Someone who the Ammei should be afraid of. Afraid enough of, in fact, that they should turn to Huginn and his people for help."

I gestured in the direction of the portal ring. "I'm the one who set off the smoke bomb so that I could slip into one of the portals out there and escape, presumably to gather an army to come back and take over the city. Fortunately for the Ammei, the Patth have just arrived"—I gestured to Fearth—"and are here to save the day."

"Very good," Circe said. Her voice was vaguely mocking, but I could also hear a hint of approval. "And why exactly does this plan require us to keep you alive?"

"Because disposing of bodies is tricky work," I said. So I *had* gotten it right, or at least was close enough. "Especially since the Ammei monitor the whole area from the Tower by day and from the portal ring by night. Even more especially since corona guns create an ungodly stink that no one is going to mistake for anything but carnage."

"So you came back and we caught and killed you," Circe said calmly. "How does that hurt the plan?"

"Why did I come back without my army?" I countered. "More crucially, who exactly shot me?"

"We did," Uvif bit out. "We saw you try to enter the portal and stopped you?"

I shook my head. "Sorry, but it's too late for that story. If you'd just happened to come out of your own portal as I was trying to escape you should have emerged triumphant from the smoke three hours ago. The way the timing works now, you popped in long after the search was over, probably while Huginn was presenting his dire warnings of what I was up to."

"It's an interesting theory," Circe said. "But it's all speculation."

"Not at all," I said. "Furthermore, I would argue that the fact that Conciliator Fearth is dressed in full formal regalia while Conciliator Uvif is in more modest clothing shows that Huginn *wanted* me kept alive. You, Circe, were to escort him into the Ammei presence while Uvif and his Iykams were to sit on me and keep me from getting lonely."

"I don't care what Expediter Huginn wants," Uvif said stiffly. "He is an Expediter. I am a conciliator. My orders supersede his."

"Calm yourself, Conciliator," Fearth put in. "The human makes a compelling case—"

"You have not had dealings with this human, Conciliator Fearth," Uvif cut him off. "Furthermore, you do not outrank me." He shifted his glare to Circe. "Nor do you, Expediter Circe. If I declare this human's life to be forfeit, it is forfeit. And I do so declare." He gestured to the Iykams. "Kill him."

"You may be right about your traveling companions not out-ranking you," I spoke up quickly. "But I can tell you who *does*."

"You?" Uvif scoffed. "Your precious Alien Portal Agency? Your human Commonwealth?"

"No," I said. "Sub-Director Nask. And he also wants me kept alive."

The room went silent. Uvif, predictably, recovered first. "Does he really?" he demanded. "You, a mere human—?"

"I, a mere human who's been of great service to him and the Patth over the years," I cut him off. "The very damn portal you took to get here was only yours because Huginn and I made a deal. I think Sub-Director Nask would be very upset if I died for no reason." I looked Uvif squarely in the eye. "Injured pride doesn't count."

The mahogany red of Uvif's face went a couple of shades darker. But this time, it was Circe who got there first. "You make a good case," she said calmly. "Especially the part about appeal-ing to Sub-Director Nask. Fine. For now, at least, you stay alive."

She looked pointedly at Uvif. "Alive *and* unharmed," she added. "Expediter Huginn has a long history of improvisation on his jobs, and he might yet find a use for our friend here."

Uvif spat something in Patth. "On the contrary," Circe said coolly. "I think he asked for me because I know how he thinks and therefore can anticipate his plans."

"Not just a pretty face, then," I murmured, just to see what kind of reaction I would get.

In one way, it was disappointing. She turned and looked at me with a speculative, almost amused expression, without even a hint of annoyance or discomfiture. But in another way, it was exactly the response I expected from a seasoned Patth Expediter. Circe knew who she was, she recognized her strengths and abilities, and she didn't need to prove herself to anyone. Particularly not to a prisoner.

As my father used to say, *Ego, greed, and stubbornness are ninety percent of the levers you'll ever need. Beware of the ten percent those levers don't work on.*

Fearth asked a question. "A few more hours," Circe replied in English. "We'll wait until it's nearly dark and the Tower watchers have been pulled off duty. When we leave we'll go out the back and work our way around the outer edges of the dead zone, get through the portal ring, and go to the Tower."

Fearth spoke again. "Not a problem," Circe said. "I can spin a story about how we got out of our portal without being seen."

Uvif put in something. "No, we're not pitching them your hunting story," she said with a hint of strained patience. "Roarke stays alive and unharmed. Understood?" she added, this time including the two Iykams in her gaze.

There were three affirmations, Uvif's clearly reluctant, the Iykams' just as clearly perfunctory. "Good," Circe said. "Everyone relax. Repack your gear if you want—when we leave this building we're on stage. Roarke, might as well make yourself comfortable. You're going to be here a while."

Fearth moved to one of the side walls and sat down. Pulling out a pair of flat body packs from under his duster, he started to lay out their contents on the floor beside him. The two Iykams also pulled out packs. Uvif gave me another couple of seconds of hard, bitter glare, then stomped over to a corner by himself and started fiddling with his own gear. I picked a section of floor that looked slightly less lumpy than the rest and eased myself down, resting my back against the wall.

"You all right?" Circe asked.

"As all right as current circumstances allow," I said. "Thanks for keeping me in the conversational loop, by the way. You could have just kept going in Patth."

"It's a politeness thing," Circe said with a small shrug. "Nothing to do with you personally."

"Understood," I said. "I still appreciate it. I'm sure Huginn would, too."

"You're welcome." Her eyes flicked over to Uvif. "I don't know how much you got from what Uvif said, but just for the record he was wrong. Huginn didn't request me for this job. It was Sub-Director Nask himself."

I frowned up at her. "Really? Why?"

She shrugged again. "No idea. You can ask him when you see him." She paused. "Assuming you survive."

I felt a knot settle into my stomach. "Any reason in particular why I shouldn't?"

"There are the Ammei," she said. "Who knows what they want and how they intend to get it?"

"And there's Conciliator Uvif?"

Her lips compressed briefly. "Unfortunately, he's right," she said reluctantly. "I can warn and even threaten, but I can't give a conciliator orders. If he chooses to defy me—and doesn't mind making an enemy of Sub-Director Nask—there's nothing I can do about it."

"I would hope Sub-Director Nask has some consequences he could bring to bear."

"I'm sure he does," Circe agreed. "But that wouldn't help you, would it? The point remains that if Uvif's willing to risk it, there's nothing official I can do."

I felt my ears prick up. So now there was nothing *official* she could do? Did that mean there might be something unofficial in her bag of tricks?

I didn't know, and I certainly wasn't going to ask. As my father used to say, *Nothing draws the wrong kind of attention than using the word* unofficial *in a conversation.*

"I appreciate the honesty," I said. "So what you're saying is that I'm in charge of my own defense?"

"That's usually how life works," Circe said. "Bearing in mind the consequences, of course."

"Of course," I said. "And I assume the Iykams you're leaving with him will obey him instantly?"

"Maybe not *instantly,*" she said. "They heard my warnings, too. But they probably will eventually."

"Got it," I said. "I appreciate the heads-up."

She gave me a sort of wry smile. "You appreciate a lot, don't you?"

"I'm just that kind of guy."

"Yes. Pockets?"

I pulled out my info pad, notebook, flashlight, and multitool and set them on the floor. Her eyes flicked over everything, lingered a moment on my empty plasmic holster, then gestured for me to put it all away again. She gave me a small nod, then turned and walked over to Fearth. She crouched down in front of him and began sorting through the gear he'd laid out, conversing with him in low voices.

I focused on Uvif. He was still sitting with his back to me, and while my knowledge of Patth body language was even less detailed than my knowledge of their facial expressions I didn't doubt for a minute that he was ready to risk whatever it took to blot out the stain of Landon Station. Or if not the entire stain, at least me.

With a sigh I slipped off my jacket and folded it into a pillow, then stretched out on my back. As Circe had said, I might as well get comfortable.

And as I gazed at the broken and warped ceiling, I tried to think.

Selene would know what had happened the instant Circe and Fearth arrived, of course. Circe had gripped my wrist and held my hand, not to mention standing shoulder to shoulder with me for three hours, all of which meant that my scent was all over her. She would know Circe had taken me and was holding me incommunicado somewhere.

But then what? Would she call Circe on it? Would that gain her anything?

Alternatively, she could play along. But would *that* gain her anything?

Muddying the water even more was the fact that Huginn knew Selene was there and that she would smell me on Circe. He must be counting on some reaction from her.

But which one?

On the other hand, Huginn presumably *didn't* know that Ixil was here. Could Selene somehow get word to him?

Better yet, could *I* get word to him?

Because wherever he'd gone to ground, he'd surely spotted Huginn's smoke screen. He'd be watching closely to see what happened next.

Unless he'd gone down to the river to link up with McKell and whatever force Kinneman had sent.

I hissed out a quiet breath. With two Patth now on the ground, plus an extra Expediter and a couple more Iykams, a show of EarthGuard muscle was the last thing I wanted.

But right now there was nothing I could do about it. Maybe after Circe and Fearth left, I'd find a way to slip Uvif's leash and find Ixil.

I looked over at Circe, still in deep conversation with Fearth. She'd said they were going to wait until nightfall.

I had that long to come up with a plan.

I'd traveled to a lot of worlds in my time as a bounty hunter, and along the way I'd learned how to quickly get a feel for the local circadian rhythms. So when Circe and Fearth finally headed out, I didn't need the single quick look I got through the house's back door to know the sun had just set in the western sky.

Which meant that the Tower beacon was about to light up.

I didn't know whether or not that aspect of the Nexus Six routine had come up in whatever private communications Circe had had with Huginn. If it hadn't, she was in for a surprise.

But that was her problem. Mine was staying alive, and with the whole city about to be bathed in gentle light Uvif's plans for me would have to go back on hold for the next two hours. Our current hiding place was too close to the portals and portal guards for him to risk killing me in here, and if there was any cloud cover at all out there the beacon's light would reflect off it and make the whole area too bright for him to risk moving me.

Which meant I had those same two hours to fine-tune my plan. I shifted a little, easing my back against the lumpy floor—

"You," Uvif said. "Human."

I opened my eyes. Uvif was standing across the room beside the doorway, the two Iykams flanking him with their corona weapons drawn. "On your feet," the Patth ordered.

I sighed. Unless, of course, he decided he didn't care about the risk. Apparently, my plan wasn't going to get those two hours of fine-tuning after all.

But that was fine. I usually ended up running things on the fly anyway.

"About time," I said, wincing as I levered myself up off the floor. Several hours of lying on a hard surface hadn't done my back any favors. "The clock's ticking, and there's something I need to show you."

Uvif seemed to twitch. "What do you say?" he demanded.

"I said there's something I need to show you," I said, taking a step toward him.

"Stop," he snapped. "Do not come nearer."

"Fine," I said, taking another short step before stopping. I was still too far away to deal with a pair of armed Iykams, but my casualness about obeying Uvif's order would hopefully impress him with my lack of fear of him, which should in turn suggest that what I had to offer would convince him I was worth keeping alive.

On the other hand, my brief interactions with him at Landon Station hadn't left an impression of great imagination. I needed to make sure that the dots I wanted him to connect were big enough. "I'll say it again. There's something you or Conciliator Fearth need to see, something the Director General needs to know about. I realize you and I have had our differences in the past, and—"

"You speak of public humiliation as *differences*?"

"—and I understand your anger about that," I continued, passing over the fact that if I hadn't outmaneuvered him the way I had, Nikki would most likely have gone ahead and slaughtered everyone on the base. "But as I say, the Director General needs to know about this, and I frankly don't trust Conciliator Fearth."

He frowned at me. "Why not?"

"Because he strikes me as the ambitious type who'll step over anyone to climb the ladder," I said. "Am I wrong?"

"What about Expediter Circe?" he asked, ignoring my question.

"I trust her even less," I said. "Expediters won't just climb the ladder over you. They'll stab you in the back on the way up."

"Yet you claim you trust me?"

I held out my hands, palms upward. "Like I said, I need *someone* to get this information to the Director General. The fact that you don't like me is actually in your favor, since you'll take an extra close look at the information I'm presenting. If you're convinced it's as important as I say, you'll be able to convince the Director General."

"And how will you benefit?" Uvif asked. "Do not expect me to believe you help the Patthaaunutth from the abundance of your heart."

"Not at all," I assured him. "I'm doing it for money, pure and simple. Sub-Director Nask will tell you that's my guiding principle."

For a few heartbeats he stared at me. The Iykams' corona weapons, I noted, hadn't wavered a single millimeter from their focus. "Tell me what this information consists of," Uvif said at last.

I shook my head. "It would be better for me to show you."

"Tell me or die here."

I sighed, letting my shoulders slump a little with resignation. I'd known this was coming, and was ready for it.

Or at least as ready as I could be. This next step was both the most crucial and the most speculative part of my story, and I'd have preferred to wait until we were at least outside before I had to take it. But Uvif wasn't going to budge without me giving him *something*. "I can tell you this much," I said, mentally crossing my fingers. "It has to do with silver-silk."

As reactions went, Uvif's wasn't all that impressive. He gave a little twitch from the waist up, a motion I'd occasionally seen on other Patth, and his lower facial muscles tightened for maybe half a second. Barely a flicker, and immediately gone.

But it was all that I needed, and was frankly more than I'd expected. My gut feeling was that he wasn't placed highly enough to know why silver-silk was so important, either to the Ammei or the Patth, but that he'd heard enough about the stuff to know that it *was* somehow significant.

Which was a shame. I didn't know how silver-silk fit into this puzzle, either, and I'd hoped I could worm some of those secrets out of him.

But as my father used to say, *You can sometimes get someone to spill the beans, but if all he's got is gravel it's not going to be worth the effort.*

Predictably, Uvif tried to bluff. "What does silver-silk have to do with the Patthaaunutth?" he asked.

"If you don't know, it's not my job to tell you," I said. "Do you want to see what the Ammei are up to, or not?"

He hesitated another couple of seconds, then gave a single nod. "If you are lying, my servants will kill you."

"Understood," I said. Not that he'd had any other plan for me, but I could appreciate a good threat as well as anyone. "We'll go out the back way, then head toward the river."

"The silver-silk is in the river?"

"It's *near* the river," I corrected, starting walking again. "It's easier to show you than to explain."

Though of course I wouldn't be explaining *or* showing. Heading straight east from this part of the city would put us a few kilometers south of the pier where our vac suits were presumably still hidden. The minute we hit the riverbank I would kick up a diversion and go straight into the water, traveling as much below the surface as I could. Once I reached the pier, I would suit up, swim back to Alpha and thence to Icarus, and do whatever groveling it took to beg, borrow, or steal enough EarthGuard Marines to storm the tower and get Selene out of there. Once we were out of the line of fire, Kinneman would be welcome to take on Fearth and Uvif however he wanted to.

The trick, as always, was to make sure neither of the Iykams shot me before the scheme even got started. That meant being docile and cooperative right up to the point where I wasn't.

Uvif and the Iykams stepped aside as I walked over to the door, reforming behind me as I walked through. "Back door's this way, right?" I asked over my shoulder, pointing in the direction Fearth and Circe had disappeared earlier.

"Yes," Uvif said. "Do not think you can escape even in the dark of night."

"With all the money the Director General is going to give me still on the table?" I countered. "Wouldn't dream of it." I reached the door, got a grip on the edge, and pulled.

The hinges gave a small rumble, much less tooth-jarring than the noise the front door had made when we first we'd entered the house all those hours ago. More importantly, it was quiet enough that the Ammei guarding the portals nearby wouldn't hear and come running. Outside, the city was bathed in the faint glow coming from the beacon's light reflecting off the overhead clouds. Letting out a breath I hadn't realized I was holding, I stepped into the doorway.

And stopped dead in my tracks.

The Ammei guards didn't need to come running. Their representatives were already here.

Facing me at ground level, spread out around the door like a crowd facing a stage show, were at least twenty of the ferret-like tenshes. Standing silent and motionless.

Gazing straight at me.

CHAPTER TWENTY-ONE

———— ✦✦✦ ————

I don't know how long I stood there. Probably only a couple of seconds, but it felt like a dip into eternity. I stared back at the tenshes, my mind flashing back to Fourth of Three taking Selene off for her tour, remembering how the tenshes accompanying him had gone into back-arched threatening mode the instant I made a move toward him.

Rozhuhu had assured us that the animals were tame. But even if he'd been telling the truth—and I wasn't exactly brimming with confidence at Ammei honesty—that didn't mean the ones in the abandoned part of the city weren't dangerously feral.

And I knew full well that there were plenty of ferret-sized creatures in the Spiral that were extremely dangerous, especially when they gathered into hunting packs.

"Why do you stop?" Uvif demanded in my ear.

"That," I said, nodding toward the silent watchers.

He made a strange sort of choking hiss. "What are they?"

"The Ammei call them *tenshes*," I said. "Seem to be little furry sidekicks."

"Are they dangerous?"

I opened my mouth to tell him, no, at least not according to the Ammei.

And then, just in time, I realized there was a much better way to play this.

As my father used to say, *If you end up in the center of unwanted attention, try to find something that worries them even more than you do.*

"If you could see their teeth and claws better you wouldn't ask that," I said grimly. "Damn. They look like they're there to stay, too."

I frowned. They *did* look like they were there to stay, come to think about it. In fact, as I looked more closely, I saw that they weren't focused on me at all, as I'd first assumed. Instead, those beady little eyes were all focused lower, specifically on the half-rotted, one-by-two-meter porch stretching out from the back door. Like they were Earth cats, and some very interesting mouse was hiding under there.

And then, I finally got it.

I shifted my gaze to the section of floor Uvif and I were standing on. Like the rest of the main house, it was constructed of more of the same wood planking. There were gaping holes in the boards, particularly at the edges and around the nail holes, but there were plenty of mostly intact chunks mixed in.

Stretching outward from where I was standing to the door's threshold was exactly what I needed: a mostly solid, meter-long board five centimeters wide and maybe three thick. "I guess we'll just have to move them," I said, motioning Uvif back from the door. "A couple of steps, if you would?"

"What do you think to do?" Uvif asked, his eyes still on the silent tenshes as he and the Iykams complied.

"Like I said, persuade them to leave," I told him. Crouching down, I slipped my fingers through a couple of conveniently placed holes and got my fingers under the edges of the board. I braced myself and carefully pulled upward. There was a muffled *snap*, and two thirds of the board came up in my hands. Beneath the house, I could see now, was a shallow crawlspace maybe fifteen centimeters deep separating the building from the ground below.

"There we go," I said briskly. I straightened up and swung the board back and forth, pretending I was testing its weight and balance. "Yes. This will do nicely."

But even as I waved the board around in an attempt to draw my companions' eyes, my own attention was on the hole I'd just made in the floor. If I was reading the geometry right, the crawlspace should also extend beneath the porch that the tenshes were so interested in.

It did. Just as I swung my board in a particularly imposing arc I saw something stir right at the edge of the hole, presumably arriving from the porch area. Two somethings, actually.

Pix and Pax.

I breathed out a quiet sigh of cautious hope. Ixil had said he would stay on Nexus Six while McKell went back to Icarus to report, but Kinneman could easily have ordered that the Kalix instead return to Icarus, an order that would likely have been delivered by a few Marines.

But Ixil was still here. More than that, he'd apparently witnessed my unplanned disappearing act and moved his outriders close enough to hear at least some of what Fearth and Circe were planning.

Unfortunately, that still left a couple of crucial gaps in my knowledge. Did he have an extraction plan ready for me? Or was he leaving that up to me and had simply sent in Pix and Pax on the off chance I could find a use for them?

As my father used to say, *Close friends are the ones you can always rely on. Make sure you're always your own closest friend.*

I studied the little creatures sitting in the darkness staring up at me. I had a use for them, all right. The question was whether I could get them to understand what I needed.

There was only one way to find out.

"Okay," I said, finishing my practice swings and turning back toward the door. "You three wait here. I'll go clear us a path."

"Stop," Uvif said quickly. "If they are servants of the Ammei, will their masters not be close at hand? If so, an overt attack will draw their attention."

"Good point," I agreed, taking a half step forward into the doorway where I could get a clearer look outside and also block Uvif's own view. With Pix and Pax no longer having a staring contest with the tenshes from under the porch's edge, the other animals were starting to lose interest and wander away. "But we can't just stay here, either, especially not if there are Ammei nearby patrolling the streets. I guess we either use the front door or give up on getting our hands on all that silver-silk."

"There are Ammei also on the other side of the building," one of the Iykams spoke up.

"Right, but their main job is to make sure no one goes in or out of the portals," I reminded him. "Still, we might have to do something about them."

I looked straight down at the hidden outriders. "A shame we don't have some knockout pills or something that we could use to put them to sleep," I added. "But since we don't, we'll have to *go*"—I leaned just slightly on the word—"with something different."

I'd hoped Pix and Pax would get the message. They did. Before I'd even finished my sentence they were off, disappearing back through the hole and presumably out the porch end. Briefly, I wondered if they would have to run a tensh gauntlet, then put it out of my mind. I'd seen no signs that the tenshes had attacked them before; hopefully, they wouldn't do so now.

"What do you plan?" Uvif asked.

I suppressed a smile. At this stage, faced with a sudden shift in the tactical landscape, Circe would probably already have a couple of alternate plans in mind. Huginn would probably have three or four. Uvif, in contrast, seemed completely clueless on what came next.

"I need to rig up a diversion," I told him. "I think everything I need is back in the other room."

He muttered something under his breath. "Be quick about it."

We returned to the relatively spacious room where we'd spent so many hours together earlier. While Uvif and the Iykams watched from the doorway, I busied myself pulling together whatever odds and ends I could find: bits of broken ceramic, a few splinters from the baseboards, and some yellowish powder that had collected in one of the corners. I wrapped all of it in a piece of the black mesh that had been left behind when the silver-silk had been harvested. I pulled out my flashlight, shone it briefly through the side of the mesh, and nodded as if satisfied.

"Okay," I told Uvif, surreptitiously checking my watch. All in all, I'd burned through about fifteen minutes. Hopefully, that would be enough. "I'm ready."

"What will that do?" Uvif asked, peering doubtfully at my masterpiece.

"You'll see," I said, walking toward them. Again, they moved aside to let me pass.

And as they did so, I gently stroked my left thumbnail into

mirror mode. Cradling my junk collection in both hands, I angled my thumb to look at the floor behind me.

I'd worried that I hadn't given the outriders enough time to get back to Ixil, upload the memory of my knockout-alternative comment, and download any new instructions. I'd also worried that Ixil wouldn't remember his off-hand comment back in Alpha when this whole thing first started and wouldn't catch what I was trying to tell him.

Both concerns had been for nothing. In my mirrored nail I saw Pix and Pax lurking motionless in the shadows near the back door, their full attention on me. Their noses seemed to twitch as Uvif and the two Iykams followed me into the corridor and we headed for the front door.

My last look, before I again repositioned my hands, was of the two outriders moving stealthily along the floor toward us.

"This is where it gets a bit tricky," I said, stopping a meter back from the door and peering out. "When the sky above the beacon is clear—like it is right now—the area's pretty dark. It's when there are clouds directly above the Tower that we get the kind of city-wide reflection we don't want."

"Then we should wait until there are first clouds, then no clouds," Uvif suggested. "The guards' low-light vision will be most impaired at that time."

"Exactly," I said, impressed in spite of myself. Between my encounter with him at Landon Station and his single-minded demands for my death here I'd come to think of him as brutish and vindictive but not especially intelligent. That suggestion showed that he did have at least a modicum of tactical ability.

I felt my stomach tighten. It was exactly that sort of flawed snap judgment that could bring a bounty hunter to a very quick and very lethal end.

As my father used to say, *Always assume the other guy is smarter, faster, and a better shot than you are. If you're wrong, you'll be pleasantly surprised. If you're right, at least you won't be taken down by an obvious sucker punch.*

"You three wait back here," I continued, taking another step toward the door. Now, more than ever, I needed to make sure my moves and timing were exactly on their marks. "I'll take a look."

That single step was all I got. Uvif snapped an order, and an instant later I was yanked to a halt, both upper arms gripped in an Iykam hand. "Hey," I protested, half turning to glare at Uvif over my shoulder. "What the hell?"

"You do try to run?" Uvif growled, his voice heavy with suspicion.

"I do *not* try to run," I growled back. At the bottom of my peripheral vision, so far unnoticed by anyone else, Pix and Pax skittered forward and plopped themselves down directly behind the Iykams, pressing solidly against the heels of their boots. "I try to give you information about silver-silk, remember? Let *go*." Turning back to face forward, I took a long step backward, dragging the two Iykams with me.

Or rather, I'd have dragged them along if their feet had been free to match my backward step. But with Pix and Pax keeping that from happening—

The alternative, Ixil had said about my knockout pills, *was for you to sneak up behind each one, crouch down, and let one of us push him over you.*

The Iykams went down like a matched set of falling trees, letting go of my arms in a frantic but futile attempt to somehow get their hands in position to break their fall. But there was no time, they were facing the wrong direction, and they landed flat on their backs on the rotten wood with soggy-sounding thuds. The impact jarred loose one of the corona guns, sending it skittering across the floor. The other Iykam managed to keep his grip on his weapon, though only until I bent down and twisted it away from him.

"Or we can continue our discussion later," I said, waving the corona gun casually in Uvif's direction. "Just relax. No one has to get hurt."

"You will die, human," the Patth said, his voice going dark and quiet. "I will kill you myself."

"We can talk about that later, too," I said, watching him as I crossed the room and retrieved the other weapon. "Right now, we're heading over to that wonderfully engineered hidey-hole Expediter Huginn set up for us. On your feet, Iykams. Let's go."

I had no doubt that any of the three of them would have tried something desperate if I'd given them the slightest hope that an attack would have even a slim chance of success. I made damn sure not to give them any such hope.

A minute later, they were tucked away behind the collapsed

ceiling section. A minute after that, I'd closed the flap behind them and wedged the power pack of one of the corona guns into the opening in a way that would prevent the catch from disengaging. "I suggest you wait until Circe comes to fetch you," I called softly through the panel. "Shouting for help now would only mean coming up with a good story to tell the Ammei."

There was no answer. I hadn't expected one.

Pix and Pax were waiting for me by the back door. The earlier crowd of tenshes had vanished, leaving nothing but derelict buildings visible in the soft glow of reflected beacon light. "Okay," I muttered to the outriders. "Let's go home."

In some ways it was like a replay of the previous night, when I'd slipped out of our designated room and skulked around the ruined city.

But for that excursion I'd waited until the beacon had shut down, the result being that I'd had to fumble my way around the area in near total darkness, painfully aware that if I ran across an Amme I would probably run headlong into him before I even knew he was there. Now, with the beacon blazing its light into the wispy overhead clouds, I could see much more clearly. It made the city easier to navigate, but also made the ghost-lit ruins that much creepier.

But even better than light, this time I had guides.

Not just guides to wherever Ixil had holed up, either. Three times during our meandering trip through the debris one or the other of the outriders suddenly spun around and ran his body into my shin. Luckily, I was fast enough to take the hint, stopping dead and dropping into a low crouch. The first two times it was a group of Ammei striding purposefully through the city thirty meters or so away, possibly hunting for me, possibly just on routine patrol. The third time it was a roving pack of tenshes like the ones who'd thought earlier that they had Pix and Pax trapped under the porch. One of the creatures at the edge of the herd paused for a long look at us, then turned back and hurried to catch up with his companions.

I grimaced as I watched them go. If the tenshes could make the same neural connection with the Ammei that Kalixiri outriders could make with their masters, the alarm was going to go up the minute any of that pack found someone whose leg they could climb up. I needed to get under cover, and fast.

Fortunately, that was our last encounter with any of the locals. Two minutes later, accompanied by the gentle rippling sound of the nearby river, we reached the half-demolished two-floor building that was our goal. The outriders slipped nimbly through cracks in the western wall; I found a half-broken door and maneuvered my way through the gap. I walked a zigzag path through a long corridor that had been rigged with impromptu light baffles and entered an inner room...

"Welcome," Ixil said, rising from his seat on a box in one corner and giving me a quick visual once-over. "I trust you're unharmed?"

"Thanks to you, yes," I told him, frowning a little as I looked around. This room seemed awfully familiar. "I'm a little surprised to find you way out here. I didn't give Pix and Pax *that* much time to bring you my plan."

"Oh, no, I was much closer to you then," Ixil explained. He snapped his fingers twice, and Pix and Pax detached themselves from my sides and trotted over to him. "I moved back here to our base after I gave them their instructions. I assume it went well?"

"Very well," I confirmed as the two outriders climbed up Ixil's jacket and settled on his shoulders. "See for yourself."

He nodded, a sort of distant look crossing his squashed-iguana face as the outriders' memories flowed into him. "Interesting," he murmured. "What did you do with the corona—? Oh, I see. You think they're hidden well enough that that Ammei won't find them?"

"They're buried pretty deep under that wood pile," I said. "I also took out the power packs before I dumped them."

"Yes, I see," Ixil said, his eyes coming back to focus. "Hopefully, that'll be good enough. If not, we'll at least learn something about Ammei sensor and search capabilities."

"Speaking of which, if the tenshes we passed report in fast enough, we're probably well within the search radius," I warned. "We might want to relocate."

"I don't think that will be a problem," Ixil said, giving each of his outriders a brief pet. "They don't seem to have that capability."

"You sure?" I asked, eyeing the outriders. "Because if they can't search the way Pix and Pax do, what good are they?"

"I don't know," Ixil conceded. "Still, Pix and Pax seem to have come to a certain tacit agreement with them."

"I hope you're right," I warned, thinking back to the silent mass of tenshes blocking our way out the back door. "The crowd that had them pinned down under the porch seemed pretty unfriendly."

"No, I don't think so," Ixil said. "I would say they were more bemused than belligerent. Intrigued, perhaps. You saw that they didn't attack, even though they could have fit through the same gaps the outriders did, and that they didn't impede their return to me after hearing your instructions."

"I suppose," I said reluctantly. "That still doesn't explain what the Ammei see in them."

"That, I agree, is still unknown." He gave me the Kalixiri equivalent of a smile. "Still, there's something to be said for simple companionship."

"The Ammei don't strike me as the cuddly type."

"I would tend to agree." He waved me to a more or less flat chunk of wood that might once have been the top of a cabinet. "But that's a mystery for later. For now, let's start with what exactly happened after Huginn set off that smoke bomb."

I gave him the complete rundown of Huginn's smoke-screen gambit, from the time we left the Tower up until Ixil's outriders made their appearance at my impromptu prison. "I assume Huginn and his Iykams set all this up before the Ammei caught them," I finished. "Planting gear where Huginn could get it on last night's midnight stroll. What his end game is, though, I haven't the faintest idea."

"He does seem to play his cards close," Ixil murmured, absently stroking the heads of the two outriders crouched on his shoulders. "But some parts are clear enough. For one thing, the Patth apparently know a great deal more about the Ammei than we do. Certainly more than Huginn has let on."

"Yeah, that one's pretty obvious," I conceded. "On the other hand, there's one thing we know that I don't think he does." I waved my hand around the room. "This room. The room Huginn picked for Circe and Fearth to hide me in. The room by the river, probably, except it's too wrecked to tell. They're all the same design." I raised my eyebrows. "*And* they all had silver-silk baseboard linings."

"Which means?"

"I don't know," I said. "But it can't be a coincidence, which means it has to be important."

"I agree," Ixil said thoughtfully. "Possibly more so than you know, in fact. Do you remember back to when Nask first captured you and Tera? Among other things, he talked about the Patth legend of Orammescka."

I searched my memory. I'd had far more pressing concerns at the time, but I vaguely remembered the incident. "Isn't he the one who captured fire and brought it back before the sun killed him? The Patth version of the Greek Prometheus?"

"That's the one," Ixil confirmed. "Except that the sun didn't kill him, he just fell to his death."

"Dead is still dead."

"True," Ixil said. "At any rate, during Tera's later debriefing she mentioned being oddly impressed by the conversation, that she sensed an earnestness in the way Nask talked about Orammescka."

"Well, we know he's big into mythology," I pointed out. "*Anybody's* mythology, actually. Just look at the way he names his Expediters."

"I agree," Ixil said. "At the same time, Tera wondered if there might be some actual history buried in the legend. With that in mind, she, Jordan, and I decided to take a deeper look at some of the other Patth myths."

"Harmless enough hobby," I said, keeping my reflexive skepticism firmly in check. Most legends I'd run into in my travels struck me as wishful thinking at best and meaningless froth at worst. But there'd been times when I'd found a buried nugget or two in the stories. "You find anything interesting?"

"Possibly," Ixil said. "There's a story of a Patth named Arammeika who infiltrated the lairs of the silver and black spiders. He stole magic webs from each of them and brought the webs to the people."

I looked over at the wall, a chill running up my back. "Silver-silk intertwined with a black mesh," I murmured.

"Interesting, isn't it?" Ixil agreed. "You told us that the Ammei don't use silver-silk ornamentally?"

"Not that I've seen," I said. "Do the Patth use silver-silk in any industrial processes?"

"We don't know," Ixil said. "But given how closely they guard their technology, it's certainly possible."

I snorted. "I think when you put components of your stardrive system into your pilots' faces you've gone way beyond *closely guarded*."

"I stand corrected," Ixil agreed. "Still, we don't have any actual evidence of such uses."

"Maybe we do now," I said, frowning suddenly. The myths had the common theme of someone wresting control of a vital resource from a higher power.

But if I'd heard Ixil right, there was more similarity than just that in the two stories. In fact . . .

"Gregory?"

I shook away the thought. I needed to do a little more research of my own before I shared such an odd thought with Ixil or anyone else. "Something I didn't tell you earlier," I said. "There's a big room in the Tower across from the library with shuttered windows where the Ammei are building something out of Icari metal. Selene says there's also silver-silk in there."

"Is that where the material they've harvested from the various houses has been taken?"

"That's our assumption," I confirmed. "No idea whether the silver-silk is being used directly in their current project or just being stored. Have you had a chance to look around the city?"

"We've done a cursory examination of some of it," Ixil said. "Anything in particular you're looking for?"

"I'm wondering about the distribution of these larger houses," I said. "Or maybe more specifically, the distribution of these silver-silk rooms."

"And?"

I hesitated. Ixil was used to me trotting out wild theories, but this one had even less of a solid foundation than most of them. "I'm wondering if—"

I broke off as Ixil suddenly lifted a finger for silence. I strained my ears.

And felt my mouth go dry. From somewhere outside had come the soft clink of a foot against a rock.

They'd found us.

CHAPTER TWENTY-TWO

Ixil was already on his feet, his hand gripping his holstered plasmic, as Pix and Pax leaped onto the floor and made for a pair of cracks in opposite walls. Ixil caught my eye, gestured in silent command toward a half-collapsed doorway on my right. I nodded acknowledgment and slipped through the opening.

I found myself in another room, smaller than the one I'd just left, with a ceiling that was completely collapsed on the side facing the river. The ceiling of our building's upper story was visible through the broken opening, that section also collapsed nearly flat. Across the warped floor was a gap that had probably once been a second-floor window but now opened just above ground level.

Ixil came up behind me. "Through the window," he whispered. "Into the river. There's a Barracuda tethered underwater to a rock at the edge of the riverbank about twenty meters upstream. Wait for me there."

I nodded and picked my way across the debris to the window. I crouched in the gap a moment, doing a quick scan of the area, then slipped outside.

I'd heard the river when I first approached Ixil's hideaway but hadn't realized just how close it was. Now, I could see that the western bank was no more than ten meters away, just beyond a line of the reeds like the ones Selene and I had seen near the dock a few kilometers farther north. I could hear more foot-steps, but none of them seemed to be coming from the stretch I needed to cross.

Which could just mean the crowd behind me with the big feet were making noise on purpose in hopes of flushing their quarry into the arms of a squad waiting quietly along the riverbank.

I huffed out a silent sigh. In which case, my best move here might be a sacrifice play. As my father used to say, *Sometimes you need to sacrifice a good position in order to leave an ally in a better one.* Circe knew I was out here but she didn't know about Ixil. If I could play stupid into their trap before they spotted him, we would still have a wild card up our sleeve that no one knew about. I gathered my feet beneath me, picking out a promising spot in the reeds—

A movement to my right caught my eye. One of Ixil's outrid-ers had emerged from the reeds about five meters upstream from me. He raised himself up on his hind legs like he was trying for a better view, then turned and looked at me.

It was as good an invitation as I was likely to get. Shifting direction, I headed toward him, keeping hunched over and run-ning as quietly as I could. He dropped back to all fours as I approached and disappeared into the stand of reeds.

With my focus on getting caught before anyone found Ixil I hadn't worried about making an obvious exit point in the reeds. Now, though, I saw that Ixil already had that covered. What I'd assumed was a single solid line of the plants turned out to be actually two lines, with a small gap between them. The outrider ahead of me had gone down an angled lane that led across the gap. I eased down the lane, trying not to break or bend any of the reeds along the way, and found myself at the water's edge.

The outrider—it was Pax, I saw now—was waiting with an air of impatience. I nodded and eased my way past him into the cold water. I reached for him, intending to set him on my shoulder for the upcoming swim, but he merely hopped past my extended hand into the water and started paddling his way upstream. Taking one last look along the river, still wondering if there was an ambush waiting, I followed.

I found the hidden gear right where Ixil had said it would be. With their combination of a three-hose scuba breathing setup, powered diving wings, and passive threat-sensor arrays, Barracudas were the tool of choice for EarthGuard's elite SOLA units. In this case, Ixil had added two sealed hamster-ball carriers big enough to safely get his outriders back to Alpha.

Assuming he and Pix were able to get here before the searchers found them. I got Pax into his ball, watched with distracted interest as he triggered the compact scrubber/rebreather, then settled in to wait.

I'd been there about ten minutes, hanging onto the rock with one hand and Pax's ball with the other, my eyes and nose just above water as I slowly froze to death, when a sudden swell sent a small wall up the back of my neck and nearly over the top of my head. I spun around as the flood subsided, blinking water out of my eyes, to see Ixil floating downstream toward me, Pix perched on his shoulder. "You all right?" he whispered as he came up to me.

"Fine," I said. "I've got Pax in his ball. I wasn't expecting you to come from that direction."

"I thought it wise to decoy them a bit," he said. "Grab one of the mouthpieces and one of the handgrips and we'll be off."

"Wait a minute," I said as he retrieved the other hamster ball and scooted Pix into it. "We can't leave without Selene."

"You told me she was a VIP among the Ammei."

"That was before I pulled my disappearing act," I said. "And before Fearth and Circe spouted off whatever lies and poison they've spent the last few hours spreading."

"I understand your concerns," Ixil said, scooping up two of the scuba mouthpieces and handing one to me. "But there's nothing the two of us can do alone. We need to get back to Icarus and work out a plan of action."

"Ixil—"

"Unless you have a plan right now for freeing her," he cut me off. "Not an intention or a desire, but an actual plan."

I glared at him. But he was right. It was just him and me, with only a single weapon between us, and without any additional resources for either combat or evasion. Even the survival supplies he'd had back in the house were presumably gone by now. Silently, I plucked the mouthpiece from his hand and set it into my mouth.

"We'll be back," Ixil assured me. "Don't worry. We'll get her out."

Twenty seconds later, with the air hissing through my mouth and the diving wing vibrating in my hands, we headed toward Alpha.

Barracuda diving wings, I'd heard, could crank up to impressive underwater speeds. In this case, though, Ixil kept the engines at low power, content to let the river carry us along toward Alpha at its own pace and maneuvering only when he felt it necessary to avoid compact schools of fish or tendrils of river weed that might telegraph our position to anyone watching from the bank.

I could appreciate Ixil's desire for stealth. On the other hand, the river wasn't getting any warmer, and I guessed Pix and Pax had limited air capacity. It was a relief when we finally came within sight of Shark Tooth Rock and the dark curve of Alpha's receiver module beside it. Ixil anchored the Barracuda to one of a set of freshly attached rings beside a darkened but open hatch, motioned me to take a final breath, then popped out his own mouthpiece, collected the two hamster balls, and pushed himself into the opening. For a second his legs flailed as his head and torso adjusted to the new gravity direction inside the module, and then he was gone. I took my own last breath and followed.

The fact that there'd been no light showing through the open hatch as we approached had worried me a little, given that the only portals I'd ever seen without that omnipresent glow had been either dead or seriously unconscious. But as I pushed through the hatchway I saw that Kinneman's people had simply gone the obvious route of rigging a blackout tent over the hatch.

Ixil was standing in the usual puddle that had collected around the hatch, waiting for me beside a flap in one of the walls. Pix and Pax were already out of their balls and back to their usual spots on his shoulders. "This way," Ixil said, lifting the flap to show yet more black fabric beyond. "I imagine he'll want to talk to you."

I felt my lip twist. "I can hardly wait."

"And keep your hands visible." Turning around, Ixil headed through the flap. I ran my hands over my jacket and trousers to squeeze out as much of the water soaked into the fabric as I could and followed.

The black fabric turned out to be a short tunnel acting as a visual airlock. We passed through it and out another flap at the far end.

To find ourselves facing a semicircle of heavy laser muzzles. Five weapons in all, gripped in the hands of five armored EarthGuard Marines, none of whom looked especially glad to see either of us.

Or maybe that was my imagination. They probably were glad enough to see Ixil, at least.

"Vatican cameos," Ixil said, lifting his hands to confirm their emptiness. I did likewise. In response, the laser muzzles lowered to point at the deck. "Is Colonel McKell here?" Ixil asked, taking a step forward.

"He's at Icarus, sir," one of the Marines said, eyeing me. "General Kinneman also left orders that if Roarke arrived we were to escort him directly there."

"That's all right, I'll take him," Ixil said, beckoning to me as he turned toward the launch module interface.

The Marine took a long sideways step into his path. "The general said we were to escort him there *personally.*"

Ixil shot a look at me. "As you wish," he said, resuming his walk.

This time, the Marine stepped out of his way. Ixil and I passed through the group, the five of them forming up behind us.

And as we walked, I gave the sphere a careful look.

Most of the tangled equipment heaps that had been created by Alpha's loss of gravity during our landing were still where Selene and I had left them. Elsewhere, though, the module had become an armed camp. The place was buzzing with men and women in EarthGuard uniforms, most of them sporting the shoulder patches of the elite SOLA combat specialists. On one side of the blackout tent were three new weapons racks, one holding half a dozen Pashnian over/under plasmic/10mms, one with the simpler EarthGuard standard-issue Sigurd plasmics, and one with four especially nasty-looking Parabel 9mm rocket-load sniper rifles. On the other side of the tent, beside the spare Barracudas, was a hanging rack of combat drysuits. Whatever Kinneman was planning, it looked like he was almost ready to go.

I felt my throat tighten. For Selene's sake—and probably for Kinneman's—I needed to persuade him otherwise.

We reached the interface and, one by one, rolled over into the launch module. Three minutes and a floating trip up the extension arm later, we all popped into the Icarus receiver module.

The first time I'd traveled here to the heart of the Icarus Group

I'd been greeted by a squad of Kalixiri soldiers resting comfortably on their backs along the inner hull, heavy lasers pointed at the spot every visitor to the portal had to pass through. Now, as had been the case when Selene and I were brought in at the beginning of this current mess, those aliens had been replaced by humans wearing the same SOLA shoulder patches as the soldiers in the Alpha module.

Not only had Kinneman turned the Icarus Group into a humans-only club, he'd populated it with EarthGuard's most elite troops.

Someone must have radioed ahead, because I rolled out of the portal into the main base to find six more SOLA soldiers waiting for us. "Mr. Roarke," one of them said, his voice briskly formal. "In accordance with Section Twenty-Eight of the Unified EarthGuard Articles, General Kinneman has ordered that you be placed under arrest, pending a trial on the charge of treason. We have orders to escort you to a holding cell until then.

"Your trial will begin in one hour."

As my father used to say, *You never know how mad someone is until he threatens you with something he can't possibly pull off.*

But as he also said, *When someone's too mad to think straight, walk very carefully. There's no satisfaction in making him sweat about where to dump your body.*

So I didn't protest or complain as the soldiers quick-marched me down the corridor. I didn't even breathe loudly.

Still, I had to admit at how impressively he'd choreographed our procession. Between me, Ixil, the five soldiers from the Icarus portal, and the six new ones we'd now picked up, we had to look like either a dangerous prisoner transfer or the changing of the guard at someone's palace.

I'd had a private bet with myself that Kinneman would have gone old-school on his brig, with cells made of metal bar crosshatches and doors opened with physical keys. But we arrived at our destination to find just the standard unbreakable plastic walls perforated by clusters of two-centimeter-diameter gerbil-cage-style air holes. The furnishings were also EarthGuard standard: a cot, a blanket, a pillow, a chair, and a sink/toilet combo.

This particular brig consisted of only three cells. I wondered if the Alien Portal Agency's troop discipline was really that good, or if this was just the VIP section and there were other spots for employees who didn't live up to the general's standards.

The center cell was waiting for me, the sergeant acting as jailer standing ready beside the open door. At his direction I emptied my pockets onto a table a meter from the cell door and stepped inside. The sergeant closed and locked the door behind me, and my escort marched out. Ixil stayed long enough to assure me he would talk to Kinneman—though considering his standing in the general's eyes probably wasn't any better than mine was I doubted that would do much good—then followed. The sergeant gave me a final look, then retreated to a duty office on the opposite side of the room.

Leaving me standing there, alone, cold, and facing court-martial, with water oozing from my wet clothes into a small puddle around my feet.

And even at that, the bitter thought clouded my soul, I was likely in a better situation than Selene.

The chair was metal and looked extremely uncomfortable. But sitting on the cot in my wet clothing would soak the mattress, and despite Kinneman's promise of an imminent trial I figured I'd likely be here long enough to sleep. But I was also damned if I would strip in front of my jailer or whoever Kinneman had watching via the cluster of cameras on the opposite wall.

Which left me only the chair. Easing myself onto it, wincing as the cold water and colder metal pressed against my skin, I looked around in hopes of inspiration.

It wasn't promising. The chair, cot, and toilet were bolted to the metal floor, and none of them could be disassembled without specialized tools. Without tools or privacy, there wasn't a single thing I could do but wait.

Apparently not for long. I was still examining my new quarters when the brig door opened. I shifted my gaze in that direction, expecting to see Kinneman here to threaten me in person—

"Hello, son."

I sighed. "Hello, Dad," I said. "Excuse me for not getting up. It's just so very comfortable here."

"Yes, I can see that," he said with a hint of amusement. "Sergeant?"

The jailer poked his head out of his office. "Yes, Sir Nicholas?"

"I have dry clothes for the prisoner," he said, hefting the satchel he was carrying. "Will you open the door, please?"

"Yes, sir." The sergeant stepped briskly into the room, crossed to my cell, and keyed it open. "I have to examine everything first," he said, almost apologetically.

"Understood." My father stepped close to him and opened the satchel.

If it had been McKell or Ixil, this would have been the moment when knockout gas puffed out, or a flash-bang went off, or the sergeant would collect a paralyzing stomach jab under the satchel's cover.

But this wasn't either of them. This was my dad. The jailer peered into the case, poked around a bit, then nodded. "Clear, sir," he said, stepping back.

"And you can turn those off," my father added, nodding toward the cameras. "A bit of privacy would be appreciated."

The sergeant hesitated, then nodded. "Of course, Sir Nicholas. But they have to go back on once he's dressed."

"Understood." My father stepped into my cell. "You can lock me in if you want."

The sergeant nodded again, closed the door and locked it, then retreated again to his office. "Here," my father said, watching the cameras as he handed me the satchel. "You can start...now."

I nodded. The little lights that supposedly showed when cameras were active were easy to gimmick, a simple trick that had brought many a prisoner to grief after being lured into blabbing something incriminating. But there were other, more subtle indications that cameras were off, and I knew all of them. These cameras were definitely off.

So, presumably, were the directional microphones inevitably associated with them.

"So we're not doing a prison escape?" I asked as I pulled off my jacket.

"No point to it," my father said, frowning. "You didn't *really* think he was serious about putting you on trial, did you?"

"Shouldn't I have been?"

My father shook his head. "He's mad, Gregory. Mad at you, mad at your friends, mad at the situation you've forced him into on Nexus Six. And you never know how mad someone is until he threatens you with something he can't pull off."

"Can't *possibly* pull off," I corrected him absently as I studied his face. "So why are you here?"

My father's mouth puckered. "To give you a heads-up," he said. "Obviously, there's nothing General Kinneman can do to you within the time frame he specified. Even martial law has strict guidelines to prevent those in power from going all Attila the Hun on people."

"So violent threats are just his idea of a bargaining chip?" I asked, dropping my trousers and leaving myself clad only in underwear.

"Basically," my father said, turning his back to me. "What he wants is for you to go back to Nexus Six ahead of the SOLA team he's prepping. You'll gather as much intel on the situation as you can: Ammei deployment, defenses, key locations, and so on. Once you've gotten everything you can and the fighting starts, you can retreat back to Alpha."

"Sounds reasonable enough," I said, dropping my underwear and starting to towel myself off. "Does that mean I'll be getting my own Barracuda and combat suit?"

"Of course," he said. "Plus any weapons you want, plus possibly some support personnel. You'll have to negotiate that latter part with the general."

"I'll at least need Ixil," I said. I finished with the towel and pulled the fresh underwear from the satchel. "You think Kinneman will go for that?"

"Considering how far Ixil is into your same doghouse, I think he'd be amenable to that," my father said dryly. "You decent again?"

"Yes," I said, getting my feet into my new trousers. "Nicely done, by the way."

He turned back to face me, frowning. "Come again?"

"Picking the moment you were turned away from me to offload all the questionable stuff," I said. "You figured I knew your tells, and hoped you could slide all that past me."

"I just turned around for modesty's sake," he insisted.

"Oh, come *on,* Dad," I chided. "Did you really not know you have vocal tells, too?"

He pursed his lips. "Actually, I didn't," he admitted. "All right, you caught me. What do you want to know?"

"I think I can guess," I said. "Everything's supposed to go exactly the way you laid it out...except that I'm not gathering intel, I'm providing the diversion. Kinneman's sending me in to get caught, and while the Ammei and Patth are all fussing over me the SOLA team hits the place. Tell me I'm wrong."

He sighed. "No, that's pretty much it," he said. "But if you look at it from Kinneman's perspective—"

"You don't need to sell it," I interrupted him. "I'm in."

"—it's a matter—" He broke off. "What?"

"I said I'm on board with being the sacrificial goat." I lifted a finger. "On one condition. The first thing the SOLA team does once they get to the Tower is pull Selene out."

"Oh," my father said, looking a little taken aback. "Well..." He sighed. "No use lying, is it? I'm sorry, Gregory, but the team's first job will be to secure the Gemini portals. Kinneman's not going to budge on that one."

"And Selene?"

"A distant second."

I felt my stomach tighten. Down deep, I'd known that would be how Kinneman's priorities would shake out. "Then let me sweeten the pot," I offered. "I know where RH is."

His expression twitched. "You *know*?"

"Yes," I said.

Because I could play fast and loose with the truth as well as he could. And really, I *did* know the other half of the portal directory was in the Tower library. Somewhere. Probably. "Once Selene is safely out, I'll get it."

For half a dozen heartbeats he just stared at me. I probably had tells, too, but at this point I didn't really care whether or not he suspected me of fudging things. If there was even the slightest possibility that I was telling the truth he would have to tell Kinneman, and Kinneman would have no choice but to play those odds.

"All right, I'll tell him," my father said. "No promises, but—"

"And there's a time limit on this offer," I said. "I don't know what they might be doing to Selene in there, but I'm not going to stretch this out while Kinneman dithers or consults or asks his prognosticator or whatever. He said he was bringing me to trial in one hour? Fine. He's got that same hour to send Ixil and me back to Nexus Six."

I never found out how that conversation went. All I knew was that, forty minutes after my father headed back to Kinneman I was hauled out of my cell, sent back through Icarus to Alpha, and poured into a SOLA drysuit. Ixil, similarly garbed, was already waiting by the blackout tunnel when I arrived, Pix and Pax back in their hamster balls on his shoulders. "We ready?" I asked as I walked up to him.

"Yes." His eyes flicked over my shoulder. "You sure you want to do this? There's no telling how the Ammei will react when you reappear."

"Sure there's telling," I said as casually as I could. "Depending on what Circe and Fearth told them, they'll be either angry or lethal. But it'll all be on me. You and the outriders are going to go to ground the minute we're ashore."

The outriders gave a simultaneous twitch. "Interesting plan," Ixil said. "We won't, of course."

"You won't?"

"I'm told you specifically asked for us," Ixil said. "Therefore, you have a plan that requires us."

"I *do* have a Plan B," I admitted. "But the current Plan A is still for you to sit tight and wait for the cavalry."

"Plan B it is, then," Ixil said, securing his helmet and tapping the radio key. "You can tell me all about it on the trip over," he added, his voice now coming through my helmet speaker.

"Sure," I said, sliding on my own helmet. "Really, you're going to love it."

CHAPTER TWENTY-THREE

He didn't love it. But he didn't hate it, either. And as my father used to say, *It's a good sign when your plan pulls a solid neutral from your allies. That way you know they'll be alert and thinking the whole way.*

The stars were starting to disappear into dawn over the eastern mountains by the time we were in place. "You're sure they'll come here?" Ixil asked a little doubtfully as I gave my chosen venue one last check.

"They will if they listen to Huginn," I said. "He talked about these big houses earlier, and he knows I'll remember that. No, he'll point the Ammei here as a likely spot for me to have gone to ground, all right." I looked down at the matte, color-shifting camo suit that the drysuit had turned into once we were out of the water. "I have to say these things are amazing. I'd expected a lot more trouble getting ashore and sneaking in here."

"Only the best for General Kinneman," Ixil said with a hint of irony.

"Of course." I gestured to the door. "Better get to cover. We'll find out soon enough if this is going to work."

"Right," Ixil said. "Good luck."

A minute later, as I peered through one of the cracks in the wall, I saw him and Pix slip beneath the pile of rubble he'd chosen for his observation spot. I looked behind me at the similar rubble where Pax was hidden, then walked over to a chunk of wall beside the house's broken-down entrance and a convenient ceramic slab. I ran my finger down the wall, tracing out the words *talk to me*, then crossed to what was left of the stairs and eased my way to the upper floor. I lay down in my chosen spot, where I could watch my wall through a crack in the floor. I pulled some heavy, drywall-like slabs on top of me for concealment, and settled in to wait.

Like most stakeouts I'd been on, this one seemed to linger far beyond the seconds and minutes my watch was ticking off. I thought a lot about Ixil and Pax, wondering if they were well enough hidden against whatever search parties were prowling around. I thought about Kinneman and his SOLA assault team, wondering if the general would wait for me to create my promised diversion or if he would get impatient and launch his attack without it. I wondered if whatever resistance the Ammei mounted against that attack would collapse before the best firepower EarthGuard had to offer, or if their lightning guns would prove the superior weapons.

Mostly, I thought about Selene.

So far, the Ammei had treated her like royalty. But now I'd disappeared, presumably abandoning her and the Ammei, and Circe and Sub-Director Fearth were on site telling whatever story they wanted about the two of us.

In the wake of all that, had Selene's status changed? Probably, and almost certainly not for the better. But until I knew the details, trying to counter Fearth's gambit would be flailing in the dark. I needed intel, I needed it badly, and I needed it now.

Which was the whole idea behind this scheme. The simplest way for the Ammei to find me was to use Selene's tracking abilities to turn what would otherwise be a massive, multi-day, city-wide search into something quicker and more focused. If she could talk Second of Three into putting her to work, and if she caught the invisible message I'd left for her on the ceramic slab downstairs, she should be able to pass on the information I needed without the Ammei knowing she was doing it.

If it turned out that such intel was too little or too late, I had a backup plan in the form of the replacement Sigurd plasmic I'd taken from the Alpha weapons rack. Dueling it out with a bunch of armed aliens wasn't how I'd planned my day to go, but if it was that or leave Selene alone and in danger I was ready to take the risk.

I'd been lying there an hour, thinking dark thoughts, working up contingency plans, and listening to the wind whistling softly through the gaps in my hideout's walls and ceiling, when they finally arrived.

To my relief, Selene was indeed leading the way, squeezing through the warped doorway. Close behind her were Third of Three and Rozhuhu, the former presumably here as the authority figure in charge of the hunt, the latter here as translator. Behind them came four of the ubiquitous armed Ammei guards, plus I could hear more of them scuffling through the debris outside. Prowling around everyone were half a dozen tenshes, weaving their way between the moving feet with impressive dexterity. They fanned out across the room, poking their little noses into the corners and various small piles of debris. I could only hope they didn't spot Pax.

I'd half expected Circe to talk her way into the hunt, either to keep an eye on Selene or in hopes of exacting some revenge on me for locking Uvif and his guards in the closet last night. But instead of our lady Expediter, the final member of the search team—

"If you ask me, this whole thing is a waste of time," Huginn growled, stopping by the doorway as Selene sniffed the air.

I felt a sudden hollow feeling in my stomach. Circe didn't know me beyond what I'd done to Uvif and whatever she'd read in various reports. She hadn't seen me in action and didn't know the sort of convoluted schemes and tactical sleight of hand I'd learned as a bounty hunter and which I liked to use against my adversaries.

But Huginn knew. Not only had he seen my stunts firsthand, but he'd been dragged into reluctant partnership in one or two of them. He would suspect I was running a game here, and he'd be watching for it. The minute Selene got my message and started casually talking about things everyone else in the room already knew, he would realize I was within eavesdropping range. At that point, all it would take would be a single word to Third to call fire and brimstone down on me.

And there wasn't a single thing I could do about it. Not without calling that same destruction down on my own head.

"We have *not* asked your advice," Rozhuhu shot back with an air of impatience. "Furthermore, you have already stated that point six times. As I also have stated that we are here at the command of the First of Three, and will not falter until our task has been completed. Selene of the Kadolians, is he here or is he not?"

"He *was* here," Selene said, walking a slow circle around the room. She reached the slab where I'd written my invisible note, passed it without pausing, and continued on. "But as I told you from the start, finding a midpoint of Gregory's path still gives us two directions to follow with no indication as to which is the more recent."

"And even if you do find him, then what?" Huginn persisted. His gaze drifted casually around the room, lingered for a fraction of a second too long on the crack I was looking through, then moved on. I got a grip on the butt of my plasmic, knowing full well I couldn't do anything with it, and waited for the inevitable. "I can tell you right now what his advice will be," he continued, turning back to Rozhuhu.

Rozhuhu made an odd sound in his throat. "You speak of counsel from a mere *bodyguard*?" he asked contemptuously. "Such surely cannot be taken seriously."

"Maybe that's not the way of the Ammei," Huginn said. "But the Kadolian concept of bodyguard stretches beyond the physical into the emotional and intellectual."

"That is not the way of the Kadolians."

"Maybe it wasn't when you knew them," Huginn said. "But it's been thousands of years since then, and things have changed. And I don't think you'll be pleased with the advice Roarke of the humans will offer her."

I frowned, part of my mind listening to the discussion, most of it focused on Huginn and his baffling lack of action. Surely he'd spotted me during his survey of the room, or if he hadn't he'd at least figured out where I had to be. As I'd told Circe, he undoubtedly had a spot for me in his plans before I'd inconveniently run out on him, and this was his chance to corral me and get me back into line. So why wasn't he jabbing a finger at the ceiling and whooping in triumph? More than that, why did it sound like he was deliberately funneling me the information I'd been hoping for from Selene?

Were the two of them working together? Or was this a subtle scheme Huginn was playing back at me?

"Because I've spoken at length with Roarke on many topics,"

Huginn continued. "I know with certainty that he'll recommend she not take the needle."

"If Roarke feels such strength of purpose against it, why did he himself lead us to the *Imistio* Book?" Rozhuhu countered.

I frowned. The *Imistio* Book? As in, the *Imistio* Tower?

"Maybe he was looking for something else and didn't know what he'd found," Huginn said. "You said the book had been returned to its hiding place. Why would he have put it back if he wanted you to have it?"

I felt my stomach curl into a hard knot. So this *Imistio* Book was the one I'd found in the Grove of Reflection. And, despite my best attempts to leave no clues of my presence behind, I'd apparently left enough of them for the Ammei to find the damn thing.

So much for the Gold One's efforts to keep it away from them.

"Perhaps he sees the *Imistio* Book as a threat to his status," Rozhuhu said.

"Right," Huginn said sarcastically. "Because if Selene of the Kadolians becomes the true Third of Three, she won't need his counsel anymore. Is that what you think?"

"Yes," Rozhuhu said. "As the Third of Three has already said."

I frowned a little harder. I'd hoped Selene would be able to dribble me some information. Instead, for whatever reason, Huginn seemed to have taken over that job.

And instead of dribbles, he was feeding it to me via firehose.

If Selene of the Kadolians becomes the true Third of Three. What did that even mean? Was the Third of Three we'd been introduced to just a regent or placeholder in the hierarchy? Was that a position that was supposed to be held by a Kadolian? That might explain why they'd been treating her so well up to now.

So how and where did this *Imistio* Book fit in? "Maybe Roarke's concerns are more subtle," Huginn said. "This is a modern Kadolian female we're talking about, and from what you and the legends say the enhancement serum in the *Imistio* Book was created eight to ten millennia ago. What if there's been genetic drift in the Kadolians over that time? What if there are metabolic changes that make her an entirely different person? What might the needle do to her?"

And then, with a horrific rush, I got it. We were talking about some drug or chemical that dated back to the height of Icari power and influence in the Spiral. *Imistio*—Selene had already said the Ammei word paralleled the Kadolian word for spear or needle.

So those hadn't been just random lines of Icari poetry I'd seen on those thin metal pages. They were parts of a chemical formula, probably accompanied with step-by-step instructions on how to mix up a batch of the stuff. An enhancement serum, whatever the hell that was, unless Huginn was just being flowery.

And First of Three wanted to inject an untested and unproven drug into *Selene*?

Not a chance. Even ignoring Huginn's warning about genetic drift, Selene wasn't going to try some millennia-old gamble if I had anything to say about it.

Unfortunately, there was a very real chance that I wouldn't.

If Selene of the Kadolians becomes the true Third of Three. So if Selene took this serum she would become one of three people in charge of Nexus Six? Including the portals and the Ammei soldiers guarding them?

If so, and whatever I thought of such an insane experiment, I knew it was an opportunity General Kinneman would grab with both hands if he ever got wind of it. Put Selene and the serum in front of him, and he'd be right there with First of Three.

"And if the serum doesn't function as expected?" Huginn demanded. "Kadolians don't drop in on Nexus Six every other week. If you damage her, you risk never having another chance. You should at least do some testing on the serum. Starting by making sure the formula is correct."

"The book once resided in the Center of Knowledge," Rozhuhu said stiffly. "It was removed and hidden by one of the Gold Ones. It *is* accurate."

My throat tightened. Accurate . . . except for the two pages currently riding around in my artificial arm. Had the Ammei even noticed they were missing?

"Again, how do you know?" Huginn persisted. "There are thousands of books in there. Who's to say you don't have an early formula that was subsequently improved on?"

Third rumbled something. "The Third of Three expresses amazement, Huginn of the humans," Rozhuhu translated. "You claim to be servant to Selene of the Kadolians, yet you do not wish her to ascend to this highest of honors?"

"I would never begrudge her such," Huginn said. "Just as I

also don't begrudge the ascension of Conciliator Fearth to the position of Second of Three. I simply wish to make certain that neither will find the darker branch of their stories."

So now Fearth was also being promoted? And to Second of Three? Did that mean the job of First of Three was also up for grabs?

I grimaced. No, of course not. What Huginn was laying out was how it must have been at the beginning: an Ammei, a Patth, and a Kadolian, running things from their neat little triumvirate. There was a sudden soft scratching sound from the stairway. Carefully, I turned my head to look.

To find that while I'd been focused on Huginn's exposition one of the tenshes had wandered up from below and was sniffing at a pile of sheetrock slabs.

I froze, my hand once again closing around my plasmic. Four meters in this direction, and the creature would be right on top of me. If that happened, I was going to have to find a quiet way to silence it and hope its owner didn't miss it.

To my relief, the tensh showed no indication of straying from the stairway's general vicinity. He looked around a bit longer, started to move in my direction, then suddenly turned and went back down the stairs. Breathing a silent sigh of relief, I returned my attention to the group below.

And felt my eyes narrow as something odd caught my eye. Most of the people down there—Huginn, Selene, Third, Rozhuhu, three of the guards—were looking at each other, their eyes level as they talked among themselves. The fourth guard's eyes, in contrast, were pointed at the top of the stairway.

And as I watched, his gaze steadily lowered until it was pointed at the floor. Not just at the floor, but at the tensh that had now reached ground level. The animal came into sight through my observation crack and scurried toward the guard, passed him without slowing, and headed toward something I couldn't see on the far side of the room. I looked back at the guard, to find him still focused on the animal.

Watching it very intently. Almost, the odd image flashed to mind, like an anxious parent watching his five-year-old child to make sure he didn't get lost on the way to school.

I'd wondered earlier if the tenshes were pets, symbionts, parasites, or Kalixiri-style outriders. Selene had suggested there was some connection between the tensh and Ammei scents. But we'd never come up with a solid answer to that puzzle.

Like an anxious parent...

No. Ridiculous. There were plenty of animal species in the Spiral where the young weren't just smaller versions of the adults, of course, tadpoles and frogs being the most obvious example. I didn't know of any sapients that followed that pattern, but there was nothing that said they couldn't.

And there was the similar armadillo-like armor plating both the Ammei and the tenshes had for skin.

Third growled something, his words cutting off my runaway train of speculation. "The Third of Three reminds us we are wasting time," Rozhuhu translated. "Where do we go next, Selene of the Kadolians?"

"We follow the trail," Selene said. "I'm not certain, but I think it's getting stronger."

Third spoke again. "You have until sundown to find him," Rozhuhu said. "After that, we return to *Imistio* Tower."

"And the serum?" Huginn asked.

"She will take it as planned," Rozhuhu said. "She and Fearth of the Patthaaunutth both. Unless you counsel Fearth of the Patthaaunutth to refuse."

"No, I can handle Conciliator Fearth," Huginn assured him. "He'll listen to my counsel, and I wholeheartedly support and embrace the glory of the Ammei. But if Selene of the Kadolians refuses, it will come to nothing. We must yet convince Roarke of the humans."

I peered down at Huginn, trying to figure out what he was trying to tell me. What the hell did the glory of the Ammei have to do with this?

"Roarke of the humans cannot counsel from concealment," Rozhuhu said. "If he wishes to speak, he may come to *Imistio* Tower and state his case."

"And if he counsels against the serum?" Huginn repeated.

"She will still receive it. The *Imistio* Book has been found, and a Kadolian and a Patthaaunutth have arrived on Nexus Six. The goal of the ages is within sight. It must now be brought into reach." He looked sharply at Huginn. "And Roarke of the humans will not stop us."

"I can convince him," Huginn said firmly. "When he is found, you must let me try. But with or without Roarke's counsel, Selene of the Kadolians chooses her own way. Even if the serum works she may not cooperate in achieving your goal."

"Do you speak, Selene of the Kadolians?" Rozhuhu asked.

"I shall await the counsel of Roarke of the humans," Selene said. "He is not here. Do you wish to proceed along his trail?"

"We do," Rozhuhu said, a hint of suspicion in his tone. "We await your guidance."

Selene bowed her head and turned to the doorway. "Then come."

One by one they followed her back outside. I thought about moving to one of the damaged sections of wall where I could watch to make sure they were leaving, decided there was an even chance I would either make enough noise to bring them back or else collapse the rest of the structure on top of me, and stayed put.

Anyway, Ixil was out there watching. As soon as it was clear, he'd send Pix to fetch Pax and me.

Between the escape from Uvif, the escape from the Ammei, the sort-of escape from Kinneman, and now the eavesdrop trap, I hadn't had a lot of sleep in the past twenty-four hours. I'd fallen into a light doze when I was startled awake by Pix's nose poking insistently at my cheek. I gave him a quick stroke along his back and headed back down the rickety stairs.

Ixil was sitting on a piece of masonry near the door, watching Pax squeeze in through a crack and join us. "We clear?" I murmured.

Ixil lifted a warning finger as Pax climbed up his clothing and settled onto his shoulder. His eyes unfocused a moment as the outrider dumped the memories of this latest recon—"They're gone," he confirmed as Pix climbed up to the other shoulder. "Let's make sure it stays that way."

He paused again, and I watched as both outriders hopped back down and disappeared through opposite sides of the building. "Interesting conversation," Ixil said, waving me to another broken slab. "I wonder what this goal is the Third of Three was referring to."

"Personally, I'm more interested in this serum they're talking about," I said grimly. "And what it might do to Selene if it isn't the right one. Or if it *is*."

"Definitely a concern," Ixil agreed. "I assume, given how eager

Huginn seemed to pass this information on to you, that he has similar fears for Conciliator Fearth."

"I noticed that, too," I said. "As my father used to say, *Enlightened self-interest is a valuable ally.*"

"Indeed," Ixil said. "I found Huginn's reference to the darker branch of their stories particularly interesting, bringing to mind the myths of Orammescka and Arammeika. You know that the first story ends with Orammescka falling to his death after obtaining fire for the Patth, and Arammeika's legend ends with her still alive after delivering the webs of the silver and black spiders. But there are alternate versions of both myths where Orammescka lives and Arammeika dies."

"I didn't know that," I said, my mind suddenly tumbling off in an entirely different direction. Had I just spotted something important, or was it just an artifact of my churning thoughts and fears? "So the stories say only one of them lives?"

"Or both live, or both die," Ixil said, peering closely at me. "That's the problem with myths and alternate endings. You have something?"

"Maybe," I said. "Just to be clear, are you saying this serum is tied in with these legends?"

"I don't know," he said. "Still, the current situation where a serum is connected to a great purpose and seems to have dual outcomes of life or death seems uncomfortably parallel to the myths. Any thought as to what the glory of the Ammei is, or what this goal might be?"

"Not a clue," I said. "But my guess is that, whatever Huginn says, he's opposed to it."

"He told Rozhuhu that he would convince Fearth."

"He also implied that a stubborn Selene would stalemate the whole thing," I reminded him. "I think he's trying to stay on Rozhuhu's good side, pretending to cooperate, hoping that Selene and I can keep Fearth from having to take this serum."

"Perhaps," Ixil said, not sounding convinced. "A pity he didn't give us more information about it."

"I'm guessing he doesn't know anything more," I said. "You saw how good he is at this game. I think he gave us everything he had."

"Indeed." Ixil cocked his head slightly. "Tell me about this sudden thought you had a moment ago."

"The sort of weird one I usually get," I said. "Did you notice that the name *Orammescka* has an *amme* in the middle and *Arammeika* has an *ammei?*"

Ixil muttered something I couldn't catch. "I missed that completely. And under the circumstances, I hardly think it's coincidence."

"Me neither," I said slowly, trying to think this through. "Let's assume I'm right, that the Ammei are connected to these legends, and try rewriting them. It was the Ammei who gave the Patth fire, silver-silk, and whatever the black mesh is that came from the black spider. An electronic matrix, maybe. If the Patth cooperate with their benefactors they have life; if they don't, they get death."

"Has there been any conflict between the Ammei and Conciliator Fearth?" Ixil asked.

"No idea," I said. "I was taken off the game board before they met. Selene might have picked up something—she knows Patth scents well enough to spot any major emotional upheavals—but we won't be able to ask her until we can get her away from them."

"Yes," Ixil said thoughtfully. "In the meantime, let me try a variant of your myth. What if fire was given to the Patth and silver-silk to the Kadolians?"

I ran that one a couple of turns around my brain. "Could be," I said. "Or maybe it's more subtle than just an either-or. When we brought Alpha down, Selene was able to track its status by smell. How it was...I know it sounds crazy, but how it was *feeling*. She could track its functional state, the changes it went through when it was coming through the atmosphere and then into the river, and when it was partially back up. I know that sounds weird."

"No weirder than many other things we've seen Selene do," Ixil said. "And she knew when it was back to full function?"

"Actually, we weren't in the portal when that happened," I said. "One other thing. When we first reached the Alainn portal, she described it as being dead."

"Interesting," Ixil murmured. "I wonder... You said the silver-silk from Alainn is organic, correct?"

"I think all silver-silk is," I said, frowning as I tried to figure out where he was going with that question. "The original stuff from Jondervais came from insects—"

And in a blinding flash of lightning, I got it. "It's *organic*," I breathed. "Way more complex chemically than ordinary metal. When silver-silk heats up, or cools down, or changes in any way, that change is reflected in its scent."

"A scent that has a much wider operational range than anything inorganic," Ixil said. "Most metals and circuit materials don't carry much odor, so any such changes would be hard to detect."

"But not impossible," I said. The pieces were falling together, and I wasn't sure I liked the picture they were forming. "She does that all the time on the *Ruth*. Sniffs out problems in the making, usually before the monitor sensors even notice."

"And on the *Ruth* she's just picking up temperature and stress changes," Ixil pointed out. "Imagine how much more detailed a picture she can get from something made of organics."

"Yes," I said. "Okay. So the Patth were the engineers who got to play with all this cool stuff. The portals, the Talariac Drive, and who knows what else. So what does that make the Kadolians? Manufacturing consultants? Quality control? Real-time analysts?"

"All those, and probably more," Ixil said. "The Patth build the portals and the Kadolians monitor their work and make sure everything is functioning properly. Where do the Ammei fit in?"

"There's only one place left for them," I said grimly. "The Ammei have to be the Icari."

"I thought the Gold Ones were the Icari."

"Are they?" I countered. "Isn't it convenient that the Ammei can point any unwanted attention at a vague species that no one has ever seen and no one has ever heard of? And yes, I took a few minutes to do a search while you and Kinneman were finding the camo drysuit for me. There aren't any known sapient species that could even remotely be called gold-colored."

"What about you humans? Some of you are shades of brown."

"Brown is a long way from gold," I said. "Besides, our ancient history is way too well nailed down to allow for a few thousand years of building and running an interstellar transport system."

"Perhaps the name refers to the Gold Ones' value or wealth," Ixil suggested.

"Their value or wealth when?" I asked. "Now? Ten thousand years ago? And who says gold was even valuable back then? But really, all you need to do is look at the numbers. Huginn said that when Fearth and Selene got the serum they'd take over as Second of Three and Third of Three. That just leaves First of Three."

"Who you've never seen," Ixil pointed out. "Could he be a different species? One of the Gold Ones, perhaps?"

I shook my head. "Selene would have mentioned smelling another species."

"Unless he was hidden away somewhere."

"You mean in a hermetic walk-in storage place like the one where they stashed Huginn and his Iykams?"

"Or on another planet entirely," Ixil said, waving his hand in the direction of the portal ring. "It wouldn't be a long journey."

I winced. I hadn't thought about that. "Point taken. I still think the Ammei are the Icari, though."

"You make a reasonable case," Ixil said. "But I can't help thinking we're missing something."

"Probably," I said. "But as my father used to say, *The minute you think you have all the pieces to the puzzle, start looking for the ones that were dropped on the floor.*"

"Interesting turn of phrase," Ixil said. "What floor do you intend to search?"

"The only one we've got," I said. Unfastening my holster from my belt, I handed it and my plasmic to Ixil and started to strip off my camo suit.

"Where are you going?" he asked.

"To make Kinneman happy," I said. "It's time to get myself captured."

CHAPTER TWENTY-FOUR

———— ❖ ————

As my father used to say, *The best way to get inside a secure facility is to be invited. Unfortunately, such invitations are likely to involve guns.*

The trick to keeping the people behind those guns from getting suspicious was to make it look like you'd succumbed to their superior skill and vigilance instead of deliberately and purposefully walking into their open arms.

In this case that should be easy. Without the fancy EarthGuard camo suit I should be quickly tagged by whoever was monitoring the city from the Tower's Upper Rooms.

Sure enough, I'd been darting between buildings and crawling behind weed clumps for barely fifteen minutes when I eased my eyes around a corner to find myself face-to-face with a trio of tenshes standing in a line pointed straight at me. I quickly backed up, as if trying to avoid them, only to be faced by five others who'd come up behind me and were standing in the same spear-like formation. I thought about making a break for it and forcing the Ammei to chase me down, decided it would just mean getting captured tired, and lowered myself onto a patch of clear ground to wait.

Up to now most of the tenshes I'd seen had been hanging around with various Ammei. I thus naturally expected that the guards handling these particular groups were close enough to be on top of me in a minute or two.

But they weren't. I ended up sitting for nearly six minutes, staring at the two sets of silent tenshes, before three Ammei finally came into sight around the building's corners, lightning guns pointed at me exactly like the two lines of tenshes. "Hello," I said, making sure my empty hands were visible as I got to my feet. "I understand you're looking for me. I don't suppose any of you understands English?"

There was no answer. One of the Ammei twitched his weapon in the direction of the Tower. "Understood," I said, turning that direction. "Nice day for a stroll, anyway."

We picked our way through the ruins to the nearest subway ramp, the tenshes ringing us in a loose escort pattern. The Ammei herded me down the ramp, where three more guards and the usual four-car train were waiting. Either I'd been under observation well before the tenshes showed up, or else First of Three was pulling out all the stops to bring me back to the fold. We all climbed aboard the train and headed inward.

The eight tenshes, their task apparently finished, stayed behind on the surface.

We reached the end of the line and headed back up to ground level. My guards steered me toward the nearest corner of the Tower, where we climbed the short ramp to the door, passed between the two guards on duty there, and once again I stepped inside *Imistio* Tower.

Or *Imistiu* Tower, as Selene's Kadolian called it. *Needle Tower.*

At least now I had an inkling of why the Ammei had named their home that.

Third of Three and Rozhuhu were waiting for us in a short, arched corridor made of intricately fitted stone. "The First of Three is angry with you," Rozhuhu said, the last word all but lost in the boom as the doors were slammed shut behind me. "Selene of the Kadolians has asked for your advice."

Third bit out something. "The Third of Three demands to know where you were hiding."

"You have a whole circle of Gemini portals out there," I said. "Where do you *think* I went?"

There was a slight pause, and I had the unpleasant sense that that might have been the wrong answer. Maybe some of the portals led to places I wasn't supposed to know about, let alone visit. "The Third of Three demands to know where you were hiding," Rozhuhu repeated.

"How about we make a trade?" I offered. "He tells me why Selene of the Kadolians and Fearth of the Patth are his prisoners, and I'll tell him where I went."

For another long moment Rozhuhu just stared at me. Then, he turned and spoke to Third. Third replied, and the discussion was on.

I looked at the guards now gathered around me. The wording of my offer had been about eighty percent bluff—Rozhuhu and Third would hardly admit out loud that Selene and Fearth were prisoners. But whether it was that phrasing or the offer itself, it was apparently not a situation they'd anticipated.

From somewhere came a melodic four-note riff. The two Ammei broke off their conversation and Third began talking quietly, apparently to himself. There was a pause, more conversation, and then Third gestured to Rozhuhu. "Come, Roarke of the humans," Rozhuhu said, gesturing my guards to move in closer. "The First of Three wishes you to witness the destruction."

I felt my stomach tighten. "Destruction?" I asked carefully.

"The destruction," Rozhuhu said, and there was something in his tone that sent a fresh shiver up my back, "that you have brought upon yourself."

Way back when Selene and I first arrived on Nexus Six—only a couple of days ago, but it felt like at least a month—Huginn and I had zeroed in on *Imistio* Tower's mysterious Upper Rooms as a definite place of interest. He'd followed up that conversation by sneaking into them on his own that first night, bringing back a limited but intriguing report.

Now, I was getting the grand tour.

The place was just as Huginn had described: a single large room divided in quarters by chest-high partitions that allowed for some privacy when seated or lying down while still offering an unrestricted view through the large windows while standing. The partitions stopped a meter or so from the walls, leaving an open outer ring to allow occupants to move from one section to another. From my angle as I was ushered in I could see a bit into the two sleeping rooms—taking up the north and south cubicles, as Huginn had said—and into the food prep area in the western section. Contrary to Huginn's description, though, the latter now boasted a small set of serving implements, as well as a group of boxes and tubes that looked like food and drink containers.

I'd guessed earlier that after Selene and I popped into town the Ammei would begin running full-day city surveillance. Apparently, I'd also been right about the Upper Rooms being the vantage spot they would choose for that activity.

Second of Three, Fourth of Three, and four more Ammei were waiting silently at the eastern side of the room. Second and Fourth were wearing their usual hats, while the other four had much smaller but equally ornate headwear that suggested they were of higher status than Rozhuhu or the guards. They were standing at the four compass points of the room, gazing out at the city through the windows.

"You have tried to bring destruction to Nexus Six," Fourth said without preamble as Rozhuhu led me to him around the outer ring.

"Have I?" I countered. "Because I urge Selene of the Kadolians to refuse the serum until it has been properly tested?"

Second said something. "How do you know about the serum and the reticence of Selene of the Kadolians?" Fourth asked.

I felt a flicker of chagrin. I'd forgotten I wasn't supposed to have been in on that conversation.

Still, as my father used to say, *Knowing something you shouldn't just means you heard it somewhere else.* "I am adviser and body-guard to Selene of the Kadolians," I said as loftily as I could manage. "Being aware of dangers to her life and well-being is part of that job."

The Amme at the south-facing window said something. "We will return to this question at another time," Fourth said, ges-turing me in that direction. "Come now and witness what you have done."

I felt my heart pounding as I again walked around the perim-eter of the room to the indicated window. If they'd found Ixil and his outriders...

But whatever drama was about to happen, the stage didn't seem to be set. The inner section of occupied buildings, the por-tal ring, the devastation beyond—it all looked like every other time I'd seen it. I looked sideways at the Amme I was standing beside, and saw for the first time that his compact hat had a set of bulky flip-down lenses or goggles that he was peering through. "I need one of these," I said, turning to Rozhuhu and pointing at the hat and goggles.

"You have no status among the Ammei."

"No, but I doubt I'll be able to see the destruction you brought me here to witness without them," I pointed out.

He made an impatient-sounding noise and gave a short command. The Amme at the western window came over to me, pulled the goggles from his hat, and handed them over. I nodded my thanks, held them over my eyes, and looked back out my window.

I'd expected the goggles to be telescopic, infrared, radar-scan, or some combination. But at first glance they didn't seem to be any of those, or to be anything else, for that matter. It was only as my eyes adjusted to the view that I saw that the image was somehow clearer and brighter than it had been without them. It wasn't anything specific I could put my finger on, but I could definitely see better than before.

Something in the ruined section near the portal ring caught my eye. I focused on it, noting that the goggles seemed to respond to my attention with an additional layer of enhancement...

I stiffened. Something was moving out there. Something I couldn't really see clearly, yet paradoxically I could tell was human-sized, was moving inward toward the portals and the Tower.

A chill ran up my back. According to every official document I'd seen or heard of, the active camo suits Kinneman had given Ixil and me were the very best stealth gear EarthGuard had available. But for years there'd been dark rumors of something better, a ghost suit that came close to an actual cloak of invisibility. For those same years EarthGuard had pooh-poohed all such stories while at the same time pestering the Commonwealth government for the additional research money they claimed they needed in order to create such a thing.

Now, as I gazed across the ruined city, I knew that the denials and the funding requests had both been blinds. EarthGuard had ghost suits, all right. And whatever strings Kinneman had had to pull, whatever deals or trades he'd had to make, he'd found enough of them to equip his SOLA assault team.

And it was going to work, I saw with a sinking heart. Even with the Ammei enhancement goggles, even knowing what was out there, I could barely see the soldier moving through the debris. The Ammei were sitting ducks—

"There," Rozhuhu said. "Watch there."

I looked where he was pointing. A dozen meters to the left of the one I'd been looking at was another ghost, similarly making his way toward the Tower. I didn't know how many troops Kinneman had brought, but with the ghost suits and the heavy weapons I'd seen in Alpha, they were setting up for an absolute slaughter—

Without warning a brilliant flash blazed across my vision. Reflexively, I jerked back, blinking away the purple afterimage.

To find the invisible SOLA soldier I'd just been looking at sprawled motionless on the ground. He was fully visible now, the ghost suit and the man himself destroyed by the lightning-gun blast.

I was still taking in that horrible sight when another flash lit up the ground. I shifted my gaze in that direction in time to see another soldier collapse, what was left of his ghost suit trailing smoke.

"See the destruction you have brought," Rozhuhu said. "Watch them, Roarke of the humans. Watch them all die."

"Stop it," I bit out. "You've proved your point. Whatever you want from me, I'll do it. Just let them withdraw."

"What the First of Three wants from you is for you to learn your place," Rozhuhu said. "What he wants of your warriors is their deaths. Watch and learn."

I clenched my teeth, suppressing the curse I wanted to spit at him. I didn't like Kinneman's attitude and tactics, but I had no quarrel with the men and women under his command. To stand by helplessly and watch them be slaughtered one by one...

I swallowed hard as another flash lit up the landscape, this one slicing clean through one of the abandoned houses on its way to demolishing its target. I couldn't save them. Rozhuhu had made that very clear.

But if I couldn't save their lives, maybe I could at least figure out how it was being done.

Because while it was obvious that the spotters up here could see through the ghost filters, what was *not* obvious was how they were communicating that information to the gunners below.

Other flashes were appearing now as the EarthGuard soldiers

realized their approach had been compromised and were shifting into counterattack mode. Resolutely, I lowered my eyes away from the carnage and over to the Ammei end of the shooting gallery. Midway between the Tower and the first ring of houses were a loose formation of Ammei guards, four of them within my field of view, lightning guns raised and ready. As I watched, one of them adjusted his aim a few degrees and fired, his shot again cutting through an outer building to take out one of the invaders.

How the *hell* did he know where to shoot?

They weren't using radio. Standard EarthGuard procedure when launching an attack was to blanket the entire radio spectrum with static. No one up here was talking, which ruled out loudspeakers or individual sonic focusers. No one was pointing, which similarly eliminated the oldest and most straightforward approach to targeting. None of them were wearing goggles like mine, and anyway their targets were often out of their line of sight before they fired.

Telepathy? But if the Ammei were telepathic, why did they bother with language among themselves? I looked down at one of the other guards, this one walking sideways toward what I assumed was a better firing position. I studied him, looking for something—*anything*—that might give me a clue as to how they were pulling this off.

Another, more subtle movement caught my eye. Five tenshes, who'd been standing somewhere on that side of the guard, were also in motion, bounding away from the Tower and around one of the bushes in the wide lawn. As the guard came to a halt, the animals settled themselves into the same arrow-straight line I'd seen an hour ago out in the city while waiting to be captured. The guard stopped behind the rearmost tensh, lined up his weapon along their line, and fired.

And at the far end of the blast, yet another ghost-suited soldier fell dead.

I looked sideways at the Amme with the fancy goggles standing next to me. Now that I was watching for it, I saw his eyes shifting from the approaching SOLA soldiers to the Ammei shooters and back again.

No. Not to the shooters. He was looking at the tenshes.

I'd been right about the telepathy. Only it wasn't between the Ammei.

Something cold and hard settled into the pit of my stomach. I'd speculated that the tenshes might be like Ixil's outriders, able to download orders and upload memories when they were linked into their master's nervous system. But I'd never been able to make that theory fit into the pattern of our interactions with both the animals and the Ammei themselves.

It had never fit because I'd been wrong. The Amme/tensh interaction was indeed telepathic, but only in one direction. The Ammei could give the animals mental commands and the animals obeyed.

And with that, the last piece of the puzzle that was Nexus Six fell into place.

I still didn't know First of Three's whole plan. But at least now I knew the players.

CHAPTER TWENTY-FIVE

◆◆◆

Kinneman had sent thirty soldiers to infiltrate the city. Six minutes of terrible, one-sided battle later, all thirty were dead.

"The destruction is complete," Rozhuhu said as the lightning guns finally went dark. "Do you learn your place, Roarke of the humans?"

I took a careful breath. Antagonizing the Ammei would gain me nothing, and could lose all of us a great deal. But it was still sorely tempting. "My place is at the side of Selene of the Kadolians," I said. "May I see her?"

Rozhuhu turned to Third, and launched into yet another private conversation. This time, Second also joined in. "You will see her," Rozhuhu said at last. "We will go now."

"Do we meet her in the secret room?" I asked as Second and Fourth started around the outside of the room toward the exit ramp.

Rozhuhu gave a little twitch. "What secret room do you speak of?"

"The room on the north side of level three," I said. "The big one across from the Center of Knowledge."

He seemed to relax. "We meet Selene of the Kadolians at the Chair of Authority."

"Which is where?"

"Follow."

I didn't have long to wonder where we were going, or whose authority we were talking about. The Chair of Authority turned out to be just one floor down, right below level nine's Upper Rooms.

Like that floor, the whole level here consisted of a single room. Unlike the Upper Rooms, though, this one didn't have any of the short dividers or multiple half rooms, but was instead a completely open area. In the center was an elaborate throne, and seated there was an old Amme with a hat that put all the others I'd seen to shame.

"Roarke of the humans," Rozhuhu intoned as I was brought to a spot three meters in front of the throne and motioned to a halt, "present honor and respect to the First of Three."

"I greet you, First of Three," I said as politely as I could, given that this was the Amme who'd wanted me to learn my place through the wholesale slaughter of Kinneman's soldiers. "Where is Selene of the Kadolians?"

There was a general stir among Rozhuhu and the others. Apparently, I wasn't supposed to speak until I'd been spoken to. "First of Three?" I prompted.

"I'm here, Gregory," Selene's voice came from behind me.

I turned. Coming up the ramp were Conciliators Fearth and Uvif, with Huginn and Circe following close behind, the whole group wrapped in a six-Ammei armed escort. Behind them, looking almost like an afterthought, was Selene with her own four-Ammei guard. Fearth, Uvif, and Circe, I noted, were sending visual daggers at me; Selene's pupils just looked tense.

There was no sign of the Iykams Fearth had brought here from the Alainn portal. My guess was that they'd probably been tossed into cold storage along with Huginn's group.

"Are you okay?" I asked Selene.

"As bright as a Gilbert's tit-willow," she said. "You?"

"Feeling a bit pear-shaped," I said, feeling my throat tighten. In one of Gilbert's musicals—I couldn't remember which one— one of the characters had talked about a suicidal tit-willow bird. Among all our fruit-and-bird code listings, that was the most ominous one. Coupled with my use of the archaic warning term *pear-shaped,* it looked like neither Selene nor I was in particularly good positions. Hopefully, I could help with that.

Or else I would just make things worse. At this point, it was probably a toss-up.

"But it's good to see you," I added. As the incoming group reached me, I slipped between the Ammei guards and Patth and reached Selene. "I missed you." Before anyone could say or do anything I moved in close and gave her a big hug.

With Selene's hyperacute sense of smell, the close proximity required for a hug was stressful at best and painful at worst. But right now comfort was at the bottom of my priority list. I needed information, and I needed it without anyone else knowing what I was doing. I pressed my cheek against Selene's, putting my lips close to her ear—

"Which is Huginn's portal?" I breathed.

"Four o'clock," she whispered back. "They're giving us the serum after we talk."

"I'll try to fix that," I said. "Get me Huginn's reactions."

A hand closed roughly around my upper arm. "That's enough," Huginn growled, hauling me bodily away from Selene. "This is a place of honor and reverence, not some dive where you and your female can frolic."

"Like *you* should talk," I snapped back, the retort coming out before I realized it made no sense whatsoever.

Or maybe it made sense to Huginn. I was still trying to get my feet firmly back under me when he again yanked me off-balance, this time pulling me right up against him. "What did you say?" he demanded, his face bare millimeters from mine. *"What did you say?"*

I was working on an answer when he dropped his voice to a whisper. "What do you need?"

"Freedom of movement," I murmured back.

A microscopic nod. "Because *no one* disgraces the First of Three," he went on at his original volume. "Understood?"

I looked over his shoulder. Everyone else in the room was staring at us, Circe and the two Patth glowering, the Ammei looking more surprised than outraged. "Understood," I said, putting sullen acceptance into my tone. I didn't know how far on my side Huginn was, but at this point I'd take even a fractional ally. "I apologize to the First of Three and the Ammei people if I unintentionally caused offense."

First said something. "The First of Three accepts your apology," Fourth said in his usual stilted English. Apparently, First didn't have a translator of his own and had to make do with

either Second's or Third's. "Selene of the Kadolians requests your
approval. Do you grant it?"

"I am happy to offer advice," I said. "To offer approval I must
first know what it is I'm approving. Tell me about the glory of
the Ammei. What is it, and what will the Ammei do with it?"

"Such is not for humans to know," Fourth said. "That knowledge
is reserved for the Ammei, the Patthaaunutth, and the Kadolians."

"Who are, after all, the First of Three, the Second of Three,
and the Third of Three," I said. "Are they not?"

Fourth shot a look at First and Second. "That knowledge is
reserved for the Ammei, the Patthaaunutth, and the Kadolians,"
he repeated.

"So you won't explain to me the glory?" I pressed.

"That knowledge is reserved—"

"Yes, I got it," I interrupted him. "Still, I think your other
guests should know the truth. If you don't wish to tell them,
perhaps you'll allow me to do so."

"You do not have that knowledge," Rozhuhu put in tartly.

"Don't I?" I took a moment to look around at the silent
assembly. Circe and the two Patth were still glaring, but Huginn's
expression was now one of carefully controlled interest. More
important, I saw that Selene had quietly moved into close sniffing range of him.

"It's quite simple," I said, turning back to First and the other
Ammei leaders. "In the room across from the Center of Knowledge you're building a portal."

I still didn't know enough Ammei expression and body language to be able to fully gauge their reaction. But the stir behind
me showed that the Patth, at least, were surprised by my revelation.

"You say untruth," Fourth said. "You have not been inside
that room."

"As I said before, I'm aware of all dangers to the life and
well-being of Selene of the Kadolians," I reminded him. "I also
know you've been working on this portal for many years. Yet it
remains unfinished. I conclude that you, First of Three, require
the services of the Second of Three"—I waved behind me in the
general direction of the two Patth—"and the Third of Three"—I
pointed at Selene—"to complete the portal and regain your glory."

I stopped, waiting as Fourth quietly translated my speech for
First. He finished, and for a long moment the room was silent.

Then, First stirred and spoke in a firm, very formal voice. "You speak truth, Roarke of the humans," Fourth translated. "Do you then give your approval to Selene of the Kadolians to accept her role?"

"Not yet," I said. "Not without further testing of the serum. *But.*" I raised a finger. "Suppose I could obtain for you an already functional full-range portal? Would you then need the aid of Selene of the Kadolians and Fearth of the Patthaaunutth to complete your version?"

This time, I could feel a stir go around both sides of the room. "I know that's what you need," I continued. "Here on Nexus Six, surrounded by twelve Gemini portals, you would hardly need to build another of those. No, your makeshift model has to be a full-range one." I cocked an eye at First. "So tell me: What do the Ammei need with a new portal? Are you trying to return to the Gold Ones?"

"Do not speak of the Gold Ones!" First snarled.

I took an involuntary step backward, bumping into a pair of Ammei guards who'd silently come up behind me. The First of Three spoke *English*?

I swallowed a curse. I'd called it, all right, all the way back at the beginning. I'd speculated to Huginn that all the Ammei spoke English, and were only pretending otherwise.

As my father used to say, *Getting your enemy to overestimate you is good. Getting him to underestimate you is better.* And here in this rustic, out-of-the-way planet filled with homey, backwater, clueless aliens who could barely even communicate with strangers, I'd fallen right into the psychological trap.

"Nice to finally hear your real voice, First of Three," I said. "So you don't think much of the Gold Ones, do you?"

"We will not discuss them," Fourth said.

I shook my head. "Sorry, too late," I said. "I've got it now. You were the Gold Ones'...what? Overseers? Conductors? Managers?"

"We will not—" Fourth began.

"Enough," First cut him off. "Roarke of the humans is correct. He knows the truth."

"Most of it, anyway," I said. Somewhere in the back of my mind I noted the curious and slightly suspicious fact that neither Patth had said a word since the beginning of the confrontation. Were they listening in stunned amazement? Or were they already up to speed, possibly even more than I was, and were just letting me take point? "Did you and the Gold Ones part on bad terms?"

"The portals were *ours,*" First said stiffly. "They were always ours. *We* ran them, *we* managed them, *we* dedicated ourselves to their function and operation."

"But you didn't *build* them," I said, watching him closely. "The Gold Ones, the Patth, and the Kadolians did that."

"They were *ours!*" First snarled again. "They betrayed us. They *all* betrayed us."

"Then what do you wish of us?" Fearth spoke up.

First turned to him. "You will take the serum," he said, his voice gone quiet and somehow even more chilling. "As the needles join with their threads and link the silver and black together, you, Fearth of the Patthaaunutth, and you, Selene of the Kadolians, will join with me to recreate the glory that was once ours. You will make the final assemblies and pattern the final adjustments. When you have finished, the Ammei, the Patthaaunutth, and the Kadolians shall once again rule together."

"If we refuse?" Fearth asked.

First gave the same kind of twitch I'd just seen from Rozhuhu. "You will not refuse."

"No," Fearth said, his voice respectful but firm. "The Director General has already decided. That era is past. The Patthaaunutth will not return to it."

"The Patthaaunutth will have no choice."

"I will not take the serum."

"You will have no choice."

"Just a minute," Circe spoke up, sending me a speculative look. "There's no need for anyone to take this serum. Roarke says he can get you a full-range portal."

I winced. The sole purpose of that question had been to get Huginn's reaction to the idea of the Ammei being loose in the Spiral again. I'd been very careful of my word choices—*suppose I could?*—to make sure I wasn't committing myself to anything, with plenty of room to backpedal should anyone call me on it.

But as First turned to face me, I realized with a sinking feeling that such subtleties were probably going to be lost on him.

Sure enough—"You know where a portal is?" he asked.

"I know of several," I said, stalling while I tried to think. During my last trip to Icarus I'd looked up the Ammei enclaves

Huginn had talked about, and I knew the planets where the four of them were located. The most obvious thing to do would be to pop off with one of those names.

But as my father used to say, *Obvious doesn't necessarily mean right.* If the Ammei had already fully searched their chosen worlds and come up dry, trying to foist off one of them as the home of my theoretical portal could quickly get me in serious trouble. Better to name some other random planet and hope for the best...

"It's on Juniper," Selene said.

I turned my head to stare at her, my thoughts and plans doing a sideways tilt. Juniper was indeed one of the Ammei worlds.

But how had she known that? She hadn't been back to civilization since we arrived on Nexus Six, and I hadn't had a chance to hand off any of that information. Worse, if the Ammei *had* searched that planet...

First muttered something. "Where?" he demanded.

"We know the general area," I jumped in. The last thing we could afford was being pinned down to latitude and longitude. "I can show you on a map later. But first we need some guarantees."

First spat something. "The Kadolians are the Third of Three," he said. "The Ammei are the First of Three. Humans are nothing. *We* rule, not you."

"I thought you said you'd all rule together," I said. "Which is it?"

"We are the First of Three," First said again.

"All are equal," Huginn murmured, just loudly enough for me to hear, "but some are more equal than others."

"Actually, it doesn't matter," I said. "Either way, you still need me. You certainly need Selene of the Kadolians."

"No," Uvif said. "You need neither of them."

I felt something tingle on my back. Uvif had taken a step away from Fearth and Circe and moved toward First. What was he up to? "You don't need Selene of the Kadolians, First of Three," the Conciliator continued. "Nor do you need Conciliator Fearth of the Patthaaunutth." He took another step forward.

Two of the guards flanking the throne raised their lightning guns warningly. First of Three held up a hand, and they lowered their muzzles to point at the floor in front of the Path. "Explain," First said.

"You need a Patthaaunutth and a Kadolian to finish your portal," Uvif said, and there was no mistaking the arrogant menace in his tone. "Very well. I welcome the opportunity to work with you and the Ammei. *I* will take the serum, and will pledge my full support of the Ammei glory."

"We welcome you, Uvif of the Patthaaunutth," First said. "But you still must persuade cooperation from Selene of the Kadolians."

"Such persuasion is unnecessary," Uvif said. "There is another Kadolian I can bring to you."

I caught my breath. No. *No.*

"Where?" First said. "What is his name?"

"He currently resides with Sub-Director Nask," Uvif said. "His name is Tirano. He comes from the world where the Ammei once gathered the precious silver-silk." He sent me a mocking smile. "And he was briefly associated with Selene of the Kadolians."

"When can he be brought here?" First asked.

"The portal will reopen in six hours and twenty minutes," Uvif said. "At that time, if you so choose, I will travel there with a group of armed Ammei and bring him to you. Do you so choose?"

There was a brief conversation among the Ammei. "I do," First of Three said at last.

"I strongly suggest you reconsider," I warned. "The boy is barely into his youthage. A serum designed for Kadolian adults could be fatal to him."

"Or it could not," Uvif said calmly. "Still, if it does, we still have Selene."

"Yes," First said, his eyes shifting between Uvif and Selene. "Yes, we will."

My eyes flicked across First and his guards, my brain blazing through a quick set of attack scenarios. If I could get to the closest guard and wrest his weapon from him before the others could get to me, I'd be in position to hold First hostage and bargain for Selene's life—

And then, for the second time in five minutes, a hand came out of nowhere and locked around my right upper arm. Reflexively, I jerked, but before I could pull away a second hand closed around the back of my collar, pinning me solidly in place. "You can all work out the details together," Huginn said from behind me. "Meanwhile, Roarke of the humans needs to be put some place where he can be neutralized."

"Huginn—" I snarled.

"I suggest the Upper Rooms," Huginn went on. "The beds there have metal frames that are anchored to the floor. I have a set of wrist cuffs, and I can secure him there."

"No," I snapped, shooting a glare at Huginn. "I'm bodyguard to Selene of the Kadolians. I must stay at her side."

"All the more reason he should be locked away," Huginn said. "Each of them is the guarantee of the other's behavior. First of Three?"

"You speak wisdom," First said. "Take him." He motioned to Rozhuhu and said something in the Ammei language. "Rozhuhu will follow and observe."

"Fine with me." Huginn twisted my arm. "Come on."

He turned me around and we headed back across the room toward the ramp. Four armed Ammei were already waiting for me with an air of expectation. We started to pass Selene and Fearth, and I leaned back against Huginn's grip, slowing our forward momentum. "I'm sorry, Selene," I apologized.

"Don't worry, Gregory," she said, the tension in her pupils in sharp contrast to her surface calmness. "Others may fear the events of the night. We do not."

I huffed out a sigh, and gave her a heavy nod.

And as Huginn, Rozhuhu, and the guards herded me toward the ramp to the Upper Rooms, I felt a small easing of my own tension.

I'd seen enough of the Ammei to suspect the *First of Three* designation meant they fully intended to be in charge of any deals or alliances they might make with their guests. I'd also seen enough of the Patth to know they didn't like playing second fiddle to anyone.

Now, with Selene's reading of Huginn's mood during the conversation confirming that hunch, my gamble looked to be paying off. Huginn was concerned about the direction this whole thing was going, and if he didn't trust the Ammei there was a fair chance he would stay on my side.

I frowned, running Selene's words back through my head. She hadn't said *others might be concerned*. She'd said *others might fear*.

Might *fear*?

Huginn was a highly trained, highly skilled Patth Expediter, not someone who could easily be frightened. Unless Selene had overstated his emotional reaction, he was well past just being worried. Apparently, there was still more going on under the surface that I didn't know about.

But that was for the future. Right now, Selene was in trouble, and it was my job to get her out of it.

Fortunately, I had a pretty good idea how to do that.

The beds in the Upper Rooms were just as Huginn had described: thick mattresses on metal frames, with the legs bolted to the floor. Huginn led us to the southern cubicle, the one farthest from the entry ramp, and gave the room a quick look. "This will do," he said, pointing to the bed and pulling out his cuffs. "Okay, Roarke. Assume the position."

"You're on the wrong side, Huginn," I warned as I lay down on my stomach, dropping my left arm off the mattress to dangle alongside the bed leg. "You better think it through while you still can."

"I've done all the thinking I need to, thanks," he said, kneeling beside me. For a brief moment his eyes met mine, and I saw in them the dark fear that Selene had already sensed from his scent. The man was indeed worried.

"Your job is to serve the Patth," I reminded him.

"My job is to serve the winners," he countered. Leaning over, he snapped the cuffs onto my left wrist and the bed leg. "If you're smart, you'll reach that same conclusion."

"I already have," I said as he straightened up. "Don't go very far with that key. I'll need to use the facilities at some point."

"Don't worry," he said, stepping back and handing the key to Rozhuhu. "Leave this with the guard at the foot of the ramp. You *are* setting a guard, aren't you?"

"There will be two guards," Rozhuhu said, taking the key. He stepped past Huginn and knelt down beside me, double-checking that the cuffs were secure.

"Make it one," Huginn said. "The Alainn portal isn't going to be an easy nut to crack. You'll need every soldier you've got; and *I'll* need all the time we've got to brief them on the terrain and run them through the attack plan. One guard, give him the key, and get everyone else to the library."

"The First of Three must approve any plans," Rozhuhu said stiffly.

"Then we'd better go talk to him right now," Huginn said, striding toward the ramp. "Like I said, you'll need everyone you've got if we're going to snatch the Kadolian kid."

They headed to the ramp, Huginn urging speed, Rozhuhu still worrying aloud about protocol. Their voices faded away, and I heard one final indistinct conversation as Rozhuhu presumably assigned my guard and handed off the key.

And then, silence.

I turned toward the nearby window and studied the slice of sky visible from my angle. About an hour to sunset, I estimated, followed by two hours of the beacon's artificial twilight before it shut down for the night. Three hours out of Uvif's six hours gone before I could even start my play.

I grimaced as I lay back down. The timing here was going to be tighter than I liked, possibly too tight to be feasible. But I had no choice. I had a way around the guards at Huginn's portal—maybe—but not if anyone who happened to look out of the Tower was able to see me. Why the hell was the damn beacon still running after all this time?

And then, abruptly, a thought flashed unbidden across my mind. Two hours, seven minutes, and a few seconds, Huginn had said for the beacon's timing. I didn't remember the precise numbers, but that was close enough to my vague memories for me to realize I'd stumbled on the truth.

The beacon wasn't just blazing out in hopes that some random galactic passerby would happen by. It was a deliberate signal to Alpha, with the period of the glow precisely matching the full-range portal's orbital period. Whatever small positional fluctuations Alpha might undergo, the one-revolution timing guaranteed that somewhere in its orbit it would be able to locate Nexus Six and the Tower.

And with that, one more lurking mystery suddenly resolved itself. I'd wondered why the Icari would set up a ring of Geminis here without having a full-range portal also set up alongside them. Only that had indeed been the case once. Alpha had been right here in the city, probably in the center of the ring where *Imistio* Tower now stood. But then someone had stolen the two halves of a portal directory, and the Icari had responded by moving Alpha into orbit where any thieves trying to come through would find themselves at a dead end.

Except that the thieves had never walked into the trap, because the one carrying RH had already sneaked through and the one with LH had died in battle on Meima and been buried in rubble before he could follow. But the trap remained, the portal left permanently open back to Meima, while the beacon kept its faithful vigil. Meanwhile, the Icari, tired of waiting, had presumably moved on.

And so matters had stood for the past five or ten millennia. The Ammei on Nexus Six, isolated from all but the handful of worlds they could reach through their Geminis, had effectively become a backwater, their former glory fading along with the city itself. They blamed the Icari—the Gold Ones—and brooded.

Until someone thought of a possible way out. If they could build their own full-range portal, they could get back into the game.

I scowled. I could follow the logic that far, but right there was where it fell apart. There was no way they could fit a thirty-meter-diameter launch module in the room I'd seen. It was possible that most of the portal's size was geared to alleviate the tidal effects arising from the artificial gravity, and the Ammei might have been able to skip that part of the design. But they would still need a receiver module if the thing was going to be of any use to them, and there was no way they could put one of those together without internal gravity.

There was still a piece missing, and I didn't have any idea what it was. But I would bet commas to commarks that Huginn did. If I pulled this off, he would definitely owe me that piece.

Two hours fifty minutes to go. Arranging myself as comfortably as I could with one arm pinioned to a metal bed leg, I settled in to rest.

CHAPTER TWENTY-SIX

The beacon shut off, and the soft glow that had filled my sleeping room disappeared. I gave my eyes two minutes to adjust to the faint starlight coming in through the windows, then got to work.

I'd already pulled my last knockout pill from my left arm's hidden wrist compartment and set it on the floor beside the bed. Now, settling the thumb and first two fingers of my right hand on the arm's quick-release points, I squeezed and twisted. The artificial skin unwove from the genuine skin of the elbow and upper arm, the forearm came off, and I was free.

I sat up and pulled off my shoes, then picked up the knockout pill. My bedroom/prison had come equipped with a small collection of Icari books, and during the past three hours I'd studied the selection and picked out the one that seemed the best size for what I needed. I pulled it from its shelf, then padded silently in my stocking feet to the meal-prep area on the floor's west side. Huginn had led me past it earlier on our way to the sleeping room, and I'd again visually picked out which of the drink tubes would be easiest to get to. Unscrewing the cap with only one hand was a bit tricky, but by wedging the tube in my left armpit I was able to get it open. I dropped the pill into the liquid, gave it a quick swish to make sure it dissolved, then gave the cap a single turn back on just to make sure nothing leaked out. I made my way back to the

ramp and crouched down by the wall beside it, drink tube under
my arm, book gripped in my right hand.

Bracing myself, I cleared my throat. "Guard!" I called, adjusting
my volume to sound like my voice was coming from the far end
of the floor. "Guard! You—Amme! I need the bathroom. Guard?
Come on, I need the bathroom."

I paused to listen. I didn't know whether everyone on Nexus
Six spoke English or it was just the fancy-hat leadership. But
surely Rozhuhu had told the guard that the prisoner would need
a bathroom break somewhere along the line and to be ready for
such a summons. I filled my lungs to try again.

And paused as I heard the faint sound of approaching footsteps.
One set of them, just as Huginn had recommended. I resettled
my grip on the book, made sure the tube was secure. A darker
shadow appeared in the opening, framed against the background
of the ramp area...

Then he was there, stepping off the ramp and turning toward
my sleeping room. He had a lightning gun slung over his shoulder,
one of the hand weapons I'd seen on the Ammei by the portal
room belted at his waist.

In his left hand he carried a small bucket.

I smiled tightly. So much for my bathroom break. Rozhuhu
had accepted Huginn's warning that the raid on the Alainn portal would require as many soldiers as First could spare, but he'd
also apparently decided I was too dangerous for a single guard
to unlock and escort to the bathroom by himself. The bucket,
a time-honored option for prisoner relief, was his compromise.

The guard got four steps before I came up behind him and
slammed the book as hard as I could against the side of his head.

The impact sent him staggering sideways toward the windows.
But he managed to stay on his feet. I hit him again as he tried
to turn around, the blow throwing him still further off-balance,
then slammed a kick into the back of his knee. The combination
finally brought him down, landing him heavily on his side. Quick
as a cat he rolled onto his back, hand fumbling for his sidearm.
I tossed the book at his face to distract him and dropped on top
of him, landing with my knees pinioning his arms. A quick turn
of my wrist got the cap off the tube, and as the guard opened
his mouth to shout a warning I dumped in the contents.

He gagged and tried to spit it out. But it was too late. Enough of the drug had gotten in to hopefully do the job. I pressed my hand over his mouth and held on grimly as he bucked and twisted beneath me. Then, abruptly, his muscles loosened and he went still.

I stayed where I was another thirty seconds, listening for any sign that we'd been heard. But there were no sounds from below. Huffing out a relieved breath, I drew his sidearm from its holster and stuck it into the back of my belt. I rolled off him, unslung the lightning gun from his shoulder, and slid it as far as I could across the floor.

The key to the cuffs was in the upper left chest pocket of his tunic. Leaving him sleeping peacefully, I hurried back to the bed, unlocked the cuffs, and retrieved my arm. Reattaching it was tricky even in a brightly lit room, and it took me a couple of tries before I was able to line everything up. After that, it was just a matter of enduring the unpleasant tingle as the artificial nerves and motor systems reconnected with the flesh-and-blood ones.

Finally, it was done. I put my shoes back on and went back to the sleeping guard, dragging him around the floor to the other sleeping cubicle. I cuffed him to that bed frame, returned the key to his pocket—making his friends find bolt cutters or a torch in order to free him would just be petty—and returned to the ramp. Senses fully alert, I headed down.

The caution proved unnecessary. Huginn's warnings regarding the upcoming raid had stripped the upper Tower of any security except for my lone guard.

The vine rope Huginn had made was still where I'd left it under my bed in our former sleeping room. A long and nervous climb later, I was once again on the ground outside the Tower.

And here was where it would start to get tricky. If Ixil was where I'd left him, or even if he'd just stayed in that general vicinity, I should be able to find him quickly enough for what I had in mind. But if I had to search the whole city for him—or worse, if he'd gone back to Alpha—my plan would die on the vine. Mentally crossing my fingers, I crossed the lawn, slipped into the subway tunnel, and headed outward.

I didn't know if the upcoming mission had drawn the usual guards away from the portal ring, but I wasn't in the mood to take chances. I eased past that access ramp as quietly as I could, then resumed my soft jog. One more stop, I decided, and I'd go back to the surface and continue my search.

I was approaching my chosen ramp when I spotted a small movement by the opening.

I came to a halt, staring into the darkness and wishing I still had those Ammei enhancement goggles. The movement came again, and this time I could see that it was something small. Probably a wandering tensh, standing right where I'd planned to come up. Possibly with an Ammei controller within view.

Or, if I was lucky and Ixil had anticipated my movements...

I eased toward the figure, aware of the weapon still tucked away at the small of my back, even more aware of the fact I didn't have the foggiest idea how to use it. Even if I did, odds were it would be loud enough or bright enough to bring the whole city down on me. I closed to five meters of the ramp...

And felt the tension drain out of me as I heard a familiar squeak. "Pax?" I whispered.

There was a soft flurry, and a moment later Pax was nosing at my outstretched hand. "Good boy," I murmured. "Take me to Ixil?"

I'd never figured out whether or not the outriders could understand English. But Pax clearly had his orders. He gave my hand one final sniff and scurried away, turning into the opening and heading up the ramp. I followed, pausing at the top to check for Ammei, then continued on across the debris field. I spotted a couple of tenshes rooting through the plants, but as usual they barely paused to give me a curious look before returning to their hunting.

Three minutes later, Pax squeezed through a wall crack in yet another of the run-down buildings. I found a broken but navigable window and went inside. "Ixil?" I called softly.

"About time," Ixil said quietly from a darkened corner. "Are you all right?"

"For the moment," I said. "But it's about to hit the fan, and there's no time to explain."

"Understood," Ixil said. "What do you need from me?"

"From you, nothing," I said. "Two questions. First: You said Pix and Pax had an agreement with the tenshes. Do you think they could get a group of them to play follow-the-leader?"

"I think so, yes."

"Good," I said. "Second question..." I hesitated. "Are your outriders claustrophobic?"

❖   ❖   ❖

I'd wondered earlier if the Ammei would continue their night guard on the portals. I still didn't know the full answer to that question.

What I *did* know now was that they *were* definitely keeping watch on the portal at the four o'clock position, the one Selene had told me led to the Patth base. That only made sense, especially since Uvif had probably told them which one they would be traveling through.

Still, there were only four guards, a low enough number that Ixil and I should be able to take them out without too much trouble.

Unfortunately, a physical attack would almost certainly end up with one or more of the guards dead or wounded and the rest of the city on full alert. Hopefully, my plan would entail considerably less violence.

"There," Ixil murmured, pointing to his left around the bush we were crouched behind.

I peered in that direction. I couldn't see anything but debris and shadows. "You sure?"

"He's there," he assured me. "You sure you don't want a plasmic?"

I shook my head. "The knife will do."

He nodded, understanding or agreement, I didn't know which. "Get ready."

Just as I couldn't see Pix, so I also didn't hear his distant squeak. But the half dozen tenshes prowling around the base of the portal clearly did. All of them simultaneously turned or raised their heads toward the sound.

Their movements were relatively subtle, but the Ammei guard on that side was instantly on it. He muttered something, and the other three hurried quickly to his side from their respective duty posts. For a moment they all peered off into the darkness, lightning guns raised. Then, abruptly, the tenshes loped off in Pix's direction.

The guards were ready. Another muttered order, and three of them headed off behind the animals, leaving the fourth to maintain his vigil.

I winced as they headed into the darkness. Right now the remaining watchman was standing directly between me and the portal. If he stayed put, I would have to circle around to the other side, which would cost time I was pretty sure I didn't have.

Fortunately, whoever had given him his orders was too smart to leave that much of the portal unguarded. For a couple of seconds he watched his fellows head away, then started walking a quick sentry circle around the portal.

"Looks like you'll have twenty seconds," Ixil whispered into my ear.

I nodded. That was the estimate I'd also come up with. "Soon as I'm gone, get back to cover," I whispered back, handing him the weapon I'd taken from the guard.

"Understood," he said, tucking the weapon away in his belt and drawing his plasmic. Neither of us wanted any bloodshed here, but if the three Ammei unexpectedly turned back, he was prepared to give me cover fire. The fact that such an action would probably cost him his life was something that had also surely occurred to him. "Good luck."

Pax was crouched on the ground beside me, dressed in the little vac suit I'd seen him wear on our first trip onto Alpha's outer surface. I gathered him into my arms and got ready.

And as the guard's path took him out of sight around the side of the portal, I rose from my crouch and charged.

I made it to the portal in five seconds flat. A quick check of the surface to locate the nearest hatch, a couple of seconds to find and trigger the release, and the hatch popped open to reveal the usual soft glow. I reached in and dropped Pax onto the deck, then leaned my head and torso through the opening and pulled myself the rest of the way in. Ignoring the brief vertigo as gravity shifted, I reached down and closed the hatch.

I exhaled loudly. "We're in," I murmured to Pax as I looked around. I'd wondered if the receiver module would be set up as a staging area the way Kinneman had done with Alpha. But the sphere was empty.

Mostly empty, anyway. Two blackout tents had been rigged, one of them three hatches over from where Pax and I had come through, the other at the top of the sphere. Entry point and surveillance, I tentatively identified them. "A good five or six seconds to spare, too," I added. "Come on."

I made my way around the curved deck to the interface, Pax trotting along beside me, and looked cautiously into the launch module. Again, the Patth hadn't left anyone to watch over this end of their portal.

And really, why should they? With the other end of the pair locked down, there was no need to have anyone on duty here.

Rolling over the interface, I crossed to the extension arm, with Pax again at my side. "Wait here," I told him as I got a grip on the arm and was pulled gently upward. "Miracles *do* still happen."

But apparently today wasn't one of those days. I reached the luminescent gray section, hovered there a moment, then began an equally leisurely descent. "Yep, it's still blocked," I confirmed. "I guess it's your turn."

I reached the bottom and once again got Pax into my arms. "Let's just hope Huginn's grinning hint about their portal lock wasn't just some general disinformation smarminess. Otherwise, this is going to be a really short trip."

Pax squeaked encouragingly. I held him across my left arm, keeping hold of the extension arm with my right hand as we headed up. I watched our ascent closely, trying to judge the right time. Half a second to the gray area...

I swung Pax around, pressing his paws against the extension arm and pulling away my own hand. He reached the gray.

And vanished.

I took a deep breath as gravity reversed and I again floated downward. I hadn't gotten through; Pax had. That strongly suggested that the Patth were using the same sort of balloon technique, and roughly the same size balloon, as the Icarus Group was. Great for keeping human-sized intruders out, but it left the center of the receiver module perfectly accessible to something the outrider's size. That left Pax sitting right now in the center of their balloon.

The crucial question was whether the balloon was made of a material that his claws could poke through.

That was the true gamble here. Ixil hadn't had a knife or anything else we could equip Pax with, and while he'd assured me that outrider claws were sharp enough and strong enough to handle anything the Patth were likely to use, I still couldn't shake the mental image of Pax floating helplessly in the middle of an impenetrable tomb until his suit's air gave out. I reached the deck, grabbed the extension arm, and started up again.

Only to reach the top, float there a moment, then start back down.

Just relax, I ordered myself firmly as I started another trip. Ixil had warned that the balloon might take a minute to slowly deflate after Pax punctured it and might still be adequately in position to block me until my third or fourth attempt. I hit the deck and started back up, muttering a mix of curses and prayers. Once again I reached the luminescent gray—

And this time the world around me vanished.

A portal trip typically only took a couple of seconds. But these particular three seconds seemed to last forever. Just because the Patth receiver was open didn't mean I was in the clear. If there were Iykams on duty in there, they could easily have realized what was going on, incinerated the balloon and Pax with a couple of blasts from their corona weapon, and were waiting for me to appear for a repeat performance. The universe reappeared—

I found myself in the center of a Gemini-sized receiver module, not a single Iykam or Patth in sight. At one side, off to my right, one of the hatches was open, letting in diffuse light and the sound of quiet conversations. Below and to my left, a slightly deflated balloon was drifting toward the deck.

I exhaled a sigh of relief. A premature one, certainly, given how much of the road still lay ahead. But at least now I wouldn't have to live with the thought that I'd caused Pax's death.

Because from this point on, if Pax died I probably would, too.

The balloon was still softly hissing its air out when I finally landed and crossed over to it. A couple of careful slashes from my knife, and Pax was free. I sheathed my knife, picked him up, and headed toward the hatch. I reached it, dropped onto my belly by the opening, and eased my eyes over the edge for a look.

I'd expected the sort of gadget-heavy research facility that I'd seen at the first Patth portal I'd visited a couple of years ago. To my mild surprise, spread out before me here was less like a science lab and more like the base camp of a wilderness expedition. Transport and exploration, not research, was apparently the plan of the day. Five Patth and a round dozen Iykams were seated at various tables, standing guard by the mouth of a tunnel, or working their way through stacks of equipment, all of them completely oblivious to my presence.

For a couple of seconds I mulled over the question of whether it would be safer to call to them from inside the receiver or to drop in on them in all my unarmed glory before getting their attention. The latter, I decided. Taking a deep breath, I again gathered Pax onto my left arm, grabbed the edge of the hatchway with my right hand, and swung my legs out and down to the deck half a meter below me. "Hello," I called, displaying my open hands. "Don't shoot—I'm unarmed."

As surprises went, it was easily in the top ten entrances I'd ever been a part of. There were at least three startled squeals from the occupants, and three chairs went skittering across the floor as their former owners leaped up and spun around to face the horrible threat that had suddenly appeared in their midst. "I'm unarmed," I repeated, raising my voice to be heard over the fresh ruckus. "I'm here to talk to Sub-Director Nask. Someone please tell him that Gregory Roarke is here and needs to see him right away. Tell him it's urgent."

I paused, looking at the ring of corona weapons that had suddenly sprouted around me. Then, giving everyone my friendliest smile, I lowered myself carefully to sit cross-legged underneath the portal hatchway. "While you do that," I added helpfully, "I'll just wait here."

The last time I'd seen Sub-Director Nask he'd been cocooned in the Patth version of an intensive care pod, slowly recovering from the bloody hijacking that had nearly killed him. He was still far from looking his old self, but at least he was moving around mostly on his own.

Of course, should he happen to stumble, there were plenty of helping hands in his vicinity ready to break his fall.

Two of those hands belonged to Muninn, Nask's other Expediter. He was bigger than Huginn, and a lot less talkative. But I'd seen him in action, and he was just as agile and deadly as the smaller man. The other twelve hands belonged to the six Iykams who had crowded into the interrogation room ahead of Nask's arrival and spread out around the walls. They were even less talkative than Muninn, but the looks they were giving me were every bit as expressive as fancy oratory would have been. As far as they were concerned, I was a loathsome insect they really, really wanted to step on.

The fact that they were probably in charge of the portal security that I'd just breached was likely a good percentage of that animosity.

Nask himself seemed a few degrees friendlier than everyone else in the room. But that was probably just because he wanted to hear my whole story before he gave the order for those shoes to go splat.

At least he *did* let me give him the whole story. Or rather, as much of the story as I was willing and able to tell.

I finished, and for a moment he stared at me in silence. Finally, he stirred. "And you expect me to believe all that." It was a statement, not a question.

"I expect you to believe me far enough to take some serious precautions," I said. "Was there anything I said that didn't make sense?"

"There was quite a bit that seemed to be absent," he said pointedly. "How you and Colonel Ixil T'adee arrived at Nexus Six, for one. I assume the outrider you brought in is one of his?"

"Yes," I confirmed. The first thing Nask had done when he arrived in the portal chamber was order Pax to be taken away and put into isolation. Given that the outriders were essentially living recorders, I couldn't really blame him. "Sorry to have popped your balloon, by the way. But as I said, I needed to get to you before your next routine portal opening in"—I consulted my watch—"one hour and forty-two minutes, at which point the Ammei attack force comes charging in."

"Yes," Nask murmured, his face clouding over. "And all this to protect us and our portal. Yet you have stated in the past that you don't like the Patthaaunutth in general and me in particular. Why take our part against a people you've barely met and know nothing about?"

"I know enough," I said. "I know that they're megalomaniacs who brag about bringing back old glory, which is never a good sign. I know they have Icari tech. I know they demanded our help instead of asking for it."

"All of which you could reasonably suggest describe the Patthaaunutth," Nask said calmly.

"I suppose," I said. "I also know that they're holding Selene against her will. *And* Huginn *and* Circe *and* Conciliator Fearth. Right now I need allies to get all of them back safely, and you're the best I've got."

"I sympathize with Selene's situation," Nask said. "As for the others, members of the Patthaaunutth Directorate know the risks their positions may subject them to. Expediters are even more aware of the dangers."

I frowned. That didn't sound like Nask at all. "Are you saying you're not interested in rescuing them?"

"Not necessarily," he said. "I merely state that there are other considerations."

"Fine," I said, clamping down hard on my impatience. The clock was ticking, and we didn't have time for this ridiculous verbal sparring. "Let's talk about Tirano, then. He *is* here, I assume?"

"He is," Nask said. "But he's in a safe location. Even if Conciliator Uvif has turned traitor, the Ammei will not get to him."

"Are you sure?" I countered. "You haven't seen those lightning guns in action. Besides, even if you keep him safe, they'll still have Selene. They've already got Uvif on their side, which seems to be two thirds of the winning combination."

Nask's eyes seemed to flash at the mention of Uvif's name. But his voice remained calm. "Selene would not accede to their demands," he said. "Her people surely remember their time among the Ammei."

"Maybe," I said. "But memories aren't much good when your life's on the line. Especially when your stalling has a good chance of leaving her in their hands for a long time."

"Meaning?"

"Meaning that if you let the Ammei charge in, even if you counter with force in the receiver module, all those lightning guns blazing around raises the possibility of the portal taking damage. If that happens, you'll be permanently locked out of Nexus Six."

"*You* have a pathway there."

"Which you can't get to."

"Perhaps," Nask said, his eyes intent on me. "That's twice you've mentioned the power of the Ammei lightning guns. Yet you've not said where or when you saw them in action."

I felt my lip twitch. I'd hoped to skip over Kinneman's incursion fiasco. "Kinneman sent in some soldiers," I said reluctantly. "The Ammei slaughtered them, one shot per, from a pretty good distance. I have no doubt they can do the same here. End of story."

"Interesting," Nask murmured. "And a Patthaaunutth force might expect to receive a similar reception?"

"If you wait for them to be ready, yes," I said. "If you go now, you'll hopefully take them by surprise. Huginn has as many of them as he can tied up with their attack plan, which should reduce the number of sentries. I trust you have weapons that are less obvious than those?" I gestured toward the line of corona weapons pointed at me.

"We have several," Nask assured me. "Lethal and nonlethal both."

"Let's go with nonlethal," I said. "I don't know how it is with the Patth, but in the Commonwealth killing someone comes with a horrendous pile of paperwork."

"It also leads to irreversible results," Nask said.

"There's that," I said, wondering if he'd missed my attempt at humor or simply ignored it. "Either way, you should be able to get to the Tower before they're aware of you."

"The Tower that, according to your reasoning, is where the bulk of their forces will be found?"

"Well, yes, there's that," I conceded. "But lightning guns seem to be designed mostly for use in open spaces. Inside rooms and corridors, they may not be as useful."

"They will certainly also have hand weapons."

"They have some kind of sidearms, yes," I again had to admit. "I haven't seen them in action, though."

"I have no doubt they're as dangerous as the lightning guns," Nask said. "I also note that your scenario would place the Patthaaunutth in the position of aggressors."

I frowned. "Seriously? With your portal and your lives at stake, you're worried about *that*?"

"The Patthaaunutth always prefer to hold the higher moral ground."

"Since when?" I demanded. "You kidnapped Tera and me, your Talariac Drive has forced small shippers out of business all across the Spiral—" I broke off. "Wait a minute. Are you afraid of the Gold Ones?"

"The *Builders*," Nask corrected stiffly. "Only the Ammei call them the Gold Ones."

"I stand corrected," I said, looking hard at him. "The question remains."

Nask hesitated. "The reign of the Builders is the past," he said, picking his words carefully. "The Patthaaunutth do not fear ghosts."

"Sure," I said. Nice statements, both of them. Unfortunately, neither was actually an answer to my question. "Well, you need to make a decision on that, and you need to make it fast. Kinneman and EarthGuard got their collective nose bloodied today, and they're not going to be in a rush to try again."

"Even with you and your colleagues in danger?"

"You vastly overestimate our value to him," I said bitterly.

"The only people at risk are Selene, Ixil, and me, and Kinneman doesn't especially like any of us."

"A curiously self-defeating point of view," Nask said. "But that's his affair. Your conclusion, then, is that their lives are solely in Patthaaunutth hands?"

"It is," I said, feeling a familiar tightening in my stomach. There'd been something in his voice right then. "Let's cut through the ground clutter. What exactly do you want?"

Behind Nask Muninn stirred, as if the question had been a little too blunt for his taste. But Nask merely favored me with a small smile. "You said earlier that the Ammei were building a full-range portal?"

"A partial one, anyway," I said. "I assume it's a full-range from the curvature of the sections they've got, though there's nowhere near enough room in there for a complete sphere. I also didn't see any sign of a receiver module."

"There's no particular reason the receiver couldn't be located elsewhere," Nask said. "Regardless, if they're building a portal, they must be working from the ancient plans." He paused expectantly.

I sighed. "And you want me to grab them for you?"

"Yes," Nask said. "I will take the plans in exchange for Selene's life."

"*And* mine?"

"You'll be going into danger alongside the Iykams," Nask pointed out. "They will protect you to the best of their ability, but I can make no deeper promises."

"No, I suppose not," I said, my eyes flicking across the silent Iykams. They still didn't like me, but I'd never seen one disobey a direct Patth order. "All right, it's a deal. One final question: Do you know what the Ammei are up to?"

"According to you, they're building a portal."

"Portals are a means to an end," I said. "I'm asking if you know what the end is."

"Why would I?"

"Because I suggested to the First of Three that I might have a full-range portal to offer him in place of the slapdash one they're building."

Nask's reaction wasn't very big. But it was definitely there. Muninn's was even bigger. "I see," I murmured. "Thank you."

"For what?" Nask asked.

"For confirming that Selene's assessment of Huginn's reaction was correct." I raised my eyebrows. "You're not just *worried* about the Ammei. You're genuinely afraid."

"Sub-Director?" Muninn said, his expression gone dark.

"It's all right, Muninn," Nask said, his eyes steady on me. "Mr. Roarke knows nothing crucial. Certainly nothing he should disappear for."

I worked some moisture into a suddenly dry mouth. "Besides which, you need me to get those portal plans?"

"There's that." Nask smiled faintly. "And truly, we've been informal colleagues through many trying events. I would not wish a hasty end to that association."

"Neither would I," I said. "Especially since the Patth usually make out pretty well at the other end of those events." I looked at my watch. "And now we're wasting time. If we're going to get ahead of the Ammei, you need to start assembling your force right now."

"Please," Nask said in a self-satisfied tone. "The force is nearly ready. Its preparation began the moment you appeared in the portal chamber."

"Ah," I said. I should have realized that Nask would have a military option already in place. "What do you need from me?"

"If you can give us any idea where in the Tower the prisoners might be located, that would be helpful," he said.

I smiled. "Oh, I think I can do a little better than that," I said. Reaching into my pocket, I pulled out the dirt-stained map Selene had given me. "The last time I saw them was in the throne room on level nine," I continued, catching a whiff of the almost-lavender dirt as I handed it to Nask across the table. "Or they might be in the portal room—level three, north end, across from the library. We might as well stop in there on our way up."

I'd noted in the past that it took a lot to surprise or impress Nask. This time I'd managed both. "Excellent," he said, glancing at the map and then handing it up to Muninn. "This will make the assault much easier."

"Glad to hear it," I said. "Then if Muninn will kindly show me to my combat suit, we'll get this thing moving."

CHAPTER TWENTY-SEVEN

———————— ❖ ————————

I'd been mostly joking about the combat suit. I should have known better.

The outfit Muninn presented me with was similar to the one Nask's previous Expediters had poured me into two years ago when they were about to send me into the Firefall portal. It was textured in mottled gray for maximum visual stealth, flexible and surprisingly light, and loaded with a matrix of strategically placed armor inserts that would provide good protection while still allowing a decent range of motion.

The helmet for that older suit, I remembered, had been a bit heavy with a tendency to fog up. This newer model seemed to have eliminated both problems.

My weaponry consisted of a long knife, a shorter push knife, and a sidearm that was a variant of a standard police stunner. It fired a pair of electrodes into a target, delivering a jolt that should cause nearly instantaneous unconsciousness. Unlike the Commonwealth version, Muninn told me, once the current had been delivered to the target there was a sharp follow-up voltage spike on the Patth model that vaporized the leads, thus eliminating any problems with tangling. The gun was semiauto, with a six-cartridge magazine, and I had two spare mags ready on my belt.

Nask had wanted me to leave Pax with him, arguing that the

potential chaos of a battle could prove fatal to the little outrider. I argued back that if things started teetering the wrong direction a Kalix lurking in the rubble was our one and only hole card, and that Pax was the only one who could quickly bring him up to speed on our assault plan.

In the end Nask gave in, though he clearly wasn't happy about it. He did make sure to deliver the outrider to me inside a sealed, opaque box.

Under other circumstances I would have privately labeled Nask paranoid. But given that Kinneman would undoubtedly have done the exact same thing, I resisted the temptation.

The rest of the assault squad was waiting when Muninn and I returned to the portal: sixteen Iykams dressed in their version of my combat suit. Along with stunners, they also carried their favored corona weapons. As we rolled one by one through the receiver module hatchway, I saw that Nask had also set another six Iykams armed with heavy lasers in the inside hull, clumped together so that they could target anyone coming through without catching each other in a cross fire. If we failed in our mission, he was making damn sure that no Ammei force got farther than right here.

"My crew and I will go first," Muninn told me as he led the way into the launch module. "While you're coming in I'll go up top, check things out, then come back in and send a group out to deal with the portal sentries. When they're finished, they'll come in with an all-clear, and we'll head for the Tower on our assigned vectors. Questions?"

"No," I said. Actually, I had a whole stack of questions, starting with how we would find Selene and the others and get them back safely to the Path base, and ending with where and how Nask expected me to find the damn portal plans. But since none of those could be answered until we were on Nexus Six, there wasn't much point in asking them. "Let's do it."

He nodded. "First crew: Go."

He and eight of the Iykams grabbed hold of the extension arm and floated up. The other eight gathered around me, poised with hands hovering near the arm. The first group hit the gray section and vanished, and the nine of us got our own grips and followed. We reached the top, and two seconds later were in the Nexus Six receiver module.

The first crew were still floating their way downward. Briefly, I wondered if the sound of eighteen pairs of boots thudding onto the deck would be audible to the Ammei guards, decided there was nothing I could do about it if it was, and concentrated on making sure the square meter of metal I was headed for wasn't already claimed by someone else.

The first crew landed with only a small thud. Muninn and four Iykams immediately headed for the blackout tent at the top of the dome. My crew was still on our way as he disappeared inside, and we were just landing as he reemerged and gestured his Iykams into the tent. He looked around the sphere, spotted me, and pointed to the other tent. I nodded back and headed that direction.

My crew and I were gathered around the tent, and I was straining my ears for any sounds coming from outside, when the tent flap opened and an Iykam popped his head in. "Clear," he said, then popped back out again. I gave Muninn a thumbs-up and headed into the tent.

A minute later we were gathered outside the portal. The four Ammei guards were sprawled unmoving on the ground, and for a moment I wondered whether Nask had kept his promise about using nonlethal weapons where possible. But while there was a slight odor of singed clothing there was none of the overpowering stench that came from a corona weapon victim. "That the place?" Muninn asked, nodding toward the Tower.

"That's it," I confirmed, frowning as a sudden thought occurred to me. On our other previous nights on Nexus Six, at least the ones I'd been here for, Second and Fourth had taken Selene to one of the inner ring houses to sleep instead of bunking her with Huginn and me in the Tower.

Had they done the same thing this evening? After all, when Rozhuhu left me chained in the Upper Rooms, he and First would assume I was out of the equation for the night. That could have led them to opt for business as usual. Equally important, if I *did* somehow get loose, I would have the whole Tower to go through before I headed out into the rest of the city to search for her. That was a good enough reason all by itself to tuck her away elsewhere.

"Change of plans," I told Muninn. "You take both crews to the Tower and find the Expediters and conciliators. I need to check out one of the houses in the inner ring first."

"That's not the job," Muninn growled.

"It's part of *my* job," I countered. "You heard the deal I made with Sub-Director Nask."

He looked back at the Tower, probably wondering why the Ammei would put the portal plans in an unsecured house when they had a big heavily guarded building available. "Fine," he said. "We'll all go and check it on the way."

"It'll take a few minutes," I warned. "More minutes than we might have. I don't know how long before someone sounds an alarm, but this grace period won't last forever."

Muninn muttered something I didn't catch. "Have your look," he rumbled. "But then catch up."

"I will," I promised. "Remember that there will probably be guards on whatever door you pick to go in. You have something to take them out from a distance?"

"Don't worry about it," he said. He lifted his arm and gave a rapid pattern of hand signals. "Watch yourself."

"You too."

He headed toward the Tower, the Iykams fanning out into an approach formation around him. I angled off their path, heading for the house I'd first seen Selene taken into on that first visit with the town's Elders. If she was there, I needed to get in quietly, eliminate any opposition, then get us both out equally quietly.

If she wasn't there, things were going to get a lot more complicated.

I reached the outermost ring of houses and paused for a long look around. None of the buildings nearby were showing any lights, but that didn't mean everyone was tucked away in their beds. Nighttime sentries loved watching their assigned territories from darkened rooms, and without knowing which houses had been pressed into service there was no point in doing a crouch-and-skulk underneath one house's windows when I would be perfectly visible from the one next door.

But as my father used to say, *When you're somewhere you're not supposed to be, act like you've got the deed to the place in your pocket and are dying to show it to someone.* Taking a deep breath, I straightened up and started walking.

No one appeared, called to me, or tried to stop me. I kept going, passing the outer three rings of houses and heading toward the fancier ones across from the Tower. I slowed as I approached, trying to figure out which was the one they'd taken Selene to. The view from here on the ground was a lot different than the one from the Tower, and the fact that the dim starlight was muting all the colors and patterns wasn't helping. All I had to go on was roof shapes, the patterns of some of the walkways, and the distribution of decorative plants surrounding the houses.

The plants.

I pulled off my helmet and took a deep breath. Sure enough, there was a hint of almost-lavender wafting through the air. I headed toward the house I'd tentatively tagged, sniffing as I tried to follow the scent. It seemed to be getting stronger, but I couldn't be sure. The house I was after had a door facing the Tower, I knew, and as I got closer I saw there was another door on the opposite side. I put my helmet back on, headed around to that side, and slipped through the gloom to the door. Notching up my auditory enhancements, I pressed the side of my helmet against the panel.

Nothing. If there was anyone inside, they were being very quiet.

But if Selene couldn't say anything, maybe she'd at least been able to leave me a message. Keying down the helmet's auditories and keying up its opticals, I moved along the side to the front corner of the house and studied the dirt and plants at the front. Given that she'd made a point about the interesting fragrance of the dirt, that was probably where she would try to leave a clue. I looked across the soil, rocks, and plants of this house, then shifted my attention to the next building over.

I frowned, cranking the magnification up a notch. Was that...?

It was. Barely visible, but definitely there, was a fifteen-centimeter-long stick in the dirt with a pair of thirty-degree arcs coming off the two halves in opposite directions.

I smiled grimly, visualizing the scene. Selene had paused with her foot planted on the middle of the stick, then turned partway back toward the Tower as if looking for someone or something, swiveling her foot thirty degrees in the process and dragging the stick to carve out the distinctive mark I was looking at.

And of course she would have done all of that it in front of the house they were taking her to.

I crossed the empty patch of ground to my new target house and pressed my helmet against the wall near the corner. The Ammei inside were being quiet, but at full power my audios were able to pick up the sounds of movement and quiet conversation.

I keyed the volume back down and crossed to the rear door. Working off my left glove, hoping fervently that Selene was still awake, I pressed my helmet to the wall and my finger against the crack beneath the door.

For about half a minute nothing happened. I keyed my audios a bit higher and pressed my finger more tightly into the gap. Sooner or later Selene was bound to catch my scent, but under the current circumstances it had better be sooner.

Then, to my relief, I heard a faint gasp. "Danger," Selene's voice came faintly. "The First of Three is in danger. Do you hear me? Do you *understand* me? First Dominant Yiuliob? Do you hear me?"

"I hear you, Selene of the Kadolians," an Ammei voice I hadn't heard before grated out in accented English. "But I listen not. You speak confusion and trustless words."

"I speak truth," Selene insisted. "Surely you haven't forgotten the awesome powers of the Kadolians."

"The powers of the Kadolians are well-known," Yiuliob retorted. "Their strengths and their limits both. *Imistio* Tower is distant and sealed. How do you claim to smell danger to the First of Three?"

"So you *have* forgotten," Selene said, and I could visualize contempt in her pupils. "Our senses are not merely of the body. They are also of the mind."

"You speak trustless words."

"Then the future will be upon your head," Selene said. "I have given the warning. I now point to the danger. See if you will. Deny if you will. But the truth will come at you very quickly."

I didn't wait to hear more. Pulling back from the door, I put my glove back on and drew my stunner. As my father used to say—and as I'd quoted to Selene on occasion—*Beware of any truth that comes to you at a high rate of speed.* However she was planning to get away from her handlers, it was clear from her warning that she would use this door or come out the front and around one of the corners. Pressing my back against the wall to be ready for either possibility, I pulled a spare stunner magazine from its holder with my free hand and got ready. A sudden group of subtle vibrations rumbled through the wall at my back, feeling like a minor groundquake or running footsteps—

The door beside me slammed open and Selene sprinted out into the darkness, her hands chained together in front of her, a trio of Ammei guards on her heels. The nearest of them caught the back of her shirt and yanked, breaking her stride. She flailed, fighting to break free and hold onto her balance.

A second later, she was fighting equally hard to keep from toppling forward as my stunner blast broke the Amme's grip and sent him sprawling on the ground. The other two pursuers didn't even have time to turn around before joining their friend in unconsciousness.

"Behind me," Selene gasped out a warning as she stumbled to a stop.

Fortunately, for once I was already ahead of the game. Even as I zapped the third Ammei I'd spun around into the open doorway, eyes and weapon trained inward. Two more Ammei were charging toward me, their faces showing sudden surprise at the armored intruder unexpectedly facing them down. Two more stunner shots, and they were down and skidding along the floor. I quick-stepped backward as the one in the lead came partially over the threshold, ejected the stunner's mag, and popped in the fresh one. I spotted two more shadowy figures standing farther back in the house, both of them belatedly aware of the threat and trying to dodge out of the line of fire.

Too late. I dropped both of them and hurried inside. A quick search of the ground floor came up empty. I considered heading up to the second floor, decided we didn't have time, and went back outside.

Selene was kneeling by the second guard I'd stunned, working a key out of one of his tunic pockets. "How is he?" she asked as I knelt beside her.

I had a split-second question of whether she meant Muninn or Nask, both of whom she could smell on my combat suit. But of course there was no reason she would worry about the Expediter's health. "Much better," I told her, taking the key and trying to figure out how it worked. "Walking slowly, but on his own and without help. I don't suppose your friend First Dominant Yiuliob had any interesting books in there?"

"There were several," she said, a sort of unenthusiastic understanding in her pupils. "Which one does he want?"

I hesitated. This would *not* be well received. "The plans for the portal the Ammei are building in the Tower," I said. "That was the price for freeing you."

294 Timothy Zahn

She didn't answer. I finally figured out the key and got her chains off. "If it's not here, I'll have to go back to the Tower," I said, standing up and offering her a helping hand. "I'd really rather not do that."

There was a sudden muted flash from one of the Tower's windows. "Especially since Muninn's team seems to be drawing fire," I added, feeling my stomach tighten. I'd hoped Nask's team would get farther inside before that happened. "Either way, we're getting you out of here. You want Nask or Kinneman?"

"Neither," she said. She looked at the Tower, then back at me, and I saw sudden thoughtfulness in her pupils. "I did see the plans once," she said. "Or at least I think I did. But Second of Three took them to the Tower."

"I hope there's a *but* coming?"

"I'm not sure," she said, some of the thoughtfulness fading. "Second of Three and Yiuliob were talking, and I *think* Yiuliob said he wanted to keep the other book on Juniper until the portal was ready."

"Really," I said, wincing as another pair of flashes came from the Tower. "So the Icari split up the plans like they did the address book?"

"Maybe," Selene said. "It could also be that the schematic books run sequentially instead of with the address book's left/right split. Maybe what he said was that he wanted to hold onto one set until this *part* of the portal is ready."

"Maybe." Or maybe, I reminded myself, he said nothing of the kind and Selene's efforts at reading the Ammei language through the filter of Kadolian had gone completely off the tracks.

But if it came to hopping over to Juniper for a quick look or strolling my way into a major firefight, there wasn't any need for a coin toss. "It's worth a look, anyway," I said. "Any idea which portal is Juniper's?"

"The ten o'clock one," Selene said, pointing across the greenery surrounding the Tower.

"Terrific," I muttered. And if anyone in the Tower happened to be looking in that direction, we would be instantly spotted and probably almost instantly fired at.

The only alternative to the open ground would be to circle through the inhabited section of the city. But while that would partly shield us from Tower snipers, it would us leave us wide open to observation from the Ammei who lived in those houses. Not to mention it would be a longer path.

"Let's hope they still don't want to risk hurting you," I said, heading toward the corner of the house. "At least not until they have Tirano in hand."

"I think they probably know by now that's not going to happen," she pointed out.

"Hope springs eternal," I said. "Besides, even with Nask fully alert there are ways the Ammei could breach the Alainn portal. Especially if First doesn't mind sacrificing some of his own in the process."

Selene shivered. "I don't think he would mind at all."

"Neither do I," I agreed, looking around. I didn't see any sign of Pix or Pax, but that didn't mean they weren't lurking out there somewhere. "Ixil, if you get this message, we're heading for the ten o'clock portal, and then will come back to the four o'clock one back to Nask. If you can provide any cover along the way, we'd appreciate it."

I took a deep breath and gave Selene's hand a reassuring squeeze. "Okay. Let's go."

CHAPTER TWENTY-EIGHT

———— ❖ ————

The flicker of lightning-gun fire continued to send bursts of light across the city as Selene and I hurried across the greenery, dodging bushes and ground dips, watching for tenshes we might trip over, and—at least for me—waiting with a tingling back for the shot that would bring our journey to an abrupt and probably permanent end.

The shot never came. Whatever Muninn and his Iykams were doing for Huginn and the conciliators in there, they were definitely keeping the path clear for Selene and me.

We reached the inner ring of houses without incident. There we slowed, my helmet's audios and opticals at full power, my stunner gripped ready in my hand. The Tower might be the ideal place for a sniper, but close-set buildings like this were prime real estate for ambushes.

But again, there was nothing. Had Huginn really managed to pull everyone in town in on his planned portal assault? If so, Muninn's own situation was looking pretty bleak, and there would probably be an awkward conversation sometime in the two Expediters' future.

Still, given that their overarching job was to provide Nask with whatever he wanted or needed, neither of them had much room to complain.

Which led to the sober reminder that if Nask was willing to sacrifice his own Expediters for the cause, he wasn't likely to lose even a few minutes of sleep if Selene and I ended up as collateral damage.

"Any idea what you're going to say when we get there?" Selene asked as we cleared the last group of houses.

"Not really," I said. "Something suitably official-sounding, probably, to get us into their library or wherever else they've got this book stashed."

"It might go better if I do the talking," Selene suggested. "I'm the one who's met First Dominant Yiuliob and heard him talking about the book."

"Or whatever else he might have been talking about," I warned. "That still isn't entirely clear."

"I know," she said. "But there *is* definitely a second book of some sort."

"So maybe you should just stick to asking for the second book without any descriptive detail," I said, frowning suddenly as a new thought suddenly struck me. "You said Yiuliob wanted to keep the book on Juniper until the portal was ready. Could it be our long-lost RH half of the Meima directory?"

"I wondered about that, too," Selene said. "But from the way he talked it sounded like this book would be needed before the portal could be used."

"Whatever," I growled. Way too much of what we thought we knew about the portals, the directories, and the Icari themselves was based on pure assumption, and I was getting tired of flailing in the dark. "And you're right. You're the one who talked to Yiuliob, so you're the one who should handle this. I'll stand off to the side as the muscle who was sent to escort you there and back again."

We arrived at the portal to find it unguarded. I picked a convenient hatch and opened it, and we rolled inside, closing the hatch behind us. We crossed the receiver module to the interface, rolled into the launch module, and let the extension arm's gravity float us upward. At Selene's warning I holstered my stunner—we were supposed to be harmless visitors, after all—and a moment later we passed through the two seconds of darkness and arrived on Juniper.

I'd assumed there would be at least a small reception committee waiting. To my surprise, the module was empty. "You think everyone forgot to tell them what was going on back on Nexus Six?" I murmured as we floated toward the hull.

"That seems unlikely," Selene said.

"Yeah." Off to my left, about a quarter of the way around the receiver sphere from the launch module interface, one of the hatches was outlined in bright orange. Apparently, that was where visitors were supposed to exit. "On the other hand, if Yiuliob was Juniper's delegate to the Nexus Six proceedings, and he was busy keeping tabs on you, it's possible the people here never got the memo that there was trouble in paradise."

"So we pretend everything's all right?"

"Sounds like our best approach," I agreed. "We're just here to bring Yiuliob and the Third of Three the second book."

"I don't know," Selene murmured, her pupils going wary. "It can't be that easy."

"I never is," I said sourly. "But we can at least try to start it off that way."

I eyed the big orange rectangle, trying to figure out my next move. If the hatch had been open, the obvious approach would be to creep over to it and use my thumbnail mirror to have a look outside. But there was nothing quiet, sneaky, or subtle about a portal hatch swinging open. It would likely catch the attention of everyone out there, and if I paused at that point to assess the situation my hesitation might look suspicious.

Which unfortunately led to the conclusion that I needed to open the hatch and roll immediately outside as if I'd done it a hundred times, or at least had been properly briefed on the procedure and local protocol.

We landed on the hull with the usual thump. "Okay, here's the plan," I told Selene as we headed toward the orange hatch. "I'll open up and roll out like I do this every day. You stay out of sight until I say *Good day*. If I say *Is there a problem?*, get back to Nexus Six as fast as you can."

"I don't know," Selene said, the concern in her pupils deepening. "If I leave, what happens to you?"

"I'll be fine," I assured her. "If I can't talk my way out, I'm still armed and armored, and I'll be right behind you. Go find Ixil if that area near Four O'clock is clear enough. If it isn't, see if our suits are still under the pier and get back to Alpha."

I could tell by the flavor of her silence what she thought about the idea of facing Kinneman again. I didn't like it much myself. But if the alternative was getting shot by some overeager Amme who didn't bother to check his target against the list of people who were vital to First of Three's grandiose scheme, Kinneman was hands down the better option.

We reached the hatch. I took off my helmet and set it on the deck, gave Selene a confident smile, and popped open the panel. Through the sudden blaze of sunlight that came flooding in I saw the opening was situated at the typical ninety-degree angle. I slid my legs through, letting the planet's gravity swivel them toward the ground, then pushed myself the rest of the way out. I straightened up, let my inner ear adjust, then turned around.

Through my various travels I'd teleported into research labs, military encampments, forests, and solid walls of packed dirt. But up to now I'd never dropped into a scene that looked like a combination accounting office and import customs station. A half dozen long tables were set up near the hatchway, each with a computer, a multi-scan deep sensor, and a stack of packaging material. Four of the tables held stacks of colorful vegetables or small boxes containing dust or pellets in more muted shades of brown or dark green, with clusters of Ammei evaluating, counting, or otherwise processing the goods. Beyond the produce tables were two rows of smaller desks where other Ammei were working busily on computers. One of the aliens in each group, I noted, wore the same sort of status hats as the upper-class officials on Nexus Six. The whole operation, portal and all, was laid out beneath a massive tent whose top rippled in the breeze and whose open sides revealed a forest scene around us.

It was the sort of busy, buzzing place that could have visitors dropping in at any hour with goods for the exotic foodstuff markets. Unfortunately, whatever their usual clientele, it was instantly clear that I wasn't it. The first casual glances from the workers quickly turned into surprised or rapidly unfriendly stares, accompanied a couple of times by mildly comical double takes. The computer operators were marginally slower on the uptake, being farther from the portal, but the sudden cessation of conversation from the sorting floor brought them snapping to the same confused attention.

The sorting floor's Hat Man took a step toward me and said

something in the Ammei language. "Sorry, I don't understand," I said in English as I took a quick survey of the crowd. There were no guards in here, at least not wearing anything like the outfits I'd seen on First of Three's soldiers. For that matter, I didn't see any weapons at all. "Does anyone here speak English?"

"Who are you?" the Hat Man from the computer group demanded as he strode toward me through the line of desks. Unlike most of the Ammei I'd met on Nexus Six, his English was nearly perfect.

"And good day to you, too," I called back. "I'm Roarke of the humans. I'm here with Selene of the Kadolians." I felt the brush of air on the back of my neck as Selene emerged and took up position on the ground beside me. "May I ask your name?"

Hat Man looked briefly at the sorting floor's overseer, then turned back to me. "I am Overseer Quodli," he said. "Why are you here?"

"We were sent by First Dominant Yiuliob to bring the second book to Nexus Six," Selene said. "Please take us to it."

"Were you sent by First Dominant Yiuliob?" Quodli asked, still coming toward us. "Or did the First of Three *order* him to send you for the book?"

A quiet warning bell went off in the back of my mind. I'd speculated there might be competing factions among the Ammei, but up to now I hadn't seen anything to indicate that might be the case.

But of course, up to now I'd only dealt with the leadership on Nexus Six. If there were interplanetary rivalries going on, we could have a problem. Especially if First of Three held one half of the portal assembly manual and First Dominant Yiuliob held the other.

Luckily, Selene was on top of it. "The First of Three may *suggest* to First Dominant Yiuliob," she said evenly. "He does not *demand* or *order*. First Dominant Yiuliob sent us himself."

"So he may have said," Quodli countered, stopping a couple of meters in front of us. "Who can tell if it is truly so?"

I winced. So it wasn't just politics between Ammei enclaves. There were apparently some internal rivalries here on Juniper muddying the waters.

"Nonetheless, we were sent for the book," Selene said. "Please take us to it."

Quodli half turned to look again at the sorting floor's Hat Man. "I will bring it," he said, turning back to us. "Tell me First Dominant Yiuliob's authorization words."

I felt my stomach knot up. *Hell*. But of *course* there would be authorization words. Even with the Ammei in control of both ends of this Gemini portal they wouldn't be naïve enough to just let some stranger wander in and walk off with their stuff. "Those words are for your ears only," I spoke up before Selene could answer. "Take us to a private place near to the book. We'll give you the code and you can then hand over the book."

"This place is sufficiently private," Quodli said. "Tell me now."

Beside me, Selene gave a small little gasp. I looked at her.

My stomach knot tightened a couple more turns. Her pupils had suddenly gone tense, her eyes flicking behind us at the portal. Clearly, someone had just come through behind us from Nexus Six... and from the expression in her eyes it wasn't a group of Iykams sent by Muninn as backup.

At the moment, the intruders were still floating toward the receiver module's inner hull. We had until they landed to get the hell out of here.

"Let's compromise," I proposed to Quodli, stepping back to the portal hatchway. "We'll all go inside and I'll give you the code there." Without waiting for an answer, I stuck my head and torso into the opening and swung my legs through.

The newcomers were four Ammei soldiers, lightning guns slung over their shoulders, hand weapons drawn and ready. They were still falling slowly toward different parts of the hull, but they were on the alert and had spotted me even before I was fully inside.

Unfortunately for them, none of them was in position to target me. I drew my stunner and fired a shot at each of them, turning them into a set of living rag dolls as they continued drifting toward the surface.

"Home?"

I looked back to see that Selene was inside and on her feet. "Home," I confirmed, leveling my stunner at the opening. "Go."

She nodded and took off running toward the interface. Quodli, clearly oblivious to what had just happened, poked his head into the sphere. He jerked to a halt as he saw the weapon leveled at his face. "What is this?" he demanded.

"Change of plans," I told him. My first instinct was to shoot him where he stood, hoping the resulting confusion in the crowd outside the portal would slow any reaction. My second instinct was my natural hesitancy to shoot anyone in the face. "Get out of here," I continued, gesturing him back. "We'll talk later."

For a moment I thought he was going to force the issue. Then, without a word, he dropped back out of sight.

And with that, the clock was ticking. Whether or not there were guards inside the sorting area, there were surely some standing on call nearby. Selene and I needed to be long gone before Quodli whistled them up, ideally without having them pop out onto Nexus Six behind us.

I scooped up my helmet from the deck and headed for the interface. I could hear a growing cacophony of shouting voices from the opening behind me as I jammed the helmet back on my head and keyed the audios. I knew several ways of closing off a portal or otherwise discouraging pursuit, but all of them required equipment I didn't have. I would just have to come up with something new before Quodli got his response organized.

Selene was already out of sight through the interface. I slowed my approach, mentally preparing myself to lean over and dive in, when I heard a soft *chuff* from behind me. I spun around in mid-stride—

To see a small cannister arcing directly toward the interface.

I didn't know what the cannister contained. All I knew was that Selene was on the other side of that opening, and that I was armored and she wasn't. I turned what would have been my final leap through the interface into a belly flop on top of it, my arms and legs extended outward in a Da Vinci pose to hold me in place over the gap, my back to the missile. Half-closing my eyes, feeling every muscle in my body tense up, I waited for the impact. The cannister slammed into the small of my back with a lot less force than I'd expected—

And the world around me exploded into thick, orange smoke.

I got just a whiff of something odd before automatic air scrubbers I hadn't been told about kicked into action, sealing the helmet around my neck and expelling the bits of gas that had made it inside. "Selene—gas!" I shouted a warning. Spinning around, I looked back across the receiver module.

The Amme who'd fired the first grenade had a second missile on the way. I braced myself, noting peripherally that the orange gas was settling quickly against the hull, and as the grenade reached me I slapped at it with my stunner. It exploded into another burst of gas with the impact.

But this time my counterblow sent the cannister arcing and bouncing back the way it had come, trailing smoke behind it like some child's rendering of a comet. The shooter saw it coming and ducked out of the opening.

He would be back, though, probably with a bunch of friends. Pulling in my arms and legs, I rolled into the launch module.

Selene was standing beside the extension arm, her pupils cringing as she looked at the orange smoke swirling around her ankles. "You all right?" I called.

"For the moment," she said. "This smells like a knockout gas, not poison."

"Not surprised," I grunted as I pulled out my knife. "Counterproductive to kill the intruders before you interrogate them." At least the stuff was heavier than air, which would buy us a bit more time. "Here—catch." I lobbed her the knife. "Can you find the controls or power line to the extension arm's grav field?"

"I think so," she said, a frown in her pupils as she caught the knife. "Why?"

"I want you to isolate and knock out the grav that takes us up the arm without affecting the rest of the arm's functions. Can you do that?"

She looked down at the extension arm's base. "Yes," she said. "Why?"

"Because we don't want them following us," I said, popping open my stunner's access panel. The capacitor that delivered the knockout juice . . . there it was. "Find it but don't do anything until I tell you."

I pulled out the capacitor and stuck it into my belt, then rolled over to look through the interface. A couple of Ammei had appeared across the way, this pair sporting gas masks. I lifted the stunner, aimed, and fired.

I wasn't sure the weapon had enough range to deliver its electrodes across the receiver module's thirty meters. To my mild surprise, it did, though the leads' path was fascinatingly twisty as they crossed the radial gravitational field. The Ammei saw the leads coming and ducked back out of sight.

With the capacitor removed, of course, there was no blast

of current for them to hide from. But that wasn't why I'd fired. What I needed to know was how strong the leads were, and how well they were connected to the gun.

It was a standing joke around the Spiral that if you wanted something overengineered you should give the job to a Patth. In this case, that derision was going to work in my favor. Holding the gun in one hand and the leads in the other, I pulled as hard as I could.

Nothing. The leads stayed intact and connected to the gun against my best efforts.

Perfect.

I pulled out my push knife, cut off the leads, and rolled back over. Selene was leaning gingerly over the extension arm's base, keeping her face well above the drifting gas, a slender cable in one hand and my knife in the other. "Ready?" I called.

"Yes."

"Good. Catch." I tossed the gun across the sphere to her. The twisty path it followed was even more pronounced than the one the leads had mapped out, but she caught it without difficulty. "Here's what we're going to do."

It took me three short sentences to explain it. "Are you sure?" she asked.

"As sure as I can be," I said. I thought about keying the helmet's optics to get a better look at her pupils, decided I really didn't want to know what she thought about the plan. "Regardless, I think it's our only shot."

"All right." She paused, took a deep breath, and sliced the wire. Then, raising her eyes and the stunner, she fired.

The electrodes slammed into my chest, the armor absorbing most of the impact. I caught the leads, wrapping the slender wires around my hand for extra grip, and started pulling.

And as the wires between us steadily shortened, we began rising toward each other.

Selene and I were nearly the same weight, and the physics of the situation said we would reach the business end of the arm together. Unfortunately, I hadn't considered the weight of my combat suit when I'd done my mental calculation. Even as I continued pulling hand over hand, I saw she would reach the luminescent gray trigger section before I did.

Fortunately, she'd also spotted the problem. Her solution was to wrap her legs loosely around the extension arm, the friction adding just enough braking to compensate for my extra weight. I kept pulling, trying to ignore the voices and scrambling footsteps I could now hear coming from the receiver module. We reached the gray trigger, both of us let go with one hand and reached for it—

Just in time for one of our pursuers to appear in the interface and stick a gas grenade gun through the opening.

Fortunately, he was too late, a point I emphasized by hurling my push knife at his face. There was just enough time for me to see him flinch back, his weapon momentarily forgotten, before the world around Selene and me vanished.

I huffed out a sigh of relief in the darkness. Three seconds later, we were back on Nexus Six.

"That was interesting," Selene said as we floated downward.

"One of my goals in life is to keep your life interesting," I said. "Toss me that, will you?"

"It really doesn't have to be *this* interesting," she assured me as she lobbed me the stunner, the leads trailing behind it.

"I'll make a note," I said. "Did you happen to bring my knife along?"

"Sorry," she said. "I needed to hold onto the gun with both hands."

"Not a problem," I said, scowling at the weapon. With both knives gone, I had no way to get rid of the dangling leads.

But I could at least get them out of my way. Coiling them up, I pressed them against the grip where they'd be tucked up under my palm. It felt awkward, but it should keep me from tripping over them. I popped the rear compartment and returned the capacitor to its place, then loaded my last magazine. As long as we didn't run into more than six Ammei, we should be fine. "So much for getting the book. Any ideas for what we should do next?"

"You said earlier I should find Ixil," Selene reminded me.

"That was if we got split up," I said. "The question is whether we head to the Tower and try to find the first book or go back to Nask and tell him we struck out."

"Do we really need to deliver that news in person?"

"Technically, probably not," I said. "But I wouldn't want him thinking I found the book he and I made a deal for and then handed it over to Kinneman."

"You should be able to give him those assurances through a StarrComm message."

"Agreed," I said. "It also occurs to me that we need to get off this rock, and that Kinneman's still mad at us. Nask may be the lesser of the two evils right now."

For a moment, Selene seemed to digest that. "You just said we have no bargaining leverage with him."

"Actually, we do," I said. "We have you."

"He has Tirano," she pointed out.

"Who's young and inexperienced," I said. "No, he needs you, all right. More important, he doesn't want First of Three to have you."

We reached the end of our gentle fall and dropped the usual final meter to the deck. "That's all well and good," Selene said as we made our way around the sphere toward the hatch we'd come in by. "But it seems to me that the best way to assure no one else has me is to drop me into a box somewhere. The same thing Kinneman is threatening."

"True," I conceded, looking around the empty sphere. Given that First of Three had sent a four-pack of soldiers chasing us to Juniper I'd assumed he would at least have a backup force standing ready here on Nexus Six in case we came back. Apparently, Muninn and his Iykams were keeping his forces too busy to bother with loose ends like us. "But Kinneman doesn't have any other pieces of the Ammei/Patth/Kadolian puzzle, so all he's got is a game of dog-in-the-manger. The Patth, on the other hand, *do* have a piece. With you in hand, they have two of them."

"So it boils down to going with either Nask or Kinneman."

"I'm not crazy about the choices either," I admitted as I popped the hatch. "Let's see what we can do about finding a different one."

Morning was still a couple of hours away, and the stars over the eastern mountains were blazing with the universe's usual indifference toward the affairs of men. I looked over at *Imistio* Tower, searching for lightning-gun flickers, but I didn't see any. "Looks like the battle's over," I told Selene. "I wonder who won."

"Maybe we should go find out," a familiar voice came from behind us.

Slowly, carefully, I turned around.

Jordan McKell was standing there, a pair of camo-suited

Marines flanking him. "Hello, McKell," I said as calmly as I could. "Here to sample the Nexus Six nightlife?"

"More likely to count the bodies," he said. "But first things first."

He seemed to brace himself. "Gregory Roarke, under authority of General Josiah Leland Kinneman, I'm placing you under EarthGuard military arrest."

CHAPTER TWENTY-NINE

$$\cdot\!\!\!\diamond\!\!\!\cdot$$

"Whoa," I said, pressing the stunner a little tighter against my leg. So far the three of them were playing it calm, but that was likely to change the minute they noticed I had a weapon in my hand. "Wouldn't you like to at least get my report?"

Though why *hadn't* they noticed? It wasn't like the stunner was a tiny palm gun designed for concealment. And up until McKell announced himself I hadn't even been trying to hide it.

And then I got it. They'd spotted the leads still attached to the stunner's business end, and even if they weren't familiar with this particular Patth model they would know that all such weapons had a mechanism for detaching those wires. The fact that I hadn't done so told them that either the weapon had jammed or was otherwise out of juice.

"I'm sure General Kinneman will be delighted to hear it once you're back at Icarus," McKell said. He flicked a look at the portal hatchway behind me. "Should we be expecting company, by the way?"

And it was at that moment, at that precise time and place, when I finally realized that Selene and I did indeed no longer work for the Icarus Group.

"We *did* stir things up rather badly in there," I confirmed. "We should probably think about getting out of the neighborhood."

"All right," McKell said, gesturing in the direction of the river. "You might as well leave that here," he added, nodding toward my half-concealed stunner. "You're out of power."

I hissed out a feigned curse as the two Marines came out from behind McKell and headed toward Selene and me, their laser rifles held ready across their chests but not pointing at us. "It's that obvious, huh?" I asked, lifting up the weapon and scowling at the attached leads still coiled beneath my hand. "Oh—yeah. These."

And as I plucked at the leads I casually brought the stunner level with the first Marine's chest and fired.

The camo suits were armored and presumably insulated against electrical weapons like these. But the Patth engineers had clearly taken that into account, possibly with sensors that adjusted the voltage to the resistance level of the target's clothing and physiology. The Marine jerked and collapsed like a dropped marionette. The second Marine had rotated back on one foot to make himself a smaller target and was bringing his laser to bear when my second shot took him down as well.

I swung the stunner's muzzle to point at McKell. His hands were still hanging empty at his sides, his expression calm and maybe even slightly amused. "Do I need to drop you, too?" I asked.

"Do you?" he countered.

I felt my eyes narrow as I studied his face. Calm, amused—it almost looked like he'd expected me to pull a fast one on his companions. "I mean do you need me to shoot you to keep Kinneman from blaming you for this?"

He shook his head. "You got the drop on all three of us, and with all the Ammei and Iykams running around the city I made the decision to surrender so that I'd be able to haul the Marines back to safety," he said. "You said something about a report?"

"Right," I said, keeping my stunner pointed at him but cranking my combat reflexes back from hair-trigger to wary. "The Ammei are building a stripped-down version of a launch module in the Tower. There are apparently two books that make up the instructions, one currently in the Tower, the other in the Juniper enclave." I nodded back behind me. "Incidentally, there shouldn't be anyone coming through anytime soon—Selene and I wrecked the extension arm grav field, and I don't think they're going to be able to shinny up the arm. Nask sent us in there to get that second book—"

"*Nask* sent you?" McKell interrupted.

I nodded. "The Ammei were holding Selene, and I needed his help to get her out. That was the price."

"Understood," he said. "Kinneman's going to have a fit about that. Did you get the book?"

"No," I said. "Sorry."

"You sure?" he asked, his eyes flicking over my combat suit.

"Trust me," I assured him. "If I had it, I'd tell you. But after I sprung Selene, First of Three apparently figured out where we were going and sent a matched set of soldiers after us. We had to beat a hasty retreat."

"Okay," McKell said. "Anything else?"

"Plenty," I said. "The portals were apparently built by, or at least operated by, a triumvirate of Ammei, Patth, and Kadolians. The Patth were the engineers, the Kadolians monitored the equipment and watched for problems, and the Ammei oversaw the system. And no, they don't have the long arms or tentacles we've all been assuming. They can telepathically order the tenshes around. They're the ones who actually push the control keys."

"Interesting," McKell said. "And you're sure the Ammei aren't the Icari?"

"Pretty sure, yeah," I said. "They refer to the Icari as the Gold Ones, and claim they're not on good terms with them."

"Could just be a layered diversion."

"True," I said. "But *someone* hid the book that had the formula for the enhancement serum."

"The stuff they wanted to pump into Selene and one of the Patth?" McKell said. "Ixil got word about that back to us."

"Good," I said. "Hopefully, all that's been short-circuited now. Another reason for me to make a deal with Nask."

"You could have come to *us*," McKell said.

"It was faster to go to Nask," I said. "Besides, would Kinneman really have committed more troops after the slaughter earlier?"

"We came in okay this time," McKell pointed out.

"Because Huginn pulled all the Ammei in to train for an assault on Nask, and Muninn and his Iykams rained fire down on them while they were conveniently bunched up," I countered. "Which isn't to say we should sit down and have tea. Like you said, there are still unfriendlies roaming the streets."

"Right," McKell said, giving the area a quick survey. "So what now?"

"You go back to Icarus with your friends," I said, gesturing to the unconscious Marines. "Selene and I go back to Nask."

"Why?"

"For one thing, to report my failure to get the book," I said. "For another, he probably wants this combat suit back."

"That's it?" McKell asked, his eyes hard on me.

"That's it," I said with all the innocent sincerity I could muster.

"Uh-huh." He pursed his lips. "You can't trust him, you know. He's a Patth, and everything he does is solely for their betterment."

"I know," I said. "But for the moment, I think our interests overlap with his."

"For the *moment*?"

"So turn it around," I suggested. "What's Kinneman's attitude going to be if we come back to Icarus?"

He hissed out a breath between his teeth. "Now that he has access to Nexus Six and *Imistio* Tower . . . to be honest, I think he'll decide he doesn't need you anymore." He raised his eyebrows. "Which isn't to say he would be right."

"Doesn't matter," I said. "Even if he's willing to admit he was wrong, by the time he does it may be too late."

"Too late for what?"

"I have no idea," I admitted. "But First of Three is building a portal, and we have no idea what it's for. Even without Selene or Tirano to fine-tune it he may be able to get it to work, and after what I saw from the Tower I'm guessing Kinneman won't be able to stop him. I'm also guessing there's an even chance the Ammei can talk the Patth Director General into some sort of deal."

"Plus there are the Gold Ones," Selene murmured.

"Plus there are the Gold Ones," I agreed grimly. "The Icari. We don't know where they went, whether they're still around, or what plans they have for the portals and the Spiral. Selene and I need freedom of movement if we're going to get a handle on any of that."

"You're not the only ones in the game, you know," McKell pointed out.

"No, but we're the ones who are most up to speed," I said. "On top of that, the Gold Ones clearly have an interest in Kadolians, and as far as I know Selene's the only one of that species who's interacting more or less openly with the rest of the Spiral."

"Yeah." McKell hissed out another breath. "I don't like it. Kinneman's going to like it even less. But I can't give you a good argument other than what I already said about not trusting the Patth."

"Understood and agreed with," I said. "Tell the good general that I was furious at you for coming after me. That should take some heat off you."

"I'm pretty sure Ixil and I are already too far gone for that," McKell said. "Good luck, and be careful."

Leaning over, he got a grip on the Marines' back collars and started pulling them along the ground. I watched until they were out of sight around a clump of bushes, then took Selene's arm. "Come on," I said. "Let's go talk to Nask, and see what we can get out of him."

"And see how deeply we've stepped into it this time?"

I sighed. "Yeah," I said. "That, too."

The battle for the Tower was apparently over. Or at least it was as over as Nask wanted it to be.

The six Iykams who'd been guarding the Alainn portal's receiver module were still in position, still ready to fire on any visitor who didn't have clearance. Or possibly ready to fire on anyone they just didn't like the looks of.

Luckily for us, this time Huginn was lying on the curved hull alongside them. "Welcome back," he called, waving off the guards as we drifted downward.

"Thanks," I called back. "Everyone get back okay?"

"Conciliators Fearth and Uvif are unharmed," he said. "Muninn and Circe took some superficial damage and are being treated." His lips compressed briefly. "Four Iykams were killed, and another five badly wounded."

I winced. Sixteen Iykams in, only seven still battle-ready. Even with the element of surprise, a better than fifty percent casualty rate. "Sorry. What about the ones the Ammei had locked away?"

"We got them out," Huginn said. "Did you get it?"

As my father used to say, *Anyone can lie. Almost anyone can evade a question. It's the ones who can evade but make you think they answered that you have to watch out for.* "I think Sub-Director Nask will be pleased," I said. "Is he receiving?"

We were close enough now for me to see the slight narrowing

of Huginn's eyes. Maybe his father had given him the same advice. "Sure," he said, getting to his feet. "Let's go see him."

He took us to the base's medical facility. Nask was there, sitting in a recliner in front of a bank of monitors, overseeing the treatments on his wounded Expediters and Iykam soldiers. "Roarke," he greeted me tiredly. Still only mostly recovered from his old injuries, I guessed. "Selene. Did you get what I asked you for?"

"Unfortunately, no," I said. "First of Three was able to send some chasers after us. Even if he hadn't, the gatekeeper on Juniper wanted an authorization code which we didn't have."

"What you're saying is that you failed to keep your end of the deal," Nask said coldly. "You promised the portal plans in exchange for Selene's release."

"Yes, I suppose you could say that," I conceded. "Though, actually, it turns out that was never a viable option, since Selene told me the plans themselves were taken to the Tower. You can send in more Iykams if you want to look for them, but there was no practical way we could have found them on our own."

"If the plans are in *Imistio* Tower, why were you on Juniper?"

"Because there's a second book there," I said. "The Icari seem to like splitting up their most important information collections."

"This second book includes additional plans?"

"Not sure what it includes," I admitted. "We just know it's connected somehow with the portal plans. But as I said, we couldn't get to that one, either." I lifted a finger. "On the other hand, I could argue that Muninn and his team didn't actually free Selene, either. I did that on my own, which kind of makes the whole agreement moot."

"But you *did* use Patthaaunutth equipment."

"True," I conceded. "On the *other* other hand, without my coming here to warn you about Conciliator Uvif, you'd have been wide open when he returned with his army of Ammei. That could have ended very badly, especially if he'd gotten to Tirano."

Nask looked over at Huginn. "Huginn?" he invited.

Huginn hesitated, then gave a reluctant nod. "He's right, Sub-Director," he said. "As far as I could tell, Conciliator Uvif was fully prepared to cooperate with the First of Three in his raid. I could stall them somewhat, but when the portal opened he *would* have led them in. They still might not have taken Tirano, but the confrontation would have been considerably bloodier."

He looked at me. "I agree Roarke didn't deliver exactly as per your agreement. But under the circumstances I think he more than justified any trust you placed in him."

"I see." Nask eyed him another moment, then turned back to me. "Very well. I declare the contract satisfied. Return the combat suit, and Huginn will escort you back to Nexus Six."

"Thank you," I said. "But I'm afraid that might be a bit awkward. Kinneman is not very happy with us at the moment."

"Would you like me to speak with him on your behalf?" Nask asked, a hint of humor peeking out.

"That would be an interesting conversation," I said. "Actually, I was hoping we could make another deal with you."

"If General Kinneman chooses to waste resources by locking you away, that's his choice and his folly," Nask said. "As for a deal, you have nothing that I want or need."

"What about Selene?" I asked. "Whatever the Ammei are up to, it's clear they need both you and the Kadolians."

"We have Tirano."

"Who's young and inexperienced," I said. "Having Selene on your side gives you a lot more bargaining power."

"There is no bargaining needed," Nask said. "The First of Three's goal—" He broke off. "There is no bargaining needed," he repeated. "The Patthaaunutth will not deal further with the Ammei. Nor will I deal further with you. You may go."

I huffed out a tired breath. I'd hoped against hope that it wouldn't come to this, that Selene and I could make this work some other way.

But Nask had closed all the other doors. I had only one card left to play.

If I hadn't already damned myself in Kinneman's eyes, this would put me solidly over that line.

"Just one more minute of your time, if I may," I said. "Huginn, back in the Tower you told me you knew we'd found something on Meima."

"Yes," he said, watching me closely. "You said it was an Icari document."

"It is," I confirmed. "As I also said, as far as I know we haven't been able to translate any of it. But we *do* know what it is."

Beside me, Selene stirred. "Gregory?" she murmured, her pupils going dark and apprehensive. "Do you really want to do this?"

"We don't have a choice," I said. "We can't go back to the Icarus Group. Not with Kinneman in charge. Not if we don't want to be charged or locked away."

"But not this way," she said, her pupils pleading.

"Then how?" I asked. "Kinneman and Sub-Director Nask are the only ways off Nexus Six. We *have* to get out of here."

"But if Kinneman finds out—"

"We don't let him," I said. "Or we disappear. But before we can do anything else, we have to get off this planet."

Selene closed her eyes briefly. "Not this way," she said.

"Then give me another option."

She opened her eyes. The anguish was still there, but there was also a reluctant acceptance. There *was* no other way, and we both knew it. "All right," she said, almost too quietly to hear. "Do what you need to."

I nodded and turned back to Nask. "What we found was the left-hand half of a portal directory."

"Which portal?" Nask asked.

"As far as we could tell, all of them."

Nask and Huginn looked at each other, their faces suddenly gone stiff and unreadable. "How do you know?" Huginn asked, turning back to me. "What does it look like?"

"Each page has a short description in what I assume is Icari script on the left-hand page," I said. "The right-hand page has a grid of colored squares that correspond to a portal's destination panel. But while a full-range portal's panel is four rows of twenty indicator lights, the book's page has four rows of ten."

"So it's half an address," Huginn said. "And they're done in red, yellow, and black?"

"Yes."

"Interesting," Nask said quietly. I had his attention, all right. "Where is this directory now?"

"Somewhere safe," I said. "Kinneman may be an unimaginative tyrant, but he's not stupid. I have no doubt it's somewhere safe and completely inaccessible."

"Then what is the purpose of this conversation?"

I took a careful breath. "I know where the other half is."

There was a long pause, silence and darkness seeming to fill the room. I let it hang there for a few seconds, then waved a

hand. "Perhaps we should start with some context and patterns,"
I said. "We don't know all the details, but it appears there was
some kind of conflict between the Icari and Ammei that came
to a head on Meima. Or maybe it was between two Ammei
factions—like I said, we don't really know. What we *do* know
is that one of the groups got hold of the two halves of a portal
directory and wanted to get them to Nexus Six."

"To Nexus Six itself?" Nask asked. "Or to one of the other
worlds accessible from the other Janus portals?"

"I don't know," I said. "Either way, the Icari apparently found
out about the plan and set up a trap to catch and strand the
courier."

"What kind of trap?"

"We're not quite sure," I hedged. I was flirting too closely
with treason as it was without telling them that Nexus Six was
Alpha's system. "The point is that the scheme went sideways. A
battle that was supposed to give the courier of one of the halves
a diversion to sneak into the Meima portal to get here instead
got him killed and left him buried for a few thousand years."

"And the other half of the directory?"

"Unbeknownst to the Icari, it was already here," I said. "It
had been brought through undetected and securely tucked away
while the thieves waited for the other half."

"Which never arrived."

I nodded. "Right."

"Where was the first half hidden?" Huginn asked.

"No idea," I said. "What I *do* know is that somewhere between,
oh, fifty to seventy years ago one of the Icari stopped by, found
or dug up the directory half that was hidden here, and moved it."

"To where?"

"We'll get to that," I said. "Meanwhile, the visiting Icari—or
Gold One, as the Ammei call them—also found out the Ammei
were trying to build a portal. He didn't want that any more than
the Patth do, so he found—"

"What makes you think we don't want the Ammei to have
a portal?" Nask interrupted.

"Basically, everything you and Huginn have said and done in
the last couple of days," I told him. "I don't know why you don't
want it, I just know you don't. Anyway, our Gold One apparently
decided hiding the book with the enhancement serum formula

would be enough to stymie the project, so he did that. Then, just
for completeness, he also cut off access to their silver-silk source
on Alainn by wrecking that end of the portal. That forced them
to cannibalize silver-silk from everywhere else it was being used
around the city, which slowed down the project even more. And no,
I don't know why they had silver-silk in all those buildings, either."

"The old defense grid," Nask murmured.

I frowned at him. "Excuse me?"

"Nexus Six once had a defense grid," he said. "Various buildings equipped with weapons and reinforcement shields to protect
the city and the portals. Silver-silk was a key component."

"That would have been useful to know," Huginn said, his
eyes hard on Nask.

"It was as much legend as history," Nask said. "Even now,
we're still learning which parts of the old stories are which."

"You might want to step up the pace," I warned. "If First of
Three is ready to start poking needles into Patth and Kadolians,
they must be getting close to finishing that portal."

"Indeed," Nask said grimly. "Enough history. Tell us about
the directory."

"Sure," I said. "First, here's what I want in exchange." I started
ticking off fingers. "You get us from here to Xathru so we can
pick up the *Ruth* and find somewhere to lie low. You provide
us with two or three false IDs, both for us and for the ship, to
make it harder for Kinneman to track us down. You give us a
high level of access to security systems, information sources, and
whatnot—doesn't have to be the full access you Patth have, but
something much better than we could get on our own. Finally,
you give us everything you have on the Icari and Ammei—legends,
history, golf scores, everything."

"Including the true relationship between the Ammei, Kadolians, and Patth," Selene added.

"Yes—that," I agreed.

"All this in exchange for the directory?" Nask asked.

"Well, half the directory," I reminded him. "That's all we can
get for you."

Nask eyed me another long moment, then gave a slow nod.
"Agreed," he said. "Where is it?"

I stood up. "Come on," I said, gesturing to the door. "Let's
go get it."

CHAPTER THIRTY

———— ◆◇◆ ————

"Imagine you're a Gold One visiting Nexus Six," I said as we walked through the corridors back toward the portal. "You may know from your archives that half of one of your precious top-secret directories vanished a few millennia ago, possibly to right here. Even if you don't know that history, you *do* know that this half-directory you've stumbled on isn't supposed to be lying around loose, certainly not in Ammei territory. So what do you do?"

"You take it away and hide it," Selene said.

"Right," I agreed. "But where? Remember, the Ammei had a relationship with the Kadolians, and Kadolians can sniff out Icari metal even through a layer of dirt."

"Hide the needle in a tub of other needles," Huginn suggested. "Put it in the Center of Knowledge."

"That's the obvious option," I said, keeping my voice casual. *Hide the needle in a tub of other needles...* "But in this case, that wouldn't work. Wherever he found it, he had to assume the Ammei would miss it and launch a search. He had to put it somewhere they wouldn't look." I raised my eyebrows at Selene. "Or *couldn't* look."

She stiffened, and I saw sudden understanding in her pupils. "Alainn," she breathed. "He took it to Alainn."

"*Alainn?*" Huginn echoed. "No. *Damn.*"

"Yes," I agreed. "Ironic, isn't it, after all the effort you went through to dig out the portal and move it off the planet to wherever we're sitting right now."

"Irony isn't the word I was thinking of," Huginn said from between clenched teeth. "You're enjoying this, aren't you?"

"A little," I admitted. "But don't worry, it's not as bad as you think. You're right, Selene, that moving the directory to Alainn and then sabotaging the portal to cut off access was his plan. But he didn't just have the Ammei to consider. He knew they would need to find a compliant Kadolian for their portal project, and as I said your people are great at sniffing out Icari metal. So...?"

We'd reached the portal now and I stopped beside the access hatchway. "He couldn't just hide it on Alainn," Selene said slowly, her pupils showing deep concentration. "Not even just bury it. With no other Icari metal around, a Kadolian could easily find it."

"Actually, that long ago, there wasn't even much *non*-Icari metal in that area," I agreed.

"So what did he do?" Huginn asked. "Travel to whatever passed for civilization on the planet, hop a transport, and take it somewhere else?"

"He could have done that," I agreed. "But where? The Kadolians were mostly nomadic—still are, as far as I know." I looked at Selene, caught the confirmation in her pupils. "Anywhere he hid it, there was still a small but finite chance that one of them would eventually stumble over it."

"He also might wish to retrieve it someday," Nask said, an intense look on his face that was now shifting to a mix of understanding and disbelief. "Are you saying...? No. Ridiculous."

"Not only not ridiculous, but practically inevitable." I waved up at the sphere looming over us. "You were right, Huginn, that you hide a needle with other needles. But you don't need to hide an Icari-metal book among other Icari-metal books."

"You can also hide it inside more Icari metal," Selene murmured.

"Yes." I gestured Nask to the hatchway. "After you, Sub-Director."

Two minutes later, we were standing together in the launch module. "The whole thing made so much logical sense on other levels that we never bothered to look any deeper," I continued. "Shutting off the Alainn end instead of the Nexus Six one kept the

Ammei from just pulling parts out of one of their other Geminis and putting the portal back in business. They presumably could go to Juniper or one of their other enclaves and travel from there to Alainn by regular ship, but only if they knew which planet was at the other end."

"The silver-silk was right there down the path from the Alainn portal," Selene said. "There was no need for them to go into any of the nearby towns or interact with any of the local people, so they never learned the planet's name."

"Right," I said. "They knew there was silver-silk there, of course, and given how rare and valuable the stuff is that should have been a big clue in tracking it down. But the Spiral's elites had decided to keep Alainn a deep, dark secret, which meant it was absent from every database the Ammei could have looked through."

"Only now they know," Selene breathed. "They know it's Alainn, and they know where the Loporri and Vrinks are." She looked at me, her pupils showing sudden horror.

"All the more reason for us to figure out what they're up to and shut them down," I said. "So, Huginn. You want to tell me where it is?"

Slowly, Huginn looked around the sphere, his eyes taking in everything. "The parts that had been removed were here," he said, walking a quarter way around the sphere and stopping beside a group of access panels. "That was the bottommost part of the module when it was buried on Alainn with its grav field off. So..." He pointed straight up. "There."

"Because no one is going to climb twenty meters through the middle of an empty ball without a damn good reason," I said, nodding. "Let's find out if you're right."

I walked around the sphere to the spot directly above him and knelt beside the largest of the three access panels in that vicinity. I used my combat suit's multitool to unfasten the oddly shaped screws and pulled off the panel.

There, half hidden beneath a group of cables, was a familiar-looking book.

Nask had come around to my side of the module and was standing over me. Wordlessly, he held out his hand.

I looked at Selene, her pupils brimming with unhappy frustration. She still didn't like this, not in the least. But like me she couldn't see any other way that would leave us not locked in a box somewhere. Silently, I handed Nask the book.

He pulled the magnetic hasp free and opened it to the middle. Huginn came around to join us, and for a minute the two of them stood side by side, Patth senior official and his human minion, looking at a prize either of them would have killed for.

As would Kinneman, the dark thought occurred to me, if he ever found out about this.

I was drifting amid a swirl of such unpleasant thoughts when I was startled back to the present by the sharp sound of Nask closing and resealing the book. "You said you wanted to be taken to Xathru and your ship," he said as I got to my feet. "I suggest it would be better to contact an Expediter in the area and have him bring the *Ruth* to a different planet for your rendezvous. That would be quicker than transporting you and Selene there directly, which would forestall any effort General Kinneman might make against you in response to Colonel McKell's report."

I pursed my lips, thinking it through. Nask's plan made a lot of sense, actually. Once McKell and Ixil delivered their reports, Kinneman would absolutely be coming after us. Getting the *Ruth* off the table was our best chance at not getting grabbed right off the blocks.

And if Nask was planning a betrayal, he could do it just as easily taking us to Xathru as he could en route to whatever Planet X he was thinking about moving the *Ruth* to. There was, after all, a lot of empty space out there to dump bodies into. "Sounds good," I said. "Let me give you the access and console codes."

"No need," Huginn put in with a faint but definitely smug smile. "We already have them."

I felt my lip twist. "I guess you probably do."

"Come," Nask said, tucking the directory under his arm. "I have some calls to make."

CHAPTER THIRTY-ONE

There were four restaurants and ten tavernos Selene and I liked to visit on the rare occasions when we were on Popinjay.

The place we were seated in today wasn't any of those. It wasn't even on our *acceptable alternatives* list.

Which was the point, of course. Whatever bits and pieces Kinneman's data divers were busily pulling from years of financial, travel, and culinary records, the Cock 'n' Bull pub would be conspicuous by its complete absence.

I could only hope it wasn't somewhere on our dining companion's list.

"He's not happy with you, I can tell you that," my father said, gazing into his iced tea as he carefully stirred his lemon sweetener into it. "First was an APB to all Commonwealth EarthGuard and law enforcement agencies, followed by an ISLE locate-and-detain bulletin. He's supposedly trying to get EarthGuard Intelligence involved, too, but he's hitting a bit of resistance from the senior officers there."

"Thank heaven for small favors," I said, giving Selene a sideways look. Her pupils showed no hint that he was lying, exaggerating, or otherwise slanting his report on Kinneman's response to our mysterious disappearance from Nexus Six. "Does he have any ideas or preconceptions as to where we might have gone?"

"Interesting you should ask," my father said, lifting his eyes from his glass to give me a piercing look. "At first he seemed to have gotten the idea that you'd headed straight back to Juniper the minute McKell's back was turned. But then the *Ruth* disappeared from Xathru, so he shifted the bulk of his focus there."

"It could have been stolen," I pointed out.

"Could have," my father said, nodding agreement. "Wasn't. Friend of yours pick it up?"

I felt my throat tighten. "Not sure we have any friends at the moment."

"Certainly not many who would admit to it," my father agreed. "Afraid I can't be one of them, either. The general still needs my help to smooth ruffled feathers among various Commonwealth officials, and I can't afford to lose that position. For the good of everyone involved."

"Plus the fact that it pays well?" I suggested.

He shrugged. "*The good of everyone* does include my own good. As I always say, *Never join a noble cause unless large payments or self-preservation are included.*"

"Right," I said. "I forgot that one. So *did* you get paid in advance?"

"Adequately so." He cocked his head slightly. "So why exactly did you ask me to come all this way and meet you? You surely didn't need me to tell you that Kinneman's full-court press is alive and well."

"No, we get hints of that at every fuel stop we make," I said. "There were just a couple of other points I wanted to discuss that couldn't be safely done over a StarrComm call."

My father settled back in his seat. "I'm listening."

"First, I wanted to see how far you were into Kinneman's confidences," I said. "I also wanted to find out how deeply into the Icarus Group itself your fingers went."

"The Alien Portal Agency," he corrected. "Reasonably far, and reasonably deep. And, yes, for a reasonably long time, at least unofficially." He raised his eyebrows. "Which isn't to say I'm free to just hand you information whenever you want it. Sorry."

"Let's not be hasty," I said. "Because that brings me to my second point."

"Which is?"

I hesitated. But there really wasn't any diplomatic way to phrase this. "I wanted to know how long you've been feeding classified information to the Patth."

He snorted. "*Really*, Gregory. Why in the world would you even suggest such a thing?"

"Mostly your history," I said. "You spent way too much of your life playing various sides against each other, usually for their ultimate benefit, always for yours. In this specific case, I believe you're the one who gave them Admiral Graym-Barker's balloon technique for blocking access to portals."

My father shook his head. "*Really*, Gregory."

"Yes, we've established that," I said. "But it's clear that *someone* deep in the organization told them. Huginn all but admitted it."

"Huginn might have been lying or deflecting," he pointed out. "Regardless, why pick on me?"

"Because of something Huginn said at my last meeting with Sub-Director Nask." I paused, eyeing him. "You don't seem surprised that I even *had* such a meeting."

He shrugged. "My face does what I tell it."

"I'm sure it does," I said. "Unfortunately for you, the same can't be said of your scent. Selene?"

"He wasn't surprised," she confirmed quietly. "Nor was he surprised or upset by your charge of treason."

My father actually winced. "*Treason* is such a harsh word," he protested. "As you said, what I do is always for everyone's benefit. And really, isn't that your own philosophy? Go with whatever benefits you and Selene, and after that do what's best for the universe at large?"

"That *is* what I said, and thanks for remembering," I said. "But I find it hard to see how giving away trade secrets benefits anyone except the recipient."

"Sometimes you have to take a step back and look at the big picture," he said. "Would your trick with Pax have worked if the Patth were using multiple small balloons to block the receiver module instead of a single larger one? Because that *is* what they were doing before I happened to accidentally drop a hint."

"No, that change was handy," I had to admit. "But there's no way you could have known at the time how we'd be able to take advantage of it."

"Not the details, no," he agreed, the studied lightness in his manner fading into something more serious. "But I know how clever you are, and I know that information about an opponent's equipment and procedures nearly always pays off somewhere. As I always say, *Sometimes the best way to know the other guy's plans is to give them to him.*"

"Maybe," I said. "But I doubt Kinneman would be impressed by such subtleties. If he caught us, you know, and made us talk."

My father raised his eyebrows politely. "Are you trying to *blackmail* me?"

"*Blackmail* is such a harsh word," I said. "But not an inaccurate one."

"I see." He took a sip of his tea, his eyes never leaving my face. "I'm listening. What do you want?"

"We'll start with information," I told him. "Like you just said, everything about your opponent eventually pays off. I want to know what Kinneman is up to, what his intel people pull up on the Ammei, the Patth, and the portals—I *know* he'll be digging into all of that—and anything else we might be able to use."

"That's all?" My father smiled. "Really, Gregory. I never said I wasn't your friend. I only said I was one of those who couldn't admit to it." He reached into his jacket pocket and pulled out a data stick. "Granted that I don't have full access to everything, this should be enough to at least give you hints as to the directions Kinneman's going. There's also a *very* private StarrComm number where you can contact me, which I strongly suggest you use sparingly. Needless to say, all your normal contacts and numbers are being monitored, so we'll have to figure out how I can safely get information to you."

I looked at Selene, noting that her pupils hadn't changed. Apparently, my father really was serious about helping us.

Whether or not he was himself being played by Kinneman, of course, was another question entirely. "Not a problem," I said, taking his data stick and handing him one of my own. "New StarrComm contact number. I suggest you memorize it and then destroy the data stick."

He nodded and pulled out his info pad. He plugged in the stick, and for a moment gazed at the StarrComm number that came up on the display. He nodded, removed the stick, and handed it back to me. "No point wasting a good data stick," he said. "Plus, as I always say, *Even information you destroyed tells the other guy that there was something there worth destroying.*"

"True," I said, dropping the stick back into my pocket. "Well. I guess that's it. Thanks for coming, and we'll be in touch."

"That's not *quite* it," he said, making no move to stand up. "Two points. First, what did Huginn say at that meeting that pointed you in my direction?"

"Something subtle enough that no one else would have caught it," I said. "He commented the best way to hide a needle was to put it in a tub of other needles."

"Not exactly a revelation from on high," my father pointed out.

"The concept, no," I agreed. "But the wording?" I shook my head. "Everyone else hides needles in stacks or piles. You're the only one I've ever heard hide them in tubs."

"Seems to me you stretched the logic a little far on that one," my father warned. "Still, as I always say, *You* can *argue with success, but it usually comes off looking like sour grapes.* Which leads me to my second point. As of six days ago, Jordan McKell and Ixil T'adee are no longer part of the Alien Portal Agency."

I felt my mouth drop open a couple of millimeters. "Kinneman *fired* them?"

My father nodded. "He apparently felt they were a little too friendly with the two of you, which in his eyes meant they weren't sufficiently friendly with the Agency."

I snorted. "Now *that* was just stupid."

"Or perhaps manipulated," Selene said.

I frowned at her. The look in her pupils... "No," I said, looking back at my father. "You? *You* got them fired?"

"I may have nudged Kinneman in that direction," he said calmly. "But it was mostly him."

"You got them *fired*?" I repeated, feeling anger and guilt welling up inside me. I'd begged and cajoled both Ixil and McKell for help, and they'd come through when I needed them. And *this* was their reward? "Damn it, Dad—"

"They were too good for Kinneman," he interrupted. "The agency didn't deserve their services and abilities."

I stared at him... and then, slowly, I got it. "But Selene and I do?"

"There's little to be gained by creating bureaucratic openings, Gregory," he said quietly. "But there's a great deal to be gained by creating allies."

He held out his hands like a stage performer inviting applause. "You're welcome."

❖   ❖   ❖

I half expected to find Kinneman and a trap waiting for us somewhere between the Cock 'n' Bull and the *Ruth*, probably without my father's knowledge, certainly without his assistance. But the seasoned manipulator who was Sir Nicholas Roarke was himself not easy to manipulate. We reached the ship, got off Popinjay, and escaped into hyperspace without anyone so much as raising their voice at us.

Selene was waiting in the dayroom when I came back from the bridge. "They're here," she announced, looking up from her info pad. "Private contact numbers for McKell and Ixil."

"You weren't expecting them to be?" I asked, snagging a caff cola and snack bar from the pantry and dropping into the chair across the table from her.

"From the way your father talked, I wasn't sure whether his description of them as *allies* was current or merely a vague future."

"With my father, a little skepticism is a very healthy thing," I agreed. "Still, under the circumstances, I'll take any flavor of allies we can get."

"Kinneman will be watching them, of course."

"Without a doubt," I said, watching her closely. "*I* certainly would if I were him. Was there anything else you wanted to tell me about the Ammei?"

"What do you mean?" she asked, her pupils going wary.

"A long time ago you told me that someone had once used Kadolians as bounty hunters and assassins," I said. "Were those someones the Ammei?"

"I don't know," she said hesitantly. "Maybe. Is it important?"

"It could be," I said. "I'm thinking of the glimpse we got of their internal politics, particularly between Nexus and Juniper. If they were nasty enough back then for various Ammei factions to hire you to attack each other, they could be just as nasty now. Internal conflicts can offer outsiders like us a tool we can use against them."

"Unless one of them decides they want me on their side," Selene warned.

"In which case we'll have *two* tools to use. And no, you won't have to actually do anything," I added hastily. "We'd just use the idea itself as a lever. And only if we absolutely have to."

"All right," she said. "If we have to."

I winced at the look in her pupils. She didn't like the idea. Not a single bit.

But she also knew the odds that were stacked against us. As my father used to say, *Underdog stories make great star-thrillers, but in real life it's the biggest and baddest who usually win the day.*

"We'll make it work, Selene," I said, trying to exude quiet confidence. "First of Three doesn't know we're still on the job. Even if he did, he'd never consider us a real threat."

"I suppose not." She paused. "Are you going to tell me about the book?"

I sighed. Of course she would have figured it out. She'd naturally smelled the *Imistio* Book's scent on me when we first met after my excursion into the Grove of Reflection, and would know I'd handled it there. But the scent hadn't faded with time, which would tell her that something from it was still with me. "I didn't know what the book was," I said, pushing back my left sleeve and opening the arm's secret compartment. "But whatever it was, I figured it would be a good idea to give ourselves a bargaining chip." I pulled out the folded sheets of metallic paper, smoothed them out, and handed them to her. "So I helped myself to a couple of the middle pages. Can you read any of it?"

She frowned down at the pages, her eyelashes working rhythmically. "The script is similar to ours," she said. "Some of the words seem familiar, too. Most of it seems to be—" She broke off, staring at me with stricken pupils. "It's part of the procedure," she breathed. "First of Three doesn't have the complete serum."

"No," I agreed. "I figured that if we get boxed in—"

"What if he doesn't realize it?" she cut me off. "What if they make it and try it on someone?"

I winced at the horror in her voice. "They'll figure it out," I assured her hastily. "They'll see the torn pages, or otherwise realize they're missing a step."

"What if they don't?" Selene asked, her pupils suddenly haunted. "What if they use it on someone?" Her pupils darkened. "What if they use it on Tirano?"

I swallowed hard. I really hadn't thought that far ahead. "They'll figure it out," I repeated. Even in my own ears the words sounded lame. "If they don't... well, we'll just have to make sure they're told."

For maybe half a minute we just sat there, each of us following our own thoughts. Finally, reluctantly, Selene seemed to bring herself back. "Yes," she said. "We will." She paused again. "What's our first move?"

"We'll check out the other four Ammei enclaves," I said. "See where they are, try to get a feel for the local conditions and politics, locate their ends of the Nexus Six Gemini portals. Maybe give me a chance to learn more about their expressions and body language, and you a better baseline for their scents. Once we've done all we can there, we'll head back to Juniper."

"That sounds reasonable."

"Good," I said. Her tone was still neutral, but I could tell that she'd put the serum behind her for the moment and was ready to focus on the more immediate problems. "One other thing. Back on Nexus you said there was a full-range portal on Juniper. Do you know that for sure, or were you just throwing out a name?"

"Mostly the latter," she admitted. "But I'd met First Dominant Yiuliob and had a feel for his relationship with Second of Three. It seemed like Juniper was more important than the rest of the enclaves, and Ammei importance seems to be tied up with portals."

"That seems to be their pattern, yes," I murmured, thinking back to the rest of that conversation. "And the fact that no one challenged you strongly suggests you were right."

"Only I don't think any of them knows where on the planet it is."

"Which gives us a *third* tool we can use on them," I said. "Especially since I hinted that we *do* know."

"Maybe." She hesitated. "It occurs to me, Gregory, that all three of the tools you mention are mostly of the *what-if* variety. It would be nice if we could find something more solid."

"I agree," I said. "That's part of what our tour of the enclaves is for. Hopefully, we can dig up something there."

Because as my father used to say, *Once you take all the options, probabilities, and possible consequences into account, the rest is still just a crapshoot.*

The dice were bouncing across the table. From here on, there was no turning back.

I could only hope we lived long enough to see if the gamble paid off.

The End